Praise for *A Good Indian Girl*

"A recipe for success: engaging, heartfelt characters, sumptuous food that awakens your taste buds, and eloquent prose that keeps you turning the pages… This one is not to be missed."

—Jo Piazza, internationally bestselling author of *The Sicilian Inheritance*

"*A Good Indian Girl* is a heartfelt exploration of learning to first survive, then thrive, after finding your life plan turned upside down… A deeply honest tale of letting go and starting over."

—Sonali Dev, *USA TODAY* bestselling author of *The Vibrant Years*

"A layered exploration of identity and living on your own terms."

—Saumya Dave, author of *Well-Behaved Indian Women*

"A delight to the senses [and] a story as mouth-watering as the recipes found within these pages. This novel needs a companion cookbook!"

—Kerry Lonsdale, bestselling author of *Find Me in California*

"A brimming story of culture, family, forgiveness, and self-discovery… Shah uses the sumptuous flavors as another character, both to tantalize and to teach. [Her] captivating voice is one to be heard."

—Rochelle Weinstein, author of *What You Do to Me*

"A truly sensory experience—you can almost taste the recipes!—that will leave you hungry for more."

—Namrata Patel, author of *The Candid Life of Meena Dave*

"A lush, sophisticated coming-of-age story centering travel, found family, and delicious food you can almost taste on your tongue!"

—Paulette Kennedy, author of *The Devil and Mrs. Davenport*

"An immersive journey of self-discovery [that] will wrap you up and hold you riveted until the last page."

—Lyn Liao Butler, author of *The Tiger Mom's Tale*

"A heartfelt portrayal of
I loved this

—Jamie Varon, autho

Also by Mansi Shah

The Taste of Ginger

The Direction of the Wind

MANSI SHAH

A GOOD INDIAN GIRL

ISBN-13: 978-0-7783-1064-8

A Good Indian Girl

Park Row Books
22 Adelaide St. West, 41st Floor
Toronto, Ontario M5H 4E3, Canada
ParkRowBooks.com

Printed in U.S.A.

To the childfree who are coloring outside the lines and changing expectations. Always remember that your story matters.

ONE

Food had always been Jyoti's strongest connection to her roots. It awakened and heightened all her senses. She took in the large stoneware dish on which the gnocchi sat in a single layer with a thin, cheesy gratin top. She heard the sizzling and popping of the hot creamy sauce settling around the pasta, the waiter warning her that the plate was brought directly from the oven to her table. The heady scent of truffle tickled her nose, followed by the nutty smells of melted fontina, Parmesan, and Pecorino Romano. She placed one of the light, airy potato pillows into her mouth and felt the warmth of it blossoming through her. Smooth potato, aromatic truffle oil, and velvety sauce made their way to the different regions of her tongue and ignited her taste buds. She closed her eyes knowing that if enlightenment were a flavor, she had just found it.

As Jyoti Shah sat at a table in the piazza outside Osteria Santo Spirito in Florence, Italy, on that warm day in late May, she couldn't remember the last time she had savored food the way she was now. Had it been when she had worked in the restaurant and was creating new menus? Maybe it had been even further back into her childhood years, when her mom first began teaching her how to cook Gujarati dishes. Today, even though she wasn't eating Indian food, she was relieved to know that the spark she felt while tasting a well-made dish hadn't been fully extinguished. Given how much she'd lost over the past several years, it was a relief that she could still count on her palate.

When the waiter had first put the sizzling plate in front of her, she was sure no single person could consume the entirety of a dish this heavy. As she ate, she realized that the truffle gnocchi somehow managed to stay light even though it was essentially a decadent form of mac and cheese. Before she knew it, she was halfway through it and her glass of crisp and fruity house white wine.

She paused, knowing she'd consume every last morsel and drop of sauce, so there was no need to rush her meal. That was the point of being in Tuscany, after all. She'd thought it wasn't smart to come for the summer when she still had to create a new life plan after her husband had abandoned her, but her best friend, Karishma Parikh, had been very insistent, and it wasn't as if she had anything waiting for her in New York. Not anymore. No restaurant. No husband. No baby. Her parents weren't speaking to her. Her sisters were busy with their own lives.

As she watched people sitting in the restaurant patios around the piazza, lounging with wineglasses in hand as they chatted and laughed with their companions, it was a stark contrast from her life in Manhattan. There, she would shove a toasted everything bagel smeared with scallion cream cheese into her mouth as she maneuvered around pedestrians while hustling through the city. The Italians had certainly mastered the art of treasuring food and each other, and she could stand to learn a thing or two from them.

"Have you finished?" asked the thirtysomething lanky waiter

in accented English while she reclined in her chair and people watched.

Jyoti leaned forward and put her arms on either side of her plate like an animal protecting its young. "Does anyone ever leave this dish unfinished?"

The waiter smiled, revealing laugh lines at the corners of his light brown eyes. "Very few."

She picked up her fork, signaling that she was not in the minority, at least not in this instance.

"I'd love another glass of wine," she said.

He eyed her not yet empty glass and she smiled. "I'm anticipating what I'll need for round two."

He laughed and promised to return with it.

She took a long sip and drained her glass. Then she speared another gnocchi, trailing it through the sauce before placing it into her mouth. So many rich dishes lost their satisfaction as one kept eating, but this plate of perfection did not. She was determined to recipe test until she figured out how they made it so light and craveable, although maybe it was a dangerous endeavor to have instant access to it. She forced the thought away, because her time in Florence was about rejuvenating herself, and that did not include criticizing her body. She'd spent enough of her life doing that already.

Jyoti relished taking time for her meals and not being in the frenzied hubbub of her life back home. Connecting with and sharing her culture through food was why she had become a chef in the first place, but that, along with so much else, had been taken from her over the last decade. She'd been so young when she'd married—a mere twenty-five years old—and now at forty-two, she could not fathom who would be mature enough to make such a life-altering decision at that age. She certainly hadn't been, but she'd done what her parents had suggested for her. She'd always been their dutiful daughter, the eldest of the three children, and the one who was expected to pave the way for not only her sisters, but also the young daughters of the rest of their immigrant community in New Jersey.

Jyoti felt the vibration of her phone in her tote and rifled through her bag to grab it. She saw an unfamiliar string of numbers with the country code +1 and had a flutter of disappointment. She'd hoped it was one of her parents calling, however unlikely that was these days. She and her mom had been at odds since her divorce—longer, if she were being honest—and her dad wouldn't stir the drama by going against his wife. She considered not answering but wondered if it could be a family emergency since she rarely got calls from unknown numbers.

"Hello?" she said, hesitantly.

"Hi," a male voice she unfortunately knew all too well replied.

She slumped in her chair, wishing she hadn't answered. She felt uneasy knowing she was now in a world in which he had numbers that she didn't know. Ones that went with his new life and new wife. She glanced at the time. It was 1:45 p.m. in Florence, so it was morning in New York.

"Why are you calling me?" she asked her ex-husband, Ashok, even though she already suspected the answer.

Nine months earlier his father had passed away, and Ashok had told her he planned to sell Taste of Ginger, the restaurant that they had run together during their marriage. It was where Jyoti had found her passion as a chef as she saved the struggling business from ruin by creating an upmarket, innovative Indian menu. She was distraught over seeing it go, so he'd said he would give her a year to try to raise the money to buy it herself. She'd applied to countless jobs, but no one wanted to hire a self-trained chef who had only worked in one family-owned establishment, so she was nowhere near having the funds she needed. Jyoti braced herself for having to confess that she wouldn't meet his deadline and there was no point in waiting out the extra few months before he sold it.

He cleared his throat and then said, "We need to talk about the embryos."

"What?" Jyoti froze with her fork midway from the plate to her mouth.

"The embryos," he repeated, his tone impatient.

Jyoti put down her fork, scrunching her face. "What about them?"

"The cryobank called me. The five-year storage fees we paid are up. So, we need to decide whether to destroy, continue to freeze, or donate them."

She felt an ache in her stomach as he unearthed the deep pain that she had tried to bury. Jyoti clenched her teeth, desperately wanting to finish her gnocchi in peace without the past adding its own sour flavor to her impeccably seasoned meal. She considered whether she should fake a poor connection and hang up. He'd certainly done worse to her. But that would mean that one unpleasant interaction would be dragged into two, so she soldiered on.

"What are you suggesting?" she asked.

"That's the thing," Ashok said. "Radha is pregnant, so I'm going to have my own kids soon. It doesn't make sense to keep those embryos anymore. It would be awkward for my kids to have half siblings with my ex-wife, you know?"

The cacophony of sounds in the piazza that she'd found so pleasant before this call seemed to fade to silence and Jyoti felt like the air had left her body in one *whoosh*. Her mind was moving in slow motion to process what he had just said. He and his new young wife were having a baby. The thing Jyoti had spent the majority of their fourteen-year marriage trying to conceive. The thing that had wrecked Jyoti's body in ways she could not have even comprehended when she'd first thought about becoming a mother. The thing that he had ultimately left her for, claiming she was broken, and he needed to find someone who wasn't. And it seemed that he had.

"Congratulations…this is what you always wanted," Jyoti said, still in a daze.

"Thanks, we were pleased with the news."

Ashok and Radha had been married for five months and she was already pregnant. *Must be nice to be thirty-one*, Jyoti thought to herself bitterly. But that wasn't fair either. She and Ashok had started trying when she was twenty-nine and they'd still had no luck. Jyoti's mind swirled with how easily things were working out for Ashok. It seemed to always be that way: the man who leaves the woman gets to move on to a new and glossier life first.

"Well," Ashok continued, "about the embryos…the cryobank needs to know our plans within a month or they will automatically charge my credit card. Obviously, Radha and I don't want that."

Money had always been at the forefront with Ashok—he had studied accounting—so Jyoti shouldn't be surprised now. During their divorce proceedings, he'd done everything possible to retain as much of their marital wealth as he could. Their accounts had been in his name, and he'd managed the finances. It turned out their marriage hadn't been any more modern than that of her parents with traditional gender-based delineations, so Jyoti had no way of even knowing if he'd presented an accurate portrayal of their assets to the court. She suspected he hadn't but had no way to prove it. She had been so depleted and desperate to have the whole thing be over that she didn't have any fight left in her anyway.

"Do we have to do this now?" she asked.

He cleared his throat. "I'm not sure what there is to decide other than destroying them."

It was easy for him to say that. His middle-aged sperm could still impregnate a younger, more vibrant egg. For Jyoti, at her age and with her series of miscarriages, those embryos were the best chance she had of having a baby one day. But would she ever want a baby that was half Ashok? She wished that she had frozen her eggs instead, so she'd have more options now. She would have saved eggs that weren't contaminated by her ex-husband's seed in a heartbeat. But they'd been told embryos were more viable, so they did what would have given them the best chance. Until now, she'd had no reason to question that decision. She gritted her teeth at the unfairness that she was at this tipping point, where it was now or never for her to have biological children, assuming she could get pregnant or somehow afford a surrogate. Meanwhile, men could have children later in life no matter what bad karma they carried with them.

She glanced at the gnocchi that had so thoroughly delighted her moments earlier and tried to keep her voice steady as she said, "It's really not a good time for me to discuss this."

"When then? I don't want to leave it until the last minute."

She squeezed her eyes shut and tried a box breathing technique that her best friend had taught her. During her marriage, she'd accepted that her needs had never been a priority to Ashok. She'd seen the same behavior between her parents with her mom acquiescing to her dad when it came to big decisions, so she'd been taught that was what marriage should be.

"I'm not sure, Ashok," she said in a clipped tone. "But I'm busy now."

"Aren't you in Italy?" he asked.

"How did you know?" she said, even though she knew that the auntie gossip circuit would have leaked that news immediately. They'd salivate over two middle-aged single Gujarati women gallivanting around Europe doing Bhagwan-knows-what, with no plans of settling down and starting a family.

"The aunties," he confirmed. "Are you there with Karishma?"

"Yes," she said. "She's built a good life here."

"She always finds what she needs."

Jyoti ignored the snide comment. She no longer had to be

diplomatic and could choose sides between her husband and her best friend.

"Just like you do," she said.

She could almost feel his recoil and her lips curled into a satisfied smile. One of the benefits of divorce was finally being able to put her ex-husband in his place after years of having to pander to his ego.

Ashok cleared his throat. "Let me know in the next couple days. We both need to sign the papers to destroy them, so you'll need to notarize and send them back. There are some virtual companies for that. I can send you a link."

And then he was gone. Jyoti stared at her phone, still amazed at his ability to center himself in every situation without compassion or empathy for her. She had put up with it for so long, like she'd thought a good wife was meant to do.

The remaining gnocchi on her plate had lost their steam and sizzle and didn't have the same inviting aromas as when they'd arrived. She'd intended on indulging in every last bite, but Ashok had thoroughly ruined her appetite. The emotional state of the diner was the sixth sense that always impacted the taste of food. She glanced around the piazza again, now focusing on the children running through the middle and parents twirling pasta on their forks and feeding it to their kids. Through the din around her, their merriment rang out as they giggled and laughed. She tried to imagine one of them being hers but could not conjure the image. As she listened to the high-pitched voices that came from different corners of the piazza, her heart felt like it was being pulled in so many directions, but one thought refused to disappear: *Who was she now that everything she'd built in the first half of her life had been taken away?*

TWO

Jyoti's breath was labored as she trudged up the three flights of stairs to Karishma's apartment across the piazza from Osteria Santo Spirito. Karishma said that her lungs would get used to it and it would be good practice for when they visited the Amalfi Coast later in the summer. Apparently, the nonnas there walked up and down four hundred steps each day. Jyoti couldn't picture these superhuman grandmas or herself joining them on this daily stair workout, but she hoped she could manage at least the three flights with more ease in the coming weeks. She let herself into the apartment and dropped her bag onto the entry table with a huff.

Karishma was seated on the couch and looked up from her laptop. "You didn't like the gnocchi? That place has become overrun with tourists the past few years." She rolled her eyes. "I keep worrying the quality will go down."

"No, it's not that," Jyoti said, kicking off her shoes. "The gnocchi were culinary perfection, just like you said. I need to figure out how they make the sauce feel so light." She put on house slippers, and made her way to the sofa. "It was the unpleasant interruption I got during the meal." She flopped next to her friend. "Ashok."

Karishma's eyes narrowed. "Oh no. Was that loser calling to gloat about the restaurant?"

"Worse," Jyoti said. "To talk about the embryos."

"Are you serious?"

"Apparently, the exorbitant fee we paid to keep them frozen has now run out and we need to decide whether to destroy, donate, or re-up the storage fees," she said, mocking Ashok's robotic tone. "I know it doesn't make sense to keep them, but there's something so final about destroying them. When I think about what we had to go through to get them…" Jyoti's voice cracked and she looked at the wide floorboards.

"Oh, honey," Karishma said, putting an arm around Jyoti's shoulders. "You mean what *you* had to go through to get them. It was your body that was being tortured."

Jyoti knew her friend was right. The toll had hit her hardest, although Ashok never recognized that. Neither had her parents. She'd developed rolls on her midsection from the myriad of hormones injected into her. She'd never had a body that would have been featured on glossy magazine pages, but she'd certainly looked better with twenty-five fewer pounds on her petite frame. If only it had been just the vanity aspect. The hormones, stress, miscarriages, depression, and anxiety had all seeped into her cells and changed her. She felt like the essence of who she was had been altered, and even after the invasive treatments had stopped, and she and Ashok had separated, she still hadn't found her way back.

"I know," she said softly. "But it's hard to think it was all for nothing."

Karishma rested her head against Jyoti's. "You can't think that way. Would you even want to have a child with that narcissistic guy with his balding head, pot belly, and chicken legs? You can find a better specimen at a sperm bank if you really want to have a child on your own. Or here! Some gorgeous Italian lover with olive skin and luscious dark hair to roll around with."

Jyoti managed a small laugh. "If only it were that easy."

"Why not? Just leave it to me to find the perfect match for you."

Jyoti envied her friend's optimism. Karishma's confidence and energy had always drawn a healthy stable of men to her, so she didn't understand how strange it would feel to even consider someone new after she'd only been with Ashok for nearly twenty years. Nor did she understand what it meant to be alone in the way that Jyoti now was.

"I don't want to be tied to Ashok forever," Jyoti said. "But given the infertility issues we had, it seems like my younger eggs are the best option and those unfortunately are already impregnated by him."

"Doctors should really freeze stuff separately given the divorce rates. You can't be the only person who wishes she could extricate that sperm."

Jyoti shot her a look that stopped her from continuing down that path, and Karishma's expression turned apologetic.

"You have some time to decide, right?"

Jyoti nodded.

"Okay, then let's have fun tonight. There are a million things you still need to eat and drink in Florence. I'll introduce you to my friends, and we'll deal with this problem another day."

Karishma was great at putting things off for another day. It was why she probably fared better in Florence, with its laid-back lifestyle, than she had in the scuttle of New York, where she'd worked a corporate job as an editor at one of the major publishing houses. The environment had been draining for a non-white woman trying to change a resistant system, so she became a freelance editor with complete control over the content she worked on. Jyoti's hands got clammy at the thought of such unpredictable work. She'd loved the certainty of going to her shift at the restaurant each day. Despite their differences, being college roommates had solidified an unshakable bond between them, one that survived even after the friendship between their mothers had stalled.

Karishma stood and pulled Jyoti off the couch.

Her eyes twinkled as she said, "If you don't want to go out for drinks tonight, then we can just stay in and do some meditation or a sound bath. I just got some new crystals that we could use."

Jyoti groaned playfully. "Fine. I choose alcohol."

She liked to poke fun at the spiritual practices her friend had found since leaving her corporate life, but she had to admit that Karishma's energy was calmer and more grounded. Crystals had been strategically placed throughout her home. A malachite tower near the front door for protection. Selenite gridding her living room. Carnelian throughout for creativity. Shungite near the electronics. Maybe there was something to the breathwork, meditation, and crystals she now surrounded herself with. Her best friend was so comfortable in her own skin, and, as much as Jyoti liked to tease her, she hoped some of that would rub off on her.

It was humid and warm on the piazza as they walked to Volume that evening. The heat that had collected in the cobbles from the day now radiated upward. She had already come to appreciate the shifting moods of Piazza Santo Spirito. In the morning, it was a quaint neighborhood with a few pop-up stalls selling fresh produce and flowers. The locals and vendors all knew each other, greeting one another by name and frequently stopping to chat. As Jyoti adjusted to a daily routine of buying produce in small portions, she was reminded of India, where the bhajiwala would stop by each morning with fresh offerings on his cart.

In the afternoon, the piazza moved into a slightly more bustling atmosphere, with people gathering outside to lounge at restaurants. By aperitivo, it was buzzing with evening energy and the hum of laughter and animated conversation. All of this was mere steps from Karishma's home. And a world away from the constant, frenzied energy of New York that had left Jyoti feeling so depleted as of late.

They selected a table on the terrace and Jyoti ordered the obligatory Aperol Spritz. She felt her sour mood improve as she brought it toward her lips, the ice clinking against the glass. She inhaled the sweet citrus scent from the orange slice and then sipped the cool, gently fizzed liquid. Simple was often the most satisfying.

She followed that first refreshing taste with a salty, briny Castelvetrano olive, relishing the firm, yet also soft, texture of the smooth, fatty fruit. Aperitivo hour was taken very seriously and was an *experience* rather than a simple pre-dinner drink. There was an impressive array of olives, tapenade, pickled veggies, marinated artichokes, and crostini that appeared along with the drinks, the waiter having carefully placed each small dish before them with a precise and practiced hand. Each table had the same bountiful spread. She was likely to lose her appetite for the main meal if she weren't careful now, and Karishma had raved about the pasta they were going to have that evening, so she wanted to be ready for it.

Jyoti was lathering tapenade onto a crostini when two men and a woman strolled up to their table. Karishma rose and delivered two air kisses to each of them.

As they sat down, Karishma began introductions.

To Jyoti she said, "These are my best friends out here." She gestured to the taller and slimmer of the men, who had dark hair trimmed short and dark brown eyes to match. "This is Enzo. A true local to Firenze. His family has been here for over six generations. I met him at an aperitivo a few years back when he so rudely asked me to move away from the pork leg at Il Santino."

Enzo shrugged and said in a thick Italian accent, "If I had known she was vegetarian, there would have been no need for me to worry about her taking the last slices of pork."

Jyoti had already heard plenty about Enzo during her weekly chats with Karishma over the years. Jyoti had pictured him as an Italian playboy because she knew about the casual sexual relationship he and Karishma had, but he seemed to be nerdier and have more substance than she had expected.

Karishma then gestured to the petite Taiwanese woman who had joined them. She had black hair tied into a trendy bun with a few wisps strategically poking out. "This is the ever-fabulous Mae. We met in language class when I first arrived in Florence and neither of us knew a word of Italian. She's since become my most trusted photographer in Italy when I need to shoot anything for one of the books I'm working on."

Enzo cleared his throat. "Are you suggesting you speak Italian now?"

Karishma threw him a faux shocked expression before turning back to Jyoti. "You'll find Italian men don't prioritize their manners."

Enzo arched an eyebrow. "As if an American should talk about manners."

Jyoti noticed how easily he had referred to Karishma as *American*. Back home, there were so many people who only saw them as immigrants. She'd always struggled with the question "Where are you from?" because her answer often depended on who was asking and what answer she thought they wanted. She was relieved that Karishma's friends had steered clear of that question.

"Nice to meet you," Mae said to Jyoti, ignoring the barbs Karishma and Enzo were tossing at each other.

Jyoti loved the easy rapport the group had, and it made her happy to know that Karishma had found good friends in Florence after moving on a whim several years ago. Jyoti had been so concerned that her friend was far from her family and the community she'd grown up with that she'd made a point to never miss their weekly chats. Now she could see that she'd worried for nothing. Maybe it wasn't impossible for Jyoti to think about starting over somewhere new too.

"Last, but certainly not least—" Karishma put her hand on the shoulder of the pale-skinned, freckled, green-eyed man sitting to her right "—this is Ben."

"Pleasure to meet you," he said to Jyoti in a British accent. To Karishma, he said, "That's all the introduction I get? 'This is Ben?' No funny anecdote or quip like the others?"

Karishma eyed him. "What would you prefer?"

He turned to Jyoti. "I'll have you know that it's a great story. We met skydiving over the Tuscan vineyards and landed in a pile of grapes, barefoot and ready to stomp them out for the harvest. It truly was a magical day."

Jyoti cocked her head. "I take it the real story is rather mundane?"

His face flushed like a personal lie detector. He pointed to a building behind them. "I live just there. People on this piazza can't help but run into one another."

Karishma smiled. "He's also quite the reliable waterer of plants when I'm away, so there's that."

He smiled appreciatively. "It's only fair for the dog-sitting I foist upon you now and again. Pretty sure I've got the better end of that bargain."

"Debatable. Your dog is very cute," she said.

"Says you and every other person. I thought she'd help me pick up women, but instead they can't help but notice that I don't measure up. I should have gotten an ugly dog that would make me look better."

"Aw, Ben," Mae said. "We love you and Roussane equally."

"Yes, but you don't fancy a date with me, do you?" Ben said, feigning hope.

"Well, no," Mae said. "Maybe if you brought your dog."

Ben held up his hands in defeat while the group laughed.

Then Enzo gestured to Jyoti and Karishma. "And how do you two know each other?"

Karishma grabbed Jyoti's arm and pulled her closer. "Jyoti is like a sister to me. We've been friends since we were kids and never looked back since."

Jyoti squirmed, knowing that while she'd always had Karishma's unwavering loyalty, she hadn't always reciprocated it as well as she should have. When her mom or the aunties had passed judgment on Karishma's "unconventional choices" over the years, and said how proud they were that Jyoti was so well-behaved, she'd accepted their praise without defending her friend. Silence is often the worst betrayal. Except in her case, she'd gone further.

She pushed the thoughts aside and exchanged pleasantries with Enzo, Mae, and Ben before they grabbed the waiter.

"Would you like another?" Ben asked, gesturing to her nearly empty glass.

She'd been drinking faster than she had realized. After years of long stretches where she couldn't drink because she was trying to get pregnant, the free-flowing alcohol was a welcome relief, and she nodded eagerly for a refill.

Mae focused her attention on Jyoti. "What brings you to Florence?"

Jyoti tensed, not knowing how much Karishma had shared with these friends. If they were her Firenze family, then perhaps they already knew everything the way she'd heard so much about each of them. Karishma must have noticed her discomfort and jumped in.

"I forced her to finally visit after all these years." She eyed Jyoti, signaling that Jyoti's secrets were safely locked away. "She's had a bit of a rough patch, and I wanted to introduce her to some new people and amazing food. She's a chef back home, so what more perfect place for her than Florence?"

"A chef!" Enzo clapped his hands. "When can we come for dinner?"

Jyoti laughed. "I haven't been a chef for some time now."

"Nonsense," Karishma said. "She has a palate that is superhuman. Her samosas will make you believe there is heaven on earth."

Jyoti gave her friend a grateful smile, because they both knew cooking had fallen by the wayside for her. It was hard to motivate herself to cook for one.

Ben patted his doughy, slightly protruding stomach. "You can't say 'samosa' around a Brit and expect us to let that go. We'll work on getting you to make those for us. We can be very convincing at times. Especially with enough wine."

Everyone laughed, and Jyoti forced a smile and raised her glass in agreement. They had no way of knowing that the recipe was her mother's and it had been too painful to make them after her parents stopped speaking to her.

Conversation flowed as easily as the drinks and Jyoti tried to relax. She felt the same way she had when she met new people throughout her twenties. She'd assumed these fast, unforeseen connections were only possible during the excitement and spontaneity of young adulthood, before life had left her jaded. But perhaps the heart was never too old, worn, or scarred to make room for new friendships.

The summer sun held on as the night progressed, and it was still bright outside when the group finished their aperitivo and walked the short distance from Volume to 4 Leoni in Piazza della Passera.

It was more upscale than Osteria Santa Spirito and the other restaurants near it, but still did not have the stuffy feeling of high-end dining in New York, even though Jyoti suspected the food would far surpass that of those places. They were shown to the back of the bustling dining room and Karishma slid into the booth against the wall, pulling Jyoti down next to her.

"You are going to love this place."

If Karishma believed that, then Jyoti had no reason to doubt her. She had not been led astray yet.

"Tonight, we are going to have the more famous upmarket version of an iconic Florentine pasta dish," Karishma said. "You have to try the original before I take you to the restaurant that I think actually has a better version. That place hasn't been blessed by Giada de Laurentiis like this one, though, so it doesn't get as much love."

Her friend had certainly done her culinary homework during her years in Florence, and Jyoti was happy to have such a thorough guide. Inside 4 Leoni, they ordered the salad specialty of the house, which had fresh peppery arugula, smooth Emmenthal cheese, creamy and firm avocado, a heap of verdant pesto, and toasted pine nuts for a satisfying crunch. Jyoti was eating more than she ever did back in New York, but didn't feel as weighed down and suspected it had to do with the quality of the produce. That, and her mood. A change of scene could do wonders.

She accepted her plate of salad and savored the nutty, herby, fresh, and creamy flavors and textures dancing across her tongue. She admired that fresh produce was the star of this dish. The pesto was divine and she appreciated that it wasn't used sparingly. This was not a "dressing on the side" country. That had been the special request that Jyoti had hated most when she saw it on tickets at Taste of Ginger. She didn't understand why the quest for a smaller size led people to choose depravation over satisfaction.

Then came the promised dish and Karishma smiled as the plate of delicate pasta satchels was placed in front of Jyoti. The whole table now turned toward her.

"What?" Jyoti asked.

Ben said, "There's something fascinating about watching a chef's reaction to food. We need to see what you think."

Jyoti had never enjoyed the spotlight, but the pull of the pear, taleggio, and asparagus pasta before her was too alluring. As she lifted the first satchel with her fork and placed it in her mouth, she noticed that, like at lunch, the luscious sauce didn't have the heaviness she would have expected. How did Italians manage to keep cheese sauces so light? As she bit into the thin al dente wrapper, the slightly sweet filling oozed out and she tasted the combination of fruit, cheese, and vegetable. The pear was ripe and succulent, marrying well with—and not overpowering—the other savory flavors, and the sprinkle of earthy asparagus and black pepper grounded the dish. The chef had used a young taleggio, delicate and light, without the sharp pungent tang she had expected to find. Karishma was right that she'd never encountered this flavor combination before. It was a dish that she would not have ordered herself because the ingredients didn't seem harmonious, but her instincts would have been wrong. She took a satisfying sip of earthy Brunello to wash it all down, the high acid and tannins cleansing her palate for the next bite.

"It's sinful," Jyoti announced to the group. "Now, please eat!"

Her dinner companions obliged. From her vantage point, Jyoti looked at couples, families, and friends enjoying their food. Meals felt sacred in Italy. Food was not something to be shoveled into one's mouth while watching television, even though this was her reality after Ashok left. She'd never expected to find herself alone, ordering takeout and eating while binging the latest reality housewives series. She knew the shows were trash, but watching dysfunctional married couples made her feel better about her own situation.

Jyoti saw a little girl who must have been four or five years old at the table across from them. She was concentrating hard on her plate and using a piece of bread to mop up some red sauce. Bread was the one thing she'd had so far in Tuscany that left much to be desired. It had no salt. Ever the editorial encyclopedia, Karishma had told her the competing explanations for this; some pointed to bread as a highly prized commodity that was heavily taxed in the Middle Ages, others to an ancient local feud between Florence and Pisa (during which Pisa prevented shipments of salt from reaching Florence), and others to a history of local bakers who forewent salt in bread to complement the salinity of Tuscan sauces. The latter seemed unacceptable to Jyoti because she firmly believed that each component of a meal should stand on its own. Regardless, the silver lining was that she had no need to waste any stomach space on bread and had more room for the other delicious, and appropriately seasoned, carbs in the city. The girl with the light brown ringlets had her little tongue out as she concentrated on cleaning the sauce on her plate with the salt-free bread, and Jyoti could not help but smile as she worked so diligently.

Ben leaned over and followed her gaze. "Do you have children back home?"

She looked at him and balked. "What? Me?" She shook her head to bring herself back to the present moment. "No, I don't. Do you?"

He shook his head. "What is it that Karishma says again? 'I'm child-free.' Mercifully. What a headache that would have been to sort out in the divorce. Kids are cute, but they certainly limit your options." He whispered to her conspiratorially. "Perhaps its uncouth to say, but I'd rather live for myself than for other people."

Jyoti knew Karishma was personally offended anytime someone asked her if she was child*less*, because she thought there was nothing less about her life without children. But Jyoti wasn't sure if she felt the same way. Her parents, Ashok, and their community had made her feel like such a failure when she couldn't conceive, and it was hard to separate their expectations from her own.

"And you?" Ben asked her. "You want them one day?"

She was sure the question had seemed harmless enough to him, but he had no idea just how complicated those five words were for her right now.

THREE

Jyoti hadn't expected to drink as much as she had, but Ben worked for a wine distributor and knew the best labels. It was hard to pass up wine from someone who could give her the entire backstory on the vineyard and bottle, although as she lay in bed the next morning, her recall seemed questionable, at best. She'd always wanted to learn more about enology and loved how wine could affect the flavors and experience of food, but drinking was such a taboo subject with her parents and in her community, especially for women. As she recounted her evening, she thought about which wines would pair well with traditional Indian food, but she was now starting to wonder not just about the wine, but how she could incorporate her Indian flavors into some of the comforting Italian dishes she'd been eating. She started imagining dishes like saag paneer ravioli, cauliflower and pea shaak risotto, and chili cheese toast pizza. And Ben could help her find the right wines to complement them.

She felt a flicker of inspiration for the first time in so long, reminding her of her early years at Taste of Ginger. She would peek through the kitchen pass whenever one of her new creations went out so she could see the look on the diner's face when they took their first bite. That expression was the unfettered truth, and from it she knew if something needed to be tweaked. People puckered their cheeks if the salt was too high or widened their eyes when the spice was too much. It pained her to know that the meals she was now conjuring would never come to fruition, because in a few months, Ashok would sell the restaurant and she'd never cook in that kitchen again. She consoled herself by saying she'd find a way to bring her culinary visions to life elsewhere because they were burning to come out of her.

Karishma's kitchen was small by American standards but large by European ones and Jyoti was grateful, especially because she knew cooking wasn't among Karishma's extensive list of hobbies. Jyoti found the equipment she needed to prepare her favorite hangover dish: bataka poha, easy to make and heavy on the carbs, acid, and spice. She opened cabinets, praying that Karishma had the ingredients on hand. Near the stove, she found the masala dabba and lifted the lid. Turmeric, chili, dhana jeeru, and cinnamon and cloves wafted up to her like a warm hug. Tucked into the back of a small pantry, she found pressed rice flakes. Grabbing a lemon and large potato, she got to work.

She tossed black mustard and cumin seeds into a wide skillet with some oil drizzled onto the bottom. They immediately began to sizzle and pop, releasing their aromas. She added in cubed potatoes, salt, green chilies, turmeric, finely diced shallot, and lemon. The smell was like coming home. Last, she added the rice flakes that she'd rehydrated with water and some cinnamon and clove powder before mixing it all together. When her mom had taught her the dish, she'd used curry leaves and

Jyoti loved the flavor those added. But it was no surprise that Karishma didn't have a limro plant lying around.

"Is that what I think it is?" Karishma's voice broke Jyoti's reverie.

Jyoti looked over her shoulder and smiled.

"You really are an old auntie, aren't you?" Karishma said, yawning. "What made you even think of it?"

Jyoti took a spoonful from the top where it was less hot and fed it to Karishma like she was a child. "It's the best hangover food."

She watched Karishma's eyes widen as the spice and acid hit her tongue. Her whole energy changed as she chewed. That was the power of well-prepared food.

"You know," Karishma said, "it *is* the perfect hangover food." She helped herself to another spoonful. "I haven't had this in years. Not since I moved to Florence, and who knows when before that."

Jyoti grinned. "Just tell me all the Guju classics you want this old auntie to make while I'm here."

She served them both bowls full of steaming, fluffy yellow goodness and they took them to the couch.

"Your friends are nice," Jyoti said through mouthfuls.

"They liked you too," Karishma said.

"You've built yourself a pretty good life here."

"It could be yours too. We could be roommates again."

Jyoti never thought the word "roommate" would apply to her in her forties. Life had a way of reminding her just how little control she had.

"Not sure it's that easy for me to pick up and move," Jyoti said. "But I suppose it's not out of the question like it would have been while I was married."

Karishma looked smug. "That's exactly the opening I need. So many things are going to open up for you now. The Universe wanted you to release that dead weight and live in alignment, and now the rewards will come. Just wait and see."

Karishma was a pit bull when she wanted something, and she usually managed to get it. Her tenacity allowed her to climb the ranks in publishing, despite her usually being the only Brown person in the room. That doggedness was also the reason she'd burnt herself out, quit, and moved to Italy. She'd meant to come for only a year, but then that turned into two, then three, then four. Now she had found herself a new home.

Karishma's phone dinged and she smiled. "I'll bet you thought everyone was too drunk to remember, but Ben is asking when the samosa party is happening."

Jyoti laughed. "Do you even have the spices for that?"

Karishma shrugged. "I have no idea what goes into them, but I can show you what I have."

Jyoti thought of the two jars she had at home, full of the samosa spice mixes her mother had taught her to make. They were the first thing she'd made that she knew was the best version of something she had ever had. It was one of two recipes she'd learned from her mother that she hadn't modified as she delved deeper into her culinary knowledge. Samosas were nostalgic and celebratory, which was why she hadn't made them since her falling out with her parents. But they weren't coming around like she'd hoped, and she wasn't going to go the rest of her life without sinking her teeth into that comforting crunchy-on-the-outside, soft-on-the-inside pastry shell filled with the tastes of home.

"I'll take a look and try to improvise," Jyoti said. "I'm assuming there's not an Indian grocery store around here?"

Karishma shook her head. "Not a huge Desi population in this fair city."

"Doesn't that bother you?"

"Sometimes. It would be nice to get a dosa or parathas every now and then, but I have my comfort food list whenever I visit my parents. More often than not, it's nice to have the separation. There are no gossiping aunties to make snide comments about why I can't do things the traditional way. With every choice, we both gain and lose something, right?"

Jyoti had basked in the aunties' praise, and she knew it had pleased her mother that, up until her divorce, Jyoti had maintained good standing in their community and had been the one everyone hoped their daughters would emulate.

"I never realized you gave that gossip a second thought," Jyoti said. "You're always so chill about it."

Karishma shrugged. "No one wants to be looked down on. What was my crime? Being open about dating and drinking? All of their kids were doing that too and lying about it. I didn't want to have that kind of relationship with my parents."

Jyoti was in the camp of having lied to her parents about those things. "Not all of us could talk to our moms the way you talk to yours though."

"I guess I'm lucky that way. But it's hard to know which came first. Was it that my mom was always more open than others, or was it that I started being honest with her at an early age so she was trained to receive that type of information better by the time we got to college?"

She had raised a fair point that Jyoti had never considered. She'd spent her life trying to make her parents' lives easier, and, for her, that meant not worrying them about things that they would disapprove of.

"Who knows?" Karishma mused. "Maybe it wasn't even that. I suppose it could also have been my pursuing a career over marriage and kids. The gravest of sins." She pressed her hand to her chest in mock horror. "The work I do matters, even if our parents' generation doesn't think it does. Getting books into the world that allow so many people to see themselves in the pages will have a far wider-reaching and longer-lasting impact on the world than many of their kids will." Karishma leaned back into the sofa cushions, making herself comfortable as she ate more bataka poha.

She knew Karishma hadn't meant anything against her, but she wondered if that's how she'd thought of her while Jyoti had been married and trying to get pregnant. Did she think that Jyoti wasn't contributing to the world because she'd believed marriage was the natural next step after college, and then children after that?

"I'm sorry if anyone made you feel like what you're doing isn't enough," Jyoti said. "The work you do—it matters a lot for the generations after us. Just think of the kids who are going to libraries and pulling books off shelves and seeing themselves on the covers and in the pages. We never had that. I went through an entire English literature degree and didn't read a single book by an author who wasn't white."

Karishma relaxed her shoulders and cast Jyoti a grateful smile. They'd often spoken about the difficulties of being the transition generation that was always struggling to find their place. It was why when Karishma began freelancing, she'd made herself one promise: she would only edit books of Indian and other underrepresented authors. She was determined to help as many as she could who were brave enough to attempt that journey through the many white gatekeepers in the publishing industry. When she'd started at her first publishing house, she'd hoped that by working within the system, she could help shepherd more authors through it. Instead, she kept getting stalled whenever she tried to introduce something innovative or emerging. The number crunchers were never ready to invest in something that didn't already have a proven track record, creating the circular loop that kept the industry mired in the same types of books and authors.

"It's fine if they don't get it," Karishma said, in a tone that suggested it wasn't. She then slung her arm around Jyoti's shoulders and gave her a squeeze. "Now that you're on the black sheep side of the fence, too, it's been less lonely. Maybe you should write a cookbook turning all the Gujarati recipes on their head, and I can help you sell it, and then we'll permanently seal our fate outside their circle."

Jyoti smiled, but knew she'd rather be back in her parents' and the aunties' good graces than cement her freedom. The aunties could be a bit much with their strong opinions and lack of boundaries, but they were also who she could count on to pin her sari in the bathroom at an event, or show her a better way to make bhajias.

"I don't know if I'm strong enough to commit to that," Jyoti said. "But if we find the ingredients, I'm in for the samosa party, as long as you help me assemble them."

Karishma saluted her. "Yes, Chef. Ben is rather resourceful when it comes to food, especially food he wants, so we can have him get anything you need." She stiffened her shoulders and took on a formal demeanor. "Excuse me," she said in an exaggerated haughty voice, "*source* anything you need. That's what you chefs prefer to say, right?"

Jyoti adopted a similar faux snooty tone. "Indeed."

They settled into finishing their food, and Jyoti enjoyed the happy sounds of spoons clinking against the bottoms of bowls.

Later that day, Jyoti found herself scrolling through social media profiles, admiring chefs and food stylists. Her mother had raised her to keep her thoughts private whenever possible, so she was a lurker on social media rather than a commenter. Jyoti couldn't believe how imaginative pasta was becoming, the humble comfort food now elevated to visual masterpieces. There were several accounts devoted to laminating fresh herbs into pasta dough, creating the most intricate patterns that appeared as if painted on. Samosa dough was much thicker, but she wondered if there could be a way to laminate cilantro into that.

She came across an influencer who used natural colors from

ground butterfly pea flower, spirulina, and turmeric to create the most artistic patterns on the pasta dough. There were modern designs with geometric shapes and intricate landscapes showing fields of flowers or trees. She could see that hours and an endless array of dirty dishes would be required to prepare these doughs that would be cooked and consumed in minutes, but her brain was excited. Seeing the turmeric dough made her think about what Indian-inspired fillings could go into the pasta to create something no one had ever seen before. Maybe she could do a saag paneer filling with a sauce that looked like pesto but had the flavors of green chutney.

Her enthusiasm mounted until she remembered she wouldn't be serving these dishes in Taste of Ginger. It seemed so bleak that she'd be able to find the money, and she would have to start letting that image of her future go.

A familiar sense of failure washed over her. She recalled her feeble endeavor of starting a food blog when, after a few years of failed attempts to conceive, Ashok had insisted the stress of her work was likely contributing to "her fertility problems" and forced her to quit the restaurant. After a couple weeks of staying at home and being a housewife, Jyoti had felt antsy and started the blog. She quickly learned that cooking for a restaurant and cooking for cameras were very different. Like any good chef, her focus had always been on flavor. But when posting online, no one could actually taste the food and very few were likely to make the dishes they saw.

While Indian food was complex, layered, and delicious, it wasn't considered pretty by Western standards. The aromatic brown gravy in her channa masala was never going to get the same traction as a perfectly twirled mountain of spaghetti with a sprig of verdant basil resting at the summit and parmesan snow around it. Given the stiff competition, her lackluster photos and captions that promised bold, tantalizing flavors were a far cry from what people wanted to see. At her peak, she'd managed to gain about 500 subscribers, most of whom had been friends of friends rather than people seeking her out. Now she saw that her last post had been eight years ago, and her subscriber count was down to 118. She could hardly blame the people who had deserted her. It wasn't like she'd done much to hold their attention.

Jyoti tossed her phone next to her and ruminated on how Ashok had always been so sure the problem was not with him. It had to be something wrong in *her* body. It irked her so much that he and Radha had gotten pregnant so quickly because it meant that he had been right and no ex-wife ever wants to think that about her ex-husband.

She picked her phone back up and logged into TikTok, knowing that was where the real magic happened these days. She had previously created an account but had yet to make a single post, preferring to marvel at others' food content than produce her own. As videos played one after another, the algorithm eerily learning which food posts would keep her engaged, she easily distracted herself by conjuring ways of presenting Indian food differently. It wasn't the type of cuisine that had a lot of fussiness with tweezers and ring molds, but that didn't mean it couldn't adapt with the times.

She switched over to her Instagram feed, but the endless stream of newborn baby photos, wedding pictures, career highlights, and family portraits dulled her spirits. She had a hard time visualizing what her future would be. She wasn't a mom. She wasn't a wife. She wasn't a chef. Who was she supposed to be when she had centered her whole life on embodying those three identities?

When they'd begun the divorce discussions, she'd somehow convinced herself that Ashok would understand how important her work was to her and let her keep the restaurant. He'd been guilted into running it but had always wanted to use his accounting degree for a regular office job with set daytime hours. Jyoti's reliance on logic had been silly given that it had started off as his family's business, but she'd thought this was his chance to unload the burden he'd never wanted. Surely, he must have recognized that her passion and efforts were what had propelled Taste of Ginger to its level of success. And that she could catapult it even further if she made it her sole focus and was no longer worried about making babies. But memories were selective in the aftermath of a failed marriage.

She considered whether she could start her own restaurant when she got back home. Something smaller and more affordable than Taste of Ginger. But the task seemed daunting. And she'd never loved the business and front of house aspects, which was why she and Ashok had been the perfect pair when it came to running the restaurant. The reality was that everything about her new life alone seemed overwhelming. Ashok wasn't perfect but having him around meant there were many things she didn't have to worry about, like appliances, finances, and who would bring her kitchari if she fell sick. Still, regardless of what she wanted, she needed to learn how to survive without help from Ashok or her parents. The divorce settlement was running dry, and she had no income outside of that. She lamented putting herself in a position where so much of her life had been dependent on her husband. She needed to figure out what a middle-aged woman with her limited skillset and job experience could do, and once she did, she'd make sure it was something no one could ever take away from her.

FOUR

Mad Souls looked like a quintessential dive bar that reminded Jyoti of her college days. It was small and had moody forest green walls. The sticky tabletops were all too familiar, but the main difference was they were coated in craft cocktails rather than cheap beer. A colorful chalkboard displayed the menu and Jyoti left it to her group of trusted advisors, Karishma, Mae, Ben, and Enzo, to pick out her drink.

Their party was too large to sit at one of the sparse tables inside, so they joined the millennials and Gen Zers who had spilled out onto the front patio of the bar. Feeling like she was in her twenties again, Jyoti sipped her chianti margarita, marveling at how tequila and chianti somehow worked together, while also acknowledging that this dangerous combination could likely lead to bad decisions.

Ben leaned toward her and whispered conspiratorially, "I've tracked down your spices. Now we just need to wait for the delivery."

"Karishma was right," she said. "You're very resourceful."

Ben nodded. "I told you, Brits don't joke when it comes to samosas."

"I'll do my best not to disappoint."

Karishma joined them with two new drinks in hand. She'd already had a couple and her steps were wobbly. She was eyeing Enzo in that way that Jyoti had now become accustomed to. Karishma would not be spending the night alone.

She thrust a glass at Jyoti, some liquid sloshing over the side. "Here, take this!"

Jyoti didn't know what type of alcohol she'd be mixing with her chianti and tequila, but she didn't care. The summer breeze against her skin and her gradual acclimation to a Florentine lifestyle left her feeling more carefree. She understood how Karishma had gotten sucked into the magic of the city.

Karishma tried to whisper in Jyoti's ear but didn't realize how loud she was. "That gorgeous guy over there has been staring at you." She turned Jyoti's shoulders so she could see the young men standing around another table.

Jyoti saw the Italian man with chocolate eyes and thick hair smiling at her. He raised his glass, and Karishma nudged her to do the same. "I could practically be his mother," Jyoti said under her breath.

"But you're not," Karishma said, "and that's what matters. Go talk to him."

"How?" Even if she had the courage to approach a man that much younger, she did not speak Italian and literally could not converse with him.

"You worry too much," Karishma said. "Just get laid. You don't need to write a dissertation with him."

Jyoti was not someone who "just got laid." But as she looked at that guy smiling at her so confidently, she wished she could be. She'd only had one boyfriend before Ashok, another Indian guy because she'd never had the desire to venture outside of her community, and had been with a grand total of two men in her life.

"I'm sure he prefers a younger, thinner, whiter woman."

Karishma huffed. "Europe isn't like America. Look at Emmanuel Macron." She grabbed Jyoti by the wrist and dragged her over to his table.

"Ciao!" she said to the three young men. *"Il mio nome è Karishma. Questo è la mia amica Jyoti."*

The man who had smiled at Jyoti said, "Saro." He then gestured toward his two friends and introduced them as Alessandro and Federico.

"Parli inglese?" Karishma asked with a flirtatious smile.

"Si, un po," Saro answered, eyes still on Jyoti.

Jyoti could not understand what this guy, who had to be around twenty-five, could possibly see in her. The bar was full of lithe, age-appropriate Italian women who had mastered the art of walking on cobbles in high heels, and he could easily spend his time talking to one of them. But she saw that Karishma was locked in, explaining to Saro that Jyoti was visiting from New York. His eyes shone. Everyone knew New York from television and movies, so they moved to easy conversations about *Friends* and *Law & Order.*

Federico brought over shots and Jyoti's stomach twisted at the thought. She was all for indulging in wine or cocktails, but she hadn't had a shot since her twenties—and with good reason. But the desire to fit in remained the same as it had back then, and she tossed back her glass with the group and choked it down. Saro kept sidling closer to her and whispering in her ear. Jyoti couldn't understand much of what he said, but Karishma kept encouraging her to reciprocate.

Am I really going to have a one-night stand with this kid? she asked herself. But then she thought about Ashok and Radha. If that pot-bellied jerk with a receding hairline could pull someone younger, then she could too. Besides, it would be a welcome change if the last person she'd had sex with could stop being Ashok. She didn't need to marry this guy, but it would be nice to replace some long-stored images in her mind. She was at that intersection of too drunk to make thoughtful decisions, but not drunk enough to pass out, so she decided to go for it.

She leaned forward and kissed him. She could tell he was taken aback, but he had no trouble adjusting to the change of pace. When she pulled away, Karishma gave her a triumphant look and slinked back over to Enzo. Saro's friends managed to make themselves scarce, too, so she allowed herself to fall into this stranger, who was looking at her with a desire that she wasn't sure her husband had ever shown. As the bar closed, Saro had his arm around her and was leading her toward his apartment while Karishma and Enzo were heading back to hers.

When Jyoti woke up the next morning and saw Saro's body tangled in the sheets, she felt her cheeks flush. She'd learned that he was sixteen years younger than her, confirming that, yes, she could have been his teenage mom. The headache she had from the mixture of booze was worth it. It had been so long since she'd been touched with lust and passion and delight.

But as fun as her foray into her twenties had been, she was ready to go back to her forties and get some ibuprofen and hydrate. She quietly dressed, and when he stirred, she softly told him she had to leave but he should go back to sleep. He did not resist, and she took one last look at him sprawled on the bed and smiled to herself before walking back to Karishma's.

The apartment was quiet when she entered and there was no sign of Enzo's shoes by the front door. She needed hangover food and she needed it now, so she began rifling around the kitchen to see what she could pull together. She really wanted sabudana vada, but she would have needed to soak the tapioca last night, so that craving would need to wait. She saw the loaf of bread, chilies, tomatoes, garlic, and shallots and let out a sigh of relief. *Chili cheese toast.* She grabbed a nondescript white semihard cheese from the fridge and smelled it. It seemed mild in flavor and would do. She warmed a skillet, buttered the bread, topped the slices with her cheese and veggie mixture, and placed them in the pan. Then she grabbed the lid and an ice cube from the freezer. She dropped the ice into the hot pan away from the toast and immediately put the lid on it to retain the steam, melting the cheese while the bottom crisped.

Karishma came into the kitchen in her robe, her hair wet from the shower. "What's on Auntie's menu today? A little something to help ease those aching sex muscles?"

Jyoti gave her a devilish grin. "Chili cheese toast."

"Is that code for hot, spicy sex with a young Italian?"

"No. It's code for hangover food that we both need. And yes, there was sex with a young Italian." Jyoti looked at her friend coyly. "Three times."

Karishma clapped her on the back. "Well done! When you get back on the horse, you really get back on it."

"You were right, Kar," Jyoti said, handing her a plate with cheesy toast on it. "I already feel different knowing Ashok wasn't my last. It's weird how quickly that switch can be flipped."

"See, there can be life after divorce, and perhaps an even better one."

"Maybe, but you know how hard it is for me to live without a plan."

Karishma nodded. "I know. But stick with it. Let the Universe guide you. You don't need to carry these burdens with you forever. Just set them down for a summer and remember what it feels like to really live again."

"Like you're doing with Enzo?" she said.

Karishma batted her eyes innocently as she picked up her toast.

It sounded so nice to be able to stop worrying, but Jyoti wasn't sure if she was capable of that. Last night was starting to show her that maybe she could let go of her need to be in complete control for a little while.

Karishma took a bite and closed her eyes. "I haven't had this since I was a kid. Until you came this summer, I'd hardly had Indian food at all, but there's something about those childhood favorites that bring you right back home, isn't there?"

Jyoti bit into hers and let the onion, garlic, and chili light up her tongue while the tomato and cheese cooled it down. Food was a carefully orchestrated dance when done well. "I can teach you some of your faves, if you'd like. Then, you don't have to go as long in between. Seems Ben could get you any ingredients you'd need."

"Thanks, but culinary pursuits were never my thing. That's why it's nice to have you here. Maybe we plan on you visiting more instead."

"I'd like that," Jyoti said.

Karishma nudged her. "Perhaps to visit your new Italian boyfriend."

"Nice try, but I'm not sure that's what this was."

"Do you have plans to see him again?"

Jyoti looked sheepish. "He put my number in his phone, but I slunk out while he was half-asleep. I'm not sure this is a repeat thing. I got what I needed."

Karishma smiled like a proud parent. "Good. You don't come to Florence to meet the man you're going to marry."

Later that day, Jyoti heard a groan from the living room and found Karishma staring in disgust at her laptop.

"What happened?" Jyoti asked, but she knew that look all too well by now.

"I had three authors who were out on submission—one who is Laotian, and two who are Indian. One was Swati. All of them are back to the drawing board."

Jyoti knew the story of Swati Doshi well because she had

been the impetus for Karishma to leave her corporate job. Karishma had gone into publishing and worked her way to senior editor because she wanted to help people like Swati who were telling stories of families from immigrant backgrounds. She'd been so excited to acquire Swati's book, but her publisher didn't want to take a "chance" on something that didn't already have a reliable audience. Karishma had become increasingly frustrated with the disconnect between the stories she wanted to acquire and the ones she was directed to take on. The powers that be were always saying they wanted more diverse content, but it had started to feel like lip service because they only wanted to lean on sanctioned tropes like immigrants leaving their "unfortunate" lives in their home countries and finding easier ones in North America. When she brought authors like Swati to the acquisitions table, whose work challenged white North America's treatment and acceptance of immigrants, there was always some vague reason why she didn't have the support to make an offer, or there were more frequent requests to revise and resubmit rather than offering a contract and doing the editorial work together. In the rare instances in which she could get someone through, the advance would be lower than it deserved and then the marketing would fall into the same cookie-cutter patterns as white authors, doing nothing to help the book find the right audiences. Karishma's pleas for more—more money, more exposure—went unheard.

What she had thought would be her dream job had turned into her having to churn out whatever was most comfortable for white audiences. All while being the public face of diversity for her publishing house and having to smile and express how *eager* her team was for submissions from nonmainstream authors. So, after she couldn't get Swati's book through acquisitions, she realized the biased systems were just too entrenched. And sacrificing her physical, mental, and emotional health wasn't worth continuing the losing battle. Once she began her freelance business, Swati became her first client and she was determined to help get her through to publication one day. Unfortunately, it had been over five years and three different manuscripts and it still hadn't happened.

"I'm so sorry things aren't working out for Swati again. Hopefully one day soon. If you believe in her this much, then it's clear she has talent."

"Can you imagine finally reading a novel about our people?" Karishma asked. "When I read her stories, I realized how much we've been missing. We've gone our whole lives without reading one book with Gujarati characters like us. Everything we know about our culture comes from our parents and aunties and uncles. And their experience with Indian culture is frozen in time from when they left India fifty years ago. They don't realize how much India has evolved since then. Wouldn't it be amazing to see other people's experiences, outside of our little enclave, that we could also relate to?"

"But you are going to change that," Jyoti said, joining her friend on the couch.

Karishma sighed. "I'm trying, but it's always the same excuse. 'There's no market for them.' I wish I could shake them and say that we need to *create* that market. Most people are influenced by what you tell them to buy. So, if we keep pushing white authors writing romance or thrillers, then of course we won't have a market for nuanced cultural family stories. But if the industry put the same money and effort into those books as it did when publishing the first legal thriller, then people would buy them. I wish decision-makers could focus on the long game."

When Karishma got into this mood, Jyoti knew the best way to support her was to just be there and listen.

Karishma continued, "The worst part is that Swati's last editor rejection came with a note that while the writing was good, they couldn't pick it up because the India wave is over.

What *wave*? There are 2.5 million people who migrate out of India every single year. A few Indian authors get published in North America over the course of decades and that is somehow supposed to be enough to cover the experiences of the entire diaspora of over 32 million people? When does the white privilege wave end? No one would ever say, 'We have too many white women rom-coms, so let's stop publishing those.'" She flashed Jyoti an apologetic smile. "Sorry. It's been a tough week of rejections."

"Never apologize," Jyoti said. "I know how deeply this affects you. Watching you go from being so hopeful about your dream job to so disillusioned was painful to watch."

Karishma touched her signature labradorite East-West prism necklace by her favorite jewelry designer, Asha Patel. She wore it daily and always sought comfort from the crystal when she was stressed. "I've worked with thirty-seven authors since I started freelancing, and only fourteen of them have gotten published so far."

"I know it's hard, but those numbers are way better than when you worked in-house," Jyoti said. "Back then you had something like thirty authors and only three of them weren't white. And you always said you had the most multicultural list on your team." Jyoti squeezed her friend's forearm. "You've changed the lives of those authors by getting them in the door. You can be proud of that."

Karishma sighed. "Maybe one day publishing will stop favoring the same stories it always has and finally understand that a rising tide lifts all ships."

FIVE

It was time. She'd been putting this off for the last couple days, and Karishma had practically poured two glasses of wine down her throat in preparation. Jyoti sat cross-legged on the bed and picked at a loose thread on the comforter as she stalled. She knew the longer she played this out in her head before making the call, the worse it would be, but she couldn't get herself to pick up the phone. Her night with Saro had been a reminder that there was life after divorce, and even though it may not look like the one she had planned, different did not have to mean worse.

With a deep breath, she hit the button to dial Ashok.

When he answered, she could hear the sounds of pots and pans and running water that had once been so familiar to her. The kitchen staff at Taste of Ginger would be getting ready for the lunch rush, and she missed being a part of that team. This time before opening was the most calming for her because it was after the prep had been done but before the chaos of diners arriving.

"Hi," Ashok said, his voice distracted.

The background noise lessened, so she figured he had moved

from the kitchen to the small back office and closed the door. It was the only place to have any privacy there.

"You can let the embryos go," she said, trying to keep her voice even as she thought about the three potential lives that could have come from them. One boy and two girls. When they'd implanted embryos in the past, they got to choose the sex and that was one part of the process that she'd never been comfortable with. It felt like too much power for any one person to determine which reproductive parts to bring into the world. She'd always let Ashok decide because she knew she'd be happy with any healthy baby that would allow them to move forward and let her body rest from the years of efforts.

"Good. I'll email you the documents."

It was so easy for him. But unlike her, he wasn't saying goodbye to parenthood—only to parenthood with her.

"I guess that's it," she said.

"Yep."

"Alright then."

She couldn't believe how stilted conversation now was with someone she had once shared a bed and future with. But not everyone was meant to be in your life for every season of it. She hung up knowing there was nothing more to say.

She took some deep box breaths and gave herself a moment to reflect on closing this chapter of her life. She'd started at the age of twenty-nine, and devoted the entirety of her thirties to this. Five miscarriages, each one more emotionally and physically draining than the one before it. Four rounds of IVF. Twenty-seven pounds added to her body over that period of time. She recalled how she'd tried to stop the fertility journey years earlier, but she hadn't been strong or convincing enough to succeed.

That day, six years ago, Jyoti found Ashok at the dining table in their home with his laptop and a bunch of papers spread before him.

"What are you doing?" she asked.

He turned toward her, his face sullen. "These medical bills have gotten out of hand. It's over one hundred thousand dollars over the past four years."

"Why don't we stop?" she suggested, sitting down next to him and putting her hand on his forearm.

"What do you mean *stop*?" he said.

"Just stop. All of it. My body is tired, Ashok. There's nowhere left to poke holes into it. We were happy before we started trying for kids, weren't we? I could go back to Taste of Ginger, and we could be a couple who is happy without kids."

"How can we be happy that way?" he asked, his voice earnest as if he really wanted her to give him the answer.

"Not everyone has kids."

"Who do we know who doesn't?"

"Karishma."

Ashok scoffed. "Her and her child-free nonsense. She never does anything the right way." He sounded like the aunties. "Who do we know who is *married* and doesn't have kids? What would we tell our parents?"

She rubbed his arm. "That we tried our best and it didn't happen for us."

"That's easier for you to say," he said. "Chaya already gave your parents a grandchild, and Tanvi could too. My parents only have me."

Ashok wasn't wrong. She did feel relief at knowing her parents' ability to have grandchildren hadn't hinged solely on her. Chaya's son, Nitin, gave her some breathing room. And there was a chance, however slim, that Tanvi would one day marry and deliver that purebred grandbaby that would finally satisfy her parents.

Jyoti sighed. "But what can we do? We've tried everything. We have to consider the possibility that we can't have children naturally." She hesitated before continuing, "If we adopt, we could give someone a good home."

He gave her a wide-eyed look, as if the suggestion were preposterous. "How do we know what kind of kid we are getting if we adopt? We can't guarantee the lineage. The child could be disturbed or handicapped, and we wouldn't know."

Jyoti hated his word choice and lack of logic. It wasn't as if parents were guaranteed to have a child who was just like them but having that type of conversation with Ashok would go nowhere. She knew her suggestion was not part of the life he envisioned for himself, so she tried to find some empathy.

"We could adopt from India. There are so many children who need homes due to poverty. And the kid would still look like a part of this family as far as our lives here go. Most people in America see brown and assume we all look the same anyway, so we could finally use those stereotypes in our favor," she said, knowing appearances mattered a great deal to him and his parents. Hers too, if she were being honest.

Ashok ran his hand through his thinning hair. "I don't know, Jyo. I really want my own kid. We don't know anyone who has adopted. It's about preserving the family line. How would my parents feel if it ends with me? Think about what people would say."

When she was younger, Jyoti had told herself she would never live her life based on "what would people say" the way her parents and their friends did. But after she married Ashok, she realized it wasn't that easy to give up the teachings of the community they grew up in. It was hard to make a decision and know you'd have to explain yourself to everyone around you for the rest of your life. Ashok wasn't wrong in suggesting that's what would happen to them. It would. But if raising children was their top priority, then wasn't it just the first in the long line of sacrifices they'd make throughout the course of their lives as parents?

"We'd have to stand up for ourselves if we went that route. With our parents, with the aunties and uncles, with the temple..."

Ashok looked drained. "I want to see myself in my kid's face..."

If it were up to her, she would have given that to him years ago. But this was not in her control. She inhaled slowly and released the question she'd been too afraid to ask. "What if we can't have children?"

Ashok looked uncertain. It seemed they were coming up against the fear Jyoti had always had: If it came down to her or having a family, which would he choose?

After a long pause, Ashok said, "Harsha and Promod did a couple rounds of IVF and nothing took, but then when they stopped everything and went back to trying the natural way, it worked for them. Maybe that's our problem too. Maybe we need to stop the hormones and let nature take its course."

"You mean go back to having sex for fun?" she asked, trailing her fingers along his arm with a sultry smile.

"We'd still need to track the ovulation cycles and make sure we are trying at the right times. That's how Harsha did it," he said.

Jyoti deflated. She missed her husband and wasn't sure she would ever have him back. Their lives had been centered around having a baby for most of their marriage now and the early years of them working as a team in the restaurant felt like a distant memory. She hardly recognized who they had become and wondered if they could ever be that couple again. It felt like Ashok wouldn't be satisfied until he had the family he'd envisioned for himself.

He looked so hopeful as he waited for her answer, and Jyoti knew their journey wasn't done yet. He'd never answered her question about whether they could be happy without kids.

It had taken another three years before Ashok finally confirmed what Jyoti had always suspected was the answer. She was now halfway around the world, sitting in Karishma's apartment in Florence, grieving the life she never got to have. Loss was painful no matter how it came about.

Karishma knocked on the door to her room and popped her head in. "You feeling okay?"

Jyoti shrugged. The memories of her marriage and fertility journey weighed down on her.

"I'm hungry and it's time to continue your culinary tour of Florence. What do you say? Don't make me eat pasta alone," Karishma said.

Jyoti was so grateful for her friend. "I could use some carbs. And vino. Lots of vino."

"I know the perfect spot."

They strolled fifteen minutes from the apartment and crossed a busy intersection to find themselves at Alla Vecchia Bettola for what Karishma promised was "the best red sauce in Italy."

They passed through the makeshift patio that Karishma said came about during the pandemic, and entered the unassuming butter-yellow building, passing through the small foyer with red and cream tiles to the main restaurant. Jyoti was instantly hit with the smell of garlic and onions. She loved how those ingredients were completely transformed by heat in a way no other ingredient was, going from pungent and assertive to sweet and luscious. With garlic and onions, it was possible to make any dish delicious. She had often marveled at how those ingredients found their way around the globe and were present in nearly every culture's food she knew of, apart from Jainism.

To their left was the bar area with large cuts of cured meats and ropes of garlic bulbs suspended from the ceiling above it. Well-used copper pans rested on the wall near the bar and kitchen, while black-and-white framed photos hung throughout the restaurant. The walls were lined with rustic white tiles and classically European fixtures. This was a place that felt like it had been the same for generations.

They were shown to a dark cherry wood table with a white marbled top with gray veining near a window that had a yellow curtain across it. It was a cozy space that they could barely slide into, but the perfect one to curl up with a bowl of warm pasta and a bottle of earthy red. Jyoti loved that this was not a country of wine lists and sommeliers and all the pomp and circumstance that came with selecting a bottle of wine in New York when dining out. Here, you decided whether you wanted red or white, and then left it up to the staff.

"I love this place," Jyoti said, sitting on the backless stool and glancing around at the satisfied diners and bucolic surroundings.

She touched the paper placemat whose hue could best be described as somewhere between dried pasta and mustard and mulled over how perfect the color choice had been. While it felt like a restaurant that had changed very little over the years, it seemed like each choice had been made to withstand the test of time. Front of the house had always been Ashok's realm at Taste of Ginger, with her offering input when he sought it or if she saw something that needed a feminine touch, but she knew they hadn't taken the same care as at Alla Vecchia Bettola. If she ever opened a restaurant herself, she needed this level of precision.

Karishma ordered the penne alla bettola for them both and a fiasco of Rosso di Toscana, which the waiter promptly brought and set on the table with two thick glasses. There was none of the pretentiousness in glassware that there would have been in Manhattan with a specific shape designated for each varietal. He left them to pour for themselves and headed back toward the kitchen.

"I never knew these bottles were called fiascos," Jyoti said, touching the woven straw enrobing the bottom half.

"'Fiaschi,'" Karishma corrected. "That's the proper word for the plural in the wine industry. 'Fiasco' is the singular."

Karishma's editorial work made her meticulous about details.

Jyoti had always thought she'd clean up at trivia nights with all the random data she had amassed over the years.

"I suspect you can recite the history too?" Jyoti said.

Karishma looked sheepish.

"Alright, come out with it. I know you're dying to tell me."

"*Fare fiasco* means 'to fail,' and sometime in the fourteenth century there was a mistake in the glassblowing process that resulted in a round bottom that couldn't stand on its own—a failure of the bottle." Karishma's eyes lit as she shared her knowledge. "Rather than throw it away, the merchants devised a straw basket to hold the bottle so that it could still stand upright and be used. Tuscany uses fiaschi more than any other region in Italy, and in the seventeenth century, Florence decided that labels needed to be applied and the straw going up the neck of the bottle was removed to expose the glass and provide for a label. That's the bottle that has withstood the test of time and that we're still using today." She gestured to the fiasco on their table with a flourish.

Karishma loved when other people got excited about her random facts, but Jyoti couldn't give her the satisfaction just yet.

She cocked her head. "It's very unlike you to have dates narrowed down only to centuries. You'd think the year could be discovered with adequate research."

Karishma looked stricken as she considered this, and Jyoti could see her mental wheels spinning as she thought about how to find the exact dates when she told this story in the future.

"I'm kidding," Jyoti said. "Don't go down a rabbit hole to find out anything else."

Two plates of steaming penne coated in thick reddish-orange sauce were placed before them. There were specks of chopped parsley sprinkled on top to give it brightness. The waiter offered Parmesan, and they both nodded eagerly as it fell like snow from up high to give an even coating.

"Get ready for magic," Karishma said.

Jyoti could feel the al dente perfection as her fork speared two noodles and she brought them to her mouth. The pasta was toothsome, and the vodka sauce had a fiery chili flake spice on the front of her palate, then a concentrated, jammy tomato flavor that tasted like the sauce had been baked rather than made on a stovetop, and then a hint of sweetness from cream on the finish. The salty parmesan lifted everything up a notch and she knew this dish was getting added to her growing list of culinary experiments from this trip. Once she learned the science behind making these dishes as they were, she could apply those techniques to other foods and flavors and create something new.

"You were right," Jyoti said through a mouthful. "This is perfection."

"You've earned it after the adulting you had to do today."

Karishma raised her glass. "A toast," she said, waiting for Jyoti to raise hers before continuing. "To living a life greater than the one you planned."

Jyoti clinked her glass. "And to the friends who will help you get there."

Twenty years ago, she couldn't have imagined that she and Karishma would be sitting in this restaurant in Florence, indulging in what was indeed the best red sauce she'd ever had, with no clue what her future held. The only thing she was certain of at this point was that she wanted Karishma and pasta in it.

SIX

Two fiaschi later, Jyoti and Karishma were drunk. They stumbled and giggled on their walk home and spilled into the apartment, depositing themselves onto the couch.

Jyoti leaned back and stretched out her stomach. "I need to digest. I'm so full of pasta."

"The only thing better would be being full of—"

Jyoti swung a throw pillow at her friend. "Stop it!"

Karishma shrugged. "You know I'm right."

Jyoti closed her eyes to keep the room from moving. When she opened them again, she sensed it was later than she thought. There was a small blanket covering her and the lights were off. Karishma's door was closed and she'd gone to bed. Jyoti sat up and realized alcohol was still coursing through her because her head was foggy. She could not believe that she felt the urge to eat again after how much pasta she'd had at dinner, but the rumbling was there. She checked her phone and saw that it was 2:40 in the morning. She then saw the email from Ashok. When she opened it and the attached form that needed to be notarized, she froze at seeing the black-and-white text and the checked box next to "destroy embryos." Her chances at parenthood and the life she tried to have were erased in a single line item on a boilerplate form. The emotion she'd tried to bury beneath a pound of penne and a liter of wine began to bubble up to the surface.

She grabbed her phone and opened TikTok. Anything to distract from her swirling thoughts, but perusing the videos of food accounts did nothing to allay the grumbling in her stomach.

She got up and began searching the cabinets for something that could be easily made in the middle of the night with the ingredients on hand. It was times like these when she missed the convenience of her fully stocked and organized pantry in New York. She'd gotten to keep the apartment in the divorce. She now suspected it was because Ashok intended to marry quickly and move into a new place. He was strategic even when his actions seemed kind.

The downside to shopping for produce daily was there wasn't much to work with at this hour. A few potatoes, cheese, some bread, butter, olive oil, a bit of fruit. She opened the small freezer and found a bag of mixed vegetables and knew that was the answer. She'd brought her pav bhaji spice mix from home. It was something she and Karishma would often eat together when they were sharing an apartment after college, and it had been one of Jyoti's favorite comfort foods ever since her mom had made it for her as a young girl. Probably because of the amount of butter. Pav bhaji needed a whole lot of butter, and so did Jyoti's broken heart right now.

She put some potatoes to boil, starting them in cold water so they cooked evenly. She placed the frozen mixed veggies in a colander to thaw. While the potatoes cooked, she busied herself with her phone again. She felt an emptiness inside her as she thought about her future. She thought about calling her sisters, but it was 9:00 p.m. at home and she knew Chaya would be busy with Nitin, who was now seven years old and had a bedtime routine that Chaya and Isaac were sticklers about. Tanvi would be out with her friends somewhere, as she always had mysterious plans that she never shared with the family.

Why aren't the right people around when you need them? Jyoti wondered.

Before she could think more about it, she saw *Mom* on her favorites and thought this was serious enough that they'd get over whatever had been going on with them since her divorce.

She felt instantly comforted when her mom picked up on the second ring.

"Hi," Jyoti said, hesitantly.

She could hear the clink of dishes in the background and knew her mom would be cleaning up the kitchen after dinner while her dad was camped on the sofa watching the nightly news.

"What's wrong? It's late there," Nalini said.

"Oh, nothing," Jyoti said, feeling her words still slurring so she tried to keep her sentences short. "I had a bad night. I—" She wasn't sure what to say, given the destroyed embryos meant her mom would be losing something too. Her voice was soft as she said, "We had to destroy the embryos."

The sound of running water stopped. "What does that mean? They just flush them down the drain or something?"

Jyoti flinched at the cruel description and her mom's typical focus on logistics rather than emotions. "I'm not sure… I didn't ask."

"Je hoy te," Nalini said. *Whatever it is.* "He's having a new baby so what does he care."

"You knew about that?" Jyoti said as she stared at the potatoes dancing around in their boiling water bath.

"Everyone knows after Sasti Masti knows," her mom said.

Sasti Masti was the name adopted by the group of uncles and aunties in their New Jersey Indian immigrant community.

Meaning "cheap fun," it had started as a way for Gujarati families to find one another after immigrating, focusing on inexpensive ways to socialize, but had become cliquish as it grew in size. Now the offshoots had grown to a dizzying number and the gossip ran more rampant.

"You knew but didn't tell me?"

"What was the point? It's done, right?" Nalini said. "Now Ashok will really learn what it means to have kids and what must be sacrificed for it. This younger generation isn't going to do as much for their husbands as I did. You think Radha is going to give up her life to raise a baby and have a clean house and hot meals waiting for him each day?"

"It would have been nice to have heard from my own mother rather than having been blindsided by my ex-husband." Jyoti's words smashed together without breaks.

"Are you drunk?" Nalini asked.

Jyoti pursed her lips tightly. Maybe if she didn't answer, her mom would change the subject.

"Jyoti," Nalini said sternly.

"I just had a little wine," she said. "It was a lot to process."

A big sigh from her mom. "Always drinking with Karishma, hah? I need to clean up the kitchen. I'm sure your friend can help you with your *processing*." She said the last word like it was poison dripping from her lips.

A sober Jyoti would have known not to call her mom drunk, but the whole point of alcohol was to numb good judgment. Now she was back to the loneliness of the night and had likely made things worse with her mom without having gotten any benefit out of it.

She opened TikTok and saw green dots next to some of her followers and even though she didn't know who they were, it gave her some sense of calm that, somewhere, someone was occupying the same virtual space as her in this moment. Maybe she could talk to them. People who didn't know her couldn't judge her any worse than her mom had.

Jyoti clicked on the "+" icon and her face filled the screen. Her hair was a mess and she tamped down what she could. She saw the redness in her eyes and didn't realize how close she was to the brink of tears.

"I'm not sure who is out there," she said hesitantly to her reflection after hitting the record button. "I can't say I've ever posted a video before, but I've got some liquid courage in me, as they say." She glanced around the room and then back at the camera. "I've also got a full pound of pasta in me but am making a late-night snack. Never trust a skinny chef, right?" Her voice was tentative, but she felt less tense as she continued to speak into the abyss. "It's probably because food is comfort. For me, it's always been that way, and I really need some comfort right now. Why, you ask? Well, this isn't the life I planned for myself. I know everyone thinks that at some point, but I'm not talking about having painted the walls blue and it turned out I would have preferred yellow." She chuckled to herself. "I wish those were the areas in which my life had gone wrong. Nope, I'm forty-two, my husband left me because I couldn't give him a child, and now he's married to a young new bride who is pregnant. Yup, that asshole got everything he ever wanted. And tonight, I had to give up my chance to even have the geriatric pregnancy I'd been preparing for because I had to agree to destroy the embryos we had frozen. Science is something else, isn't it? You can take a little baby slurry and freeze it to use later. You can't even do that with cream sauces without them breaking, but you can do that with a human life." Jyoti sensed her potatoes were ready and propped her phone up while she turned to the stove.

"But I no longer get to order up one of those embryo babies like it's a lunch special. It's just as well anyway. Who wants a baby with their ex, right? But when you're forty-two, single, unemployed, and your biological clock is telling you it's over, you start to feel the walls closing in." She peeled the hot potatoes without flinching and discarded the skins. She took a skillet and warmed some butter in it. When she saw the bubbles form, she added minced garlic, diced onion, and a chopped tomato until they smelled fragrant, then poured in the defrosted cauliflower, green beans, peas, and carrots and a liberal sprinkling of salt. "Divorce is a brutal thing. So much is lost during the process, and I think the worst part for me are the choices that were taken away. At the end of the day, I want a say in my own life and not to have my options just expire." She added the potatoes and her pav bhaji masala and began mashing the mixture with the back of a serving fork, creating the consistency of chunky mashed potatoes.

"While I'm sitting here feeling sorry for myself, I decided to cook something that would take the edge off. Because food can do that...the perfect bite can make everything seem a little bit better." Jyoti tasted the bhaji and added some red chili powder and more salt to round it out. "When I'm missing home—or the people who are supposed to feel like home—I always come back to these flavors that remind me where I came from, and it makes me feel less alone." She added a generous amount of butter to the bhaji and then a squeeze of lemon and removed it from the heat. She put another skillet on the flame, dropped in some pats of butter, and placed two thick slices of bread into it to toast until golden. She brought it all to the table and sat down while looking at her reflection on her phone.

She closed her eyes and smelled the bhaji. "My mom taught me this recipe. I'm a chef—or at least I used to be—and this was one of two recipes I learned from her that I never changed. But we've been having a tough time, which is why I'm on here instead of talking to her. I often wonder what happens to people like me. People whose parents have essentially disowned them. People without families of their own. What place is there in society for us? Especially in the Indian community where family is everything? I've never seen people living like that in books, or on television, or in movies. Do those people find other ways to be happy?" She salivated as she piled more bhaji onto her pav. "What I've never said out loud before is that I think I could have been happy without a child. I loved my job, my husband, my family. Why wasn't that enough? But then I went down the road of ovulation sticks, fertility treatments, hormone injections, depression, and everything else. No one can stay happy with that amount of stress. Maybe I'm wrong, and some can, but I couldn't. Trying to get pregnant was the most miserable I'd ever been, so why am I so sad now that I know that I never have to do that again? People are funny, huh? Always wanting what we can't have." She took a bite and closed her eyes as the spice and citrus lit up her mouth. "At least, for this moment, I have this." She moved the pav bhaji toward the camera. "And maybe this is all I need."

She stopped recording, posted her video, and then finished up her meal. Then she packed the leftovers and put them in the fridge for Karishma to have in the morning, leaving a pile of dishes in the sink. She was too tired to do them now, and hoped Karishma wouldn't mind the slight bit of disarray to her normally tidy home. Even after her spicy food, she could still taste wine on her tongue and knew she was in for a long day tomorrow. She hoped the bread and butter would soak up some of the damage she'd done to herself.

SEVEN

Karishma bounded into Jyoti's room and flounced on the bed with a huge smile on her face.

"What are you doing?" Jyoti asked, rubbing sleep from her eyes. She glanced out the window at the daylight pouring in. "What time is it?"

"Noon," Karishma said. "I've been waiting all morning for you to wake up."

"Why?" Jyoti asked, rubbing her head. "Aren't you hung-over?"

"Nope."

"Why are you so perky?" Jyoti squinted at her.

"Because you are amazing!" She bounced on the bed.

Jyoti groaned as the movement made her brain feel like it was thrashing around in her skull. "Seriously, what is with you?"

Karishma unplugged Jyoti's phone from the charger and thrust it at her. "Look."

"At what?" Jyoti hadn't heard anything ringing.

Karishma pulled Jyoti to a seated position. "Check. Your. Phone."

Jyoti unlocked it and saw that TikTok notifications kept flooding in. She sat straighter. "What is this?"

"That video you posted last night!" Karishma said. "I would have been mad about the dishes, but when I saw this, all was forgiven."

Jyoti wasn't following her, and Karishma took the phone and pulled up Jyoti's drunken pav bhaji post. "Look." She held the phone for Jyoti to see. "You have over two million views. And counting. There are over a hundred thousand comments. You have gone viral." She handed Jyoti the phone and clapped her hands.

Jyoti recalled pressing the red recording button after talking to her mom when she was making food last night. But surely Karishma was wrong. Jyoti didn't have even 50 followers on TikTok. She looked now and saw her follower count was at 245,367 and climbing.

"How can this be?" she said.

"Who cares? Social media is a crapshoot, but you just hit the jackpot." Karishma paused and looked upward, thinking aloud. "Actually, craps doesn't have a jackpot, so that's not a good metaphor."

Jyoti began reading the comments.

@wanderer4ever: I've been divorced for six years now, and we also couldn't have kids. This hit so deeply!

@julienathan: I've struggled so much with fertility. Even though I had a child eventually, the treatments and miscarriages before her are still with me every day…

@rishikesh50: What a jerk! I'd never leave a woman who can COOK! DM me, lady!

@homecook8605: I'm so sorry for everything you went through. And can you please share that recipe??

@desigirlNYC: I'm not sure if I ever want kids and am terrified to tell my parents. Thanks for sharing your story.

@bengaliforlife: for me, childfree means business class tickets, and there's nothing better than that!

There were countless messages, and Jyoti couldn't believe the outpouring of love and support she was getting from this community of strangers. So many people chiming in and sharing their stories of divorce, infertility, and fears. She felt more connected than she had in so long and she didn't even know their names.

"I can't believe all these people saw this," Jyoti said.

"We need to capitalize," Karishma said.

Jyoti looked up. "What does that mean?"

Karishma grabbed a notepad and pen from the small desk. "You have eyes on you right now. What do you want to accomplish?"

Jyoti looked skeptical. "It's not like I had a goal when I made this video. In the light of day, I would have had the good sense not to."

"Then I'm glad you got the munchies in the middle of the night. Jyo, you have been searching for something to work toward, and I think this could be it."

"Work toward what? Making drunk videos?" Jyoti said.

"Not necessarily *drunk* videos, but people are interested in your story, and they are also interested in your food. Do you have any idea how many publishers find authors on social media? I found two that way when I was working in New York. You could develop a following and parlay that into something more. Something you really want to do with your life moving forward."

Jyoti stared at her. "You make it sound easy, but I'm sure it's not."

"No, it's definitely not. Keeping the attention of people while they are doomscrolling is a nearly impossible task. But what do you have to lose? So you try making some videos and it fails. So what? You aren't any worse off than when you started."

"I'd just make cooking videos?" Jyoti asked.

"I think what people are connecting with is that you are telling your story *while* cooking. So yeah, include a recipe and make something, but also talk about yourself as openly and honestly as you did last night. There might even be a part of this that is cathartic for you, even if nothing else comes from it."

Jyoti liked the idea of unburdening herself of her own pain. It had felt good to let some of that go last night. Maybe Karishma had a point. There wasn't anything better she was doing with her life and her heart lifted at knowing her story had helped others. She wanted to respond to each message, so that each person knew she had read it and they were not alone, but they were coming in at such a rapid pace that it seemed nearly impossible. She would have to play catch-up when they slowed down.

"You think I could do that?" Jyoti asked.

"I know you could. Food has always been your way of connecting with people. It's how you show love. Now you can show some of that love to yourself and share it with this community of women who are craving it. People go through so much in private and are so afraid to say what they are really feeling. Especially people who look like us. You're showing people it's okay to go against what we've been taught and let our emotions out."

Jyoti welcomed the idea of having a purpose, of being able to find meaning in the last decade of her life, but she worried about going against the grain. With a level head, she'd have dealt with her pain in private like she'd been raised to do. But as the messages kept coming in, many from the South Asian diaspora, supporting what she'd said, she thought that maybe she could do this. She'd had fun cooking since she'd gotten to Florence, and it had been so long since she'd felt that. Granted, she'd only been cooking for her and Karishma when they needed a break from pasta, but she loved bringing the joy of food to other people. And this was a way to do that, even if not the most conventional. People could learn some of her favorite recipes and be exposed to Gujarati food they might not have seen otherwise. Maybe her mom would be happy to see her bringing their food to the masses since this was definitely different from the restaurant work that Nalini deemed "servant class."

"How would I make the videos?" Jyoti pondered.

"Just like last night. Keep it authentic and raw. People are so sick of seeing the fake lives people post. I think that's why you went viral. It wasn't planned or staged. It was you being genuine, no filters, and most people are afraid to show that to the world these days."

Jyoti laughed nervously. "It sounds scarier when you say it that way."

"Again, what do you have to lose?"

The excitement and possibility in Karishma's eyes felt infectious.

Suddenly, Jyoti's phone vibrated with an incoming call. Mom flashed on the screen. Eyes wide, she showed it to Karishma.

"Maybe she saw your post, and is finally ready to let this grudge go once and for all." Karishma held up her hands in prayer. "Answer it," she said, leaving the room to give Jyoti some privacy.

Fueled by optimism, Jyoti answered. "Mom?"

"What have you done?" Nalini's voice boomed through the phone.

"What?" Jyoti said.

"Thane budhi nathi?" *Do you have no brain?*

Her mother was coming in hot, a change from the coldness the night before but not in the right direction. Any optimism she'd felt for a rekindling was quickly snuffed out.

"I thought you might be calling because you saw my post," Jyoti said, deflated.

"I *am* calling because I saw that garbage! Have you no sense? Telling people we have *disowned* you? Loko shu khese?"

And here Jyoti was. Back to her childhood when she wanted to wear American clothes to the temple, her teenage years when she started developing crushes and wanted to date, her twenties when she started working as a chef at Taste of Ginger, and her thirties when she couldn't have a baby and had gotten divorced. Her mom's biggest concern was always what others would think. Jyoti had hoped there would have been an age where her mom outgrew that, but she was seventy and Jyoti was still waiting.

"I tried to call you to discuss this and you told me to go *process* it somewhere else, so I did. Didn't you listen to what I actually said?" The words left her before she could reflect on them because the answer was clear. This *was* what her mother was worried about. This was always what she worried about.

She heard her mom sigh and imagined the corresponding eye roll.

"Hai re baap. You've done enough to drag this family through the mud, Jyoti. Do you know how hard it is for us to go to temple and community functions knowing people are gossiping? Divorced," she spat out the word. "That is for white families. So is alcohol. And now you're posting drunk videos… I can hardly recognize you."

"I never asked to be divorced. You should have this conversation with Ashok and his parents," Jyoti shot back like she always did whenever her mother raised the divorce. They'd gone round and round with this same fight since Ashok first told her he was leaving her. No matter her age, she was always a teenage girl when fighting with her mother. "I wasn't the one who left the marriage."

"It's done now. We need to move on from this. Not advertise it to strangers online. We were just starting to have this in the rearview mirror and don't need any of this talk of these embryos bembryos, okay?"

It was Jyoti's turn to sigh. "I'm glad you feel that way. As you may recall, though, I'm still dealing with it, and you didn't want to help me through that."

"Jyoti, I'm serious. Take this video down before we become the laughingstock of the community. Was this Karishma's doing? She's always filling your head with ideas. You need to erase it from the internet. These are private matters to be discussed behind closed doors. Ahka gam ne nathi kevanu, okay?"

Jyoti felt her cheeks flush with embarrassment at being scolded as she replayed her mom's words. *Had she told the whole world?* She glanced at her rapidly ticking view count on her video and guessed her mother wasn't far off. But was it so wrong? People were reaching out with an outpouring of compassion and empathy that she could only dream of getting from her parents. Maybe everyone pretending these things weren't happening was the problem and giving voice to them was the best way to heal.

Her mom spoke again, "Jyoti, are you there? Can you hear me?"

She swallowed. The tone her mother was using was the one she often used with Tanvi and sometimes even Chaya, but rarely with her. "Yes, I can hear you."

"You need to take this down, okay? Right now!"

Why was it that even as a middle-aged woman, her mother giving her an order made her knees weak?

"Is that all you called to say?" Jyoti asked.

Her mother harrumphed. "What could be more important than that right now?"

Jyoti's shoulders slumped. "Nothing," she said flatly, not able to continue the fight.

She hung up and leaned against the pillows with her eyes squeezed shut while her phone continued to vibrate with more notifications.

"What did Nalini Auntie have to say?" Karishma said, eyeing Jyoti warily as she emerged from the room.

Jyoti flopped onto the couch next to her with dramatic flair.

"Uh-oh," Karishma said.

"She wants me to take it down."

Karishma looked at her phone. "You've got over three million views and still climbing. You can't take it down."

"I'm worried this will be the nail in the coffin if I don't. We had a bad conversation before I made this post, so that also isn't helping. Is this video worth that?"

Karishma brushed her off. "Your mom will be off to the next thing she disapproves of in no time. It's like an auntie superpower to be genuinely outraged one minute and then making dal bhat the next like nothing happened. You know my parents have been less than thrilled with my life choices, but they still call every Sunday complaining about the neighbors and who brought a cheap gift to the last wedding function or whatever."

Jyoti met her gaze. "But mine stopped calling. Over something completely out of my control. How long do you think the freeze will be for something that I have the power to take down in a second?"

"Do you want to?" she asked.

"No."

"Then leave it up. It's not like Nalini Auntie said all is forgiven if you take it down, right?"

"No, but the implication is that the war wages anew if I don't."

EIGHT

It had been two hours since her mother demanded she take down the video and the view count was now over four million. The number was staggering to Jyoti, but even more so was the support pouring in. She'd spent her life avoiding sharing anything personal outside of her inner circle. Her family kept their business within their walls, and she'd assumed that was normal. Seeing so many people willing to share their stories in the face of these few minutes of vulnerability from Jyoti made her realize how badly people wanted to bond with one another. It made her aware of how much *she* craved connection rather than burying everything inside in the hopes that it would never reemerge. Trauma always found a way to rise to the surface.

Chaya's face popped up on her phone with an incoming video call.

"How bad is it?" Jyoti asked.

"Let me add Tanvi here too," Chaya said.

Jyoti groaned to herself. If Tanvi was being asked to participate, then it was a Family Code Red. Once the three sisters were on the screen, Chaya took over.

"Going down in a blaze of glory?"

"That wasn't my intention," Jyoti said. "Obviously, I wasn't at my finest decision-making when I filmed it."

"Yeah...that part didn't help," Tanvi said.

Chaya shushed her. "You know the community doesn't like to think of us drinking at any age, especially as women."

Tanvi rolled her eyes. "But drunk sketchy uncles are fine."

"I'm in my forties," Jyoti said, even though she knew Chaya was right. "And did you see the comments? Did you see how many people have opened up after watching my video?"

"Yes." Chaya's tone was very businesslike, as if she were conducting a quarterly fiscal meeting at work. "But that's not helping either. It took no time for the Sasti Masti aunties to get a hold of it. I think every Gujarati in the tristate area knows about it now."

Jyoti sighed. "Do we really care what Sasti Masti thinks?"

Her younger sisters looked at her as if she'd said the world was flat.

"I think you know Mom and Dad care deeply," Chaya said.

She did know that. But it was the first spark of life she'd felt in a long time, and she was trying everything she could think of to make it seem like things weren't so bad.

"Jyo," Chaya continued. "You have to take it down."

Jyoti's shoulders slumped. "It will blow over. The aunties will get bored and move on."

Chaya stared directly at her. "Even if they do, Mom won't. You said she *disowned* you."

Jyoti flinched. "Maybe I shouldn't have used that word, but is it that far off?"

"Look, she's had a rough couple years with having to explain family issues as it is," Chaya said. "Posting about your thoughts and feelings is never going to line up with whatever tale she's woven with her friends to try to explain your divorce. Not only is she going to have our family's dirty laundry aired, but her friends are going to find out she lied to them."

Jyoti hadn't thought about what her mom would have been saying to do damage control about the state of Jyoti's life within the community. Chaya was right that whatever Nalini had said was unlikely to resemble the truth. It couldn't, because Jyoti had never shared her true feelings with her mom.

In a faint voice, Jyoti said, "I feel like I'm finally starting to find some light through the darkness. I went through so much with Ashok. Releasing everything that has been pent up for so long has been cathartic."

"That's good," Chaya said. "But can't there be another way to heal that doesn't involve publicly humiliating Mom and Dad? Maybe therapy?"

Jyoti chewed her bottom lip.

"The family can't take this rift right now," Chaya nudged.

"Mom and Dad are fighting nonstop about this," Tanvi added. "It sucks being at home while they're like this."

Jyoti always had an urge to protect her sisters. When she was younger, she'd hoped that, over time, that would balance and they'd be able to support her like she'd always supported them, but the caretaking role of being the eldest sibling remained a constant and they were all used to these patterns.

"You really don't think it will blow over in a week or so?"

They both shook their heads emphatically.

"If you take it down and say you're sorry, that will go a long way with Mom," Chaya said.

Her heart sank at their pleading faces. Jyoti understood what was being asked of her, but she wasn't sure if she could deliver.

"You'll never guess what I just got?" Karishma said, thrusting her phone at Jyoti as she emerged from the bedroom.

Jyoti read the message from Ushma Auntie: "Beta, is Jyoti doing okay…anything I can do to help? We are so worried."

Ushma Auntie's message, while seemingly nice, was far from sincere. She had crowned herself queen of Sasti Masti and was involved in the majority of its gossipy threads, even if—and maybe especially when—it included her best friend, Nalini.

Karishma laughed as Jyoti tossed back the phone. "She must be desperate for information if your parents aren't talking. I don't think she's ever reached out to me since my parents found a new Desi circle, and she certainly doesn't call me *beta*."

Her heart skipped a beat at the mention of Karishma's parents and their newfound community. Part of her wanted to address this, but she knew this wasn't the time. "My sisters said it's pretty bleak over there. The aunties are in full gossip mode and you know how much my mom hates that kind of attention."

"All over a video?" Karishma shook her head. She sat at her dining table and began peeling an orange, the citrus notes filling the room as her nails pierced the skin.

"They all have TikTok accounts now too," Jyoti said.

Karishma groaned. "Just what we need. A whole group of aunties filling social media with comments in all caps and no punctuation."

Jyoti couldn't help but smile as she recalled the many conversations she'd had with her own parents about that when they'd learned to text.

"What are you going to do?" Karishma asked her.

"I think we both know what I need to do."

"It's such a shame. You hit social media stardom and are giving it up. Influencers go their entire careers trying to achieve the algorithm gold that you struck overnight."

"The price is too high. Everyone is so unhappy."

Karishma offered her an orange segment and Jyoti joined her at the table and popped it into her mouth, letting the sweetness and acid soothe her.

“Maybe I can find another way to connect with people that doesn’t start a family feud,” Jyoti said.

She deleted her post and wondered just how much she was giving up for her family this time, while trying to ignore the voice in her head asking why they never gave up anything for her.

NINE

After she had taken down the post, Jyoti had clung to her phone, hoping for a call or even a text from her mother, but neither came. She shouldn't have been surprised because her mom firmly believed that family didn't say *thank you* to each other. Chaya had reached out with prayer emojis on the sisters' group chat, but that was the most that had come from it.

Karishma came into Jyoti's room a few days later when she was scrolling through TikTok looking at other people's videos. People whose parents seemed to exert less control over them than hers did. Karishma flopped onto the bed and took Jyoti's phone from her.

"Enough of this," she said.

Jyoti feigned innocence but didn't speak.

"I've checked the weather and it's absolutely beautiful in the Amalfi Coast right now. I think it's time for that Praiano trip we've been talking about."

"I'm not sure I feel like parading around in a swimsuit," Jyoti said, thinking about the fertility attempt rolls she'd be carrying next to all the lithe Italian women.

Karishma cocked her head. "Seriously? You need a change of scene, and I have a break while I'm waiting for some of my authors to do their rewrites, so we are going to take advantage of this downtime. You'll see. The waters in Amalfi will heal you."

Jyoti was skeptical, but she could see that Karishma was not going to relent. A couple days later, they packed their wide-brimmed hats and swimsuits and took the train to Naples.

The views along the winding cliffs from Naples to Praiano were breathtaking. There was no place Jyoti had been on the East Coast that could even compare. They were driving at an elevation that was much higher than the shore, and the azure waters of the Tyrrhenian Sea sparkled beneath them like gemstones. She realized these stunning vistas came at a price and Karishma hadn't been exaggerating when she said even the nonnas climb hundreds of stairs each day. Jyoti's lungs constricted at the thought.

"Praiano is the quieter, less touristy part of the Amalfi Coast," Karishma explained, as they entered the small town.

A two-lane road with a very narrow sidewalk along the seaside meandered through the town and appeared to be the main thoroughfare. Their driver deposited them and their luggage outside Hotel Tramonto d'Oro, a family-run hotel where Enzo knew the owners. The front of the building and reception area had looked rather unassuming, but when they opened the door to their room, Jyoti gasped. She understood the hype.

White curtains swayed softly in the breeze and framed the most picturesque and serene views Jyoti had ever seen from a hotel. Luscious green mountains met shimmering blue water all around them. Small white boats left traces in the sea as they crossed back and forth. Jyoti walked as if in a trance past the two beds that were positioned toward the water, stepping onto the balcony and taking in a deep breath of salty ocean air. She could almost taste the calm as she filled her lungs.

"I told you," Karishma said, joining her and inhaling slowly. "Praiano can heal anything that ails you. There is nothing more peaceful than meditating on this balcony."

Jyoti nodded as she marveled at how high they were. It was the elevation that allowed for such pristine and panoramic views. In the background was the sounds of birds. They sat in the wooden chairs with blue-and-white-striped cloth waiting to catch their weight. There was a white table between them with blue and white chevron tile. The simplicity allowed the guests to focus on what mattered most: the view. Jyoti knew she could spend hours sitting exactly as she was. Maybe even she could get into meditation here. Or maybe she'd rather have a glass of chilled white wine to complete the serenity. The family troubles that had been plaguing her were already starting to release their hold as she took in the natural beauty of the world around her.

"How do you feel?" Karishma asked.

"Is it too soon to say transformed?" Jyoti stared at the scene before her.

Karishma laughed. "Nope. I felt the same way my first time. Now you know why this is my usual summer spot. Enzo has been spending every summer here with his family since he was a kid, and I must admit that I'm rather envious."

"It's amazing to think that we grew up in New Jersey never even knowing this place existed, and now it's part of your life," Jyoti said. "Had I stayed married to Ashok, I think I'd have died without ever seeing this view."

Karishma nodded as she gazed at the water. "It's so easy to get stuck in our familiar routines and never break out of that Gujarati New Jersey box."

Jyoti couldn't wait to start exploring and sampling the local cuisine so she could *really* learn about this place. Breathtaking views were enticing, but the soul of a place was found in its food.

"It's really amazing to see the home you've built for yourself in Italy," Jyoti said. "When you first said you were moving away, I was so worried for you. But now I get it."

"Sometimes we need to build new homes, and they can be even better than we expected," Karishma said. "I needed a place that would help bring my nervous system back into alignment after the toxicity of corporate life in Manhattan. Now it's hard to imagine that I was ever part of that rat race. While I was in it, though, I had the blinders on and felt like the only way I could change the industry was by joining the corporate conglomerate. It's only after taking a step back that I saw new options."

"You did find a better way to do what you always wanted to do. I can see how much it has lifted your spirit, health, and general well-being."

"It's a shame that I had to let it get that far though." The breeze gently swirled her hair and she tucked the strands behind her ear. "Those last years were the worst because the industry finally started saying it wanted diversity and I told myself this was what I was waiting for. People were ready to listen to what I'd been saying for years. But they wanted the appearance of diversity rather than the actual results from it. They wanted to parade me out when courting authors or employees of color, so the company looked better than it was. No one understands the weight of that type of tokenism until they experience it firsthand." She shook her head. "I felt so duped."

Jyoti wished she could erase those years for her best friend. "You made the right decision to leave. You can interact with the publishing industry on your terms now and help the people you care about."

"I am. And I think you can do that with your cooking too." She met Jyoti's eyes. "Restaurants aren't the only way to share your food with the world."

"Maybe not. But it's the way I'm most comfortable with. And that has to count for something too."

Jyoti thought about the video she had deleted. Despite it being gone, she continued to receive messages from people who had seen it and had to resist the pull she felt to interact with that community. She kept reminding herself that she couldn't choose strangers over her own family.

"It's different for you," Jyoti said. "You can do what you love as a freelancer. It's not like I could earn a living off TikTok even if I wanted to post videos all day...and I'm not even sure that's what I'd want to do. Maybe I could be a private chef or something, but I've never done that either and wouldn't know how to start."

"What I know for certain is that you're going to find your path." Karishma stood. "Now, enough of living in the past." She dusted her hands against her thighs as if she was removing the grime of those memories. "This view is amazing, but I've got an even better one for you, and it comes complete with cocktails."

"Not saying no to that," Jyoti said, rising to join Karishma. She silenced her phone so she could be present with her friend, trying to ignore the ongoing surge of TikTok notifications.

As they emerged from the back entrance of the hotel, Jyoti realized the building was perched quite high on the bluff and many of the local homes were situated downward toward the sea. They descended a narrow cobbled stairway and found themselves in a small courtyard.

"These are called piazzetta," Karishma explained, and the name made perfect sense.

Along the walking paths they saw golden-hued water faucets poking out of stone tiles painted a deep ocean blue that poured into sinks carved from stone. Planters with flowers, herbs, and tomatoes were scattered about, seemingly belonging to the community rather than any one person. In the piazzetta, the white walls had ceramic fish hanging on them and some planter boxes with bright red flowers underneath. Praiano was homey. Jyoti suspected that would be the theme for their trip and she was ready to embrace it.

Karishma directed them to the right and Jyoti basked in the calming energy from the ocean views, quaint pedestrian walkways made of cement with a thin strip of terra-cotta tiles outlining diamond shapes, vibrant flowers in white-stone planters lining the short wall facing the sea, and charming homes nestled into the cliffside with white iron fences or stone ledges. They walked past terraces brimming with potted plants soaking up the summer sun. One had ropes of bright red tomatoes and garlic with soft purple stripes hanging along the wall to dry. Jyoti marveled at what it would feel like to try a sundried tomato straight from one of the ropes, rather than out of a jar where they were packed in oil. She could almost taste the burst of sunshine and sweetness.

They walked a short distance to a modest bar on the left with a sign that read Café Mirante. If Jyoti had still been in New York, she would have kept walking past a place like this. But she trusted in the magic of Amalfi and Karishma's track record as a tour guide thus far. Karishma ordered them the basilico, and while they waited for their drinks, they nibbled on fresh bruschetta, potato chips, and green olives.

When the basilico arrived, Jyoti smelled the heaps of fresh basil that had gone into their cocktail and salivated. They clinked glasses while taking in the oranges, pinks, and reds before them, tinting the sky with such purpose that it looked like painted brushstrokes. The first sip was captivating. Gin, fresh lemon, and home-grown basil. That was it. Perfection without any frilliness.

"Do you ever wish your parents would come visit you, and not vice versa?" Jyoti asked Karishma, as they stared out at the natural beauty on display before them. "It's too bad that they've never seen this or your life in Italy."

She shrugged. "I guess so. But they never travel anywhere other than India."

"I know," Jyoti said. "It's a shame they don't want to see places like this. I guess I get it. If you moved me out of America, then I'd want to go back and visit as often as I could. But they don't get to see the rest of the world the way we do."

"Do you think they even want to?" Karishma asked. "I never hear my parents wishing they could travel to Europe or South America. I think once they mentioned a safari when watching a documentary, but it was such a passing comment that I knew it wasn't something they would actually do."

Jyoti sipped her cocktail as the sky began bleeding into vibrant warm hues. "I sometimes wonder if my mom wanted something more than India all the time. When we were younger, I remember her suggesting we take family vacations to Europe or even Canada, but there was never enough money and my dad only ever wanted to save what we had for India trips."

"I wonder if you and I travel to other places because there's not one place that feels like where we belong," Karishma said. "If I had a place that accepted me fully and I never had to think twice about that, then I guess I'd be racing back there every chance I could too."

Jyoti thought about how little she knew of her parents' lives before she and her sisters were born and wondered what dreams, if any, they'd had to give up. Were there any? She thought of how she'd had to give up her professional career to focus on conceiving. Her parents had never shared anything like that with her while she was going through that journey, but she also realized that she had never asked. Children can be inherently selfish, even as adults, it seemed.

TEN

Jyoti had to earn her way to the sea the next day. The worst part about the four hundred steps they had to climb down was that Jyoti knew they had to take those same four hundred steps back up. The stone stairs were uneven and slick with use, and her casual flip-flops—with zero traction—were not the right footwear for the job. Or so she thought, until she saw nonnas zipping by them, arms laden with groceries, effortlessly navigating the terrain in casual sandals while she was clinging onto the railing.

When they reached the bottom and made their way past Praiano's most well-known beach club, One Fire, Karishma jumped up and down, calling out "Frankie!" A fortysomething man in a Zodiac waved back at her and blew her a kiss.

This was the famed Frankie whom Jyoti had heard so much about. Frankie was a year-round resident of Praiano, and he and Enzo had been good friends as children. Frankie looked like the quintessential Italian with his dark hair, olive skin, and wide smile.

Karishma stepped onto the boat and gave him two air kisses before introducing Jyoti. "Frankie knows all the secrets of the Amalfi Coast. I'm not kidding. He knows every nook and cranny along the shore and the best spots to swim, snorkel, or take in the view. When the rest of our friends get here, we'll do a boat day. In the meantime, and most importantly for you, he loves to eat and knows where to take us for the best food." Turning to Frankie, Karishma said, "Jyoti is a chef and is ready to sample all the local cuisine. The vegetarian part, of course."

Frankie laughed. "You make my job harder with this vegetarian nonsense, but I do my best."

Karishma gave him a faux pout. "You know perfect pasta doesn't need meat."

Frankie shrugged. "Okay, okay. I take you somewhere good."

"I was never worried," she said, placing their bags in the storage bin. It was clear she'd spent a good amount of time on this Zodiac with Frankie.

As he revved the engine and guided them away from the shore, Jyoti closed her eyes and smiled, feeling the sun on her face and the wind in her hair. Crystals may have been one of Karishma's healing techniques, but being on water made Jyoti feel grounded, and she already sensed there would be something rejuvenating about this place. The salty spray tickled her skin and frizzed her hair, but she felt at peace.

Karishma pointed toward the striated light gray cliffs rising from the water. "Dolomite limestone from the Mesozoic period. Can you believe we are looking at something that old?"

Jyoti took it all in. It was hard to fathom how short human lives were in comparison to the permanence of nature. She'd live her whole life with whatever successes and failures were in store for her, and these cliffs would still be here long after she was gone. Her time in Italy—especially the Amalfi Coast—was beginning to give Jyoti some perspective, and her constant thoughts about her rift with her parents and her uncertain future didn't feel as overwhelming.

"Karishma knows all the facts," Frankie chimed in. "She can give the tours for me now."

Jyoti smiled. "She knows all the facts about everything. Don't challenge her at trivia."

Frankie's laugh was free and unencumbered. Jyoti couldn't recall the last time she had felt so unburdened, but if she lived here, maybe it would be her normal too.

Green peppers were an overwhelming flavor, and Jyoti had never enjoyed them much because they threw off the balance in dishes unless they were expertly orchestrated. So, she was hesitant when Karishma insisted that was what they should order. She was skeptical of most of the Da Adolfo beach club so far, to be honest, and didn't understand why it was so coveted.

Frankie had deposited them there for lunch and a lazy afternoon. He and Karishma swore that while it was touristy now, the authenticity of the food remained intact. The restaurant and beach club were nothing fancy: a few rows of sun loungers that they'd had to reserve and rent, and an open-air restaurant with simple wooden tables and chairs and paper placemats that doubled as menus. The establishment was accessible only by boat, which meant crowds were regulated, so that was a nice touch.

She and Karishma perused the menu while they waited for peaches in white wine, which they'd ordered immediately upon arrival.

"The first sip of this drink is the sign that it's really summer," Karishma said.

Jyoti hadn't been led astray by her friend yet, so she was eager to try it.

To start, they'd ordered grilled mozzarella on lemon leaves and she could smell the citrusy essential oils as the colorful stoneware plate landed on their table. It was such a simple concept, but it was brilliant to allow the mozzarella to be flavored by the leaves on the grill. Jyoti put a charred leaf holding a bed of melted mozzarella onto her plate and cut off a section of the cheese with her fork. She could taste the citrus, char, and creamy fresh cheese and savored the combination. It reminded her of saganaki that would be sprinkled with lemon juice before eating, but the citrus was more subtle. She would think of other leaves and cheeses she could use in this preparation. Fig leaves might also be interesting.

There was a large group sitting behind them with several children at the table running around and causing a ruckus.

"It would be such a different experience being here with kids," Jyoti said.

"How are you feeling about that?"

"Better than before. Ashok wanted something that I couldn't give him. And now I can see new paths ahead of me that wouldn't be possible with a child."

"His emotional development was really that of a child anyway," Karishma said. "Maybe that's why he was so desperate to have kids. Then he'd have someone in the house who was at his level."

Jyoti loved her loyalty. "I know. Remember when I showed him the adoption pamphlets and he stared at them as if they were poison and asked if I had those because the doctor had said I was barren? I should have walked away from him then." She shook her head. "Instead, I kept trying to please him and our families."

Karishma leaned over and touched Jyoti's arm. "It was easy for him to keep trying. His body wasn't the one being used as a pin cushion."

"Back then, he kept saying how it would be worth it when we had our baby. I always agreed, but the truth was that I wasn't sure it would be. I'd lost so much of who I was already. I'd convinced myself that I had to make this work because otherwise I'd have nothing to show for it. Each time I was pregnant, something in me shifted and prioritized the new life growing inside of me. My body and hormones were so discombobulated when the pregnancies ended earlier than full-term. I knew Ashok didn't think of them as babies yet, but my maternal instincts kicked in from the first weeks of conception. And then the overwhelming grief that followed had been so lonely. There was so much pressure from our families, so I don't think there was any room to think about what would actually be best for us individually."

Karishma swallowed the bite she'd been chewing. "Marriage and kids are all our parents ever knew. It's hard for them to picture anything else. It's not like they had the option of pursuing passions or moving to Italy when survival was their main focus."

"That's so true. Passion is a privilege, and we're lucky that our parents' sacrifices gave us that option. It's just so ironic that the thing they worked so hard to give us is now the thing that separates us from them."

A large stoneware pitcher with the red fish logo landed on their table. It was full of white wine, with luscious large chunks of white peaches floating in it. Karishma eagerly poured them two glasses.

They raised to toast, and Jyoti said, "To our parents. Who lived to survive so that we could now live to thrive."

Karishma clinked her glass. "You have no idea how happy that makes me to hear. You're going to thrive, Jyo. I know you hate when things aren't mapped out for you, but it just means that anything is possible. Just have faith that you're going to live a richer and fuller life than you could ever have imagined."

Jyoti hoped her friend was right as she brought her glass to her lips. The first sip was sweet and satisfying with a hint of peach and the acidity of the white wine. She needed to make this at home. She loved seeing the produce sing, instead of taking a back seat to complex spices and herbs. It was different from her usual Indian cooking, but she knew there was much she would take with her from this trip and bring into her kitchen going forward.

Karishma held up her glass. "To being child-free."

While Karishma had made that toast many times, this was the first time Jyoti considered that it could be something for her to celebrate too.

The busy waiter then placed two plates of spaghetti pesto di peperoncini verdi before each of them with a *buon appetito* before he raced off to the next table.

As soon as Jyoti twirled some spaghetti onto her fork, she could tell it was the perfect al dente. Jyoti took a careful bite, expecting to be overwhelmed by a taste similar to bell pepper, but she was surprised to taste a sweetness and herbaceousness in the pesto. It wasn't any type of green pepper she had tasted before, and Karishma told her they were called friarielli and were small peppers that looked like shishitos but were sweet rather than spicy. Jyoti wondered where she'd be able to find those peppers back in New York or if she'd need to buy seeds from here and take them back to grow her own.

Like the grilled mozzarella before it, the dish was delicate and perfectly balanced. Jyoti knew she could eat a bowl of the pesto by itself and discover the tasting notes. The nuts didn't taste like pine nuts, and she wondered if the chef had used marcona almonds. The basil was likely freshly plucked from one of the abundant pots near the kitchen that had soaked up all the rich Amalfi sun. The Parmesan was nutty and added depth and salinity. She would try to re-create it but she already knew her fresh ingredients sourced in New York would not have such full flavor. And when cooking with only a few ingredients, the soul of the produce mattered most.

Recognizing that theirs was one of the only child-free tables at the restaurant, Jyoti became more comfortable with the life she had waiting for her. Around them, moms were mindlessly shoving food into their mouths while simultaneously doing the same for their kids. She couldn't imagine eating purely for sustenance rather than pleasure. She'd had a short taste of that after Ashok left her and she was too depressed to feed herself. Children were a cyclone tearing up everything in their wake, and she was starting to feel ready to give up that dream. She twirled another forkful of the pesto spaghetti and savored it while she chewed slowly and deliberately, welcoming all the nuanced flavors. Her empty tank was starting to be filled by the energy of the Amalfi Coast and she was excited for what would come next.

ELEVEN

It was hard to say goodbye to the stunning views from their room at Hotel Tramonto d'Oro, but they were just relocating a bit further down the cliff to Enzo's house. Besides, Jyoti was happy they'd have fifty fewer steps to deal with to access the sea. Enzo had met them in the hotel to help bring their luggage down the stone stairs, and within a short distance, they were transported to another part of Praiano.

He led them to a three-story home built into the cliffside with sea views from nearly every room. The decor was more rustic and traditional than the modern interior of the luxury hotel—the main floor had white tiles displaying lemon leaves, contrasting with the rich blue tiles of the kitchen backsplash. There were terraces on each level with an abundance of terracotta planters, each holding various herbs, fruits, and vegetables. Jyoti smelled the basil and thought of their cocktails at Café Mirante. It felt like a local home that was lived in and well loved, and Jyoti couldn't wait to sit on the terraces and take in the sunset from new angles. She was also eager to get some local produce and prepare a few meals in the small, yet homey kitchen.

When they stepped onto the main level terrace, they found Mae and Ben seated at the patio table, soaking up the sun.

"Fancy meeting you here," Ben said, standing to greet the women with kisses on the cheek.

"It's so nice to be back here," Mae said, looking out toward the stunning landscape before them.

"I know," Karishma said. "I think Jyoti is already hooked on this place."

Jyoti nodded. "Hard not to be."

Enzo smiled. "Summer wouldn't be complete without being here."

"You're so lucky to have such ready access to this," Jyoti said, gesturing toward the vista.

Karishma nudged her. "Move to Florence and you could have it too."

Jyoti sighed. "If only life were that easy."

"Speaking of not easy," Ben said to her, "I've got a surprise for you. Or maybe it's for the rest of us."

Jyoti watched him dash back inside the house and then reappear with two canvas grocery bags. "What's all this?" she asked.

He began pulling out packets of red chili powder, mango powder, cloves, cinnamon, cumin and coriander seeds, and other familiar spices. Jyoti could see where this was going. He then pulled out flour, semolina, potatoes, onions, and shelled peas. She began rifling through the spice packets, holding them up to the light to get a better look at their color.

"You found all of it?"

"Everything from your list," he said with pride.

"How did you get it so fast?" Jyoti asked, inhaling the fragrant cloves to assess their quality.

"Had my mate ship it over from London," Ben said.

Karishma whistled. "You are certainly committed to the job."

Ben saluted her. "For samosas, no length is too great."

Jyoti laughed. "Great. I'll be counting on you for manual labor when it comes time to assemble them."

"If Ben helps, does that mean I'm off the hook?" Karishma asked. "The kitchen can only hold two people."

"I'll leave it to you two to duke that out," Jyoti said.

She looked at the array of spices before her and recalled the first time she had made the blend herself. Her mom had thought she was silly for weighing the ingredients by grams to have the perfect recipe to use in the restaurant. Their cooking styles were very different when it came to that. Nalini was purely intuitive and didn't think about how to achieve the exact same taste time after time when she was just cooking for family and friends. Cooking for a business required precision and the batches had to be consistent. Jyoti stared at the ingredients before her and knew that without a scale and her exacting recipe, she'd need to cook like her mom to make the samosas this time. She wished she could call her mom with questions, but after their last conversation, she knew she was on her own for this.

She started with the easy parts and put a pot of cold water on the stove before lighting the flame to boil the potatoes. Then she turned the other burner on full blast so she could shred the onions near it and avoid them causing her eyes to water, another trick learned from her mother. She began to open the spice packets, breathing in each one to assess its pungency. She started blending the proportions by memory, creating two spice blends, and spooning a tiny amount into her palm to sample and tweak as needed until she tasted the familiar flavor. This had become her signature item at Taste of Ginger, and it was bittersweet cooking something that was so near to her heart but also completely entwined with her family.

As promised, Ben appeared in the kitchen like a dutiful sous chef when it was time to stuff them. She struggled to use the long, thick rolling pin that was designed for pasta, a different shape than the velan she used back home, but she managed to roll out some circles from the dough. She cut one in half and showed Ben how to fold it into a cone and press the seams together, before filling it and pinching the top to create a perfect triangle.

Ben's brow furrowed in concentration, even though his movements were clumsy and hesitant. "Like this?" he asked, presenting a lumpy misshapen triangle on his palm.

Jyoti smiled. "Let's call that 'good enough.'"

His face grew long as if she'd given him a low grade on a homework assignment, but he continued with the next one. Jyoti knew she'd eventually need to jump in and help because she could fill and shape them in a quarter of the time, but for the moment she enjoyed just being in the kitchen with a friend who was interested in her food.

"Do you cook much?" Jyoti asked.

Ben looked sheepish as he placed another samosa next to his others, each one like a snowflake with no two looking alike.

"I'd say my eating skills are far superior to my preparing skills," Ben said. "How did you learn to cook?"

"From my mom. She loved experimenting in the kitchen. When she and my dad came to America, she had to make the Gujarati food they grew up eating because it wasn't available anywhere outside the home. It might be different in London, but where we lived, the Indian restaurants mostly served Punjabi food, which is very different from what my parents were used to eating. My family considers that 'party food' because it's eaten on rare occasions, like at weddings, so we mostly ate at home. She said she'd always been passionate about cooking even before marriage, so maybe it wasn't such a hardship for her to spend so much time in the kitchen."

Ben paused, looking up at her. "That's fantastic that you have that connection with your mum."

"Had," Jyoti corrected, deciding in that moment to be fully transparent.

"I'm terribly sorry to hear that," Ben said, gaze lowered.

Jyoti realized her mistake. "No, no, it's nothing like that. She's still alive. But we aren't speaking much right now."

Ben met her eyes and waited for her to continue.

"But even before that, she had a love-hate relationship with my chef career. When I started working in my ex-husband's restaurant, she was so upset. Said it was servant work and she was disappointed to have her daughter doing it after all they had sacrificed to come to America and give their children a better life. But at the same time, she was always so proud of the new recipes I'd create and wanted to learn them. Seemed like there was no pleasing her."

Ben put down the samosa he'd been working on. "That's a bit confusing, no?"

"I thought so," Jyoti said. "But I've given up on trying to understand my mom."

"That's fair enough. Hard to know what is simmering beneath the surface, but parents seem to always think what they're doing makes sense in some way."

"Are you close to your parents?" Jyoti asked. She started to help him with filling and shaping, now that she had rolled out all the dough and covered it with a damp cloth.

"I suppose so. We see each other at the holidays and ring each other once a week to check in. Not too many deep conversations, but I suppose that's a hazard of being British in the first place," he chuckled. "My divorce ended up being really hard for them to swallow in their small community."

Jyoti nodded in understanding, her hands deftly working through the samosas as if she were on an assembly line. "Some things are the same no matter where you live. My divorce was the start of this rift between my parents and me because they were so concerned about what their friends would think."

"That's why we divorcés have to stick together." He nudged her with his elbow. "It's a grueling process, no matter the reason or who's at fault, and only those who have been through it can fully understand."

"True. It's that bond that you hope to never have," Jyoti said.

"I'm not sure about never," Ben countered. "I'd much rather be a member of this club than still be in the unhappily married one."

"Knowing what I know now, I'd say the same."

With Jyoti helping him, they made fast work of preparing the remaining samosas and she placed a damp towel over them to keep them from drying out. She then tested the temperature of the oil by slipping a thumb-sized piece of dough into it, checking to see if it quickly floated to the top. Once ready, she placed the first four into the hot oil, bubbles forming around the dough as they cooked. After they were golden on one side, she flipped them over and then moved the cooked ones to a paper towel to drip off the excess oil.

Ben reached over and grabbed one, tossing it from one hand to the other to keep from burning himself while it cooled.

"Wouldn't it have been easier to wait a bit?" she asked.

Ben shook his head. "We menfolk don't think that way."

He blew on the pastry and then took a small test bite from the corner. Determining it was now cool enough despite the steam rising from the inside, he took a larger one with the filling and closed his eyes as he chewed.

"This is brilliant," he said with his mouth full.

Jyoti smiled. There was nothing she loved more than watching someone enjoying something she had made. "Did it live up to the hype?"

"And then some. You've ruined me. How will I ever buy a takeaway from one of those carts outside the tube now?"

"My mom might be offended by the comparison," Jyoti laughed.

He stared inside the pastry as if studying it. "It's such a perfect blend of seasonings. And the texture of the pastry—crunchy on the outside and chewy on the inside—is the perfect vehicle." He took another bite. "You should bottle this mix and sell it. I think even I could make these on my own if I had your spice blends."

He wasn't the first who'd suggested that to her. She'd had many customers at Taste of Ginger ask for the same. "Maybe one day," Jyoti said. "For now, I just love making them and seeing the smiles on people's faces when they taste their first one."

After they fried up the remainder, they took the platter to the terrace where the sun was beginning to set. Enzo had prepared Limoncello Spritzes for the group. Limoncello would complement the citrus in the samosas and was the perfect choice of beverage.

"It's not the usual aperitivo fare, but hopefully this will do," Jyoti said, placing the platter before her friends.

"More than do." Karishma bent over the table to snatch one.

Enzo and Mae shared Ben's sentiment that she needed to bottle the spices and sell them, because they were indeed the best samosas either had ever had. Jyoti loved introducing them to a part of her culture. Food was her biggest connection to her Gujarati roots. It was the part of India that her parents had been able to bring with them and introduce to their children. Smells and flavors could transport them back to the world they grew up in, and it allowed them to have their American-born children experience their ancestral home. Jyoti knew her love of cooking had been one of the greatest bonds she had with her mother. Her sisters didn't have much interest in the family recipes, so it was something only the two of them shared. It was also the thing she had been most excited to pass down to her own children one day.

"I've got an idea," Ben said, polishing off his fourth samosa. "How would you like to cook while you're in Italy?"

"What do you mean? I'm already doing that," Jyoti said.

"If this is any indication of how good you are in the kitchen, then so many people would love to taste your food."

"She's so good," Karishma chimed in.

Ben continued, "One of the wineries I work with is organizing summer dinners in their vineyards for their most prestigious clientele. The owners are looking for a chef to prepare the meals. I'm arranging the wine pairings once the menu is decided. Would you be interested? I could pull some strings."

Jyoti processed the information. She'd only ever cooked at a restaurant, with tickets coming in sporadically, having to manage the line to make sure everything was ready at the right time. She'd never cooked in the type of setting Ben was suggesting, as a caterer preparing a tasting menu. She was excited at the thought of cooking for people again. And it was her first opportunity for income since the divorce, and could help her get the money she needed to buy Taste of Ginger. She'd certainly never planned on finding work here, but this type of ad hoc service seemed to be something she could actually provide without having a work permit. But then apprehension crept up inside her. She wasn't used to Italian dining preferences and didn't know what they would want. She knew exactly what her patrons in New York were interested in and could deliver winners. This would be a guessing game, though, and it was too risky to put herself in a position where she could not only let herself down, but her friends too.

"I don't know," Jyoti said.

Karishma bounced in her seat. "You have to do this. Think of how much fun it would be."

Jyoti knew Karishma's intentions were good, but she also knew that Karishma would love to see Jyoti get entrenched into Italian life and make the leap to join her as a permanent resident. As she gazed at the four eager faces staring at her expectantly, she began to tense up even more.

"We'd pay you, of course," Ben added.

Jyoti knew that was the main reason for her to do it. She'd come to Italy to make peace with the fact that she wouldn't be able to buy the restaurant. But if she could generate some income, maybe she could save enough to buy, if not Taste of Ginger, then a smaller place that would be her own someday.

"How would I even know what to make?" Jyoti asked.

Ben waved away her concerns. "You'd have full control. The owners just want their guests to have a lovely experience eating delicious food that enhances their wine. You'd do a prep meal for them to sample the dishes in advance so we'd know if anything needs to be tweaked."

"Would I make Indian food?"

"I'd suggest you put these on the menu," Enzo said, holding up a samosa.

Ben nodded. "I think the Indian flair would make you stand out. The other people they are talking to would be focused on Italian food, but that's obviously been done before. I love the idea of having something unique, and I think they will too."

Jyoti couldn't wrap her mind around how she could pull this off by herself. She considered what her parents would think if they found out. *Acting like a common caterer that we would hire in India*, her mom would surely say. For some reason, this felt like it would be a bigger slap in the face for Nalini than Jyoti cheffing in a restaurant. She could not shake the fear of failing and letting down Ben and Karishma, along with the people who'd be eating her food. As much as she tried to convince herself this could be fun, she hadn't managed a way past the horror that everything could go wrong.

"It's such a kind offer," Jyoti said, "but I don't think I can. I've never cooked in that setting or prepared a tasting menu that would be fancy enough for wine pairings. I'm a chef who makes Indian comfort food, and it's not what the Western world thinks of as 'pretty' or 'fancy' or 'upscale.'"

"Are you sure?" Ben asked. "They're having a dinner series, so there would be more chances throughout the summer if things go well at the first one."

"Think about how nice it would be to work again. You'd get to create whatever you want," Karishma added. "You loved when you got to do that at Taste of Ginger."

Jyoti had enjoyed devising new specials, and her crippling apprehension now made her realize how far she had veered from who she was and how long the journey would be to get back. "I know, and I'm flattered that you'd even ask. But I don't think I'm ready for that yet, and I'd hate to let either of you down. It's been ages since I've worked in a kitchen, and I'm afraid I've been out of the game for too long."

Karishma deflated, but Jyoti knew she could tell that she had made up her mind.

Ben sighed. "That's too bad to hear. I'm sure you'd be really great at it. I hope this doesn't mean you won't cook for us anymore either."

"That part I can do." Jyoti grinned, already feeling relief. If she didn't try, then she couldn't fail.

TWELVE

That night, she lay in the double bed she was sharing with Karishma, trying not to move and wake her. Jyoti's mind had been swirling. She tried to think of menu items she could have made for the dinner Ben had suggested but was drawing a blank. This was why she'd been right to turn it down. She used to be full of ideas and just never had the time to execute them. If she'd taken the job and made a disappointing meal, then it would have reflected poorly on him and that was the last thing she wanted to do. But she couldn't help but wonder where the spark she'd felt during her first weeks in Italy had gone. She'd been so excited to try some fusion dishes, and when she'd been offered a blank canvas, her first instinct was to run.

She'd done the same thing when she'd started to have some traction on TikTok after posting her first—and only—video. She knew she hadn't wanted to take it down, but she was too scared to cross her mother. She glanced at her account and the ongoing message notifications. It was true that nothing was ever deleted from social media. Some people had managed to save her post and shared it around and she was still hearing from new users who wanted recipes, or comfort, or just basic human connection. She felt like a coward ignoring them.

She thought about how brave she'd been at other times in her life. It took courage to step into Ashok's restaurant for the first time as a chef, despite her lack of experience. But Ashok had faith in her, so she did too. Sometimes, if someone believed in her a little more than she believed in herself, it gave her the boost she needed to move forward. It was during their first year of marriage that Ashok had taken over the Indian restaurant his dad had owned for decades, formerly called India's Tandoori. When the head chef and Ashok had butted heads, the chef quit, leaving Ashok with no one to cook the next day. Jyoti had always been good in the kitchen, having "inherited her mother's hand," as their relatives liked to say. Ashok had asked her to step in and she'd discovered a passion and career she'd never considered.

She'd started off by making the traditional dishes served in India's Tandoori for many years, which had provided a stable middle-class income for Ashok's family. But diners' tastes had been evolving, and Ashok's father had a hard time keeping up with the trends, so business was on a steady decline. Jyoti started elevating the presentation of familiar Punjabi food and creating new dishes that fused Indian flavors with more familiar Western cuisines. The clientele began to change, and the restaurant began to pick up business. After a hard-fought battle with Ashok's father, they were allowed to rebrand the restaurant and Taste of Ginger was born, with Jyoti at the helm in the kitchen, creating her unique spin on Indian cuisine.

Ten years ago, she'd been experimenting with a cardamom pumpkin crème brûlée for the holiday season when Ashok had first insisted that she stop working to improve their chances for a healthy pregnancy. They'd already been trying for three years without success, and Ashok felt like their odds would be higher if she wasn't working on her feet all day. She'd been so reluctant to give up the one place in the world that had felt like hers. The kitchen had become her source of confidence and her place of ease. He didn't understand that her creativity would not flow in the same way if she were in their apartment, trying to devise recipes on a pregnancy-centered timeline. But she'd eventually relented, as she always did, because she wanted to keep the peace. And she'd known that having a baby would delight not only Ashok, but their parents too. That was the first time she realized that no one else in her life valued her career the way she did.

She now worried that when she'd left her chef role in that kitchen a decade ago, she'd left behind her confidence along with her knives, because the old Jyoti would have jumped at the opportunity Ben had presented to her. She'd never have doubted whether she could make a memorable and delicious menu. She'd never have retreated out of fear.

She eventually managed a fitful sleep and woke up feeling quite groggy the next day. The drinks they'd had the night before probably didn't help either. When she walked upstairs to the main floor, Mae was sitting on the terrace, cleaning her camera lens with a microfiber cloth.

"Sleeping Beauty has arrived," Mae said, offering her some espresso.

Jyoti eagerly took it and let the warm, bitter liquid awaken her body.

"What time is it?" Jyoti yawned.

"Nearly 10:30."

"Where are the others?"

"They got an early start and headed down to One Fire."

Jyoti took another sip. "You didn't go with them?"

Mae glanced out toward the water. "I wanted to get some

shots from up here while the lighting was good. The beach club isn't going anywhere. They are saving us beds for whenever we feel like joining."

Jyoti loved the idea of spending a day moving from water to sun lounger and back again, but she knew the price was the hundreds of stairs between her and One Fire. She could only imagine how fit she'd be if she lived here. No wonder the nonnas along the coast lived so long. A Mediterranean diet plus mandated exercise seemed to do wonders for the body and soul.

They sat in comfortable silence for a minute, both lost in their thoughts, until Mae turned her head back from the view. "Even though I come here every summer now, it still inspires awe every time I return."

"Did you get the photos you wanted?"

Mae put her camera on the table. "I'll have to see when I get them on my computer. I like looking at the full-scale images to decide. But it's not the end of the world if I didn't. There's always tomorrow." She picked up her espresso and took a sip.

"How did you get into photography?" Jyoti asked.

"I feel like it got into me," Mae said with a laugh. "I was always the one in my family who wanted to take photos and preserve precious moments. My parents indulged it when I was young. It seemed like I had a knack for it. Plus, it kept me busy and out of trouble at family events. They had nice pictures at the end so it was a win-win for everyone. Things changed when I got to university, and they wanted me to get a 'real' education."

"I know a lot about family expectations," Jyoti said, looking out at the shimmering water.

"My parents said I needed to take the 'smart' classes if I was ever going to meet the right husband."

Jyoti smiled. It wasn't something her parents had ever said to her, but she suspected they'd have agreed with the logic.

"And did you?"

"No. Even though I took the classes they wanted, in addition to the art classes I wanted. I don't think it's as easy to order up a husband as they thought it would be."

"Finding my husband wasn't that hard," Jyoti confessed. "Probably because my parents did that for me. Keeping him was an entirely different matter. No one had really thought about the fact that old traditions might not survive modern times."

"Do you wish you'd kept him?" Mae asked.

"It's complicated, I guess. That was the only life I had ever known or thought I had wanted. It's the one that my family and community understood and accepted, and I've always loved being a part of our Gujarati community back home. Divorce changed all of that." Jyoti paused to gather her thoughts. "But now that I'm here, I'm starting to open my eyes and feel a bit lighter, so I guess that's a step in the right direction. I'd always thought community was something you built with your husband, but I love what you all have found in each other here."

Mae smiled. "Finding community is such an essential part of life. If I'd stayed in Taiwan, it would have been so much harder. The mountain of expectations and judgment would have been too big a strain. I go back there maybe once a year, and I think it's better for us to have the distance. They don't have to see me living differently than they'd want, and I don't have to see them wishing I'd made other choices. And for one week a year, we can catch up and just be happy in each other's presence."

Jyoti considered this. "I suppose it's similar with Karishma and her family too. For me, I don't know who I am without my family and culture. I don't think I could do one week a year after having had them so close for all of my life."

"You don't have to choose the same life that Karishma and I have. There are so many paths, and you'll find the one that makes sense for you."

"I hope so," Jyoti said. "I'm not sure I've ever spent much

time thinking about what makes me happy, so maybe that's why it's so hard to start now."

"I can understand that. So many Asian cultures are that way. It wasn't until my thirties that I started to think about what I wanted to have for myself."

"What happened then?" Jyoti asked.

"Absolutely nothing," Mae said with a smile. "And that's when I knew I needed more. Karishma is single by choice. She's had men come through her life who would have happily married her. I am single by default. I had really wanted to have the husband and kids and live that life, but it didn't work out for me. I wasn't meeting men who I could see a future with, even though I'd tried everything I could. My parents kept telling me I was being too picky, but I knew that wasn't it. Nothing ever clicked. I'd even told myself if I had to give up my photography career to please the right man, then I would do it, but I never met anyone who was worth that sacrifice."

"It's amazing that you had that self-awareness so early in your life," Jyoti said. "I feel like I'm still trying to figure out who I am and what I want."

"We all have to go through our own struggles to find those answers. I even thought about having kids on my own when I hadn't found the right partner, but I knew I didn't want to live as a single mom."

Jyoti nodded. "I've been going through that same debate now. Ticking biological clock and all that. I spent a large chunk of my life trying to have a child, so it feels a bit like giving up or failing to not have one."

Mae gave her an empathetic look. "I'm sorry you've had to go through that."

"It's okay," Jyoti said. "I never thought I'd want to be a single mom either. I think I only debated it to have someone after my divorce. Almost like if I couldn't find someone willing to be with me, then I'd *make* someone so I wouldn't be alone." She let out a wry laugh. "And that's not a good reason to have kids."

Mae shook her head. "No, it's not. But it's great that you saw that before it was too late."

"How did you get out of that mindset when you were in Taiwan?"

"I stopped waiting for my dream life to find me, and I started traveling the world to see if I could find the place where I belonged. I focused my photography on showcasing food because it brings people together, regardless of where they are. Then I expanded to landscapes and travel. I loved meeting new people and seeing new places. I wasn't sure where I'd settle, but then after coming to Florence, I felt like I was ready to have some roots again."

"Do you ever miss not having that family life you'd wanted when you were younger?"

"I'm forty-seven now, and I'm good with where I am. I know part of me wanted that because it was what I thought I was supposed to have."

"You have no idea how deeply I feel that." Jyoti let out a sigh. "Society puts so much pressure on women to be one thing."

"That's why it's so important to find people who can support you on the journey you're on, rather than the ones who are trying to move you along their path."

"Very well said."

Jyoti thought about how well-intentioned her mom had been about wanting to help her conceive, but Jyoti suspected it was because she couldn't see any other path for her daughters.

THIRTEEN

The next day, Frankie took their group to have lunch in Amalfi, and from there they took a bus up a winding road to the small clifftop village of Ravello, situated around a main square with a charming concert hall. Jyoti pictured the ambiance at night, beautiful lights and music filling the air, and knew it would be magical. She was amused by the signs advertising "Wine & Drugs," and could not wait to grab a gelato for their walking tour of the town.

Enzo led them to Villa Cimbrone, where he said the gardens and views far exceeded the price of admission. Situated directly along the cliff side, Villa Cimbrone had the most startling vistas Jyoti had ever seen. It was one thing to be on a boat and see the buildings crawling up the cliffs, but something else entirely to have that opposite perspective, looking down toward the water. She had a better sense of their elevation as they neared the cliff's edge and walked along the stone wall of the Terrace of Infinity, which was guarded by white sculpted busts. Along the wall were interspersed balconies filled with tourists taking selfies. The group posed for the obligatory photos before continuing through the expansive gardens.

Karishma came up to Jyoti and fell into step alongside her. "How are you doing?"

Jyoti gestured around them. "It's hard not to gain perspective with this around us. Seeing your life here and talking to your friends has helped too. I had a really great conversation with Mae yesterday, and was shocked by how similar we used to be in our outlooks and expectations for ourselves."

"I know," Karishma said. "It's nice to connect with people on a similar path, and I knew the two of you would have a lot to talk about. That's why I wanted you to come spend the summer with me. You get to meet people who can expand your outlook for your future. And I get to have you here for a nice, long time."

"We have missed out on a lot over the last few years. But you had to go somewhere that felt good for you. I can understand why you chose this place and these people."

"I'm grateful every day. But I do miss you a lot. There's something to be said about the people you grew up with who understand the different parts of you."

Jyoti gave her a side hug. "I'm always here for you, but I do know what you mean. Even though I stayed in the world we grew up in, it's different not having you there. There are so many days when I'll see something and think to text you but know it won't be the same by the time we connect. The time difference makes it hard to share the day-to-day."

Karishma hugged her tighter. "You should send me those things anyway. So what if it's time-shifted?"

Jyoti smiled. "I can do that. And maybe instead of a weekly call, we do it twice a week. Especially after a summer together.

I can't go back to living without you with just a snap of my fingers."

For the first time, Jyoti considered that Karishma might want more companionship too. She'd always been such an independent free spirit, and Jyoti had often felt like she was putting too much of a burden on Karishma's time with her neediness, especially these past few years. Karishma had these wonderful people here who had become her local family, but they didn't know what her relationship with her family was like, or the foods she'd grown up eating, or the holidays she'd celebrated. Her life was about adapting to this new world and finding a way to blend in, just like they'd done growing up in America. While at the restaurant or moving through the streets of Manhattan, Jyoti had done her best to fit into a world that was not fully hers. Even when she socialized with friends from other parts of India, they still didn't share the same language or foods, so the default in those situations was still English and pizza. It was only when she was with her family, Ashok, or other Gujarati friends that she was able to let go of the constant need to assimilate.

They made their way back toward the group where Ben, Enzo, and Mae were trying to discern what type of fruit grew on a tree Jyoti had never seen before. Mae scampered around looking for a sign, certain there must be one, while the men posited uninformed guesses to each other. Jyoti felt her phone vibrate and saw her least favorite name on the screen.

She tilted her phone toward Karishma and rolled her eyes. "He's probably calling to say he's not waiting anymore and selling the restaurant."

Karishma made a face, signaling for her to decline the call, but Jyoti stepped back from the group and answered.

She heard Ashok sigh deeply on the other end. "I've been mulling over whether to call you," he said in a tone Jyoti found overly dramatic.

"What do you need?" she asked curtly.

"What is going on with you?"

His tone took her aback. He sounded concerned, but she wasn't sure why.

"What do you mean?"

"I saw the video you posted on TikTok." His voice was hesitant. "What were you thinking? It's not like you to be that messy."

She felt her blood boil at the same time as her heart sank. Of course, Ashok would have seen the video before she'd taken it down. His parents and the aunties had no doubt raced to tell him about it. She wouldn't put it past him to have recorded it to save for future blackmail. But she also resented him thinking that he knew who she was now. She looked at the sea beneath the bluffs and her friends chatting in the gardens and knew it was a far cry from the life she had once shared with Ashok. She was angry that he saw her openness and vulnerability as weaknesses, just like her parents did. Just like so much of their community did. *Hide your shame. Never let anyone see you struggle.* Those were the mantras she had grown up with, and she was beginning to realize just how damaging they were.

"I didn't know my actions affected you still," she said. "I'm not your responsibility anymore."

"Jyoti." His voice was sincere. "We spent the formative years of our lives together. I don't wish you any ill will just because things didn't work out. I really want you to be happy."

His words were kind, but she gritted her teeth. It was hard to just disregard the years of tension and apprehension that came with being married to someone—especially someone like Ashok—and even harder not to bring that past into every conversation with him. Even more so when she had been the one left behind to pick herself up while he moved on to his new life. Once Ashok's parents knew the marriage was over, they made quick work of finding him a new wife to keep his transition as smooth as possible.

"Uh, thanks," she said, wondering when she could hang up and get back to her lovely Amalfi afternoon.

"I've been doing some thinking," he said.

She braced herself. Here it was. The real reason for the call. She knew the sincerity in his voice had just been to butter her up for whatever blow he was about to deliver. She remembered when he'd given her such lavish praise about the green curry tofu and noodle recipe she'd concocted and had been so proud of, before telling her that he was leaving her and wanted a divorce so he could find someone who wanted the same family as he did. She hadn't eaten Thai food since that day.

Ashok continued, "Given how much you seem to be spiraling right now, I do feel quite bad about how everything turned out. It's hard to watch you not having the same joy as I'm having in this second phase of life."

Her jaw was clenched, her words ready to leap out and tell him off. At the same time, she was hurt that he could so easily dismiss their sixteen years together as a lesser time of his life.

"So, after discussing with Radha..."

Oh, spit it out, Jyoti thought. It was not lost on her that he'd never felt the need to consult her on decisions when they'd been married. But that was the thing with first wives—they were merely training their husbands for the next marriage.

"I'm going to hold the restaurant for you until the end of the year, so you have more time to gather the money and try to buy it before I sell it to someone else. I know it's expensive and still may not be enough time to save up, but consider it an olive branch."

Jyoti's head spun. Part of her was processing the fact that she could still get the restaurant, and the other part wanted to shove his patronizing remarks down his throat. He was right that she still needed a lot of money, and perhaps four additional months wouldn't make any difference, but his offer seemed genuine. Even if misguided in his reasoning.

She broke her silence. "What's the catch?"

"No catch."

This was a huge opportunity for her. As backhanded as Ashok was being, she had to swallow her pride and focus on the fact that she'd always wanted that restaurant. And if she got it, then she'd never have to deal with Ashok and his smugness again.

"You'll just hold it for me?" she asked hesitantly.

"Only until the end of the year," he said. "I have to get rid of it before the baby comes because I can't be doing those late restaurant hours. Radha wants to make sure I'm here to help her out."

Jyoti doubted that he'd have taken that same collaborative co-parent approach with her, but it didn't matter. She wanted to focus on being able to get *her* baby back and restore it to its former glory.

"Will that make a difference?" he asked. "Will you be able to buy it then?"

Jyoti looked over at Ben and thought about his offer from a couple days ago. "I'll find a way."

"Good," he said, sounding surprised by her response. "And if at some point you realize you can't do it, just let me know so I can unload it sooner."

Her heart shuddered at the thought of the restaurant becoming yet another nondescript pizza place or Chinese restaurant. In a softer tone, she said, "Thanks, Ashok. Really."

"It's okay," he said. "That business was never my dream. You made that place what it is, and you deserve the chance to take it back."

He had never conceded her involvement and accomplishments before. During the marriage, he'd been too wrapped up in pleasing his father and growing the business for them. Then, during the divorce, it was impossible to be honest about anything, both of them posturing at every turn to win each small battle. Jyoti had always wanted some acknowledgment that she'd made a difference, but he'd always denied her that. She hated to admit it, but maybe being with Radha had made him better. She could feel more empathy from her ex-husband now than ever before.

After hanging up, she closed her eyes and breathed in the cleansing sea breeze. This place was affirming on so many levels. It seemed like just being here was bringing more positivity into her life. Maybe Karishma was onto something with this "energy" and "alignment" world she was always talking about, and Jyoti simply had to surrender her doubt and believe.

She made her way back to the group and approached Ben.

"Does your offer still stand?" she asked.

He cocked his head, a confused look on his face.

"I'd love to be considered for the winery dinners," she said.

"It does, but what changed your mind?"

"Possibility."

FOURTEEN

The group had one final surprise for Jyoti on their last day before heading back to Florence, and it was clear they had saved the best for last. Frankie met them in the morning and took them on a boat tour along the Amalfi Coast showing them his favorite spots and giving them an experience that very few tourists would be able to have.

"You like to swim?" Frankie asked Jyoti.

Jyoti wasn't sure her movements in the water could be properly classified as swimming. "I like being in the water. Does that count?"

"That's what matters." He steered them toward a small opening in the cliffs and stopped the engine. "Inside there is a huge cave. If you are brave, it's worth seeing."

"Brave" wasn't a word anyone other than Karishma would have used to describe her, and she felt her pulse quickening. "How do you get into it?" she asked, looking at the narrow slit between the water and the rock wall above it. The entrance seemed hardly large enough for a fish, let alone a human.

"Once the tide pushes out a little, you swim in. After a few meters, it opens widely. But it's a bit cold getting into there. *Refreshing*, not cold," he said with a smile.

Karishma, Enzo, Mae, and Ben jumped into the water without a second thought.

Jyoti leaned over the edge and marveled at how pristine the water was. So many shades of turquoise and emerald green melded together, creating a mosaic. But clear waters were deceiving because she didn't know the depth. Karishma and the others were waiting for Jyoti, so she knew she had to overcome her fears. That's what this whole trip was about. She sat on the edge and counted to five in her head before squeezing her eyes shut and sliding into the sea.

It was colder than she expected, but she immediately felt the clean water envelop and surround her with protection. She felt weightless and agile. While submerged, it seemed as if anything was possible, like her muscles would allow her to run a marathon, something she couldn't fathom on land. Underwater, she actually felt her lungs relax and realized how agitated her breath had been for such a long time now. She took wide strokes away from the Zodiac and toward the cave, bobbing her head above the water's edge when she needed air.

"Good, right?" Karishma called out from where she was treading water.

Jyoti nodded eagerly. "Colder than I thought, but it's exactly what my body needed."

"Look around us," Karishma said, gesturing toward the cliffs. "You cannot be in these waters and not feel their healing power."

"I've never understood her energy-healing rocks and things, but there is something about these waters," Enzo said. "You could feel it even as a child."

Frankie waved to them from the boat and pointed toward the small opening to the cave, which seemed a tad bit larger now that she was in the water and closer, but still not wide enough for a human body to fit through. Mae motioned for them to start swimming in that direction. Jyoti obliged, even though the magic she had been feeling was now replaced by apprehension. Tight spaces had never been her friend.

"It's going to be really chilly while you dive underneath. It's a weird cold pocket, but it warms up inside. You ready?" Karishma asked.

Jyoti was decidedly not ready. Her mind swirled with what would happen if the water level rose too quickly and she didn't make it to the other side. Or if she couldn't hold her breath for long enough and hit her head trying to get air. Or if she panicked and lost her sense of direction and went sideways rather than into the cave and could not get to air. She thought of all the ways that ended with her not getting air. Water was healing, but it was also powerful, and she was at its mercy.

"You've done this before?" Jyoti asked.

"Many times," the group assured.

"It's one of the best spots on the coast and very few tourists get to see it because they don't have someone like Frankie to show them," Ben said.

The longer they waited and the more they encouraged her, Jyoti felt her fear building rather than subsiding. She'd just given herself the chance to get her restaurant back. Was it worth doing something senseless that killed her? One big risk per trip seemed like enough to her. She didn't really want to try to cram herself into a narrow opening surrounded by rocks while at the mercy of the tides. Karishma and Enzo swam over to her, and each took one of her hands. Jyoti gripped tightly and let them steer her toward the cave.

"Just take a big breath and dive under," Enzo said.

Jyoti squeezed her eyes shut, tightened her grip on their hands, and let her friends lead her into the unknown. She felt the cold pocket she'd been warned about and her limbs tensed.

Her pulse quickened, but knowing she was not alone helped her feel safe.

After what felt like no time at all and also an eternity, they reached a warm pocket and popped their heads above the water. Jyoti gasped for air and then looked around. Inside was the purest deep blue water she had ever seen, glinting like an endless sapphire. The water was so tranquil, gently rocking them back and forth. There was a sliver of white sand transitioning from the water to the gray rocks. Thus far, Jyoti hadn't seen a sandy beach on the Amalfi Coast and had only seen pebbles and rocks leading to the water's edge.

The calm around her was captivating. No technology, no sounds other than lapping water and her breath, nothing but nature as it was meant to be enjoyed. Unlike Karishma, Jyoti had struggled with spiritual endeavors. When her family got together for pujas, she recited the bhajans she'd learned as a kid, but she didn't know what any of the Sanskrit verses meant. Her participation was based on memorization and it didn't feel like something divine to her. But here, with her body submerged in the pristine water, she felt connected to the Earth in a way she never had before. She was grounded and centered and felt like she was exactly where she was meant to be at this moment in time.

She would have stayed there for hours if she could have, but Enzo warned that they needed to head out at the right water level to return to the boat. The swim back through the narrow passage wasn't nearly as bad as the entry because nothing was ever as scary as the unknown. Frankie gave them a thumbs-up as they emerged. Jyoti knew the smile on her face said everything. She felt invincible, like life was full of possibility and she was ready to embrace it all. Starting with the dinner for Ben's client. It was the gateway to her future and she was ready to tamp down any fears and claim it.

FIFTEEN

When they returned to Florence, Jyoti felt more invigorated than she had in years. She and Ben were at the dining table in Karishma's apartment, discussing the menu. Sunlight streamed in from the open window and warmed her hands as she took notes. She had two weeks to prepare a rehearsal menu for the owners to try, and the event would take place a few days after that.

"What type of menu do they want?" she asked.

Ben shrugged. "Something unique. Something they haven't seen before."

She touched her pen to her lips as she searched her brain. "Indian food isn't generally the easiest to pair with wine. The flavors can be overpowering, and you want the wine to be the star."

He nodded. "Yes, that's the ultimate goal. They want to sell wine. But they also want to give their exclusive guests a memorable experience too. This is a perk for their most loyal members."

Jyoti felt the pressure of what she'd agreed to. She didn't

know this upscale wine connoisseur clientele at all, had no idea what they liked or didn't like, didn't know their tolerance for spices and bold flavors. There were a lot of variables she hadn't factored in when she'd gotten off the phone with Ashok and made her decision with dollar signs in her eyes. Food needed to be prepared from the heart to have soul and she'd been thinking only of her bank account.

"The menu I'd done at our restaurant in New York had been mostly Indian. Some modern twists and I leveled up the presentation, but I'm not sure if it would suit an Italian palate."

"I'm sure whatever you make will be great. This is a food-loving crowd, so if you've wanted to try anything edgy, now is the time," Ben said.

Edgy? He clearly did not know her at all.

Jyoti walked along the Arno River trying to clear her head in the hopes that inspiration would strike her. It was humid and warm, and her thin summer dress clung to her legs as she walked. She'd treated herself to a black sesame gelato to improve her mood. It had quickly become one of her favorite flavors since arriving in Florence. She'd never had anything like it. The rich nuttiness of sesame expertly layered into the smooth, sweet, luxurious texture of gelato. She had tried it on a lark assuming it was a novelty that couldn't be good, but she'd been so wrong. As she let the gelato melt on her tongue, she realized this was her mission. To make a menu that the diners would experience the way she had when she took her first bite of black sesame gelato. Easier said than done.

Samosas and chutneys seemed like they needed to be part of the starters. She'd always pleased people with those and it was something she was comfortable with. But she worried about how they would pair with the wine given their spice level. She could make them milder, but having that many spices in any quantity trying to compete with a delicate glass of white wine seemed difficult to balance. She'd make sure Ben could find the right one.

Did she dare try some of the Indian/Italian fusion dishes that had been circling her mind but had never made it to a plate? She'd been so excited to experiment during her first weeks in Florence, but that was when it would have been just a fun, low-stakes project for her and Karishma and their friends. She hadn't planned on anyone paying money for those dishes. With anything new, it took her several rounds of tweaking until she got it just right and then at least five practice rounds to figure out if she could deliver consistency, but she didn't have time for that here.

She wished she could discuss it with her mom. Better yet, she wished she could cook with her mom and have her taste. Her mom had always been good at bouncing ideas even if her focus was on traditional Indian food. She had a discerning palate even if she didn't cook with much opulence, and she was really great at figuring out what was missing when something fell a bit flat. She'd helped Jyoti sort out how to elevate flavors or add unexpected ingredients while still maintaining the integrity of a dish.

It had been almost two weeks since her mom called her to take down her viral video. Two weeks in which nothing had changed. They hadn't resumed their daily phone calls. There hadn't been any texts or emails. Her sisters hadn't mentioned anything further. They'd been so adamant that Jyoti delete the video, but now she was back to where she was. As she strolled along the Arno, finishing off the last bits of her cone, she wondered if she needed to let go of her wounded pride and make the effort to see the changes she wanted. Waiting out her mom hadn't been a successful strategy so far and there was so much riding on this dinner that she could really use her help.

She paused along a quiet stretch of the Ponte Amerigo Vespucci and let the sun shine on her face while she closed her eyes and took several deep breaths, inhaling for four seconds and then out for seven, just as Karishma had taught her. Being the bigger person required so much energy and she had to put her ego aside for the greater good. She unlocked her phone and hit the top contact on her favorites. After a few rings, she wondered if her mom wouldn't answer, but then there was her rushed voice on the other end.

"It's me," Jyoti said.

"I know. Your name shows up on the phone," Nalini said.

"How are you?" Jyoti tried ignoring the beeps and cheers in the background. Her mom was likely watching her morning game shows, and this one sounded like *The Price Is Right*.

"Fine."

"It's been a while, so I thought I'd call."

"It's not so long," Nalini said.

Jyoti couldn't figure out if her mom was being difficult or if she had simply adapted to the drastic shift in their communication over the past year.

"I got a job," Jyoti said.

"Oh?" Her mom's voice perked up and the background noise ceded.

"Well, sort of," Jyoti clarified. "One of Karishma's friends asked me to cook for a dinner party one of his clients is having."

"That's what you call a job?" Nalini said. Jyoti could again hear the sounds of the television in the background. "Being the hired help for your friend's party? Let me guess, this was Karishma's idea."

Jyoti winced. Why had she hoped her mom's attitude about cooking for money would have changed simply because this was not a restaurant?

"It's at a nice vineyard. Her friend is going to pair wines with my courses," Jyoti said, her tone deflating.

"So, the people will be too drunk to even know what you made." Nalini harrumphed.

Alcohol had been a sensitive subject since Tanvi's graduation so she should have known not to go there.

"Your father will be so disappointed to hear this." Jyoti could picture her mother shaking her head.

This was a familiar deflection by her mother, attributing the disappointment to Dharmesh, rather than claiming it for herself.

"Mom, it's not such a bad profession. And I'm good at it. Can't you just—"

"Not all of us have the luxury of pursuing everything we are good at, okay?" Nalini said. "We have to think about how our actions affect others. Jyoti, our reputations are all we have. I have made plenty of sacrifices for this family and none of you seem to appreciate them. Who is making sacrifices for me, hah?"

Jyoti had heard these sentiments before, but her mom's voice had a steelier edge this time. Jyoti had no doubt that her mother had given up so much for them. She thought back to when they were struggling financially. She had seen her mom mending her own underwear and socks until they were practically threadbare and could no longer be restitched. But Nalini always made sure Dharmesh, Jyoti, Chaya, and Tanvi never wore mended undergarments. Theirs was not a family that spoke openly about those things, so while Jyoti appreciated her mom in private, she'd never vocalized this to her. So, reverting back to their familiar patterns when emotional issues like this arose, Jyoti did what she always did, and what her mom seemed most comfortable with. She changed the subject.

"I'm having trouble coming up with the menu," Jyoti said. "I was hoping you could help me think through it, like we used to when I needed new specials at Taste of Ginger."

She heard the hiss of the pressure cooker whistle in the background. One of the most familiar sounds from her childhood. No Indian household was complete without it. Jyoti's whistle had more short staccato bursts than her mom's drawn-out hiss. She heard the sound recede as the heat was turned off.

"I don't know how I can help with something like that," Nalini said. "I don't cook those fancy bancy things you're talking about."

"But you could give me some ideas and maybe some flavors—"

"It has been a long time since I have thought about cooking something other than dal, bhat, rotli, shaak," Nalini said.

Jyoti perked up, sensing that her mother actually wanted to help her think through this.

But she was wrong. "I need to start the lunch and not waste time on these things," Nalini said curtly. "Was this all you wanted?"

Jyoti's face fell. *No, there's so much more,* she thought to herself, but could never say aloud. Instead, she said "Okay," and hung up.

In hindsight, she shouldn't have seen the call going any other way, but she'd been filled with such hope. She'd never technically made it to motherhood, but she didn't think this was how a parent should act toward a child, regardless of what they disagreed about.

She texted Chaya and Tanvi, feeling the need to have someone in her family show up for her for once. Chaya responded that Nitin was having a meltdown and she couldn't talk. Tanvi didn't respond at all, but that was the norm. Jyoti knew her mother thought her sacrifices went unnoticed, but Jyoti had often felt that way with her younger sisters too. Jyoti and her mom had so much more in common than either was ever willing to admit to the other.

Jyoti made her way back to Karishma's apartment and immediately felt its emptiness. Karishma was at Enzo's. She'd been giving him yoga lessons—the true Indian spiritual kind and not the version that had been appropriated throughout the Western world—and Jyoti didn't know how long she'd be gone. She felt like she needed someone and turned to her phone. She scrolled through Instagram to see what others were doing. People out and about with huge smiles on their faces, couples on vacation in various corners of the world, only the best photos of kids and pets looking adorable and well-behaved. Even the food accounts posted only about their success stories, and never the previous ten tries that had failed. Social media was a community where perfection was the currency. Jyoti suspected that was why she'd never made it a serious part of her life. For her, adulthood had always felt like a struggle to stay afloat, and she didn't need to be faced with others' manufactured posts of them "flourishing."

She recalled how much less alone she'd felt when people had responded to the vulnerability in her TikTok video. She craved that feeling now. It was the only time social media had supported rather than disappointed her.

She opened TikTok and her finger hovered over the recording button as she considered the consequences of sharing her feelings publicly, again. Her mother and sisters would be upset, but it wasn't as if any of them were available to console her when she was down. Why shouldn't she be allowed to reach out to others to fill that void? And this time she wasn't drunk, so she'd be more careful.

She clicked the button and saw her face reflected back to her.

"Hi there," she said hesitantly into the abyss. "I'm back, except this time I'm not drunk and not making food. Just wanted to see who was out there because I've had a bad day and the last time I shared, this community was so supportive." She chewed her bottom lip. "Do you ever wonder what social media could be if we all just opened up about our lives? I was thinking about that today. My life is far from perfect so I don't share much about it. Who wants to see a middle-aged woman who's still trying to figure out who she is? So many people deal with their failures privately—or maybe they don't deal with them at all and that's why everyone needs therapy. But I feel like when I'm lonely, there's not really anywhere to go…does anyone else feel that way?" She paused before continuing. "I guess you'll tell me in the comments if you do.

"In the meantime, I wanted to share that I got a job here in Italy that I'm excited about. I get to cook for people again, and it's been a long time since I've done that. It used to make me so happy to see the joy on someone's face when they tasted that perfect bite, knowing that I had a hand in bringing a positive moment into their day." She turned from the camera and stared out the window for a moment at the bustling piazza outside. "It's hard growing up as the eldest child of immigrants. The pressure to honor their sacrifices falls most squarely on your shoulders. And don't get me wrong, I'm grateful for all my parents have done for me. I know their lives were harder so that mine could be easier. I tried to do everything they wanted, but it never seemed to be enough or the 'right' thing. And now I have to ask myself…when does it end? When do I get to stop paying them back? I'm thankful for the life they have given me. I really am. But I'm forty-two now. Can I start living for myself?"

She smiled at the thought of people listening—really *listening*—to what she had to say. "Thank you all for being there. Maybe this is the age when I trust who I am and start living for myself."

She ended the video and felt lighter. She couldn't pretend she was fine when she knew she wasn't. Her mom might be able to bury her feelings deep inside of her and be okay, but after a lifetime of trying to emulate that, Jyoti's own emotions were beginning to fester and rise to the surface. In that way, she was not her mother's daughter.

Comments began to appear underneath her post.

@LAgirl425: Yesss…more of this!

@cookingfrenzy: So hard to be real when everyone else is being fake.

@desigirlNYC: More authentic videos please!

@rishikesh50: Where you been lady? We've been missing you.

@homecook8605: You're back! Can you send us the recipe from that last video?

She smiled at seeing users who had commented on her last video. She'd assumed a few weeks of silence was a lifetime in social media years and everyone would have forgotten her and moved on to new accounts by now. She had tried to keep things vague and not give too many personal details, thinking that maybe there was a middle ground between the things she'd said while she was drunk and engaging her TikTok community. She hoped she'd struck the balance between getting what she needed from the platform while not upsetting her mom. Either way, she knew it would not be long before someone in her family or Sasti Masti would see that she'd posted again, and then she'd have her answer. Maybe this time, she'd find the strength to stand her ground.

SIXTEEN

The Sasti Masti aunties were fast. It took less than five hours before the entire community seemed to know that Jyoti was back to airing "dirty laundry" on the internet. Chaya, who'd been so busy earlier, now had time to talk.

"What is going on with you?" she asked, her face registering concern as they looked at each other on the screen.

"I needed someone to listen," Jyoti said.

"But why so publicly? Can't you just talk to us, or friends, or a therapist?"

A therapist probably was not a bad idea, but they weren't exactly available at a moment's notice the way a social media audience was. And they weren't free.

"I tried reaching out to you after I was upset from my call with Mom," Jyoti said. "You were busy."

Chaya flinched.

"It's okay," Jyoti said. "You have a kid. A husband. A job. I don't expect you to be at my beck and call, but sometimes I need to get these feelings out of me. And I tried to be respectful this time and not so...messy." She hated that she was using Ashok's word, but, upon reflection, it seemed the most accurate.

"I'm sorry I couldn't talk then. But you know how this affects Mom, which then affects the rest of us. She spins off into a tizzy and then no matter how busy we are, we have to figure out a way to calm her down. It's hard having to always mediate between you two."

Jyoti held her tongue at her sister's use of *always*. It had been Jyoti who had spent decades of her life negotiating between their parents and her sisters. She had been the one who calmed their parents when they were distraught about Chaya wanting to marry Isaac, wringing their hands over what the community would think if their daughter married a dhoriya. After they'd married and Chaya had leaned more into his white Jewish culture than her own, Jyoti was the one assuaging her parents' concerns. It was okay if Chaya didn't cook Gujarati food or celebrate Hindu holidays, as long as she and Isaac were happy. She didn't think it was too much to ask for her sisters to carry the load for some part of their lives, but they never seemed to recognize how much Jyoti had done to pave easier paths for them.

"I don't know how to connect with her anymore."

"What did you guys fight about?" Chaya asked.

"I got a job."

Chaya looked puzzled. "Shouldn't that be a good thing?"

"I thought so. I'm catering a dinner here for one of Karishma's friends. I was really excited about it."

Chaya nodded slowly. "She likes your food but doesn't like you calling it 'work.'"

"Exactly. And I don't get it. She loves to cook. I learned this from her. We should be bonding over this, especially since you and Tanvi have shown no interest in learning our food. But it's clear she'd rather have me back in a dead-end customer service job for a corporate conglomerate than doing this."

"I eat Gujarati food," Chaya said, looking defensive.

Siblings always focused on the part that affected them. "I didn't say you don't, but it's not like you are going to be teaching Nitin how to roll out a perfect rotli."

"I don't need to teach him. That's what I have you for," Chaya said.

Jyoti stared at her like she had just proven her point.

Chaya continued, "Anyway, creative professions don't jive with her. But we've always known that. Nothing has changed."

I've changed, Jyoti wanted to say. *Everything feels uncertain and I need my family to support me now more than ever. I've let you all lean on me when you needed, but now that it's my turn, everyone is gone.*

As much as she wished otherwise, they weren't the type of family who shared these sentiments with each other, which was why she had turned to strangers online.

"Cooking is the one thing I have left that makes me happy," Jyoti said. "I can't lose that too."

"You don't need to stop doing it, but maybe don't broadcast it so much. We don't need to rock the boat right now," Chaya said.

Rock the boat had always been Jyoti's big sister admonition to Chaya and Tanvi. She'd said it when they'd wanted to date in high school, when she'd caught Tanvi drinking during her freshman year of college, when Chaya wanted to tell their parents about Isaac and Jyoti had told her to wait until she was sure it was real. *Rock the boat* was code for "don't burden our parents with anything unnecessary." They'd grown up knowing that, as immigrants, their parents had been through unimaginable hardships, and it was their job to ease that burden. Jyoti had always taken that responsibility seriously, and she bristled at Chaya using her own words against her.

"So, will you take it down? And not post anymore? You can always make a video and send it to me if you want to get the feelings out."

How could Jyoti tell her younger sister that she didn't think she could relate to what Jyoti was going through? Chaya had a perfect life with a doting husband and precocious child. Those things had come fairly easily to her. She didn't really understand the pain and loneliness that Jyoti had gone through for so many years. And she definitely did not know that she had contributed to it. Not intentionally, of course, but watching Chaya take step after step into the future Jyoti always had envisioned for herself wasn't easy.

"Thanks," Jyoti said, her tone hollow. "I appreciate it, but I'm not sure being on or off TikTok is the solution to what's going on here."

"I'm not saying it will cure everything, but it would help."

Help who? Jyoti wondered to herself. Certainly not her.

"I'll think about it," Jyoti lied, knowing this time she wouldn't compromise her own happiness to keep up appearances.

Jyoti would never forget the day Chaya called a "family meeting." She sat with her sisters and mother in the living room of their childhood home, holding steaming mugs of chaa and snacking on a plate of khari biscuits. Chaya fidgeted as she sat next to Jyoti on the couch. Tanvi was scrolling through something on her phone as she normally did.

Nalini and Chaya exchanged a look, the kind Jyoti and her mom usually did when they were in cahoots. The relationship between her mom and Chaya had been strained over the past few years after she'd brought Isaac home, so this was curious.

"What?" Jyoti asked, breaking the silence.

Chaya took a deep breath. After a long pause, she said in a cautious but optimistic tone, "Isaac and I are pregnant."

Tanvi stopped scrolling and looked up. Jyoti felt everyone's eyes shift to her, breath held as they waited for her reaction.

Her little sister was going to have a baby before her. Gujarati families like hers were steeped in traditions, including that children were married in order of age and had offspring in that same order, but Chaya had long shown that those cultural norms wouldn't dictate her life. She'd married Isaac for love and had embraced his culture more than her own after she'd seen the lukewarm reception toward him from her parents. Jyoti, on the other hand, had allowed her parents to present her with the biodatas of eligible Gujarati men, from which they'd all agreed Ashok was the best match, as they already knew his family. It didn't feel like a sacrifice because Jyoti had known she wanted to end up with someone from her culture. It eliminated a lot of the guesswork and her having to explain her customs. Dating was hard enough without having to question if someone of a different race was interested in her for her, or if her skin color played some conscious or unconscious role in his decision. She wondered if Chaya had ever asked herself whether Isaac was one of those white guys who thought it said something about him if he dated someone from another race, but Chaya had always been more self-assured than Jyoti, so maybe the thought had never crossed her mind.

Jyoti forced a smile onto her face. "That's great news!" She leaned forward to give Chaya a hug. "I'm so happy for you!"

Chaya's shoulders relaxed and her face brightened. "Thanks! I wasn't sure how you'd react given everything..."

Jyoti kept the smile plastered on her face. "Just because I'm having problems doesn't mean we can't celebrate your good news." She could hear that her voice was an octave too high.

Jyoti had been in her ninth year of marriage and fifth year of consistently trying to get pregnant. Chaya and Isaac had wed two years earlier when Chaya was twenty-nine. She'd waited longer than Jyoti because of the many rounds of *What will people think?* she'd gone through with her parents about Isaac not being Indian, but eventually, Nalini and Dharmesh had relented. Marrying anyone was better than her being thirty and single, after all. They'd never been overly warm or accepting of Isaac as they had been with Ashok, whom they'd instantly considered one of their own. But now, Isaac was bringing them the ultimate offering: their first grandchild. His virulent white sperm were sure to change the pecking order.

"I know you just started trying a few months ago…how far along are you?" Jyoti asked.

"I know," Chaya said apologetically. "We were worried it might take a while given all the…you know…but then, it happened really fast."

Jyoti's pregnancy struggles had been a family affair and she hadn't considered that her troubles might be a warning to Chaya and Tanvi. But she shouldn't have been surprised that her younger sisters' roads would be easier than hers. It had always been that way. Jyoti followed the path set by their parents while her sisters skipped along doing whatever they wanted.

She got through the afternoon talking about Chaya and Isaac's plans. They wanted to keep the sex a secret. She was due in seven months. She'd waited so long to tell them because she wanted to make sure they were near the end of the first trimester and had less risk of miscarriage given the "you know." She'd continue working at her finance job during her pregnancy since everything looked fine with the baby's health so far. She had no intention of being a stay-at-home mom and ignored Nalini's side-eye when she said that.

Their father came home with a box of mithai from the Indian store and a small sheet cake from the grocery store to commemorate the occasion. Theirs was not a designer, overpriced fancy Manhattan bakeshop family that would spend $200 on a cake if it had the right branding. Nalini quickly made shiro, and then they went to the small puja area they had in the corner of the guest bedroom, and the five of them sang bhajans and bowed their heads to wish for a healthy pregnancy. Then they took turns feeding Chaya and each other shiro, cake, and mithai.

Once they had finished, Jyoti and Nalini went to the kitchen to clean up while the rest of the family watched television in the living room. Jyoti didn't flinch at the steaming hot water running over her hands, and Nalini came to turn off the faucet and took Jyoti's hands in hers.

"Don't worry, beta," she said. "Utavle amba na pake."

A rushed mango won't ripen.

Her day would come when the time was right. It was the most comforting thing her mom had said to her since she had begun trying to have a baby. Jyoti appreciated that her mom knew Chaya's news would be hard for her. Looking at the years since then and all that had happened, if she were being honest, maybe it was the most comforting thing her mom had ever said to her. And now, she wondered if her mom had been speaking about Jyoti herself rather than a future baby.

SEVENTEEN

Jyoti was perusing the stalls at Mercato Centrale on the other side of the Arno River to get some inspiration for her menu. Finding out what was in season and available in decent quantities seemed like a good starting place. The historic building was two stories with produce, meat, and dairy on the ground floor and ready-made food stalls on the second floor. The lower level was filled with locals, Italian being the dominant language, and the second with tourists speaking English and various other languages. Jyoti enjoyed quietly loitering amongst the locals. She remained careful to stay out of their way as they went about their shopping, knowing she was a guest in their home.

She moved past the meat vendors, assuming Ben knew she'd be preparing a vegetarian menu, but suddenly realizing she hadn't actually discussed it with him. She'd always left cooking meat in the restaurant to the staff. She'd never eaten it and wasn't willing to taste those dishes, so while Ashok had insisted it needed to be served for their American clientele, she steered clear of it. That was why she wanted to do an all-vegetarian menu when she got her restaurant back. The decisions would be hers alone for the first time in her life, and she knew she could make vegetarian fare that would keep diners coming back for more. It would be nice to not feel the need to pander to the expectations of others for once.

The tomatoes in the market were large, vibrant, juicy red orbs that needed to be served. Basil perfumed the air and she was reminded of the Amalfi Coast. She saw the friarielli peppers from the pesto at Da Adolfo and decided she would try to use them for something with her own spin on it. She bought a few so she could taste them in their pure form and then determine how to prepare and pair them with other ingredients. Long fingers of zucchini were stacked into pyramids, their skin smooth and glossy. Next to them, sun-kissed zucchini blossoms, all but begging to be stuffed and deep fried.

Paneer, she thought to herself. She'd fill them with an herbed paneer. Something that looked like a classic on the plate but had a twist when biting into it.

"Are you planning to just look at the food?" a man asked, interrupting her thoughts.

She turned toward the voice and saw one of the vendors was speaking to her from behind a pile of artichokes, their long stems still attached. He looked to be in his forties and was bald, sporting a close-cut beard that was mostly gray. His face had weathered lines that hinted that he worked outdoors.

"Sorry," she said, feeling exposed under his constant gaze. "I am just trying to think of my menu."

He nodded. "For what? Dinner tonight? With your husband?" he glanced down at her hands to see they were absent of rings.

She instinctively touched her thumb to her finger where her wedding band used to be. Men were so forward in Italy and Jyoti had a hard time getting used to that. Not that she'd been dating in New York before she'd left, or really at any other point in her life. But from the stories Karishma told about her own exploits and the way Italian men were portrayed on television, she was convinced they were more assertive than American men and definitely more than the Indian men she knew. Ashok would have never found her or Radha, if not for his parents intervening.

"No husband," Jyoti said, looking down and picking up an artichoke to break from his gaze.

The leaves were tight and it felt heavy. She knew they were fresh and it was an ingredient she'd want to invest the painstaking labor of serving thinly shaved and raw to preserve its natural elegance. But it was such a strong flavor unto itself and she wasn't sure how she could make it work with Indian spices.

The man raised his brow suggestively at her. "You are visiting?"

She nodded.

"But you are choosing to cook? Firenze has some of the best restaurants in the world," he said.

"I agree." She smiled as she mentally scrolled through the dishes she'd had thus far. "But I'm a chef, and I'm cooking a meal for some Italian guests."

He looked amused. "You are making Italian food for Italians?"

She laughed. "Not exactly. I mostly cook Indian food, so I'm here to get inspiration for how to incorporate that into the great summer produce you have here."

"That sounds interesting," he said. "Perhaps I can help you." He gestured toward the artichoke she was holding. "One of the best items of the season. In fact, I have something in back that you might find interesting." He disappeared behind the stall and Jyoti heard him moving some crates. He then reemerged with a bouquet of strange flowers and handed them to her. They had thick green stems, a round green bulb, and from that protruded a vibrant purple flower that reminded her of sea anemone. "Have you seen this?"

She hadn't, but she immediately knew what it was and couldn't believe she had never seen them before. Why hadn't she? She knew most produce had flowers.

"They are beautiful," she said, taking them from him. She couldn't detect a smell, but her eyes were fixated on the bright purple flowers. "I didn't realize what artichoke flowers looked like. We only eat them before this stage, so I never knew."

He smiled. "One of the oldest vegetables in the world, they say. Like a woman, thorny yet beautiful on the outside, but if you do the work to find the heart, that is where the magic lies."

Jyoti resisted the urge to roll her eyes like she would have in New York. She'd gotten accustomed to catcalls and men laying it on thick while walking around Italy. She chalked it up to the culture, and as an outsider, she felt she had no right to pass judgment on it.

"It really is a stunning flower," she said.

"Perhaps you'd like to have some for your dinner? There's nothing more unique than artichoke flowers on the table."

It was a fantastic idea. She could picture the settings now, and knew she wanted to display these flowers, while also finding a way to make an artichoke dish. She loved knowing that there was still so much she could discover about produce and its life cycles. The learning was part of what captivated her about food. It was limitless. New varieties of fruits and vegetables were being bred daily. New cooking techniques and spices could change the textures and flavors. The combinations were endless.

"I'd like that very much."

"Tommaso." He gestured to introduce himself.

"Jyoti."

He rolled her name around on his tongue as if tasting a new fruit. "I've never heard this name. Very exotic."

Jyoti bristled at the word but decided to give him the benefit of the doubt for not being a native English speaker. She suspected if she tried to converse with him in Italian, her mistakes and misuses would far exceed his. He took her number and said he would text her about the flowers. She had a feeling that he'd be messaging about more than that, but she again tried to channel her inner free spirit. There was no harm in getting more than centerpieces out of this exchange.

Her step was lighter as she took her sack of groceries back to Karishma's and laid them out on the counter, debating where to begin. She decided on squash blossoms because she knew they would be part of the start to her meal. After all, fried food was never a bad idea.

She had to make paneer, so she poured whole milk into a large pot and turned on the stove. She had lemon juice next to it so she'd be ready when it reached the right temperature. Waiting for milk to heat always took longer than she expected and then once it hit, she had to act fast before it overflowed and left a mess on the stove. There was nothing worse than having to clean up burnt milk. She decided to jump back onto TikTok while she waited.

Her last video had not gone viral by any means, but she was still reaching and resonating with a widespread audience. She decided to post again and waved to the screen after starting the recording.

"Hi! I know my last video was just me talking, but the reality is that I love talking to you all when I'm cooking. It makes me feel like I've got friends in the room with me. Today, I'm recipe testing for these gorgeous squash blossoms." She brought the orange and yellow flowers closer to the camera. "Which means I need to make paneer, so I've got milk heating on the stove. You wouldn't believe how easy it is to make. Similar to ricotta, but made only with milk rather than a mix of milk and cream. It's amazing how the same process can lead to ricotta or paneer, depending on which dairy you start with and how you press it at the end. Also, I use lemon juice rather than vinegar to separate the curds and whey. For me, citrus is a better residual taste than vinegar."

She stirred the milk in the pot to keep the temperature even throughout the liquid. "Vinegar doesn't have much of a place in the Gujarati cuisine I grew up eating. Lemon and lime juice were definitely the acids of choice." Jyoti laughed to herself. "I recall a while back when I had to teach my mom that limes were a different fruit. She'd been calling them green lemons and didn't realize it was another species altogether. It's funny the moments that stand out about our parents. I often think about how hard it must have been to be an immigrant. I'm often treated like one in America because of how I look, but I'm not a true immigrant like she was. I don't have the language barriers or same jarring contrast from growing up in a different culture. It makes me wonder if she thought some lemons were just green when she was in India, too, or if that was another language issue that evolved after coming to America. She's an excellent cook. I got her hand, as my relatives often say, so it surprises me that she couldn't taste the difference. But I suppose there comes a time when we surpass our master, and I think that has happened for me. Maybe because I made it a profession and took the best parts of both cultures and brought them together. And now I'm throwing in parts from other places like Italy."

She touched the wooden spoon she had used to stir to feel how hot the milk was, and knew she was still a couple minutes away from adding the lemon. She pointed her camera toward the milk that was starting to form small bubbles at the surface. "This is when you know you are getting close. When it starts to bubble consistently, that's when you know it's time to add the acid to separate the curds and whey."

She turned the camera back on herself and smiled. "Does anyone else always think of *Little Miss Muffet* when they hear 'curds and whey'? It was my younger sister's favorite even though she shrieked at the thought of the spider coming down every time she heard it. It's funny how you go from being the big sister to just "sister" when you and your sibling both reach adulthood. The age gap becomes irrelevant. In the same way that I surpassed my mom with my kitchen knowledge, my sister surpassed me in life. She's three years younger, but she had a baby before me, despite my best efforts to do things in the right order. I can't blame her given what was going on with me, but when that happened, I made sure her day was still perfect. I buried the fact that she'd so easily done what I'd spent the last five years trying to do. I didn't bring up the pain of the three miscarriages, or what my family referred to as 'the you know.' I even kept a straight face when she started talking about her pregnancy in terms of *we*—a huge pet peeve of mine and something I would have never done had I been pregnant. I did what a good sister would do and kept my tears inside me until I was on the train home, alone."

She eyed the small bubbles forming at the top of the milk and turned the camera to show her pouring in the lemon juice and stirring vigorously.

"No matter how old we get, I feel like I'm supposed to be the big sister that comforted her every time she squealed about the spider in *Little Miss Muffet*. Any other oldest siblings out there feel that way? So, when you're the oldest and there's no one looking out for you, you figure out how to get yourself to a better place on your own. And part of getting better," she said, stirring as the curds clumped together and the whey separated into a greenish tinged liquid, "is eating fried food. So, I'm going to finish this paneer and think about how I want to season it before stuffing it into these delicate flowers and then giving them an oil bath. If anyone has any ideas for flavor profiles they'd like to see, please drop them in the comments."

When Karishma arrived later with Enzo, they went straight to the plate of fried squash blossoms, and Jyoti watched them carefully. She had already predicted what would happen. She knew their expressions would first register surprise, but was more fixated on the moment *after.* That moment would reveal whether it was a good surprise or a bad one before they could edit their response for Jyoti's sake.

As if on cue, she could see the question flicker across their faces and then a pause before their lips curled into an expression of curiosity followed by a smile. She'd nailed it.

"This isn't ricotta," Enzo said, staring inside the fried blossom.

"It's paneer," Karishma said. "But I can't tell what the flavoring is."

Jyoti moved a bowl toward them. "Mint, lemon zest, cumin, and a hint of green chili. I've got a cilantro mint chutney to spread across it instead of pesto."

"Never seen green chili inside of these," Enzo said, dipping one into the verdant green chutney.

"You like it?" Jyoti asked. His opinion mattered more to her than Karishma's right now because he had been raised on the same diet as her future clientele.

"It's good. Not something I'm used to, but not bad. I think Ben will love it."

She clasped her hands together. "It was so fun to make. So exciting to use my brain in that way again. I'll come up with a few other things and then invite him for a test cook."

"You should take pictures of what you're making," Karishma said.

"Why? I'll remember how to make it."

Karishma nodded. "Sure, but what if you want to post on your TikTok or something one day?"

"I actually already posted another video," Jyoti said sheepishly. "I can find the steps on there."

Karishma looked at her quizzically. Enzo looked back and forth between them, seeming to sense this was a more loaded statement than it appeared.

"Long story," Jyoti said. "But I missed that community."

"And Sasti Masti? And Nalini Auntie?"

Jyoti shrugged. "I kept it tame."

"If you say so."

"I tried to keep it about the food, so they can't be too upset about that. My mom and her friends find cooking videos on YouTube all the time."

Karishma cocked her head at her and said in a mock auntie voice, "I don't care what other people's children are doing. I only care what mine are doing."

Jyoti fidgeted. "I had to find an outlet and this seemed like a good middle ground. I can't live in a bubble for fear of upsetting her all the time."

"You sound like me," Karishma said.

"I know. That's what my mom was always afraid of."

Karishma touched her heart in mock horror. "The gravest of evils."

"Depends who you're asking," Enzo chimed in.

"When it comes to aunties, independence is a cardinal sin," Karishma said.

"She's right," Jyoti said. "A self-sufficient woman without a man is their greatest fear."

Enzo looked between them, amused, as if they were exaggerating. He had no idea.

EIGHTEEN

It hadn't come as a surprise to Jyoti that Tommaso had texted her about more than the artichoke flowers. He'd invited her for aperitivo, and Karishma squealed when Jyoti told her. The next thing she knew she was being pushed into the bathroom, makeup brushes forced into her hands, while Karishma rummaged through her clothes for a suitable—casual yet chic—option.

"You're going on a date," Karishma gushed as she helped Jyoti get ready.

"It's not a da—" Jyoti started to say. "Okay, I guess it is."

Tommaso had been rather direct with his intentions, which Karishma said was normal for Italian men. None of this vague "hanging out" or "meeting up" or "getting together" language that dripped off the tongues of the men back in New York. In Italy, you knew if you were on a date, and you knew it before you got there.

"I haven't been on a date since before Ashok and I were

married," Jyoti said, nerves creeping into her voice. "And I've never been on a date with a white guy."

"No, but you have slept with one, so there's that. That should help you get past your nerves."

Jyoti gave her a stern look. Her one-night stand with Saro had assuredly not been a date. "I'm serious. Should I avoid Gujarati stuff? Will he think it's weird if I talk about how we grew up or what kinds of food we ate? He probably has no concept of arranged marriages and will think my parents were related because they had the same last name."

"Whoa, slow down there. This is a first date. He's not writing your memoir. Talk about things you like to do and joke around. Keep it light. Movies, TV shows, travel destinations… that type of thing."

Jyoti sighed. "Maybe I shouldn't go. I have no idea what I'm doing."

Karishma gave her a compassionate smile. "So? You have to start somewhere. You're not going to spend your life alone just because you got divorced."

"Would it be so bad to do that?"

Karishma gave her an empathetic look. "No, if that's truly what would make you happiest. Yes, if the reason you are choosing that is because you are too afraid to take a risk. I'll support any choice you make that is authentic and in alignment with your soul. Personally, I think you are too interesting and talented to not share that with someone else. And gorgeous, too, but I hate when people lead with that. Although, Italians often do, so be prepared for a lot of *ciao bella*."

It wouldn't be the worst thing if someone wanted to call her beautiful. She could admit that her ego could use a boost in that department. Saro had helped in that regard, so maybe Tommaso would too. It wasn't like she needed to marry these men. Although, she would have to see Tommaso again because she was set on having artichoke flowers for the dinner.

★★★

They met at Caffè degli Artigiani, which was an unassuming spot across the piazza from 4 Leoni. Jyoti was beginning to understand how small Florence was, especially for locals. Tommaso explained that he lived on his family's farm and vineyard about thirty minutes outside Florence and would drive in for work and for "special ladies" like her. She was glad that Karishma had warned her that the men were prone to laying it on thick. In another world, this type of flattery would have come off as insincere to her, but she tried to keep an open mind.

They sat at a table in the back. The decor consisted of shelves of bottles of wine and some red accent walls, but it was clear that interior design had not been the main focus. Jyoti marveled at the trust Italian restaurants had in their patrons. She could not fathom a world in which Taste of Ginger or any other restaurant in New York would have unobstructed shelves full of alcohol from which anyone could grab a bottle. It felt idyllic to Jyoti after coming from a place where they were guarding the liquor—not only from patrons, but from staff as well.

"What made you pursue farming?" Jyoti asked, picking up her Aperol Spritz.

"Family business."

"Did you ever consider doing anything else?"

He shrugged. "Not really."

His tone reminded her of her cousins in India. Most of them had gone into the family business and pursued a degree that would complement it. She envied those who didn't go through the balancing act she'd had between trying to find her passions and pleasing her parents. Her cousins, and likely Tommaso, had avoided that drama by staying in their expected lanes. He told her about how he cared for his parents, still lived under their roof, and would do so until they passed and the home became his. He talked about how food was the center of their lives and how, each Sunday, they gathered for a meal with the extended family. She and Tommaso might look different on the outside, but Italian and Indian cultures seemed to have a lot of similarities.

"And you? Cooking is your family business?"

She almost spit out her drink. "Definitely not."

He looked at her curiously, but she wasn't going there yet.

She feigned nonchalance. "Just something I picked up after college."

To her relief, he moved on. They talked about Karishma, and he seemed amused by the spiritual practices Karishma was introducing her to like crystals, meditation, and breathwork. None of these were part of his repertoire. She told him what she had done since arriving in Italy and raved about her time in Praiano.

He reached out and touched her forearm while she spoke. "Praiano? You are exploring the best parts of Italy. I have lived here all my life and have not been to the Amalfi Coast."

Jyoti wondered if it was money, time, or both that had prevented his domestic travels. Her experience thus far had been carefully curated by Karishma and Enzo, and it seemed clear that Enzo was part of an upper-class Italian family. Jyoti wasn't sure what the class demarcations were in Italy but was sure they existed. Every culture had a way of separating people into categories and inequitably distributing privileges.

"Is there somewhere you'd like to go?" she asked.

He stroked her arm. "Maybe I will go to India if all the women are as beautiful as you."

She laughed. It was too thick even with the cultural differences. "You don't have to try so hard."

He looked wounded. "What do you mean?"

"Only that I don't need so many compliments."

"It is our way," he said, reaffirming what Karishma had already told her. "But I try to stop if you don't like it so much."

"Maybe just a little less. I'd rather get to know you."

"What would you like to know?"

"Anything."

She was trying to think of questions, but everything that came to mind was a landmine that she didn't want to answer herself, like if he had ever been married, if he had children, if he'd ever dated someone who wasn't white, or someone who was vegetarian. Why couldn't she think of anything that led to an interesting conversation, but that didn't also include a subject that would make her squirm? She wasn't touching her ex-husband and their infertility struggle. Based on what he'd said about the Amalfi Coast, travel seemed like a bad topic. She hated explaining to meat eaters that vegetarians could still be very good chefs, having to drop in the history of Alain Passard's famed three-Michelin-star restaurant Arpège to get them to back off. Books? She sensed he wasn't much of a reader. Could her life really be boiled down to a handful of subjects?

Fortunately, Tommaso didn't need a prompt from her, and began to speak about how he had convinced his family to start making wine on their land and the challenges of beginning that process. Wine was something she could always get on board with.

"You should come to the farm and vineyard," he said.

Her curiosity made her want to jump at the invitation, but she also worried about whether there were strings attached. Did she even care? Should she be channeling her inner free spirit? Or even better, *Karishma*'s inner free spirit. She knew what her friend would say.

"I'd love to," she said. "I've never seen how wine is made."

"You've never seen the process?" he asked incredulously.

"Only on TV. Not many vineyards in Manhattan. Would be hard to cultivate vines through cracks in the sidewalks."

Tommaso shook his head . though he could not fathom such a life. For her part, Jyoti couldn't imagine having been raised in a lush countryside with endless rolling green hills, where you could walk for miles only hearing the sounds of the breeze and the birds.

"Then you must visit. A chef must know where her ingredients come from."

"I couldn't agree more." She thought back to the artichoke flowers, thinking that produce was like people, with many stages of growth and development. Just like the bright purple flowers that bloomed only after the plant became inedible and no longer appeared useful, the later ones were often the most surprising and beautiful.

Jyoti returned from her date in good spirits. She hadn't expected to find her mojo in Italy, but perhaps Karishma had always known that she would.

Her friend was going through her full moon ritual of cleansing her crystals by placing them on selenite slabs under the moonlight. Jyoti had to admit that the energy of Karishma's apartment was always calming the second she stepped into it, and those beautiful stones situated throughout felt like they had to be part of the reason. Karishma put the last piece of selenite in the windowsill and turned to Jyoti.

"Are you aware of what the aunties are saying?"

Jyoti shook her head. "I silenced my phone so I wouldn't be rude at the table."

"They are having a field day with you expressing yourself." She tucked her legs underneath her and settled into the couch. "As if it's a national emergency that someone should be honest about their feelings."

"I'm not surprised."

"It's very melodramatic. A lot of baap re baaps and stuff like that." She rolled her eyes. "You aren't twelve, and posting about making paneer isn't some big scandal."

Jyoti gave her a look. "I didn't realize you followed their chats."

"I don't," Karishma said. "They are messaging me directly. Can you imagine how desperate they are to meddle that they actually reached out to *me*?"

Jyoti sighed. "Just ignore them."

Karishma gave her a side-eye. "Are you kidding? Of course I'm going to stand up for you. I told Ushma Auntie that they should be doing the same. They should be helping your mom understand that her daughter's happiness and fulfillment matter more than anything else."

Jyoti felt her cheeks flush. *Of course I'm going to stand up for you.* She thought back to when she'd come home for winter break during her final year of college. She and Karishma had been roommates for all four years at that point. Her mom had sat her down and told her to be careful about Karishma because there were rumors beginning to surface about her drinking and going out with boys. Jyoti had been doing those things too—or at least attempting the latter—but she had been more discreet, not wanting to disappoint her parents. Besides, boys rarely seemed that interested in her, especially when Karishma was around. She'd needed her parents to introduce her to someone like Ashok who wasn't swept up in Karishma's charismatic cyclone and preferred Jyoti's quiet and subdued demeanor. "A good Indian girl," he'd often called her, and the compliment had made her beam with pride. That's why it had been such an ordeal when she'd been out day drinking with him the day of Tanvi's high school graduation and missed the ceremony. She'd thought she'd have plenty of time to sober up and make it home beforehand, but the alcohol won that battle and they'd lost track of time. By the time she noticed her phone battery had died and it was much later than she'd thought, she'd missed her train to New Jersey, and graduation was over by the time she returned.

Her mother had been livid, not understanding why Jyoti's phone was off when she'd called repeatedly to find out where she was.

"You're drunk," her mom hissed, venom on her tongue as she smelled the alcohol on Jyoti's breath. "How could you be so irresponsible? It was Karishma, wasn't it? She doesn't take anything seriously, so you don't either? I knew it was a bad idea for you to live with her. She is a terrible influence."

Jyoti opened her mouth to defend Karishma but then closed it. She suspected a proposal from Ashok was coming, and she didn't want to change her parents' minds about him. Family events were sacrosanct, and someone who would encourage her to drink on such an important day might not be husband material after all in their eyes. So, Jyoti remained silent and let her mom think that Karishma had been responsible for her missing her baby sister's graduation. Jyoti had underestimated how much her mom would make it her personal mission to ensure the Sasti Masti aunties knew what a bad influence Karishma was. From there, the rumors spiraled. And with Nalini's impeccable reputation, coupled with a preexisting prejudice against Karishma for not following a traditional path, it became easy for the community to shun not just Karishma, but her entire family. It didn't happen overnight, but was more gradual. Clipped conversations followed by a series of "forgotten" invitations. The most painful cuts often happen little by little before anyone realizes how deep they've become.

Karishma had asked Jyoti about it once because her own mother had been so confused by the change in her friends' behavior. Jyoti was sick with guilt but convinced herself the truth wouldn't change the outcome. And that Karishma had never needed community approval in the way that Jyoti had. Eventually, Karishma's parents began to spend time with Gujaratis outside the Sasti Masti circle and didn't even bother to exchange pleasantries with their old Sasti Masti friends during holidays like Diwali or Rakshabandan. Paths that had once been so closely linked simply diverged.

Jyoti felt shame wash over her, wishing that all those years ago, she'd stood up for Karishma the way her best friend did for her. What was the worst that would have happened? Her parents would have been upset with Ashok? Maybe they wouldn't have approved the match? In some ways, that could have been a saving grace. Although maybe it wouldn't have even come to that given how badly they wanted their eldest daughter married. At the time, it had felt like an innocent white lie that would flow off Karishma like water, but it had changed Karishma's family. Jyoti had never forgiven herself and she suspected Karishma wouldn't either if she knew.

Jyoti was struggling to devise some new recipes and couldn't get out of her own head, all the while knowing creativity never flowed that way. When Chaya's picture flashed onto her screen for a FaceTime, she welcomed the distraction.

"Hi," Jyoti said.

"Do you have a minute?"

Jyoti's eyes narrowed. This was always the prelude to Chaya delivering serious news.

"It's nothing bad," Chaya quickly assured her, the high-pitched sounds of a children's show playing in the background. She was moving through the house and found a quiet room, closing the door behind her. Chaya met her eyes, and inhaled quickly before saying, "I saw your video. The one about my pregnancy."

"Right," Jyoti said flatly. "Sorry about that. It was a tough day."

"It's okay."

Jyoti was surprised by her sister's gentle tone.

Chaya continued, "I didn't think about how hard that was for you. I mean, I was younger then and pretty wrapped up in what I had going on. But I didn't think about how hard it must have been for you to be as supportive as you were. And you definitely were. That's what I remember most about that day. I hate the thought of you crying on the train home after I dropped you off."

Jyoti swallowed the lump in her throat that was beginning to form. It wasn't Chaya's fault that she'd never suffered a miscarriage, or that everything went so smoothly for her. But it had been really painful and wasn't a memory she liked to revisit. It was always bittersweet when you worked tirelessly for something that came so easily to someone else. She'd never told anyone what Ashok had said when she returned home that day, sharing Chaya's big news. *"That's good, right? At least we know women in your family can get pregnant, so you probably don't have a genetic defect."*

Jyoti shook the memory away. "It's okay," she said in an octave higher than intended, trying to mask the emotion creeping into her voice. "It was always going to sting watching people getting pregnant easily whether it was my sister or not."

"Maybe. But as your sister, I wish I'd paid better attention to what was really going on with you and your marriage at that time. I figured things would eventually work out for you and if you didn't want to share something with me, then it was none of my business."

"Sharing isn't exactly the family motto." Jyoti laughed quietly.

"I know. But I should have pushed harder to know what was really going on. We're sisters. We don't have to act like Mom and Dad and bottle everything up." She took a deep breath. "I called because I do want to share something with you… Isaac and I are pregnant. Again."

Jyoti took a deep breath and absorbed the words, just as she had eight years ago. She even cut Chaya some slack for her irksome wording, suggesting that Isaac was also—miraculously—pregnant. She could tell that Chaya had been scared to share this with her, especially considering Jyoti's latest TikTok post. But as Jyoti took a beat to check in with herself, she realized how differently she felt the second time around. She was happy for her sister, and happy that Nitin would have a younger sibling. She was looking forward to being masi for a second time. Most notably, she was letting go of her own expectations for motherhood and could envision a different future. So, this time, when the smile spread across her face, it was genuine and wouldn't be followed by tears.

"I'm happy for you," Jyoti said. "Is it a boy or a girl?"

Chaya let out a sigh of relief. "We are going to keep it a surprise again."

Jyoti nodded. "That's really exciting, but was it…planned?"

Nitin was seven and she had assumed they were done having children.

Chaya laughed. "No. I'm pushing forty and wasn't thinking about a life with diapers again."

She pictured Chaya's future and saw an unkempt house, Nitin running around wreaking havoc, and a newborn crying in the crib. The life she'd so desperately wanted now seemed exhausting. She'd much rather pore over ingredients in complete solitude, a glass of Montepulciano waiting for her afterward.

"When are you due?"

"It's early. We're not due for seven and a half months."

Jyoti marveled at her sister's ability to share the news this early. Jyoti had become so afraid of complications that she vowed to stop telling anyone anything unless she somehow made it past the first trimester, which she never did.

"I can't wait to meet the new baby," Jyoti said.

"That's not the only thing I wanted to tell you."

Oh no, Jyoti thought. Was it twins? Triplets? Chaya had always been the overachiever amongst them.

"Isaac and I have been talking about what happens to our kids if…well…you know." Fear flickered across her face.

Jyoti's stomach dropped. "Is something wrong?"

She waved off Jyoti. "No, nothing like that. Just more that Isaac has an overwhelming need to have our paperwork in order. You know how he is. And, well, we wanted to ask if you would be the guardian of our kids if anything should ever happen to us."

Jyoti's mouth fell slack. *Had she heard that correctly?*

"Hopefully nothing ever does," Chaya quickly added, "but he's right that we should be safe and plan for the worst. We really should have done this when Nitin was born, but somehow the years passed."

"Why me?" Jyoti asked, still in shock, not understanding why her sister would want to leave her children to someone single and jobless.

"We'd want someone who is family to raise them. And someone who has good values. Doesn't hurt that you're a great cook and could introduce them to our food." Chaya grinned at her.

"But it's just me."

"Yeah, for now. But it may not always be that way. And even if it is, it doesn't mean we'd want someone else raising them."

"Sorry, I'm stunned," she said. "But I'd be honored to do it. I mean, I hope I never have to and you're seeing your children's children and their children. But I never thought you'd want someone like me to raise your kids."

Chaya brushed her off. "No one would give them a better home. You love children and care so much. That matters more than anything else."

Jyoti realized there were many ways to have children in one's life, and her single focus on having her own for so long had blinded her to the wonderful kids who were already in her life. She vowed to spend more time with Nitin when she returned home and to shower this new baby with all the love and joy in the world. This was possibly the best-case scenario. She could have children around her when she wanted to and give them back to their parents when she didn't. Not having her own finally seemed like a blessing, and it was such a relief to feel that old pain leaving her body. She felt lighter than she had in years.

She hung up the phone and felt a burst of creativity surge through her as she started sketching out the concept for a turmeric-scented fettucine with a saffron-infused cream sauce.

NINETEEN

Jyoti got into a routine of stopping by Tommaso's stand at the market. She loved the inside scoop he would give her about the other vendors and farmers: *Don't buy tomatoes from that one because their crop had leaf miners. The sun had shone gloriously on the summer squash plants so they were likely to be succulent and sweet. The woman who made fresh ricotta had been up all night with a colicky baby so she might have been off her game today. Better to try her products later in the week.* Like Jyoti, Tommaso believed the energy one carried when tending to food made its way into the final product. She took everything he said to heart and shopped accordingly.

She returned home and washed the earthy spinach, mustard greens, and Tuscan kale she'd purchased. She was finally ready to tackle the saag paneer ravioli that had been dancing around her mind since her first week in Florence. Her mom had always made palak paneer, insisting on a purist form with only spinach, but Jyoti preferred the complexity that came with a medley of greens, so she'd always opted for saag in the restaurant. She didn't think most non-Indians understood the difference between palak and saag when they saw it on a menu, but she did, and she had to make dishes that satisfied her as much as the diners.

Kale would be a new addition to the pureed greens, but it felt wrong to leave out such an iconic Italian staple, especially when it looked so fresh and vibrant. She took her mixture of greens and blanched and shocked them to set in the color. It took some extra steps to preserve their verdancy, but she hated when greens were overcooked and developed brown hues.

She slow cooked onions, garlic, ginger, and tomatoes in a sauté pan, taking a small taste and adding more garlic. The garlic in Italy was sweeter than what she was accustomed to in New York and she wanted to make sure there was enough of a bite. Besides, was there ever enough garlic? Not to her. She opened the masala dabba and began adding the spices, relishing in the aromas of cinnamon, cloves, and cardamom as the heat coaxed out their fragrant oils. In the restaurant, Jyoti had prepared individual blends of masalas for each of their dishes. She didn't believe in a catchall "garam masala"—something she'd only seen during the past few years but had never heard of when she was growing up. She'd been confused by an ingredient called *hot spices*, which could mean anything, when she'd first seen it.

When she had the seasoning just right, she squeezed in some tomato paste to enrich the flavor and added her pureed greens. She zested a lemon to bring in floral citrus notes rather than adding the juice, which could have turned it brown. She removed her paneer from the fridge and debated crumbling it into the saag versus cutting a thin square and creating a layering effect. Crumbling was easier, but when it came to food, Jyoti rarely went with easy. She queried whether the paneer would soak up enough of the saag seasoning if it was separated from the greens. Flavor should never be sacrificed for appearance.

She groaned as she realized she was going to make them both ways and do a taste test.

"It looks like a tornado hit this place," Karishma's voice rang out, the front door closing behind her.

"Recipe testing. But I'm glad you're back. I'm going to need tasters in a bit."

"Always happy to supply that," she said. "I'm sure Ben wouldn't mind coming over either."

"Great idea. I'm trying to figure out the sauce that makes the most sense with this." She scrunched her face and looked between her saag and the ingredients spread out on the counter.

"What are you aiming for?" Karishma asked, taking a closer look.

"Saag paneer ravioli. I'm going to laminate the pasta dough with some cilantro, so I don't want a sauce that will cover that up. Something that's more of a drizzle than a douse."

Karishma nodded. "Keeping it Indian?"

"Trying for some kind of fusion where the flavors are Indian-inspired but the appearance is reminiscent of Italy, so it has that familiarity." Her eyes darted around the kitchen as she pondered her options. "Maybe I could do dollops of a yogurt-based sauce and also a spicy tomato one so people could choose their own adventure with each bite. Hot and cool on the same plate, but would still mix together nicely."

"Sounds delish," Karishma said.

Jyoti began to ponder what that would look like as a finished product. She'd need to sauté the ravioli with something—perhaps some olive oil, garlic, and chilies—to prevent the dish from being dry and boring. Or maybe even a subtle green chutney sauce? And then the yogurt and spicy tomato sauces to tie it all together. *Yes*, she nodded to herself, envisioning the final product. Once she perfected this menu, she couldn't wait to make it for her family when she went back home. Chaya and Isaac always loved her creations, and surely, she would be back on good terms with her parents by then.

Karishma looked down at her phone. "Ben said he'll be here in a couple hours."

"Good. It will take me that long to finish sauces and plating. Want to help me roll out pasta?"

Karishma washed her hands and let Jyoti put her to work. "You know this kitchen stuff isn't my strength."

"I do." Jyoti smiled. "I just need some clean hands to help catch the dough."

Jyoti began rolling out her fresh pasta in the machine Ben had sourced for her, making it thin enough that she could laminate it with cilantro leaves before giving it a final pass through the rollers. She then made some raviolis with the paneer cut into a thin square to give the two-layered effect she'd imagined, and lastly made another batch with a mixture of the saag and crumbled paneer.

There was nothing more satisfying than seeing the finished product come to life just as she had pictured. She plated six raviolis on each dish and they glistened with a silky green chutney and ghee sauce, and she used her squeeze bottle to add perfect circles of a smooth, spicy tomato sauce and a lemony yogurt sauce. She finished the plate with a few carefully placed cilantro leaves because she always liked to have a fresh element for earthiness and brightness.

When Ben arrived a few minutes later with Mae, his eyes were wide as he took in the dish in front of him.

"It's simply marvelous," he said. "I knew I picked the right person for this job."

"You haven't tasted it yet." Jyoti shifted her weight from side to side as she always did when waiting for the verdict. The anticipation and nerves bubbled within her. Of course, she'd tried it herself before serving it and loved it, but once a plate went to a diner, it stopped being hers and became theirs.

Karishma was seated next to him, fork poised to dive in.

"Wait!" Mae said. She reached for her camera and took some glamour shots before they ate. "It's too pretty not to photograph first. And this way, you'll be able to re-create it if this one is the winner."

Jyoti appreciated Mae's enthusiasm, but she also knew that she never forgot the look of a winning dish, or, frankly, a losing one. She remembered all her culinary exploits with pinpoint accuracy. When Mae showed her a few of the pictures through the viewfinder, though, Jyoti was amazed at how they'd turned out. She now realized that the ones they'd taken of the dishes at Taste of Ginger could have been vastly improved with a better photographer. It was something she'd focus on revamping once she got it back.

But for now, she was waiting for that crucial moment, right after their first taste and just before their open reactions. The three of them speared their first ravioli—starting from left to right, as instructed by Jyoti. She was trying to figure out which filling option she should choose and wanted them to eat the same one at the same time to control those variables. Ben trailed his ravioli through both sauces, Karishma dipped hers into one and then the other, and Mae tried hers without either. The way people ate said so much about who they were. As they took their first bites in unison, she looked at each of them and waited for that moment. Then, as if the clouds had parted from their faces, she saw it.

This dish was a winner. Just as she'd hoped. On their faces was surprise, intrigue, a slight puckering from Ben and Karishma who had included the tangy yogurt sauce, but most importantly, a quick return to the plate for a second bite. The time elapsed between the first two bites also spoke volumes. Sure, there were foodies who savored each bite, letting the flavors linger on their tongue and closing their eyes for a few moments after swallowing. But unless you were a food critic, most people were eager to immediately return to something they'd liked.

When they moved on to the next ravioli, which was now filled with the paneer mixed into the saag, she even more astutely observed their faces. They were still enjoying their food, but she wasn't sure she could discern a significant difference in their reactions.

"Which do you like better?" she asked.

The three looked at one another, as if trying to ascertain what the right answer should be.

Karishma cleared her throat. "They are both good and so similar. Hard to say."

Mae nodded. "There's so much flavor going on, so I'm not sure it makes a big difference. Maybe isn't worth the added work for the layering."

Jyoti waited for Ben, whose opinion mattered most for this event.

"Agreed," he said. "The taste is so good with the mixture. Not sure it's worth the extra effort for something that people will consume in minutes before moving on to the next course."

Jyoti wasn't sure if she was relieved or annoyed. Part of her always gravitated to the prettier, more difficult option, as long as taste wasn't sacrificed. But even she had to admit that practicality needed to play a role as well. Ashok had always been warning her of that when she was creating new recipes. "Keep everything manageable," he'd say. But he'd never seen food as art the way she did.

In this instance, it didn't feel like a personal sacrifice to take the easier road, so she didn't fight them the way she had when she and Ashok disagreed in the past. She felt like she had another dish for the menu that she was really proud of. Now, only six more to go.

A productive day in the kitchen always put Jyoti in a good mood, and she was excited to see Tommaso that evening. When she walked into Coquinarius, she had more bounce in her step.

She'd strolled across the river and was meeting an Italian man for a date at a restaurant she'd already been to with Karishma. She was feeling like a local and was becoming more susceptible to Firenze's pull. It was small enough that it felt charming and quaint, but still large enough that she could blend into a throng of strangers. She was inching her way closer to feeling like she could belong.

The restaurant felt open and warm with its high vaulted ceiling, cream walls, orange decor, and dark woods. There was a cute bar toward the back with geometric wooden planks, giving it a modern look. Behind it, servers and cooks were milling around as dishes were placed at the pass ready to be served. Along one wall were seemingly endless bottles of wine on floor-to-ceiling shelves, and she again marveled at how trusting restaurant owners were in Florence. Faith and a belief in human decency were part of the city's magnetism. It was a far cry from New York, where pharmacies locked up basic sundries like toothpaste and deodorant behind glass panels.

Tommaso was already seated and stood when she arrived at the table. The top of his head glistened and she had the urge to touch it but held back. She wasn't sure he would appreciate her rubbing his head like a genie. She'd never dated someone bald. Ashok had been trending in that direction and it would have been a matter of time, but he hadn't been willing to concede that the circle of bare skin forming at the top rear of his skull was widening each month.

"Ciao, bella," he said, kissing her cheek. He smelled of earth and sun, and she wondered what his day on the farm had been like.

She sat in the wooden chair and her stomach growled at the smells of fresh pasta and melted cheese wafting around her. She knew exactly what she'd be getting and they ordered quickly. When the white plate with the pasta satchels was placed before her, she could not wait to dive in. This was the more down-home version of the pear and taleggio pasta she'd tried at 4 Leoni during her first week, but this one was all comfort and no frills. No herbs or asparagus to muddy the waters. It was the type of dish that would rarely be served in New York, because it looked beige and bland—just pasta wrapped around a pear-and-cheese filling with some grated parmesan and hints of black pepper, sitting on a butter sauce. Nothing more. Utter perfection. Sometimes food should be about the taste and nothing else, and that's what this dish was to her. The purses of dough made her think of bags of money she'd seen on cartoons as a child, and she couldn't help but think that the contents were just as valuable here. She debated whether she could incorporate Indian flavors into a dish like this, but decided this was one item that was best left alone.

They ate in silence for a few minutes, and she appreciated that they both loved food enough to give each other that individual experience. The pasta practically melted on her tongue. So many people rushed through their meals without thinking about what they were eating or where it came from, and she loved to savor her first few bites without the distraction of conversation and focus her senses on the food.

"You look happy." Tommaso smiled, finally breaking the silence.

"I am," she said. "I love the simple elegance of well-made pasta."

"Are you making a pasta dish for your menu?" he asked, twirling his thick pici noodles with veal ragout.

"Definitely. I'm just not sure how many yet." She told him about her saag paneer ravioli experiment from earlier that day.

His brow was furrowed. "Those aren't typical spices for ravioli."

"I know. I wanted to make something that looked familiar but tasted different."

"It is a risk, no? You don't think people prefer what they already know?"

Jyoti felt her uncertainty over her menu creep up. Ben had told her that this fusion direction was exactly what they were looking for, but she wondered if people would have more of Tommaso's expectations.

"You think Italians won't like Indian flavors?" she asked, worrying her bottom lip.

He shrugged. "Some maybe, yes. Some maybe, no. If an Indian woman cooks Indian food, then sure, we expect that taste. But we don't really expect it when we see our food, you know?"

"You don't like bringing cultures together through food?" She tucked her hair behind her ear self-consciously. "For me, it's always exciting to create something new."

"Italian food is the best in the world, so I never have to look for anything new," he said.

Jyoti suspected there were many cultures who might disagree, but she understood the pride and nostalgia one took in the food of their heritage. She certainly loved hers. She was always trying new foods, but dal or kitchari were always the flavors she came back to when seeking comfort. But even as he made his comment, she wondered how much exposure he'd had to other cultures in general. She suspected he'd spent very little time outside of Italy. It was easy to believe the small microcosm in which you existed was the center of the universe when you'd hardly experienced anything outside of it.

"Maybe you just haven't tried enough new things yet?" Jyoti said, keeping her voice playful.

"For food, maybe that's true," he said, matching her tone and reaching out to take her hand. "For women, I know I like Indian."

She laughed in spite of herself. Flirting seemed to be his fallback anytime there was a communication barrier.

"I don't know," she said. "You can't tell a chef you don't like her food and expect to get away with that."

"Next time, you call me for a taste test," he said in a way that suggested he was speaking of more than the food. "I'm sure you can find a way to convince me."

"Okay," she said, feeling her cheeks flush.

"I hope to see all the produce I've shown you put into action." He winked, eyes glimmering.

Having someone flirt with her after so recently separating from her husband felt exciting but also strange. And this was different from Saro because she wasn't approaching it like a one-time thing that would be done in a few hours. She dared to think to herself that she was *dating* this man. Tommaso had been straightforward from the start, and Jyoti knew it was up to her to decide how far to take this. The question was, how far did she want to take it? Could she actually date someone? Could she date *him*? Any romance had an obvious expiration date because she would have to return to New York at the end of the summer. Even if she wanted to stay, she couldn't without a visa and those were not easy to come by. She could hear Karishma's voice in her head telling her to have fun and not worry about it, but worrying was what she did best, a trait she had unquestionably inherited from her mother.

He reached across the table and put his hand on hers, and she enjoyed the warmth of his calloused hand on her smooth skin. "This is nice," she said, trying to be present in that moment and stop her swirling thoughts.

"Good," he said, squeezing her fingers. "Shall we get another bottle?"

She looked at the nearly empty bottle of red wine on their table, and couldn't see any reason why not. They ate and drank and talked and laughed, and it wasn't until she rose to leave that she realized how much wine she'd had. She swayed a bit as she took a step. Tommaso immediately took her arm and lent his body for support as they walked outside into the pleasant summer night. They strolled along the river and he leaned her against a wall and kissed her.

Jyoti tensed, just like she had the first time with Saro, trying to acclimate to the unfamiliar lips against hers. It was a strange feeling kissing new men at this age, but she needed to get used to it. She relaxed her shoulders and allowed herself to have fun with it. She didn't hold back and fell into Tommaso, thinking about what brought her pleasure rather than fixating on what would please the man—the way she had with Ashok. It was liberating to focus on her needs for once.

TWENTY

There were few things in life more comforting than risotto, so Jyoti tried to think of how to add that to her menu. How could she change such a classic and add her own spin? It was a blank canvas as long as there was a creamy rice component. She debated whether she should try to move it from savory to sweet, but questioned whether that was what she really wanted to do for dessert. It would have been easy to turn risotto into a saffron-studded rice pudding like kheer. She could practically taste the flavors, but she'd never been a fan of kheer. She found the texture off-putting, but perhaps using arborio rice and allowing it to remain toothsome would make it better. *No*, she decided. She couldn't convince herself to prepare a dessert that she wouldn't enjoy.

Now that she was back at savory, she realized it wasn't so far off from kitchari, and that made things easier for her to consider. She thought about flavors she could bring together to make something unique. She envisioned a good vaghar with curry leaves, black mustard seeds, and maybe some jeeru seeds.

She could see that being the finishing element of the dish, so then she began to work backward to think of what flavors could make up the main part of the risotto. Turmeric seemed essential both for color and its floral notes. Lemon for acidity and brightness. Green chilies were a must to break through the creamy nature of the dish. She'd just need to make sure the spice didn't overpower an Italian palate. She pondered the vegetable that would fit well with those flavors and settled on roasted cauliflower. She could find the colored heirloom varieties to help give the dish some pops of purple, green, and orange. Satisfied, she grabbed her shopping bags and went to the market to stock up.

Tommaso smiled the second he saw her and rose to greet her with a soft kiss. "Did you miss me?"

Jyoti still hadn't gotten used to flirting or being vulnerable, but she nodded slightly before lifting her empty shopping bags.

He laughed. "Ah, so you miss the produce, and maybe me just a little."

She still felt light and happy after their date a couple nights earlier. It seemed like the Universe was showing her that she could take on this new life that she'd been thrust into and it wouldn't be so bad. Life still held surprises for her, and that was starting to feel more gratifying than scary.

"Maybe just a little," she said with a half smile, knowing that being coy would be cute for only so long. She needed to overcome her apprehension eventually and find ways to show him that she reciprocated his feelings if she had any hope of keeping his interest.

"Good," he said, pulling her in for another kiss.

She let herself melt into him without thinking about the fact that they were in public and anyone could see them. It was more a concern for him anyway, as she hardly knew anyone in this city, and he didn't seem to mind. She and Ashok had been long past public displays of affection, but she supposed that was what a decade of fertility schedules and treatments and failures would do to any couple. With Tommaso, she was free of that baggage, and she reveled in it.

When they parted, she got straight to business. "I need heirloom cauliflower, and maybe some fresh peas." She suddenly wondered if a smattering of green would also make sense in the dish and wanted options. "Maybe some tendrils too."

Tommaso scanned the produce and picked up a couple of purple cauliflowers to compare their weights before selecting the heavier one. He then did the same with a spiky green Romanesco, as he didn't have green cauliflower. She didn't see any orange cauliflower, but given that was more for aesthetic, it wasn't essential for the test run. He put peas and tendrils into a bag and handed it to her.

She thought back to his words at dinner the other night, and before leaving the market, she said, "Do you want to come by this evening and taste test?"

He grinned at her while rearranging the cauliflower to fill the gap from the one she bought. It was like he wanted to make her squirm for a bit, knowing how difficult it was for her to put herself out there. After finishing his cruciferous pyramid and admiring his handiwork, he came to stand next to her.

"I thought you'd never ask," he said. "I'd be delighted."

Jyoti's shoulders relaxed. "Great. Karishma and some of her friends may be there too. I need to make sure everything is perfect with the menu." She wanted to make sure he wasn't expecting a romantic date.

He waved goodbye, and she walked home with her groceries, suddenly extra nervous. Not only was she throwing a date into her recipe testing, but she reminded herself that this specific date didn't seem as open-minded to her cooking. She always tried to avoid developing new dishes when she was feeling unbalanced, but she'd invited him and there was no way to take it back. So, she had to move forward with cooking him something she had never made before. And then endure Karishma's endless questions after meeting him.

As she prepped, she found herself back on TikTok to help quell some of her nerves.

"It's been a while since I've dated," she said as she chopped the cauliflower and Romanesco into small florets. "But I guess that's a good thing since I was married for so long." She laughed uncomfortably. "But here I am. Halfway around the world, and a guy who seems nice is actually interested in me. When you're getting divorced, you don't really think about the fact that you'll have to go through all the same emotions, awkwardness, anxieties, and insecurities that you had when you were younger. You'd think they go away, and that somehow by aging, you naturally shed them, but that hasn't happened for me. I'm still just as awkward as I was in high school."

She took her florets and rinsed them in a colander.

"But flirting seems to be a skill people are born with or not, and I'm definitely in the 'not' camp. Fortunately, this guy seems to be looking past the ways I'm being weird about it—at least, for the moment. And now I'm cooking for him tonight, and that's scary and feels like I'm completely exposed. I've never cooked for someone who was a romantic interest before—other than my ex-husband, of course. But that was different. I picked up this career during our marriage, so it's not like it was something I had used to woo him. And I already knew we were together so whether he liked the food or not didn't matter much. I mean, it's always nice when someone likes your food, but you know what I mean. At this stage of my life, it's taken on a different weight."

Jyoti moved to the stove with her phone so she could start the risotto. "This community has been so great for listening, and I can't thank you all enough. It makes some of these scary moves feel a little less intimidating knowing I've got nonjudgmental followers supporting me through them." She dropped ghee into the skillet to toast the arborio rice. "I'm making an Indian-inspired cauliflower shaak risotto tonight. Taking the classic techniques and adding a new twist by using turmeric, curry leaves, chilies, mustard seeds, and lemon. Along with this gorgeous heirloom purple cauliflower." She held up the florets for the camera. "I love how the same ingredients have found completely different flavor profiles across cultures. The humble cauliflower can be cooked a million ways and each one will resonate with a different part of the world.

"Whenever I think of cauliflower, I think of my mom chopping hers and how differently she preps vegetables from me." Jyoti flashed her large chef's knife toward the camera. "My mom has no idea how to use this thing. She never cuts with a sharp knife against a cutting board the way I do. Instead, she uses this small dull blade that she has had since before I was born and cuts in her hand, bringing the blade against her thumb. All of the aunties in her generation do it that way. Somehow, she never cuts herself, but I know if I tried to do it, there would be a trip to the emergency room. I learned to cook from my mom, but never learned to use a knife the way she can. I never went to formal cooking school, so I wonder why I developed different knife skills. Maybe it was all the food shows on television, but it's always been weird to me that we prep fruits and veggies so differently."

Jyoti began separating florets from the cauliflower by turning it upside down on her board and following the natural lines of the vegetable. "The key to not having cauliflower bits all over your kitchen when you chop is to never go through the middle of a floret. If you keep the base of each segment intact, then the cleanup is a breeze." She smiled at the camera. "Or, you could be like my mom and chop the vegetable over a bowl, using your thumb for stability, but that is only if you are a seasoned auntie. For most of you watching, I'm guessing my method will be the one you choose."

She finished carving evenly sized florets and held the bowl to the camera. "Maybe our varying knife skills say more than I'd ever considered. Maybe having different ways of getting to the same place doesn't mean one of us is wrong and one is right. There are simply multiple options that lead to the same final product." Jyoti brought the camera closer to her. "Enough musing for one day. Now I'd better go focus so I can make sure I don't botch this dish. I'll report back on how this turns out—with both the meal and the guy."

She posted and read a few of the comments before taking some deep breaths and turning her focus to the kitchen.

@solotravelerfromca: Dating is so hard these days.

@nicegirlsfinishfirst: Good for you for being out there!

@nowornever: I've been divorced for five years and still haven't gone on a date.

@pastalover: What are you cooking?

@paulakimmie: Dating is a group effort…we are all in this together.

@hungrygal: That sounds delicious. Wish I could taste it!

@cookingwithfire: That's so creative, send the recipe.

@nicolefromthebay: He's going to love it. How could he not?

Tommaso, Ben, Mae, Enzo, and Karishma were gathered around the kitchen table. It was a tight squeeze, but it was also nice to have an impromptu dinner party. Jyoti loved how easy-going Karishma was with those things. She'd been delighted when she heard she would get to meet Tommaso and get a home-cooked meal out of it. But once she learned Tommaso would be there, Karishma wanted opinions from the entire crew, and none of them were about to turn down a free meal.

Jyoti had placed the shallow bowls with the creamy risotto in front of each person. After Mae snapped magazine-worthy photos of the meal, they took their first bites. She watched as they breathed in the aromatic vaghar, which was far from what one would imagine for a risotto dish. She'd been heavy-handed with the curry leaves and mustard seeds; one, because she loved both flavors, and two, because she wanted to know how far she could push that profile with her guests.

Tommaso and Ben were seated next to each other, so it was easy for her to focus on the two people whose impressions mattered most to her. Ben took his first bite and she could tell that he loved it. He was more familiar than some of the others with Indian flavors, so she expected this wasn't too far off the mark from what he enjoyed. Tommaso was a different story, and she found it very difficult to tell what he was thinking.

"It tastes like fancy cauliflower shaak," Karishma said, immediately understanding what Jyoti was going for.

She nodded. "Exactly what I hoped you'd say."

Karishma took another bite. "It's really good. So different. Shaak is so dry and this creaminess is so unctuous. It's like you combined two different comfort foods into one dish."

Jyoti clasped her hands together. "That is the best compliment you could give me."

She then turned her attention back to Tommaso, who had not spoken yet. She was desperate to know what he thought as he took another bite. Did he not understand that recipe testing meant she wanted to know what he thought about it? Of course he did. Maybe his silence meant he was trying to think of something polite to say. He hadn't hidden his views on fusion cooking so she'd known inviting him was a risk. But cooking was how she showed love and affection so she needed to see how someone she dated would accept that part of her. She began wringing her hands as Tommaso's deliberate chewing continued.

"It's another winner for me," Ben said. "I can't think of a time when I've had anything quite like this. There's nothing more exciting than innovation when it comes to a meal."

Mae added, "I love the hint of spice. It cuts through the richness along with the lemon and makes it so addicting. You just keep going back for another bite."

Tommaso remained quiet and everyone now seemed to be staring at him. *It's okay if he doesn't like it*, Jyoti told herself. It's only one dish. She had countless others in her repertoire. She'd find another that he would like.

He cleared his throat. "Ben is right. I've never had anything like this. Not what I expect when I think of a risotto. I'm not so used to these flavors, but I think it must be good."

Jyoti felt herself deflate. It sounded like he was trying to be polite. She knew she shouldn't be upset. He was unfamiliar with Indian cuisine, so she couldn't expect it to be comfort food to him.

"Don't you just love when you can try new foods?" Karishma jumped in, trying to throw him a lifeline.

Tommaso's face suggested he didn't, but he raised his glass of wine in Jyoti's direction. "Of course. To the chef!"

Jyoti joined in the cheers, but it niggled at her that he didn't seem that interested in expanding his palate. She again wondered if her menu was too Indian for a dinner full of Italian guests. Wouldn't they be more like Tommaso? She turned to Enzo to gauge his reaction, given he was the only other purebred Italian in the room.

"What do you think?" Jyoti asked, wringing her hands again.

Enzo swallowed and said, "Different, but good. It's nice to have a change. It also doesn't feel as heavy as risotto can sometimes be. You've got a tasting menu, no? I think lighter dishes are better with so many courses."

Relief flooded through her. Enzo seemed to genuinely enjoy it and had delivered a more thoughtful answer than Tommaso. But Jyoti tried not to be too hard on him. Tommaso was surrounded by strangers and unfamiliar food, and, as charismatic and confident as he seemed, maybe he was nervous too.

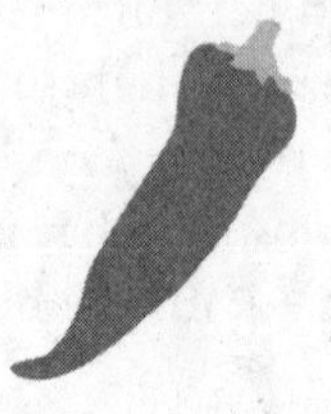

TWENTY-ONE

Jyoti stared at her sisters' faces on the screen.

"Really, Jyo?" Chaya asked. "Really?"

Jyoti feigned nonchalance. "What is the big deal?"

"You know."

"I get why people were upset about the first one, but now it's just sharing recipes and connecting with people about my life," Jyoti said. "Mom can't be so upset about that."

"You know how she is," Chaya said. "She needs time for the dust to settle."

"You mean she needs time to get back into the good standing of Sasti Masti," Jyoti said.

Tanvi held open her hands as if that were obvious. "That's always what matters."

Jyoti rolled her eyes. "Maybe it shouldn't. Would it be the worst thing if she found new friends who were less gossipy?"

She thought about how Karishma's mom had found new friends who seemed less judgmental after losing Sasti Masti. While she wished the whole thing had never happened, Jyoti knew that Karishma was closer to the aunties in that circle than she'd ever been with Sasti Masti. Maybe Jyoti's mom would be happier with a more inclusive community rather than being fueled by the gossipmongers.

"But that's not the way it is," Chaya said. "Can we please focus?"

Chaya had seemingly taken over the big sister role that Jyoti held for so long, and Jyoti had to admit that she didn't mind the shift. She was getting a taste of how their lives had been, never worrying about what their parents thought because they knew their older sister would always smooth things over. Now it was Chaya's turn to mediate the emotions and Jyoti could finally start living her own life.

"What is to be gained from talking about random stuff to strangers online?" Chaya asked. "Do you really want these stories etched in stone forever? What if whoever this guy you're talking about sees it? Or the next one?"

Jyoti hadn't been worried about Tommaso perusing her social media accounts. He'd made it clear that world wasn't for him. But Chaya raised a fair point about future prospects. It hadn't entered her realm of consciousness because she hadn't thought about dating as a continued action. She hadn't thought about meeting people and things not working out and then having to start over. Possibly again and again and again in a vicious loop.

"I can always delete the videos later," Jyoti said, half responding to her sister, half reassuring herself.

"Just think about if this is really worth the drama. Do you really want Sasti Masti gossiping about your love life?"

Jyoti most certainly did not want Sasti Masti involved in any aspect of her love life, but she'd lived enough decades to know that meddling aunties would always find a way. She turned her attention to Tanvi's face on her screen.

"Tanvi, you post things all the time," Jyoti said. "How come you don't get harassed about it?"

Tanvi chortled. "Because I'm smart enough to use incognito

accounts for anything that I don't want people talking about. And I never post dating stuff online."

She was right about that. Jyoti and Chaya had often discussed Tanvi's lack of apparent interest in anything having to do with romantic relationships and they'd both concluded that Tanvi would decide to venture down that path one day or not, but it was her decision to make. Jyoti was certainly coming around to the idea that marriage and kids weren't for everyone, and Tanvi just might be one of those people. But Jyoti was surprised to learn that Tanvi had other accounts. She wondered what was on them that she and Chaya were missing. Or maybe it was just her who was out of the loop now.

"I wonder if I should do that," Jyoti mused aloud.

"It's too late for you," Tanvi said. "People are already onto you and will go looking if the content suddenly disappears. No offense, but I don't think you're TikTok savvy enough to pull that off. I think your options are to delete it, or own it and continue."

It sounded simple when phrased that way, but it felt far less so. Jyoti looked at her sisters' faces. "And you both want me to delete it?"

Chaya quickly nodded. Tanvi shrugged. It wasn't an unequivocal answer, but it was clear where her lean was.

"I'll think about it," Jyoti said. But this time, she had no intention of acquiescing.

Satisfied, Chaya smiled and said, "So tell us about this guy."

Jyoti felt relief flow through her. There was tension over her videos, but they were still sisters at the end of the day. Jyoti gave them the highlights of her few dates with Tommaso, careful to avoid the parts about how he'd reacted to her food. She hadn't quite accepted that reaction yet and her sisters would pounce on her doubts. She didn't want to tread back into murky waters when she was finally having a fun conversation with them for the first time in what felt like years. And she didn't want to give voice to her feelings about how his reaction to her dish had disappointed her. As much as she tried to make excuses for why her food might not be pleasing to his palate, it didn't change the fact that every chef wants her food to bring people joy, especially those who might become a bigger part of her life. Her food was an expression of herself. She never wanted people to lie for her sake, but she couldn't help but feel that his lack of interest in her food was also a lack of interest in her.

Tommaso invited Jyoti and her friends to visit his family's farm and vineyard that weekend, and she was equal parts nervous and excited. Her chef side was ready to see how all the produce was grown, how the grapes were fermented, how the bottles were stored. The young woman inside of her was very nervous as this felt like going to her new boyfriend's home and meeting his family. Her only prior experience with that had been meeting Ashok's parents shortly before they got engaged. She'd perched awkwardly on the edge of their sofa in her best silk panjabi and let them study her as if assessing the ripeness of a mango. She wasn't sure if Tommaso's family would be there during the visit, but she had to prepare herself as if they would be. While she knew that this meeting might not have the same import to Tommaso as it would to Jyoti given their different cultural backgrounds, she still felt the need to impress.

She'd purchased a yellow wrap sundress with a floral pattern that hugged her curvy hips and chest in the right places. Karishma had lent her one of her favorite citrine bracelets and her labradorite prism necklace. Feeling the delicate gold chain against her skin from the necklace Karishma wore nearly every day made Jyoti feel like she was borrowing her best friend's steady confidence as well. She decided not to take any chances with her natural curls and used a hairdryer to blow her hair out into a straighter, smoother, white-culture approved style. She wanted to look like she belonged with this Italian man.

The five of them had squeezed into Enzo's car for the thirty-minute drive outside of Florence to Tommaso's farm. Jyoti marveled at the rolling hills of perfectly spaced and staked grapevines that appeared as soon as they left the city. It was an endless and uninterrupted stream of local vineyards and olive groves in all directions. The sun was shining and the car windows were open to let in the warm summer breeze. She closed her eyes and thought about how different her life was now. Had she still been married to Ashok, or had she had a child, she would not be having this moment. Each step in one direction meant a step away from another. She wanted to start appreciating rather than begrudging the path that had led her here.

She was prepared for Tommaso to be standoffish, the way she would have been if she'd brought someone home for the first time, but he cupped her cheeks with his hands and drew her in for a kiss as if he didn't have a concern in the world. After greeting Karishma, Enzo, Ben, and Mae, he led the group away from the rustic main house to the gardens. There was a hum of birds and insects as they moved through the rows of beans, artichokes, squash, leeks, eggplant, and cucumbers. There were raised beds overflowing with basil, marjoram, chives, thyme, rosemary, and other herbs that perfumed the air.

"This is a chef's dream." Jyoti knelt by the herbs and inhaled.

Tommaso laughed. "I never thought of it like that, but it is a nice place to live."

"Far cry from the city, mate," Ben said, clapping Tommaso on the back as he moved past him. "Now I see where all your produce has been coming from." He winked at Jyoti.

She smiled. "Only the best for your clients."

Ben put his hands together to thank her as they walked along the dirt path.

The group continued until they found themselves along the grapevines on the property. Tommaso led them to a two-story stone building with green ivy clinging to the sunny outer walls. Inside were three large clay vats with steel lids that looked like giant matla, and the smell of fermentation hung heavy in the air. They then went belowground to the cellar and Jyoti felt goose bumps on her arms. It was much darker and cooler and the walls were lined with eight gigantic barrels on their sides, each with a small spigot coming out of its center. Tommaso took some wineglasses and led them to one of the barrels on the right. He turned the spigot so that some medium-hued red wine flowed into the glasses and he passed them around for the group to taste.

It smelled rather acidic but Jyoti took a small sip. Her face puckered.

Tommaso swirled his glass and inhaled the bouquet. "Chianti Classico." He smiled at them. "This is not what we expect when we drink it, of course. This is halfway through the fermentation process, but I thought you might like to see how it evolves. We leave it in these barrels for at least eighteen months before transferring it to bottles. We actually buy used barrels from America because a lot of the burnt oak taste will have been removed in the prior storage. We don't want that taste in our wine the way the Americans do, and the barrels are cheaper to purchase after they are used."

Jyoti cast her eyes downward to say she was guilty of this offense, and Tommaso gave her a knowing glance before slinging his arm around her shoulders for a side hug.

"Now we taste the finished product," Tommaso said, leading them into another room with many bottles of wine stacked along the shelves on the wall. He picked up an unlabeled bottle and peered into it, but Jyoti was not sure for what purpose. It seemed impossible to look through the thick glass. She was sensing that, like cooking, winemaking was as much art as it was science.

Tommaso guided them toward a table in the center of the room and pulled a few labeled bottles off the shelves. He gestured for them to sit.

"And this," he said with a practiced pull of the cork, "is our signature Chianti Classico." He poured them each small tastings and passed them around. Then, he swirled his glass before breathing in the bouquet, finally taking a sip.

Jyoti caught Mae and Karishma giving each other a look before doing a half swirl and diving in to taste. Ben studied the wine for color and clarity before smelling the bouquet, and then eventually swished it around in his mouth to complete his test. Jyoti wasn't nearly as sophisticated as Ben when it came to these matters, but she knew what she liked, and her mouth immediately salivated as the tannins hit her tongue. She could tell this was an ideal wine to have with cheese or any other fatty, heavy food, but it wasn't a sipping wine. The rich earthiness would have paired nicely with her samosas because the wine had enough heft to withstand those assertive, spicy flavors.

She raised her glass in Ben's direction and tapped the side of it. "I could see something like this going well with the samosa course."

Ben nodded. "I'll check for that the next time I'm at Fausto's vineyard. Will that be the spiciest dish on the menu?"

"I think so," Jyoti said. "I'll tone it down a bit from what we had in Praiano. I don't want to blow people's palates in those first few courses."

"Don't hold back," Ben said. "This is your chance to show them something different from the normal fare."

Jyoti smiled before turning her attention back to Tommaso, who was opening the next bottle and pouring it into a glass decanter.

"This one," he said, "is my favorite. It's the one that you can sip on the veranda while reading a book or chatting with friends."

"Sign me up," Karishma said, holding out her glass. She took a small swirl before taking a sip and closing her eyes. "Smooth. Very smooth."

Tommaso nodded appreciatively, and poured for the rest of them. The nose was fruit forward with a hint of spice—maybe black pepper. After taking her first sip, Jyoti revised her assessment to green pepper. This was an easy drinking wine, without as much tannin as the first, and a finish so sleek that she forgot it was alcohol.

"A blend of Sangiovese, Cabernet Sauvignon, and Colorino grapes for this one," Tommaso explained.

Ben cocked his head before beginning his tasting routine, and then came to the same conclusion as Jyoti and Karishma.

Tommaso beamed. "I love to see the joy on your faces. That is why we make wine. To bring people together in comfort and satisfaction."

Jyoti's heart warmed as she realized that he made wine for the same reason that she cooked, and she held up her empty glass for another pour. "You've definitely made your family proud with these wines."

His eyes twinkled as he refilled her glass, and her cheeks grew warm.

"Sorry I'm late," a woman announced as she entered the room with a tray filled with bread, charcuterie, cheese, and olives.

She appeared to be around their age, wearing simple blue jeans and a loose-fitting mauve tank top, with gray-streaked dark brown hair bound together in a messy bun atop her head. She rushed to place the tray on the table before them. Tommaso kissed her cheek and pulled out a chair for her.

"This is my sister, Paola," Tommaso said. "She cannot be on time no matter the occasion."

She rolled her eyes at him in the way that siblings do. "As if you have no flaws?"

"Is it not true? You were late for your own wedding."

Paola brushed him off. "Does it matter? No wedding can start without the bride."

Tommaso went around the table and introduced Paola to their guests. When he got to Jyoti, she wondered how he'd introduce her, or if he had already said something to Paola and she knew who Jyoti was. She'd forgotten how much dating led to overanalyzing every small thing. In the end, she needn't have worried about a long, drawn-out preamble, because Tommaso got to her and said, "This is Jyoti," just like he'd said for all the others. She wasn't sure if she was relieved or disappointed, but she suspected both.

The group sat around the tasting table and nibbled on the aperitivo fare as they sipped their wine. Paola nudged the charcuterie plate toward Jyoti.

Jyoti shook her head. "Thanks, but I don't eat meat."

A look of confusion crossed Paola's face. "But Tommaso said you are a chef, no?"

It seemed Tommaso had mentioned Jyoti to his sister and told her a few things, so there was some comfort in that, but then she felt herself tense at the assumption that a chef must eat meat. It wasn't the first time she'd been faced with this line of questioning and she knew it wouldn't be the last, especially given Italy's cuisine, but she reminded herself she was on their turf.

"Yes, I'm a chef," Jyoti said. "But Indian food is often vegetarian and my family grew up with those traditions, so that's what I cook."

Paola considered this and then shifted her attention to the rest of the group. Jyoti's shoulders relaxed. She'd been in plenty of situations where people had challenged her culinary competence upon learning she was a vegetarian chef. She'd always been satisfied that, even though they offered meat dishes at the restaurant, it had always been her vegetarian plates that had been the most popular. Customers could always taste the heart that a chef brought to her food, and her love was in the vegetarian cuisine she created with her own hands.

Jyoti turned to Paola. "And you? Do you help Tommaso with the vineyard?"

"From time to time," she said. "I grew up in the fields with the fruits and vegetables, so I spend more days there." She gestured around the wine cellar. "This was Tommaso's dream. He wants to make a Bianchi empire."

"Would that be so bad?" Jyoti asked.

Paola shrugged. "He can do as he pleases. We have what we need."

"And your family lives here on the farm with you?"

"No, no." Paola quickly shook her head. "My husband and I live on the next plot of land. His family had the land next to ours, so we grew up together. Once we married, the lines blurred and now we treat the two properties like one big farm. The kids can go from one house to another easily. It's good for everyone, you know?"

"Wow," Jyoti said. "You've known your husband that long?"

She laughed. "For as long as I can remember. We local kids ran around together, and then once it was time to get married, we decided we were a good match."

Paola's response mirrored those of other people in Jyoti's community when it was time to get married. Jyoti hadn't grown up with Ashok, but did decide he was a good enough match when her parents had suggested him.

"And Tommaso? His first wife was local too?" Jyoti asked.

Paola scoffed. "No, Tommaso prefers women to be more exotic. Local women never suited him."

Jyoti bristled at the word "exotic," recalling that Tommaso used it when they had first met. She could see from the look Karishma was giving her that she, too, had heard the comment.

When the group finished their wine and headed back toward the main house, Karishma fell into step with Jyoti and they hung back from the group.

"You caught that 'exotic' comment, right?"

"Couldn't have missed it with you staring me down," Jyoti said.

"'Exotic' is a word that can be used to describe flowers or fruit. But not people." Karishma's expression was hard.

"I know, but it's not like Tommaso said it," Jyoti said, all too aware that she was withholding information from her best friend. "He can't be responsible for his sister. And maybe there was a language barrier."

Karishma gave Jyoti a stern look. "English isn't a problem in this country. At least not nearly as big as fetishism." She put an encouraging hand on Jyoti's shoulder. "You just need to be careful. Dating is new to you. Dating non-Indians is *completely* new to you. There's a whole different set of worries and standards when you branch out like that. It doesn't mean there aren't good guys, Enzo for one, but there are a lot of unwittingly misguided ones and it's up to you to learn the difference. This country is amazing in so many ways, but its history isn't much better than America's when it comes to people who look like us. Ask the right questions and listen to the answers."

Jyoti knew her friend was coming from a good place and she was right about Jyoti's inexperience with men. It was easy to get wrapped up in the novelty of everything around her and readily accept others' targeted attention. It was too soon to tell if Tommaso was a good choice for her, so she would tread carefully. Something felt off about the way his sister had spoken about his dating history. She knew better than anyone that siblings often knew people better than they even knew themselves.

Paola returned to her family for the evening but had left them a simple dinner of caprese salad, orecchiette with pesto, and gelato, all of which she'd prepared earlier. Tommaso certainly had a cushy life staying on the family farm. It seemed he rarely had to think about meals, cleaning, and so many other things that would have been a part of his day had he ever moved out on his own. Once the group had satiated themselves and the stars had filled the night sky, they began to discuss heading back to Florence before Enzo became too comatose to drive. Rather than all five of them cramming back into the car, Tommaso offered to drive Jyoti so they could spend some time together.

In Tommaso's small Fiat, he played soft instrumental music

and covered Jyoti's hand with his free one when he didn't need to shift gears. His touch was comforting and she'd missed having these small gestures with someone.

"You enjoyed yourself today?" he asked.

She beamed at him. "I loved it. Seeing the farm and produce growing naturally was so exciting. I've always known green beans, squash, peppers, and eggplant are fruits, but seeing them actually growing from flowers on a plant was something I won't forget. And the process of grape to bottle was fascinating. I can see why it would become an obsession for you to make sure you get the formulations right."

"'Obsession' is perhaps too strong a word," he said. "But yes, I have a fear of telling my family that I failed after having convinced them to invest in that area."

"I think we all worry about letting our families down."

He nodded. "This is true."

"It was nice to meet your sister."

"I'm glad you liked her. Paola is the key to my family approval because she will immediately go gossip to everyone," he said, winking at her. "I hope she was well-behaved."

Jyoti thought that was an odd choice of wording for a middle-aged woman.

"You've never told me much about your dating history. Was your ex-wife a neighbor like Paola's husband?"

Tommaso laughed. "Absolutely not. Italian women..." He gestured with his hands like he was trying to find the right words. "I prefer not to date them, you know?"

She'd certainly known Asian women who only dated white men, and while it wasn't her preference, she couldn't really fault them because Western society and media sent the clear message that those were the most coveted attractiveness standards. But it was interesting to hear Tommaso talk about Italian women in this way because Tuscany didn't have the same plethora of multicultural options available as a city like New York.

"What type of women do you prefer?"

He laughed again, trying to dismiss her question. "What kind of question is that?" He brought her hand to his lips and kissed it. "I like women like you."

She wanted to fall into the romance of the words and not belabor the point, but she worried about his evasiveness.

"What exactly is it about me that you like?" She tried to keep her tone light and playful, but she planned to listen very carefully to his answer.

"I love your passion for food, and the way you look after your friends, always making sure they are happy," he said.

Her shoulders relaxed, and she touched the smooth labradorite stone on her borrowed necklace with her free hand. Maybe she'd been overreacting because she had Karishma's voice in her head.

"Thanks. That's nice of you to say."

He kissed her hand. "You are also very easy to look at."

Physical compliments were always hard for her to take, so she went with her fail-safe option of deflecting.

"Where was your ex-wife from?"

Tommaso raised an eyebrow like he was surprised by the question. "She was from Indonesia."

"How did you meet someone from Indonesia here?"

He shrugged. "She was a tourist passing through. We were young. My parents had been pressuring me to marry, and I think they didn't expect that I'd grant their wish with someone like that."

"You were trying to rebel against your family?" Jyoti asked, mulling over what he meant by *someone like that.*

"I don't know about that. I loved her, sure. Also never hurts to put the family in their place too," he said with a chuckle.

Jyoti thought about how she'd always been focused on pleasing, rather than upsetting, her family. "What didn't your parents like about her?"

He squeezed her hand and quickly met her eyes. "Does it matter so much? I don't really like talking about an ex with someone I am dating."

It was a reasonable request, but she really did want to know more. She hated dating. All the balancing of what was too much or too little was nerve-racking. She tried a softer approach.

"Have you dated much since your divorce? That must have been a long time ago."

He whistled. "*Si*, over fifteen years ago. I don't know what to say about dating. I don't see too many women I like. It's mostly local women coming into the market, and, as you see, too many people who have known me since diapers on the farm."

"I know what that is like. Our Indian community was very small and close. There was a lot of pressure to always be the good Indian girl."

"I like a good Indian girl," he said, smiling at her. "You grew up with your ex-husband?"

She shook her head. "Not really. He was part of another Indian community near us, but our parents introduced us. So, I didn't need to worry about families liking each other since that part was already done."

"And why did that marriage end?" he asked.

She looked at him out of the corner of her eye. "I thought we weren't talking about exes."

He glanced at her with an amused expression. "I didn't expect that from you."

"Why not? It's only fair, right?"

Tommaso laughed and kissed her hand again. "This must be your American side."

Before she could delve further into what he meant, they had pulled up to Karishma's place. Cars couldn't linger on her small street, so Jyoti had to say a quick goodbye and table their conversation for another time.

TWENTY-TWO

The next day, Jyoti woke up feeling unsettled. She stared at the blank page in her notebook with new menu items, but as she perused TikTok for inspiration, she kept getting distracted. Something about the day with Tommaso had irked her, but she couldn't quite put her finger on it. She should have been over the moon after witnessing wine production for the first time, spending time in a vast and luscious garden, and meeting his sister, but something felt off. It didn't have the same feeling as when she'd been welcomed into Ashok's family. She knew the situations were vastly different, but she supposed she had wanted it to feel special, and instead it had felt rather ordinary. She wondered if she was trying to manufacture problems where there were none to protect herself from getting hurt. Even this short foray into dating reminded her of the pain of her divorce and losing Ashok after so many years of familiar comfort. It was difficult for her to accept that nothing in life was guaranteed and she had no control over it.

Her phone rang and Ushma Auntie's name flashed on her

screen. Jyoti couldn't imagine the reason for her mom's best friend to be calling her and her mind raced through various tragedies.

"Hi, beta," Ushma Auntie cooed into the phone.

"Hi, Auntie."

"Were you sleeping?" Auntie asked, concern in her voice.

Jyoti propped herself up so her voice would sound more normal. "No, just doing some work."

"Work?" Ushma Auntie asked, surprise in her tone, but then dismissed it and pivoted quickly. "Beta, how are you? You know, we are worried about you."

Jyoti feared that Ushma Auntie was calling to stage some sort of intervention, and Jyoti could not think of anything less appealing at the moment.

"I'm fine, Auntie."

Ushma Auntie sighed deeply. "Beta, you must think about your parents and how hard it is for them to watch their eldest daughter go through such challenges. No parent wants to experience this."

Jyoti wasn't sure which specific challenges Ushma Auntie was referring to as there were a plethora to choose from, but it didn't seem to matter.

"Auntie, this is not the life I planned for myself either, but it's the one I have. I'm doing my best to figure out how to move forward."

"We know that. We all want that for you. Maybe we can help you find a nice boy to settle with. Another man who took a divorce might be the best answer, so we don't have to worry about that part, hah? Oh! Or maybe a widower. It happens young sometimes. Then we don't have any issue about what's wrong with him that he is divorced."

Jyoti swept past the fact that her auntie clearly thought that something was wrong with *her* that she was divorced, and actually considered Auntie's suggestion for a few beats longer than she would have if not for the day before. Given her insecurities about her track record, she wondered if maybe outsourcing things to Sasti Masti to find someone within their community was a better plan than trying to date on her own outside of it. But she knew it would not be that simple because nothing in life ever was.

"I don't need help finding a husband, Auntie," Jyoti said.

"Oh yes, I saw you were dating someone there. Is this Karishma's idea?" Auntie's voice was laced with syrup, clearly fishing for information.

"No." There was a bite in her tone. "Why do you all assume I'm incapable of making my own choices?"

She could sense Ushma Auntie's surprise. Jyoti was not someone who talked back to her elders.

"S-sorry, beta," Auntie stammered. "I was just trying to help and thought maybe this could bring your family back together. It's hard on us, too, seeing you and your mother fighting like this. You have always been so close. The perfect example for even our own daughters."

Jyoti felt bad for being so terse with a woman in her seventies. She knew Auntie meant well, and this type of solution would make sense to someone from her generation, but she was tired of placating people and felt like she'd run out of cheeks to turn.

"I don't think finding a new husband is going to solve my problems," Jyoti said, her voice calmer. "Or magically bring me and Mom back together. If the last few years have shown us anything, it's that there were issues brimming beneath the surface and we ignored them for too long."

"As you wish, beta, but do take care of yourself. There is a lot of life still to live, and it will become hard if you try to do it all alone."

Ushma Auntie had gotten under her skin. Jyoti hated that she was so impacted by what her parents' friends thought, but she'd known these women all her life. The aunties could be a handful but they were well-intentioned, even if they often fell short when it came to execution. Finding a nice Indian man wouldn't be the worst thing for Jyoti or her family so maybe she should stop frolicking around Italy with Tommaso and think more seriously about her future. For once in her life, though, she wanted to make her own decisions. So, she met Tommaso at the Duomo that night, determined to focus only on whether *she* thought they were a good match.

The iconic Renaissance building sat in the center of Florence with its white walls adorned with red, white, and green marble geometric designs that gleamed in the golden hour light. It looked newer than it was, with the white background and rust-colored dome roofs having been well maintained for centuries. The delicate carvings and sculptures on the facade were true artistic mastery and craftsmanship, reminding Jyoti of the Taj Mahal, and she wondered how long it would have taken to complete construction of the Duomo given the intricate details. The surrounding piazza was crowded with tourists gazing up in awe and locals bustling past on their way throughout the city. It was easy to take for granted what existed in everyday life, just as it was possible to magnify the import of something that was new.

As she sat with her Aperol Spritz, Italian beau, and the majestic Duomo as the backdrop, she felt like life was opening up possibilities for her. It had been a long time since she had felt that.

Tommaso looked around at the clientele. "I know there are many tourists here, but I still like to come."

Jyoti nodded. "Do you ever get used to the tourists?"

Manhattan had plenty, but it felt different because of its vast size and population. In Florence, north of the river, the city seemed oversaturated with tourists wearing sneakers and taking selfies, barely any locals in sight. She understood why Karishma and her friends preferred the neighborhoods south of the river.

Tommaso shrugged. "They are good for the commerce, so it's okay. It also helps me to meet women like you."

He always found a way to bring things back to a compliment. Ashok had never been that effusive in his praise of her, but she couldn't help but wonder if the right balance was somewhere in between the two.

"Is that how you met the last woman you dated too?" Jyoti asked.

Tommaso's eyes narrowed. "Why so many questions about history?"

"Our pasts make us who we are," Jyoti said. "Aren't you curious about mine?"

He bobbed his head in a noncommittal way. "I believe who we are today is most important. Would you want your past to define you?"

She thought about her fertility treatments, her marriage, and her longstanding role as peacemaker in her family.

"I can't think of how it wouldn't," she said. "My family, my culture, and even my ex-husband are such a big part of who I am."

"Culture, yes," Tommaso said. "It defines us all. I will always be Italian, just as you will always be Indian."

"It's not that simple for me," she said, swirling her straw in her cocktail. "Growing up in America made me question a lot of who I am."

"What do you mean?"

She could sense that he had no idea what it meant to straddle two cultures and not know whether you belonged to both or neither. Life as an immigrant meant she had to be a chameleon, adjusting to her surroundings and choosing the identity that felt most safe.

"People who look like me in America don't get treated like we are American or have a right to be there. But then in India, people don't think of me as Indian." She held up her hands in defeat. "No country seems to claim me."

He looked at her curiously, and she could tell he didn't have much to add to this conversation.

"Did you ever go to Indonesia? With your ex-wife, I mean."

Tommaso shook his head. "No, we met here, so our life was here too."

"You never wanted to understand where she was from? What her family was like?"

He sipped his Campari and the ice clinked against the glass. "She preferred to be here, so there didn't seem much point to go there."

Jyoti considered if their roles had been reversed. "If you'd been in New York and we'd met there, I'd still want to know what your life in Florence was like. For me, that's part of the history you must learn before you marry someone."

"So, if we marry, I have to come to New York? Or do I need to go to India?" he asked.

She couldn't help but notice he'd sounded as if either would be a chore. It was something she hadn't needed to consider with Ashok. They were part of the same culture, so there wasn't any way to assess if he'd have wanted to learn about who she was, had she been raised in a different faith or community.

"I guess I'm not sure why you wouldn't want to know those things. Especially if you are with women who aren't Italian. There's a whole world beyond the borders of Italy."

He looked wounded. "Of course, but is there something wrong with being proud of my country? Italy is my home. I cannot see myself ever being anywhere else."

"Maybe it's different for me because I've always felt like I'm on the outskirts of wherever I am," Jyoti said. "I've never felt this unquestioning sense of belonging that it sounds like you've had in Italy. In some ways, that must be really nice. In others, I could see a lot being taken for granted if you are never out of your comfort zone. If I'd only stayed in New York, then I'd never have been here or met you."

He took a long sip. "Okay, but it's different, no? Everyone

wants to come to Italy. Firenze is one of the best cities in the world. Especially for a chef like you. The food is unparalleled."

She suspected there were quite a few regions in the world that would beg to differ. She felt her annoyance mounting, thinking of their last conversation coupled with this one. There wasn't one single comment that stood out as being particularly offensive, but something about his overall philosophy seemed to collectively show someone who was different from what Jyoti had hoped for when she'd started spending time with him.

"I don't understand why you date women who are not Italian, when it seems so clear that you are only focused on your own culture," she said tersely.

"It's not that I don't like other cultures. I've dated women from many cultures," he said, his tone defensive.

"That part I know," Jyoti said, folding and refolding her napkin. She saw the Duomo behind him and had a feeling her Italian love story wasn't going to have a Hollywood ending. "I guess the part I'm not clear on is why."

"I think darker skin is beautiful," he said, tracing his finger along her forearm.

Her pulse quickened at his touch, but not for the same reasons as before. She suddenly felt like a zoo animal on display and it made her stomach turn. Jyoti racked her brain for reasons that his words could be chalked up to a language barrier. Was this what dating across cultures was? Trying to find excuses for things that the other could not understand?

Her blood started to boil, and she took a sip of her spritz so she could remove her arm from his touch. "I hope there's something more you noticed about me other than my skin color."

"The Indian women I meet have good family values. They are good with the home and children, and, yes, their husbands too. These seem like such good qualities to me to have a peaceful life."

Tommaso was staring intently at her face, but it felt like he wasn't actually seeing her at all.

"There are a lot of people from India. I doubt everyone falls into the stereotypes you have in your head." She folded her arms across her chest. "The more we talk, the more I think you might want to end up with an Italian woman. She might understand your values better."

He flailed his hands as if trying to ward off an attacker. "If I choose an Italian girl, then maybe I don't end up with an Indian risotto, but that's a small price for being with someone like you. Risotto is easy to learn. I can teach you the right way." He winked at her.

Jyoti sank into her seat, arms tighter across her chest. It was clear that he believed women should adjust to him and that he did not believe in blending two cultures. Worse yet, he'd basically admitted that he did not like her food. She thought back to their original meeting and now could see more clearly that he wanted someone who *looked* "exotic," but who would then mold herself into the woman he needed her to be. Someone with no self-esteem or individual identity. It was starting to feel too reminiscent of Ashok. Jyoti may have put up with men like that in the past, but she wasn't about to do it again.

Jyoti cast him her best forced apologetic smile. "I think I'm starting to feel a bit sick, and will just go home and rest today."

He looked concerned. "What has happened?"

She touched her forehead. "I feel a headache coming on."

Tommaso insisted on walking her back to Karishma's building, and she didn't feel good when he reached for her hand. He hadn't seemed to notice the energy shifting between them at drinks and she found even holding hands to be too intimate with someone she knew she could no longer date. But she didn't want to make a scene, so she allowed his hand to envelop hers, her skin growing clammier by the minute. She was so relieved that Florence was such a small city and the walk from the Duomo was less than twenty minutes. When they arrived, she tossed a quick "thanks" behind her as she rushed toward the front door. She was out of breath by the time she raced up the three flights of stairs and found Karishma and Enzo practicing tadasana in the living room.

"You're back earlier than I expected," Karishma said, coming to standing. "I thought I might not see you until the morning."

Enzo exhaled sharply as he rose as well, beads of sweat dotting his brow.

Jyoti looked between them, not sure how comfortable she felt saying what she really wanted to in front of Enzo. She decided it didn't matter. If Karishma were maintaining any type of relationship with him, then Jyoti knew that he was nothing like Tommaso.

"I think you might have been right about the fetish thing," Jyoti blurted out.

Karishma gestured for her to pull up a chair from the dining table while she sat on the couch and pulled Enzo down next to her. "Tell me everything."

Jyoti recounted the odd comments and the way they'd made her feel. Karishma leaned forward and began tapping her foot against the floor. Enzo also looked tense as he heard more.

"That is so gross," Karishma said, giving Enzo a look. "He seriously said out loud that he likes darker skin?"

"I'm sorry," Enzo said to Jyoti as if he felt the need to apologize on behalf of all Italian men.

"How do I keep finding the same type of man regardless of what country I'm in?" Jyoti asked.

"Because there are crap people in every country," Karishma said.

Enzo sighed. "You have a good heart and believe the best in people. It's easy for people like Tommaso to take advantage."

Jyoti appreciated his sentiment but also didn't want to feel like being good was somehow connected to playing the fool. She wished her good intentions could lead her to someone who had similar beliefs.

"I don't know," Jyoti said. "Do you think I'm overreacting? Maybe there is a language or culture barrier and I should be more open-minded." She looked to Enzo for his thoughts.

He shook his head. "His views are outdated—"

"Were never meant to be appropriate regardless of time period," Karishma jumped in, nudging him with her elbow.

Enzo held up his hands in surrender. "Yes, those views should never have been okay." He looked to Karishma for approval before continuing. "But the truth is that a lot of people here still have them. Especially those who are more isolated and living in the countryside where change is slower to occur. You have to be careful with people like that."

"Or," Karishma jumped in again, pressing her elbow more forcefully into his side. "We don't put the onus on the people who aren't doing anything wrong to *look out* for the bad people and we live in a world where bad people learn to be better humans."

Jyoti could see Enzo squirm, but could also tell this hadn't been the first time they'd discussed something like this and he was accustomed to her unapologetic views. It was no surprise that she hadn't fared well in an archaic corporate publishing environment.

Jyoti knew she could help him out though. "While that's a nice idea, Enzo is right. People who lack self-awareness aren't going to be the ones who change themselves. The sad truth is that I do need to look for the signs, but I haven't dated in decades and it's hard to know what they are."

Karishma looked like she wanted to argue, but she backed off. Jyoti knew that as much as Karishma wished the world were a certain way, she was also pragmatic in knowing that it wasn't.

"You can't let one bad experience affect the rest of your dating life," Karishma said.

Jyoti didn't think they were still talking only about Tommaso. "I know. I just don't want to end up in the same place again."

Karishma met her eyes. "The truth is that you can't protect yourself from that. Relationships involve two people, which means fifty percent of it is completely out of your control. You'll have to rely on your intuition to tell you if someone is being genuine based on the information presented to you. And some people are damn good liars, especially when they don't even realize they are doing it, so you'll be wrong sometimes. But you're stronger than you think, and you'll pick yourself back up whenever that happens."

Jyoti wasn't so sure. Her experiences thus far had suggested the opposite.

That night, she lay in bed staring out the window at the moon illuminating the sky. She didn't think Tommaso had a clue how much she'd been impacted by their conversation, and she knew she was going to have to tell him something at some point. Florence was small enough that she wasn't going to be able to avoid him if he sought her out. But she couldn't simply walk away from him right now because she was dependent on him for ingredients for the vineyard dinner. Even though the thought of seeing him again made her seethe, she didn't have enough time to find a new vendor.

She considered opening TikTok and unburdening these thoughts to her online community, but this felt too vulnerable, even for her. Social media had been a helpful crutch to her thus far, but talking about her marriage or cooking was one thing. She didn't dare assume she'd get such a warm reception if she tried to talk about racism and bias. Her family didn't speak openly about their struggles as immigrants in America, even though her parents had surely had hardships upon their arrival in New Jersey. Jyoti had tried to learn more over the years, but her parents didn't believe in dwelling on the past and would shift subjects quickly. She had no doubt that if her mom had been upset about a video of her making paneer, then this subject was even more off-limits. Tommaso was not worth instigating any more ire from her mom, so she brooded on her own.

As much as Karishma and Enzo tried to console her earlier, she felt foolish. She had been with a man who seemed completely different from Ashok, but had many of the same qualities when she scratched beneath the surface. Both men were ultimately interested in women who they felt they could control and slot into their lives without any regard for what *she* wanted. She didn't want to be drawn to these types of men, but no matter how far she ran, she seemed to find them. When the common denominator was her, it was hard to blame the men.

TWENTY-THREE

She still hadn't decided what to say, but she was on her way to see Tommaso because the rehearsal dinner was the following day and she needed to pick up the produce she had ordered. She'd managed to avoid him for the past few days by saying she was focused on the menu for Ben's clients.

Her legs were leaden as they took her across the river and to the market. She hated confrontation. She wished she could do a contactless pickup and not have to see him at all, but this wasn't Manhattan and that wasn't in the cards. The sun was streaming down on her and perspiration began to soak through the thin fabric of her navy-and-white-checked summer dress.

"You can do this," she said to herself, pumping her fist while she stood outside Mercato Centrale. "You just pretend you are in a rush and everything is fine, and then after the vineyard dinner, you don't have to see him again for anything."

She saw Tommaso and he waved to her with a smile, still oblivious to how she'd been feeling. He leaned toward her for a kiss as she neared him, but she turned her face so he got her cheek. Her pulse quickened.

It's just another six days.

If she were hired for new events beyond the first dinner, then she'd find a new supplier.

"What's the matter?" he asked, his smile disappearing.

"Nothing," she said, eyes cast toward the floor. "I'm here to pick up my order. I've got a lot on my mind for the dinner tomorrow, so I need to get back as soon as I can."

He grabbed the bags from the back and placed them next to her, before putting his hands on her shoulders and turning her to face him. "Something is wrong, no?"

She forced herself to meet his eyes. In many ways, she felt bad for him, because he wouldn't understand what had changed or that there were things about him that made her uncomfortable. She realized as she looked into his brown eyes that she couldn't even get through the next few days keeping up this charade. She'd find a way to source ingredients for the actual dinner without Tommaso. It wasn't fair to either of them for her to keep pretending.

"I think we are better off not seeing each other anymore."

His puzzled expression appeared instantly. "Why do you say that? We've been having fun, no?"

"I don't know," Jyoti said. "Maybe...but it's not a good idea to continue."

"Did my sister say something to you? She's always trying to get me into trouble."

She could see him trying to problem solve, unable to fathom that *he* was the problem. She weighed how much she needed to tell him the truth with whether she could dodge with a lame excuse like she wasn't over her divorce. That seemed like a lifelong get-out-of-jail-free card.

"I started feeling like you liked me because I'm Indian." She opted for honesty and standing up for herself, channeling her TikTok voice.

"Is it wrong that I don't mind that you're Indian?"

Even the way he'd said "don't mind" confirmed she was making the right call.

"I don't really want to be with someone who thinks of me as exotic. It's not a very nice thing to say. And it's weird that you won't date Italian women. Who says they won't date someone from the same culture as them?"

He looked taken aback. "You think it's a problem because I like women like you?"

"There's something very off about the way you speak about women who look like me," she said, her voice becoming steadier. "It's as if you think you are doing the world a favor by choosing us."

He scoffed, then his eyes narrowed. "*Dio mio.* Some men prefer blondes to brunettes, or short or tall. What is the big deal to prefer dark skin to light?"

The fact that he thought those were appropriate comparisons to make was enough to convince her that he'd never understand.

"Being Indian is an entire cultural ethos. It's not like hair color. What you're doing comes off as racist."

She hadn't intended to throw around the *R* word, but it was now out of her mouth and hanging between them, heavy and sharp like the blade of a guillotine.

Tommaso looked shocked. "Racist? Because I like you being Indian? That's absurd. I wasn't saying negative things about you. It was the opposite. I said it was a good thing."

As if racism was that simple.

"There's no point in discussing it further. You won't get it." Her voice was flat.

He ran a hand over his head. "How can you know that if you don't even bother to explain to me what the problem is?"

She wasn't about to waste her breath. His implication that it was on her to explain her discomfort was the final nail in the coffin. Tommaso wasn't the type of guy who was going to go read anti-racism books to be able to catch himself *before* he said or did inappropriate things. He was the type of guy who might listen if she took the time to walk him through each misstep that he made. But that would be a full-time job for her.

"Tommaso," Jyoti said in a lifeless tone, "we are up against centuries of ingrained biases and behavior. We just don't have enough time on this earth to try to undo all of that."

His expression turned cold. "Maybe I was doing you a favor. How many suitors do you have lined up to marry a divorced woman who cannot have kids and has no job?"

Her mouth fell slack. Her body went into fight-or-flight mode, and she knew she needed to grab her groceries and get out of there. She picked up the bags and hoisted them onto her hips before turning to leave, knowing she'd never return here again. This was why people shouldn't mix business with pleasure.

"No Italians are going to like your weird Indian mixed flavors here," he called after her. "We like our food the way our nonnas made it."

She kept moving along as quickly as she could until she was out of the market and felt the sun against her face. She took a deep breath and tried to go back over what had happened. Why did she feel like she had done something wrong when she was just trying to express what had made her uncomfortable? *Because people who look like me in America are taught at an early age not to say or do anything that might make white people feel uncomfortable.*

She hoped that her words sunk in enough that he might take more care with the next non-white woman who came along. Because it was clear he had a type and there would be a next one. But she already knew the answer: when it came to matters of race, people didn't want to hear that they had more work to do. That they weren't already perfect in matters of equity and inclusion.

And she knew that as she navigated dating in whatever capacity from here on out, she would need to look for these signs to make sure she didn't end up with someone like that. Even if Tommaso's bias was unconscious, she could choose to walk away. And she could choose to avoid men who were going to assume their thoughts and opinions mattered more than hers, so she never ended up in a relationship like her marriage again. It seemed that there were plenty of land mines in the romantic realm, whether she chose to date within or outside of her race. Maybe it was better to avoid it entirely.

Jyoti was sweating profusely after carrying her groceries across Florence in the summer heat. She rushed to get the produce into the fridge to keep it from wilting. Nobody liked limp carrots. Her head was swirling with confusion, anger, and a bit of shock. She paced the small living room, unable to settle down. She wished Karishma was home so she could vent, but the apartment was silent. She grabbed her phone and tuned in to her online community. She knew broaching this subject on social media was risky, but she needed to clear her agitation so she could get to work. She'd just be extra careful with her words.

"Hi, everyone." Her voice was still breathy as her words fell over each other. "I've had a weird day, and I should be mad—well, I am mad—but I'm also super proud of myself. I stood up for myself today. In a way I never expected to, and there's something exhilarating in that. Oh, and you won't be hearing about that guy I mentioned before. He's definitely not in the mix. He thought I was this exotic thing to have on his arm, and that felt…inappropriate? Gross? Demoralizing? I guess all of it. But I didn't let him gaslight me into thinking that his views were okay. So that's my real victory here. I stood up for myself and I knew that no matter what he thought about the way the world worked, I have a right to feel respected for who I am. And I'm proud that I know I won't let myself end up in another relationship where I lose that. Where I sacrifice myself because it's what the man wants, and because it feels easier to bend to his will. I'm not doing that anymore. For anyone. And it's liberating."

She took a deep breath. "Thank you all for listening. And for being so supportive. It's weird to share so much with people I haven't met before, but it's also nice to see how connected we are even if we are strangers. So many of us are going through the same thing, and I'm grateful that we can lean on each other."

Jyoti posted the video and, within minutes, saw comments start to appear.

@manisha42: Way to go!

@desibritlife: Gaslighters are the worst...so daft.

@spiritualrocks: Always be true to yourself.

@solomooner: Who needs men anyway?

@jkncwb: People don't even realize how much gaslighting goes on in this world...

She felt herself calm down a little. This community was so reliable. She only wished her family were the same way.

TWENTY-FOUR

Even though she knew Tommaso had been the wrong guy for her on many levels, she couldn't get his last words out of her head. He'd criticized her flavors and it had been gnawing at her. She didn't doubt that they were good, but was he right that they weren't the best choice for this audience? He was a local Italian, a vintner, and, for better or worse, similar to the people who would be attending the dinner. She'd known from the first time that he'd tried her take on risotto that he hadn't enjoyed it. She wondered if she should be cooking for his type of palate rather than hers.

So much was riding on the success of this rehearsal dinner and she had to get it right. The only hope she had of buying back the restaurant was if she could convince the vineyard owners to make her the regular chef for the rest of the dinners they had scheduled, which Ben had said were eight in total. And now that she'd told herself to give up on dating, her career felt like all she had left. This pressure on top of her fears of ruining Ben's reputation made her mouth go dry.

She gathered her ingredients for the recipes she'd been testing, including her trusted masala dabba, but then threw in some additional Italian staples as well. She was feeling so unsure of herself. Was new always better? Different always preferred? Or at the end of a long day, did people just want the food that reminded them of home—*their* home, not hers. It was crystal clear what Tommaso would have wanted. She changed into a wrap dress, and eyed herself in the mirror for longer than she would have if she hadn't been feeling so insecure about everything else in her life. When she was feeling low, every lump and fold that had developed over the course of her marriage and fertility treatments seemed to magnify. Her phone buzzed to let her know Ben had arrived, so she cast one final look in the mirror and tried to tie the waist of the dress in a way that would make her seem smaller before she went to meet him.

Once they were seated in the car, Ben turned to her. "What's wrong?"

Jyoti sighed. "Long story, but I won't be seeing Tommaso anymore."

Ben began driving them outside of the city. "I can't say I'm all that disappointed to hear that. He seemed like a bit of a cad, if you ask me."

Jyoti laughed. "Thanks, Ben."

"I'm serious," he said, quickly meeting her eyes before turning back to the road. "I'm not saying that only because you broke up with him."

She could sense that he was telling the truth. "I know. It's just so frustrating that apparently people other than me could see through him."

"Don't be so hard on yourself. We need to make our own decisions in matters of the heart. And the opinions of anyone other than yourself are irrelevant."

"You've never been part of an Indian family, have you?"

Ben smiled. "Can't say that I have."

"Everything is a family affair. And extended family affair. And larger community affair."

He laughed. "You and Karishma seem to be managing okay."

"She does a better job of it than I do." Jyoti looked out the window. "She doesn't care what people think."

Ben scoffed. "Bollocks. You've known her your whole life. I can't imagine you believe that tough exterior."

Ben was right. Jyoti knew Karishma cared even though she pretended she didn't. She'd wanted to believe her friend's cavalier attitude, but also knew the blinders Karishma put on to let herself do it were a matter of necessity. It had started as a defense mechanism to ward off the negativity from the Indian community while growing up, and then became her armor as she tried to navigate her career.

"She's stronger than I am," Jyoti said. "I couldn't be without our community the way that she can."

"As long as we can reconcile our choices for ourselves, the rest doesn't matter."

Jyoti was having a hard time reconciling the choices that brought her to this point in life, but she was here now, and she needed to accept it. When they arrived at the vineyard, Ben introduced her to Greca and Fausto, the wife-husband duo behind the Fattorio Vineyard.

Greca gave Jyoti two air kisses, starting with the left, and Fausto did the same.

"We are so happy to meet you," Greca said, her light brown hair blowing gently in the breeze. "Ben has told us so much about your food."

Fausto patted his round belly. "We have saved our appetites for it."

Jyoti looked around the sprawling hills and greenery and was taken by the stillness and beauty of the land. "I'm honored to be cooking for you."

Fausto, Greca, and Ben had a conversation in rapid Italian

that she couldn't follow, and then Ben was unloading the groceries from his car and escorting her to the main house. Greca led the way and showed them the kitchen on the ground floor. The decor in the home was classic rustic Italian with wood-beamed ceilings, butter-colored walls, and red clay floor tiles. It reminded her of Tommaso's home, and her doubts about the menu rose to the surface again.

While Jyoti stayed in the kitchen to prepare their meal, the threesome went to tend to some of the vineyard business. Ben wanted to see how the harvest was coming along and Fausto and Greca were eager to show him a new blend they'd been concocting.

When Jyoti glanced around the inviting kitchen, she could picture the nonnas who had lived in this very home, rolling their pasta on the long prep table that filled the middle of the room. She could almost smell the flour, water, and eggs coming together. She stared at the copper pots and pans hanging on the ceiling rack, similar to what she'd seen at Alla Vecchia Bettola. She took in the thick stoneware dishes with bright blue, red, and yellow decorations adorning them.

This is a family that believes in tradition, she thought to herself, *and who was she to change that*? Suddenly grateful that she had thrown in extra cans of vine-ripened tomatoes, semolina flour, and ricotta, she pulled those ingredients out first. At the bottom of the bag sat her masala dabba, and she left it there.

She got to work prepping fried artichokes instead of samosas, a traditional asparagus risotto topped with squash blossoms filled with herbed ricotta cheese instead of paneer, spinach ravioli instead of the saag paneer–inspired one with her Indian spices, and a mushroom fettuccine instead of her saffron and turmeric pasta. For dessert, she made a molten lava cake and left out the cardamom, chili, and cinnamon she'd intended to add.

She plated everything, carefully wiping down any stray spots that ruined the aesthetic and asked the Fattorios' housemaid to help her carry the dishes to the outdoor dining table. As she stepped outside, she was greeted with smiles from the Fattorios and Ben, who were already seated with several wineglasses in front of them. Ben nodded at her encouragingly.

After setting the plates before the group, she saw a quizzical expression cross Ben's face, but he remained silent.

"Where are the samosas that we'd heard so much about?" Greca asked.

Jyoti hesitated. "I thought your guests might prefer a more traditional Italian meal, so I decided to prepare food that would be more familiar."

"Oh." Greca looked disappointed as she added risotto and a zucchini blossom to her plate.

Ben followed suit. "It looks great."

As they cut into the stuffed zucchini blossoms, steam rose from within and they each took a slow and deliberate bite. Jyoti had tried everything herself and knew it tasted good. In the zucchini blossoms, she'd added a bit of lemon zest and chopped parsley to cut through the richness. She knew everything was perfectly seasoned, but she kept her gaze on their faces. She could see that each one was taking a measured and reserved position, and that wasn't good. She looked to Ben for help, but his expression was unreadable.

"Are they okay?" Jyoti finally asked.

Fausto nodded slowly. "*Si*, they are fine. A perfectly good fried blossom and risotto."

Jyoti felt the tension slide from her shoulders. As long as they liked the food, her hope for the life she wanted to build back in New York was still alive. They had similar reactions to the rest of her dishes, stating that they liked them and the flavoring was good, but not doling out effusive praise. Jyoti didn't want to seem too needy, but she would have liked a bit more reaction. Every chef wants her food to be met with adulation. After finishing the sample dishes, the Fattorios spoke to Ben in

Italian and Jyoti could tell from his tone that he was responding with polite diplomacy.

"It is so kind of you to have come all this way and prepared these dishes for us," Greca finally said to her.

Jyoti could tell she wasn't getting the job, but she wasn't sure why. What had she missed? She was certain everything was cooked to perfection.

"Was there something wrong with the food?" she asked.

Greca and Fausto exchanged a look, and then the two of them looked at Ben before deciding how to proceed.

Greca gently cleared her throat. "We'd been hoping for a more innovative menu. Ben had mentioned that you created some beautiful dishes fusing Indian and Italian flavors, and we didn't see that come through."

Jyoti's eyes widened. They had actually wanted the original food she'd thought up and been working on for weeks.

"I'm sorry," Jyoti said, realizing her doubt and worry had carried into her food. "I thought you might prefer something that was more familiar and comfortable."

Fausto coughed. "With respect, if we wanted traditional Italian dishes, we would hire one of the many Italian chefs we know. This is Tuscany. Every household can make delicious fresh pasta and sauces."

Jyoti's face fell. They were right. She was the last person in Tuscany to hire to make traditional fare. She saw Ben squirm and knew she had let him down. That was one of the worst parts. She dreaded the thought of breaking the news to Karishma. She saw Taste of Ginger slipping from her grasp and wished she'd never had this opportunity—this *hope*—from which she'd now have to recover again.

"She really does make excellent fusion dishes," Ben said to the Fattorios, shooting Jyoti a concerned look.

Fausto wrung his hands. "You had been so certain, Ben, that

we didn't plan on a backup and the dinner is in a few days. We aren't sure we have much time to go in a different direction."

Jyoti swallowed the lump in her throat. She didn't want to be their choice by default.

"I'm so sorry," she said. "I looked around your home and thought you might prefer something more typical of the region. I made the wrong assumption. But I have worked on dishes that are more of what you had in mind."

"It's getting late," Greca said, glancing at the sun that was beginning to creep lower in the sky. "I imagine you don't have the time to make those dishes." She turned to her husband with her shoulders slumped. "We might have to go with something like this."

Jyoti would stay here until midnight if she had to, but the problem wasn't time, it was ingredients. She'd used up most of what she had brought by making these plates, and she couldn't cobble anything new together without a run to the market.

The Fattorios whispered to each other in Italian, but Jyoti knew they were thinking of ways to salvage the situation and seek out reputable chefs at the last minute. She'd have done the same thing.

Jyoti and Ben drove back in uncomfortable silence. Ben looked contemplative, and she could see his mind trying to work things out while still maintaining his politeness.

"I'm so sorry," Jyoti finally said.

"What happened? You had planned such a great menu."

She sighed. "I got stuck in my head. I worried that people wouldn't want my Indian flavors to ruin the dishes they loved so much."

"Why would you think that?"

She initially shrugged, but then felt she owed him an answer. "Tommaso didn't like my food—he made sure I knew that yesterday. I walked into the villa and felt like the Fattorios would be more like him and would be happier with something more conventional. I made the wrong call."

"Fausto and Greca are new vintners who have been trying to innovate and create wines that aren't the typical Tuscan options. That's what made them so interested in your food, and why I had suggested you for the job. They didn't want traditional." He met her eyes quickly before turning back to the road. "And they are right that if they'd wanted that, there was no need to hire an Indian chef from New York."

Jyoti winced. "I see that now."

"All you had to do was be yourself."

Maybe that was the problem, Jyoti thought. After decades of trying to please the people around her, she'd never really learned who she was. It had started with trying to blend in during her school-age years, and that carried into college, and then into her marriage. After her divorce, she'd been untethered to anyone and had felt completely adrift. The truth was that she'd been afraid to cook her food because she wasn't sure if it would have been good enough. She wasn't sure if *she* would have been enough.

"I'm so sorry that I didn't give them the right impression. I know this affects you too," she said softly.

"It's okay. These things happen. We will figure something out."

Jyoti lamented her poor judgment for the remainder of the quiet car ride home. She admired Ben for not losing his cool and lashing out at her when he would have been well within bounds to do so. This was his job. And he took it very seriously. She'd appreciated so much that he'd gone out on a limb for her when he hardly knew her and hated that he was now second-guessing himself.

She thanked him for the opportunity when he dropped her off, shoulders hunched as she entered the apartment. When she told Karishma what happened, she had a good poker face and was nodding in understanding, but Jyoti noticed her touching her labradorite prism pendant the entire time. Something she always did when she was stressed. It was so messy when friends and business intertwined, especially when it didn't go well.

That night, Jyoti navigated toward the website for Taste of Ginger and reflected on the photos of the dining room. She couldn't believe she'd had the perfect opportunity in her hands and then squandered it away. She cursed herself for letting Tommaso get inside her head and shake her confidence. She was convinced the Fattorios would have loved the original menu she'd been planning, if only she'd had the courage to make it. She tossed and turned all night, feeling so unsettled about how many people had been affected by one poor decision. As the first rays of sun streamed through her window, she knew she had to make things right.

TWENTY-FIVE

Jyoti returned to the apartment, arms laden with groceries from the Santo Spirito market. Karishma came out of her room, rubbing sleep from her eyes, and found Jyoti frantically washing produce.

"What are you doing?"

Without stopping, Jyoti said, "Fixing things."

"By making a ruckus in the morning?"

Jyoti tossed an apologetic look over her shoulder. "I'm making the original menu that Ben and the Fattorios were expecting. I know they'll love that, and then Ben is in the clear, the Fattorios don't have to find a new chef, you and Ben don't have any awkwardness in your friendship, and I have a chance to buy back Taste of Ginger."

Karishma's lips curled into a half smile. "That's a lot riding on one meal."

"That's why it has to be my best."

Karishma joined her near the sink and snuck her hands under

the water. "Put me to work, Chef. You're going to need some help."

Jyoti had never been so grateful for her best friend.

The two of them spent the morning chopping, mashing, pureeing, and making fresh paneer, pasta dough, sauces, and chutneys. Karishma helped her assemble the saag paneer raviolis so they only needed to be boiled. By the end of it, Karishma's kitchen looked like a tornado had hit it, and Jyoti knew that the true measure of how much she loved Jyoti was allowing her to create that mess in her home. And, worse still, leaving her to tidy it up, because as soon as the food prep had been done, Jyoti called Ben.

"I know you're going to tell me this is a terrible idea, but I—" Jyoti cast a glance at Karishma "—Karishma and I have spent all day prepping the original meal I should have cooked for Greca and Fausto. If we can go back to their vineyard and I can prepare these dishes for them, then I think we can get everything back on track."

There was silence on the other end. Jyoti wondered if Ben had already found them a new chef. She knew how efficient he was when it came to his job.

"If you can pick me up and take me over there, I promise I won't let you down this time," Jyoti said.

"You'd better do it," Karishma called from the background. "I'm blaming you if this mess in my home has been for nothing."

Ben laughed. "Sounds like I don't have much of a choice."

"You do," Jyoti said. "But you've tasted these dishes and you know how good they are. If innovative is what they want, then this is the menu. That's why you asked me to do it in the first place."

"I'm on my way."

Ben had called Greca and Fausto to make sure they were home and amenable. While hesitant, they allowed Jyoti and Ben to stop by to present the new meal. Jyoti chewed her bottom lip while holding the containers of prepped food on her lap so that nothing would spill. Her heart, soul, fortitude, and redemption were in these dishes and she wasn't taking any chances. When they arrived at the villa, Ben jumped out and ran around to her side of the car to help her unload. She'd carefully organized the containers into the shopping bags as if they were Tetris pieces to ensure the least amount of movement. She delicately handed the bags to him, jostling them as little as possible. Ben secured them and then took a step back to let her out of the car. He stepped onto uneven ground and lost his balance.

Jyoti's eyes widened as she watched him stumble and the bags swung wider than they should have. She pictured her carefully assembled food in a jumbled mess inside their containers. She couldn't let that happen. She quickly leapt out of the car and reached to steady the bags, which in turn allowed Ben to regain his balance.

Her hand flew to her rapidly beating heart as she tried to calm herself.

"Is the food okay?" he asked, his cheeks flushed.

Jyoti's pulse was still racing as she peeked into the bags to assess any damage. Relief flooded over her when she saw lids with just a bit of splattering and nothing too extreme. "We're still good."

Greca and Fausto greeted them with a bit of apprehension compared to yesterday, but each of them resumed their prior posts with Jyoti in the kitchen and Ben and the Fattorios sipping wine at the outdoor dining table. Jyoti heated the frying oil and organized her containers. She pulled her hair back into a bun, silenced her phone so nothing would distract her, and opened her masala dabba. She took a deep breath.

"These dishes are my culinary journey and whatever happens, I know I represented myself this time," she said to herself.

She was now ready to prepare the most important meal of

her life. She worked quickly, knowing her guests were waiting and, while they'd been gracious and accommodating, the big dinner was only days away. Time was of the essence.

She beautifully plated her potato and pea samosas with their mint pesto and tamarind sauces, herbed paneer–stuffed squash blossoms, cauliflower risotto with curry leaf vaghar, and saag paneer ravioli. Before leaving the kitchen, she closed her eyes and slowly glided her palms above the dishes as if they were prasad and asked Bhagwan to bless them. Saying her final prayer, she asked the housemaid to help her bring them outside.

As she set the plates before her guests, Ben smiled and she saw the tension in his shoulders slip away. He leaned in and looked to Greca and Fausto encouragingly. They took in the food spread before them with care before turning toward Jyoti.

"My family is from a part of India called Gujarat, so I wanted to incorporate our flavors into each of the dishes to give them a twist, while also retaining some of the familiar elements of Italian food since we will be dining in the breathtaking Tuscan countryside." She wrung her hands together and looked at the Fattorios. "I'm sorry the meal I made for you yesterday wasn't this one. This is me on a plate, and this is the food that comes from my heart the same way your wine comes from yours. The perfect pairings for any meal are love and confidence, and I hope you can see both of those shining through when you taste the food."

They offered her warm smiles, and she knew that, from here, everything was out of her hands. She'd cooked food that represented her. How that food was received was beyond her control.

Fausto picked up a samosa and placed it on Greca's plate and then took one for himself. Jyoti studied them as they bit into the crispy exterior of the pastry. Greca's eyes widened and she started slowly nodding her head. Fausto turned to his wife while he chewed, mirroring her reaction. They trailed the samosa through the various sauces for their next bites and nodded appreciatively after each one. Fausto began tasting the wines before him between bites and Jyoti and Ben smiled at each other.

Unlike yesterday, Fausto was working out the pairings as he ate and Jyoti knew she had done it. She had served the dishes that had once lived only in her mind, a menu she had never seen in a restaurant anywhere in the world, and these local Italians were enjoying her food. There was nothing more she could ask for as the sun began to set, casting orange and red hues against the purple and green hills around them. She breathed deeply and took in this moment.

"You were right." Fausto broke the silence. "I can't say I've had many samosas in my life, but this is indeed the best one." He held one up between them.

Ben jumped in, patting his stomach. "I've had many, and I can assure you that your assessment is correct."

Jyoti bounced a little. "I'm so happy to hear that."

"Is it a family recipe?" Greca asked. "You can taste the care in them."

Jyoti's mood flickered for a moment as she felt the absence in her heart before she answered. "Yes, it is. I learned from my mother who learned from hers and samosas are the first of her recipes that I mastered."

Fausto dabbed his mouth with a napkin. "You always know when recipes have been passed down. They are rooted into us, just like the vines in the soil."

Jyoti nodded, grateful to be around people who fully understood her vision and food. They tried each of the next dishes with the same gusto, and Jyoti knew she was in the clear because they delivered their comments in English, ensuring she could understand them. There was no rapid Italian like the day before. She knew from experience that when there was something difficult to say, it was much easier to retreat to one's native language, especially when you didn't want to offend the person in front of you. She and her parents and sisters had slipped into

Gujarati countless times when they'd been at stores or school for that very reason.

After finishing the food before them, Greca and Fausto leaned back from the table and turned to Ben.

"Now we understand what you had in mind." Greca's eyes moved to Jyoti. "Both of you. Our guests will never have tried anything like this and it will be perfect to highlight the innovation in our new wines. We have so many interesting spicy notes and unique blends, and I know this is going to be an exquisite pairing." She smiled warmly at them both. "Thank you for taking the time to come back and show us what you can do."

Ben gestured to Jyoti. "It's all her. She couldn't leave her customers unsatisfied and had to make things right. That's the type of person she is. A fighter."

Jyoti felt her cheeks warm at his kind words. She'd never thought of herself as a fighter, but maybe she needed to give herself more credit. She'd been through so much and she was still standing. That should count for a lot.

"I'm so happy you enjoyed the food. These are the creations from my heart and there is no better feeling than sharing them with people who appreciate it."

"Our guests will love this," Fausto said. "Thank you for letting us show them something they won't find anywhere else in Tuscany. Maybe even anywhere else in Italy."

There was something so satisfying about crafting something that hadn't existed before she'd conjured it. But that was the most beautiful part about creativity—she got to leave the world with something it hadn't seen and hopefully inspire others to do the same. And with her menu approved and the job secured, her heart swelled at the fact that as long as the dinner went well, she'd be hired for the remaining ones. She'd finally be in a position to buy Taste of Ginger. Jyoti would soon have her small place in the universe where she could serve more food that flowed from her heart to the plate.

★★★

On the ride back to the apartment, Ben was in high spirits, a stark contrast to the day before.

"You really smashed this one!" he said, pumping his fist.

"Thanks," Jyoti said, relief flooding through her. "I was terrified when I thought I'd let you down." *And Karishma and myself.*

"A bit of a bump in the road, but we've passed it now." He grinned. "Just don't go making any changes between now and the dinner in a few days."

Jyoti laughed. "Only the food you've tried thus far, I promise."

She tried to imprint the way she was currently feeling into her cells so her body would remember it later. Food had always been her way not only of connecting to her roots, but of allowing others to have a glimpse into that world and enjoy it too.

She rolled down her window and noticed the stars starting to come out as twilight transitioned fully to night. The air was so clean and fresh here compared to her urban life back home, with the heaviness of auto exhaust, cigarette smoke, and a chaotic mix of take-out food permeating the air. She realized her old life felt like it was more than four thousand miles away. She had to strain a bit to recall the feeling of walking down crowded New York streets, and ordering groceries online rather than going in person, where she could select each item by smell and feel the weight of it in her hands. She couldn't stay in Florence forever, but she knew her time here would affect the way she felt about her routine in the city. She'd make sure to keep some of the Tuscan life with her wherever she went.

As they neared the apartment building, Jyoti envisioned herself in her new restaurant. She thought about how she'd cook seasonally by going to the farmer's markets herself, rather than just having her vendors deliver. But her reverie was interrupted when she caught a glimpse of a familiar figure at La Sorbetteria, the gelateria next to her building.

She shook her head to clear it, knowing her mind must be playing tricks on her. All Jyoti could see was the woman's back as she stood at the counter and gestured to the flavors in the case. *It must be a tourist with a similar build*, she told herself as they passed the gelateria.

Ben pulled over. "Do you want any help managing the bags upstairs?"

"The containers are mostly empty, so I'm good. And besides, now it doesn't matter if I drop them."

He grinned sheepishly. "Right. Crisis averted back there, no doubt."

She laughed. "It all worked out in the end. I'll see you in a few days for the main event, and I'll definitely need lots of help with cargo then."

She slung her bags over her shoulder and waved off Ben before turning back to the apartment. As she neared the door, she heard an unmistakably familiar voice that stopped her dead in her tracks.

TWENTY-SIX

"There you are," Nalini said, spooning gelato into her mouth like it was a perfectly normal thing for her to be standing outside Karishma's apartment in Florence.

Jyoti froze, wondering if she was hallucinating. Maybe she was delusional from the heat in the kitchen or from the exhaustion of the last couple of days.

"Mom?"

Her mother gave her a look as if to say *who else would it be?*

"What are you doing here?"

"I thought I should have some gelato. You kept posting about this place on your Facebook account," her mother said.

"TikTok," Jyoti said robotically.

"Je hoy te," Nalini said, flicking her free hand. *Whatever it is.*

"I mean, what are you doing *here*? In Florence. Halfway around the world. And where is Dad?"

Jyoti looked past her mom, expecting her father to pop out. She could not get over the strangeness of the situation, especially since her mother barely visited her apartment in New

York without advance notice. Nalini always made a plan and spent her day methodically going through her to-do list.

"He's not here," Nalini said, taking another bite of what Jyoti could see was the stracciatella gelato—their shared favorite. "But you are right. This gelato is exceptional."

"Let's go upstairs." Jyoti grabbed her mom's elbow and pulled her toward the door, glancing around as if she were secreting a fugitive.

Jyoti's head was spinning as she climbed the stairs. What could possibly bring her mother here? Did someone die? But if something had happened to Chaya, Tanvi, or her father, she couldn't imagine her mom casually eating gelato. And even in those situations, she would have called. Perhaps her mom was sick? Panic struck Jyoti as she realized how much time they had lost together over these past few years. By the time both had finished the three flights of stairs, they were huffing and out of breath. Jyoti didn't know what was more of a workout—carrying the bags or catastrophizing.

Karishma was on the couch scrolling through her phone when they walked in.

"You found each other," she said slowly, looking up at them.

Jyoti glanced at her friend searching for a sign, but Karishma gave a subtle shrug. She had a feeling Karishma knew as little about this impromptu visit as she did. Karishma rose from the couch to help Jyoti put the bags in the kitchen.

"Auntie just buzzed from downstairs a little while ago, so of course I let her up," Karishma whispered. "I texted you, but doesn't look like you saw it."

Jyoti realized her phone was still silenced and reached for it, even though it was too late to see the warning.

Karishma turned to Nalini. "Are you sure you don't want any chaa, Auntie?"

Nalini waved her off. "Not right now. Maybe after this gelato."

Jyoti was bewildered at the way her mother was acting. Karishma had to be polite, but as her daughter, Jyoti had the right to cut through the formalities.

"Mom, what are you doing here? Is everyone okay?"

Jyoti and Karishma met each other's eyes, both of them recognizing that only something serious would result in such drastic behavior.

"Everyone is fine," Nalini said between bites of stracciatella.

Her mom was acting stranger than Jyoti had ever seen her, but not necessarily in a bad way. She seemed…lighter? Freer? That was the part that was so confusing. Her mother was typically very regimented and tightly wound. It had been no surprise that Jyoti had been that way for much of her life too. But this woman standing before her seemed to be as carefree as Karishma.

"Mom," Jyoti said, exasperation in her voice. "What is going on? Are you sick? Is Dad sick? Chaya? Tanvi?"

Nalini sat at the dining table, and Karishma and Jyoti followed suit. She pushed her now empty cup of gelato away from her and stared at the table.

"I left your father."

Karishma's eyes bugged out and she looked at Jyoti, who was certain hers were doing the same.

"What?" Jyoti tried to make sense of the words, but they felt like a foreign language she was struggling to grasp.

"I left him," Nalini repeated with a shrug.

"Why?!"

Nalini lifted her gaze from the table to meet Jyoti's. "You were right. I heard you in your podcast that you aren't going to sacrifice who you are and what you want for a man, and I've spent my entire life doing that."

"It's not a podcast," Jyoti said numbly, unable to help herself.

"Je hoy te. I started to see my own mistakes in your videos, and I began to look at my life ahead of me. I'm seventy years old and have lived according to Dharmesh's life since I was twenty-five. If not now, then when? I no longer wanted to… how did you say it…bend to his will."

Karishma cleared her throat and rose from the table. "I'll leave you two to talk."

Jyoti was both grateful and alarmed at having to continue this conversation without a buffer. Once Karishma had closed the door to her room, Jyoti turned back to her mom.

"What did Dad say?"

"Oh, you know him. He doesn't say much."

"I'm sure he had something to say about his wife leaving him," Jyoti said, reaching for her mom's hand.

As they touched, Nalini's eyes glistened with tears and so did Jyoti's. Some bonds could be strained but not fully severed.

For a moment, Nalini looked more innocent and helpless than Jyoti had ever seen her. "It's like you said, beta, I've sacrificed who I am for my whole life because it's what Dharmesh needed or what you girls needed and now most of it has passed me by. When do I get to live? When do I get to travel and see the world like I want to? Dharmesh doesn't enjoy any of those things and you girls are grown now, so what is keeping us together at this point?"

"But you don't believe in divorce." Jyoti recalled the multitude of conversations they'd had when she'd gone through hers. The number of times her mother would resolutely say, *Indians don't divorce, that's for Americans.*

"Who says we need to divorce? We are in our seventies. It's not like I'm looking for a new boyfriend. So what if we live separately?"

Jyoti swallowed the lump that had formed at the thought of her mother dating. The image was too unsettling for her to make peace with.

Nalini continued. "I want to live the life that I want for once."

Jyoti couldn't argue with that sentiment, as much as she wanted to. She was learning that same lesson for herself after having spent only fourteen years married in the way her mom was describing. She had bent herself to fit Ashok in so many ways, but it was what she thought marriage was supposed to be, especially in their culture, because it was what she had seen her mom doing for all of their lives. She didn't know much about who Nalini was as a person, apart from being a wife and mother. She didn't know if her mom had any passions or dreams that had been cut short or were never even attempted because of the life she had chosen instead.

"I thought you were happy with Dad." Jyoti tried a different angle.

"What is happy? Who knows? We lived our lives, we raised you kids, and now that is over. What do we do when it's only the two of us in the house and after more than forty-five years married, we hardly know anything about each other apart from what we like to eat? At least, I know that about him. Maybe he doesn't even know any of that about me since I do the cooking and he just shows up at the table when it's time."

There was no arguing that her parents had culturally traditional husband and wife roles, but Jyoti had always thought they were happy enough. Theirs had been an arranged marriage, and as Jyoti went through her divorce, she'd often wondered if her parents' generation had done it right. Eliminated the emotion from the decision and made practical choices based on what was best to have a family: education, health, financial security, shared culture. It was all about the next generation and there wasn't much thought given to the two people living in this moment. It was because of Hollywood, Western magazines, and books that Jyoti even had the idea that love could be the most significant component of a marriage. With Ashok, she thought she'd gotten lucky and managed to appease both the Western and Eastern values in one man. She'd loved him, and he was also a good match based on the standards her parents had relied on for their own marriage. It had seemed like a win-win, but then having had that love between them made it even harder when things didn't work out. In this specific situation, she wondered if her father would be more distraught about losing his familiar life rather than losing Nalini.

"What did Chaya and Tanvi say?"

"I haven't told them yet."

"Are you serious?"

Nalini sat straighter. "I wanted to tell you first, since you inspired this in me."

Jyoti shook her head emphatically. "No, no, no! I did *not* inspire this, and if you tell them that, they are going to kill me!"

"Why is this bad? I've watched all your videos. You are encouraging so many people to live in their truth and share their feelings and be open and honest. Why can't your mother be happy too?"

Jyoti slumped in her chair. She did believe the things she'd said on social media and she wanted them for herself. But she'd never considered that her words could impact her mother and family in such a profound way. She'd wanted Nalini to watch the videos and be able to understand and empathize more with Jyoti so they could be closer, *not* so that she'd internalize the messaging and rip their family apart. But if what her mom had said were her true feelings, then shouldn't Jyoti be supporting her the way she'd wished Nalini had done for her?

As if reading her mind, her mom turned to her. "I'm sorry I wasn't there for you in the way you needed. All I have wanted for you is a safe and secure life. A woman alone wasn't an option that my generation considered. But now I, too, am speaking my truth, as you kids say, and I see how much weight I've carried all this time without ever having a moment to put it down."

Jyoti's heart broke for her mom, and at the fact that she didn't know how long it had been going on. Had she felt that way when helping her and her sisters with their homework or doing the dishes or driving them to doctor's appointments? Had she felt that way each night when she slept beside her husband for nearly half a century? Or when she would cook a feast for Dharmesh's clients to introduce them to Indian food, but would have to dial back the traditional flavors so as not to overwhelm them? Jyoti wore a mask when navigating life in America, but she'd always been herself within the safe walls of their home. She now wondered if her mother ever had the chance to take the mask off.

"I didn't know you felt that way," Jyoti said, her voice barely above a whisper.

"I know, beta. It's not your fault. The world was different then, and we all got used to it. But these days, your generation is so open with your feelings and sometimes it forces us to look at things we've long locked away. The problem is that when you peek inside those places, it becomes hard to forget them again."

Jyoti looked at her mom and tried to muster the same compassion she would have had if one of her social media followers had left a similar comment. In that context, she knew her heart would have broken for that person, and she would have summoned all the empathy in the world. Why was it so much harder to do that with her own mother who was sitting before her? She suspected it was because this decision affected her, her sisters, her dad, the community, relatives in India. It was easy to summon pure compassion and empathy when a person's decision had no effect on you. Nalini wasn't a rash individual, and she had shared more of her emotional journey with Jyoti in these last few minutes than she had in the entirety of Jyoti's life prior. She knew her mom well enough to know that these were steps she hadn't taken lightly, so it was up to Jyoti to show her the compassion and security that her mom hadn't been able to show her when she had gone through her own divorce.

She knelt next to her mom and put her arms around her. As she did, tears slid down both of their cheeks.

"If that's how you feel, Mom, then we will figure this out together." Jyoti met her mom's eyes and offered a wry smile. "We're going to have to because you know Sasti Masti is going to kick our family to the curb faster than the uncles can clear out a platter of samosas."

Nalini chortled and brought her hand to cover her mouth. "But who is going to make them without our masala blends?"

Jyoti joined in on her mom's laughter and the two of them held on to each other as they giggled through their tears. They had both spent the majority of their lives prioritizing their culture and traditions, and now here they were in Italy, on the precipice of a life ill fit for the community in which they'd been raised. There would be many hurdles as they proceeded, but if they could lean on each other, then they wouldn't be alone.

Jyoti's phone buzzed and Chaya's face flashed across the screen. She held it up for her mom to see.

"They must know," Jyoti said. "We can't ignore them."

Jyoti pressed the button and both of her sisters' faces filled the screen. It looked like they were sitting side by side at Chaya's kitchen island.

"Is Mom there?" Chaya asked in a panic.

"She's here."

"What is going on?" Chaya demanded. "Dad said she *left him* and was coming to Italy to see you. None of this sounds right."

Jyoti looked to her mom, seeking permission to include her on the call and her mom relented. Now Jyoti and Nalini both filled their side of the screen.

"See, I told you she was fine," Tanvi said to Chaya. Turning back to the screen, Tanvi said, "Chaya thought maybe you had some brain tumor or something and that's why you were being weird."

Nalini sighed. "I don't have a brain tumor."

"Is it something else?" Chaya asked, her expression filled with worry.

Nalini shook her head. "There is nothing medically wrong with me. I realized the life I'm living right now isn't one that I'm living for me. I live for Dharmesh, and you girls, and for Ushma Auntie and Sasti Masti, but I'm tired of making everyone else happy. I don't know how many years I have left, and it's time to spend them on myself."

Chaya's and Tanvi's jaws dropped.

"Mom, aren't you a bit old to have a new beginning?" Tanvi asked.

Jyoti stared at her sister intently. "Delicate, Tanvi. Seriously. At what age do we just accept the crappy lot we've been given and resign to suffering through it?"

"You think *we* are the crappy lot Mom has been given?" Chaya looked aghast.

"That's not what I meant. Only that Mom has sacrificed more than we know so that all of us could be happy and maybe we should support her if this is what she wants now."

Chaya brushed right past this. "Mom, who is going to take care of Dad? You know he doesn't do anything without you. He would probably never leave the house except to get milk for chaa if you don't come back. Is that really what you want?"

Nalini frowned. "Dharmesh is not an incapable man. He can figure out how to take care of himself. Wouldn't your husband be able to do that if something happened to you?"

"Probably, but he's not from your generation. And he's not Indian."

"What about me?" Tanvi chimed in. "Dad has no clue what is going on right now and is walking around the house all confused as if he's never lived there before."

"He'll be fine. It's a shock, but he will manage," Nalini said.

"I don't think he will," Tanvi said. "And what am I supposed to do? Just leave him there next week?"

"What's so special about next week?" Jyoti asked.

"I'm moving out."

Jyoti looked at her mom and realized this could not be a coincidence. Had she just been waiting for the last child to move out of the house and Tanvi finally obliged?

Chaya jumped in. "Of all the things that would have required a family meeting, this is at the top of the list. How could you do this without talking to us? Family meetings were your rule and now you've broken it."

"You're right," Nalini said. "I should have talked to you about it, but I knew you'd have this reaction."

"So you ran to Italy to see *Jyoti*? You've barely talked to her for months. You've been complaining to us about everything she's been doing."

Jyoti looked down at her fingernails, trying to hide her discomfort.

"And you both kept telling me to give her a chance," Nalini said. "So, I watched her videos and is it so bad that what she said spoke to me too?"

Their eyes widened at this information. Jyoti braced for impact, but a part of her warmed to hear that her sisters had been supportive of her the whole time.

"This is your fault!" Chaya pointed a finger at the screen. "I told you those videos were a bad idea. Were they really worth all of this?"

Jyoti held up a hand. "I think Mom has been feeling this way for a long time. It's not just the videos. If she's unhappy, then we need to figure out why and how we can change that."

"Doesn't sound like those videos helped," Tanvi muttered.

"I didn't even know Mom would ever see them," Jyoti said.

Chaya crossed her arms over her chest. "Well, now you know the impact words can have."

"Girls, please," Nalini scolded. "I'm sitting right here so you don't need to speak as if I can't hear you."

"Why don't we all take a couple days to calm down and think, and then we can reconvene?" Jyoti said.

"A couple days!" Tanvi said. "What am I supposed to do with Dad in the meantime? This affects me more than anyone else. I'm the one at home with him."

Jyoti felt for her sister because she was right, but there wasn't much she could do from Italy. And Chaya had her own family to take care of, so Tanvi was going to have to rely on herself for a way to cope with this one.

"You'll figure it out," Nalini said. "You're hardly at home anyway."

Tanvi sulked. "What am I supposed to do about food for him?"

Their dad was used to Nalini's home-cooked Indian food and had never developed much of a taste for Western take-out, like pizza and tacos.

"I put thepla, dal, and shaak in the freezer, so he just has to defrost it and then he's fine for a few weeks."

Jyoti managed a half smile. Only her mother would be thoughtful and prepared enough to freeze food for the husband she was leaving.

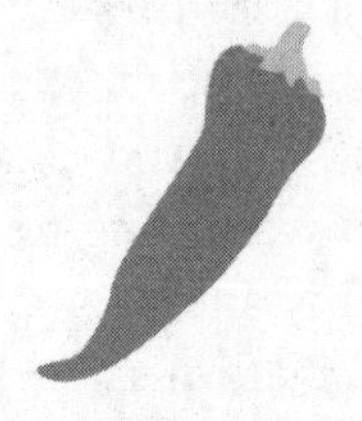

TWENTY-SEVEN

There wasn't even a question of whether Nalini would be staying in Karishma's apartment and sharing a bed with Jyoti. It would certainly be more cramped, but it was the Indian way and neither Jyoti nor Karishma had expected anything otherwise. Jyoti recalled when her white friends' parents had visited and they stayed at hotels. It was always incomprehensible to her that such a thing was acceptable. In her culture, it was a show of respect to have your family stay with you, regardless of whether it was impractical or inconvenient. And even Karishma wouldn't consider bucking that tradition. The biggest problem with the arrangement was that, in the small apartment, it was difficult for Jyoti and Karishma to have a private conversation.

While Nalini slept off her jet lag, Jyoti and Karishma slipped out and went for a walk.

"What do you think is going on here?" Karishma asked as they made their way across Piazza Santo Spirito toward the river.

Jyoti shook her head. "I have no idea. She's never done anything like this. But with everything she's said, it makes me wonder if I've ever really known her at all. I never sensed she was carrying any deep regret about a life not lived."

Jyoti fell behind Karishma so they could walk single file along a narrow strip of sidewalk as cars passed alongside them.

"We never think of our parents that way," Karishma said. "Who knows what lives they had before us? My mom has surprised me in so many ways over the years. But this definitely doesn't seem like Auntie. Could your videos have made that much of a difference?"

Jyoti felt heavy as she considered this. "They can't have, right? She's hardly listened to anything I've said for the last decade, and now, all of a sudden, my words have such weight? There has to be something else going on, but she almost seems too fragile for me to pry."

Karishma nodded as the cars cleared and they fell into step side by side again. "It definitely seems like she's having some late-in-life crisis."

"I wonder what really happened. She and my dad have always been fine. It's never been some fairy-tale love but it was never meant to be. Neither of them was looking for that. You heard her, they wanted to raise a good family, and they did that, and now she seems to be regretting something, but I'm not sure what. And I have no idea what my words could have done to spark that."

"I'm surprised we haven't gotten texts from Sasti Masti about this," Karishma said.

"I bet they don't know yet. She didn't even tell Tanvi in person and Tanvi lives under the same roof. My dad is certainly not going to run around town sharing it. Who knows what excuse he would make up if someone asked him? I'm sure the truth isn't going to fall from his lips right now." Jyoti's phone buzzed and a photo of her and her dad from many years ago flashed on the screen. "Let me see if he has more info," she said, taking a few steps away and leaning against the wall along the Ponte alla Carraia.

"Dad, what's going on over there?"

"I don't know." Her father's voice sounded strained. "She said you made some videos and now she wants to find a different life and then she was gone. What did you say?"

Guilt flooded through Jyoti. "I don't know. I was talking about my own experiences with cooking and what I was going through. I don't know what could have been relatable to Mom."

"You said something," Dharmesh said in a stern voice that she hadn't heard from him since she was a little girl. "Think about what it was so we can fix this. We've been together forty-five years. People our age can't start over now."

Jyoti felt for her dad because she knew how true that felt for him. He'd enjoyed the privileges that came with the traditional roles he and Nalini had performed until now. Those roles meant that he worked and brought in money for the family, but at their age, those skills were no longer needed. Nalini, however, had focused her entire life on survival skills to keep their family going, and she was better equipped to live on her own if that's what things came down to. Jyoti had never thought about it, but upon retirement, it did appear that the balance of power had shifted.

"Dad," Jyoti said gently. "Is there something she wanted to do when she was younger and you didn't let her or something like that?"

"How can you say that? I gave her everything, and same to you kids. I worked around the clock to provide for this family, and this is how I'm being treated now. In India, the aging parents are treated like royalty, you know that? They stay with the eldest child who takes care of them until Bhagwan says it's time to leave this Earth."

She knew that was the expectation where her parents had grown up, but it wasn't the world they lived in now. She would certainly be there to help them when they could no longer care for themselves, but Dharmesh was talking about something different, and she couldn't deny that she wasn't interested in the burdens associated with having her parents under her roof before it became necessary.

"Dad, we know that, but just try to think. It feels like she has some regret that it's too late to fix and maybe that's what is causing this. And maybe Tanvi moving out…do you know why she's doing it now?"

"Tanvi is thirty-five years old. She should have moved out a long time ago," Dharmesh said.

"Yes, but she didn't. And you guys weren't exactly pushing her out the door, so why now?"

Her dad grunted. Jyoti had long suspected that as much as her mom liked to complain that Tanvi was unmarried and still at home, a part of her liked having a child she could take care of under her roof.

Dharmesh cleared his throat. "I don't know, Jyoti. Tanvi said she wanted to live in the city and get out of New Jersey and was going to move in with her friend. This is what we wanted from her for so long, so what was there to talk about?"

Jyoti considered what he'd said and suspected that had to be at least part of what was going on with her mom. The timing was too much of a coincidence.

Nalini was awake when Karishma and Jyoti returned to the apartment, and Jyoti found her in her bedroom, looking at her notebook with the recipes she'd been preparing for the Fattorio Vineyard Dinner. Her brainstorming felt as private as a journal, and she suddenly felt exposed.

Jyoti moved forward and grabbed the notebook from her mom's hands, just like she would have when she'd catch her mom snooping through her room as a teenager. "Mom, what are you doing? You can't just go through my things. I'm an adult now."

Her mom gave her a look as if to say *so you think*.

Jyoti bit her tongue. Given Nalini's delicate state, she didn't want to instigate another fight. Instead of the sarcastic tone she would have normally taken in this situation, she said plainly, "It's just some things I've been working on."

"For what?" Nalini pressed.

Moms had zero boundaries when it came to their daughters, regardless of age. Jyoti debated how much to tell her.

"I was going to make a dinner for Karishma and her friends before I go home."

Nalini stared at her hard. Jyoti had always been a terrible liar and melted under her mom's gaze. Some things never changed.

Jyoti sighed. "It's for that job I told you about earlier that you didn't want to talk about."

Nalini raised an eyebrow. "You are still doing that? Are you going to work here longer?"

"I hadn't planned on it, but the opportunity came up, and since I hadn't gotten any work in New York…"

"You want to live here like Karishma?"

Jyoti hadn't thought about moving to Italy permanently so the question surprised her. "No, not live here, but I needed to make some money." She sighed, knowing that the floodgates had already opened. "I know you won't like this, but Ashok called me a few weeks ago and said that if I got the money to buy Taste of Ginger by the end of the year, then he'd sell it to me. Otherwise, he's going to line up a buyer because his new wife doesn't like him keeping restaurant hours and he wants a desk job somewhere."

"Now he cares what his wife wants?"

Jyoti curled her lips into a smile. Regardless of what had happened between them over the past years, the two of them were aligned in their dislike of the way Ashok abandoned Jyoti.

"Apparently so."

Nalini scoffed. "That woman is so high-maintenance. All

the aunties think so, even his own parents, although his mother is too proud to say anything in public."

Jyoti was thrilled that they'd landed on this Ashok-bashing tangent instead of her mother having a conniption about Jyoti buying a restaurant and cooking again.

"Whatever she is, she's his now. I couldn't give him the life he wanted and she can, so they deserve each other."

Nalini shot her a look, but let it go. "I didn't know you wanted to buy Taste of Ginger."

Jyoti looked at the floor. "I've always wanted it. It was the thing I tried hardest to get from the divorce but Ashok wouldn't give it to me. I've always loved bringing our food to people and watching them enjoy it."

Nalini looked wistful. "You have always been a very good cook."

Jyoti sat on the bed across from her mom. "Thanks. That is a skill I definitely learned from you. But it's more than the cooking. For me, food is the way I'm closest to our culture, so that's why it matters so much to me to share it with other people."

"For me too," Nalini said. "When we left India, the kitchen was the only time when home didn't feel so far away. The same smells of vaghar with rai or ajamo or jeeru could make me forget we were half a world away from our families and friends and the bungalows we grew up in. I couldn't show you girls India when you were growing up, but I could make sure that you could taste it."

Jyoti smiled and took her mother's hand. "And you did. And at least for me, those were the flavors that always comforted me because they were what I associated with our home."

Nalini smiled. "I think you have surpassed what I taught you."

"Maybe in terms of presentation, but not in terms of soul." After a pause, Jyoti said, "Is that what this is about? Do you want to go back to India? Do you miss being home even after all these years?"

Nalini's face scrunched as if she'd smelled something sour. "No. We made a choice and America is my home now. But it doesn't mean I need to be stuck in the same dull life as before."

"That's the part I don't understand. What is the life you're looking for that you don't have?"

Nalini sighed. "I don't know exactly yet, but it felt like time for me to stop hiding and find something for myself. I never got to see the world or try new things. Your father would never want to take a trip to Italy or something like that. We always went to India like he wanted, but I don't want to die never having seen the Eiffel Tower or tasted gelato from a real gelateria."

It wasn't much of an answer and Jyoti was still just as confused as her dad. She could see her mom's point about Dharmesh not being interested in vacations to anywhere other than India, but did her mother need to leave a whole marriage for that? She could have just booked the trip and said she'd be back in two weeks. She saw the weariness on her mom's face and decided to pay attention to the signs that her mother had often missed when Jyoti was going through her divorce. Nalini needed space rather than being inundated for answers she did not have.

The next day, Jyoti was in the kitchen prepping for the Fattorio dinner when her mother stumbled out close to noon, still catching up to the time difference. An array of containers was spread on the counter, along with several piles of ingredients that were washed and ready to use.

"What's all this?" Nalini asked.

"Prep for the dinner."

"Do you need help?"

Jyoti hesitated. It had been so long since she had cooked alongside her mother—memories she would always cherish—but it had usually been her helping her mom, not the other way around. She wasn't sure how their dynamic would be with Nalini as sous chef, but she nodded, gesturing toward the large pot of paneer that she had made earlier. It needed to be drained to separate the curds from the whey. Her mom washed her hands and joined her daughter in the kitchen.

"What exactly are you making?"

Jyoti hesitantly explained her Italian-Indian fusion menu and awaited her mom's reaction. This was the type of food her mom would normally call fussy fancy food.

Today, her mom simply said, "Very creative."

"I know it's not the type of thing you would make, but it still has familiar Indian flavor profiles, so I think you'll like it."

"When is the dinner?"

"Two days. I'm trying to prep as many chutneys and sauces as I can ahead of time so the flavors can meld together, and so there's more assembly and less cooking the day of."

This, she had also learned from her mom. Their home had been the coveted invite for Diwali each year because Nalini prepped everything from scratch, carefully detailing the menu on a large piece of paper, calculating how many days in advance certain components of the meal could be prepped. Jyoti's mouth watered as she remembered her mother's gravy for channa masala. This was always one of the first items from the menu that got prepped because it tasted better the longer the blended ingredients married together before cooking.

"Who is helping you on that day?" Nalini asked.

"They have a housemaid, but it's only fourteen people so I was planning to do it myself with Karishma. That way I can make sure it's done as I want. This dinner is like an audition of sorts for me to be able to do more of their dinners. I'd need to book the ones they have remaining for the summer if I have any chance of buying back Taste of Ginger."

Her mom's jaw tightened and, given the gravity of this dinner, Jyoti ignored it. She pressed forward as the two of them worked quietly in the small kitchen, pureeing mint and cilantro for the pesto to accompany the samosas, and then grinding dates, cumin, and tamarind into a paste for another sauce.

TWENTY-EIGHT

Jyoti had been feeling good about her progress and that her mom was there to help her. It had been nice experiencing that familiar bonding ritual again, especially now that she was starting to feel like herself after so many years of trying to be what Ashok and her parents had needed her to be. Her dad and sisters had been texting her constantly to find out if she'd learned anything more about what was going on with Nalini. She truthfully told them that she hadn't yet, and they all needed to give her some time. It had only been a few days after all, so she suspected her mom had hardly registered what she had done.

Jyoti was sketching the table settings in the dining room when Karishma burst out of her room and pumped her fists into the air.

"It finally happened!" Her smile spread across her face.

"What did?"

"Swati got a book deal!" Karishma danced in the open area between the living and dining spaces.

Jyoti's eyes widened and she stood up and joined her friend's dance party. "That is amazing!"

"It took us six years and three manuscripts, but her Gujarati stories are coming to the world. And guess what?"

"What?"

"It's a two-book deal. They are buying her first and last one, and depending on how those do, there's always an opportunity for the second one to get sold too. I guess the India wave isn't over after all," she said with a victorious look on her face.

"That's amazing. I can't wait to see them in print and go to her book signings and see your name in her acknowledgments. This is so exciting. You helped change her life."

Karishma stopped bouncing around and caught her breath. "I'm so proud of her. She has pushed through so much to get here. There were points at which she'd had offers that were contingent on her changing elements of her stories to make them more palatable to white audiences, but she made the difficult and brave decision to hold out for the right opportunity that would allow her to be authentic. And now, it's paid off and she gets to do that."

"I know how much you've wanted this for so long. I'm so happy for both of you. And maybe everything happens for a reason. Maybe this is the right time for her stories to be told because the audience is ready to hear them. Who knows if six years ago that would have been the case?"

"That's true. The world is becoming more open every day. Even if we'd made her an offer when I was still working in New York, that was only the first hurdle. Then she would have needed the right marketing support, and audience reception, and a whole host of other things that would have been hard to change overnight. Her books have a better chance now, and I hope they are so widely read that she becomes a household name."

"One book can help so many people feel seen. You should be so proud of yourself."

"It is such a relief to see her get published. The way my company treated her was awful. This finally feels like validation that leaving was the right thing."

"Even if this hadn't happened for her, you did the right thing. I've never seen you so happy and comfortable with your life. And after the time I've spent here, there is no doubt that this is your home, even though I miss you terribly in New York. Doing work that makes a difference is what lights you up."

"Thanks, Jyo. That means a lot. It's been nice seeing you find your path here too. Cooking is how you connect with the world, and I can't wait to watch you in action in a couple days. Whatever your food journey holds, you're going to bring joy to people, and I know how much you want that."

They hugged each other and Jyoti felt so grateful for how far they'd come.

Jyoti let her go, and said, "You know what the best part about her new book deal is?"

Karishma looked at her expectantly.

"That I can finally read one of her books. She'll be my first Gujarati American author, and I can't believe it took until my forties for me to be able to read one."

Karishma left to share her good news with Enzo, and Jyoti had returned to her obsessive planning for the dinner tomorrow when she saw an incoming call from Ashok. She could practically hear his voice telling her that he was going to sell the restaurant earlier than he'd said. It would be just like him to yank this away from her when she was on the cusp of getting it. She considered declining the call. Regardless of what he said, she needed to successfully complete tomorrow night's dinner service and anything he had to say would surely be a distraction, but she figured it was best to know.

"Hi," she said dryly as his face filled the screen.

"Hey," he said, his tone warm as he drew out the word. "Are you busy?"

Since when had he cared if he was interfering with her schedule?

"I am in the middle of some things, but can talk briefly if you make it quick."

She didn't want to prolong him telling her that the dream she'd been building in her head of her revamped restaurant was no more.

"I'm not sure if you've heard…" he said, running a hand through his thinning hair.

Jyoti wondered if somehow the community had already learned about her mom leaving Dharmesh. She was grateful that her mom and Karishma had gone out to grab pizza. Nalini wouldn't want to hear that Sasti Masti had turned on her and she'd already become the center of gossip.

"Heard what?" Jyoti asked noncommittally.

He looked conciliatory and Jyoti sat a bit straighter.

"I split up with Radha."

Jyoti stared at him as if he'd said he was walking on the moon.

"Did you hear me?"

"Yeah," she said, wondering why he was calling her. "But why would you do that? What happens to the baby?"

His face flashed with pain, and she'd rarely seen him look that way. Ashok was always in control and seeing him without it was disarming.

"That's the thing…it turns out the baby wasn't mine."

Jyoti was certain she had misheard him. "What do you mean?"

"She—" His voice broke and he gathered himself before continuing. "It doesn't really matter. The baby isn't mine."

Jyoti was stunned. Radha had become pregnant with someone else's baby and Ashok had no idea? It seemed like such a stretch for their community. If he was calling her, then enough people must know that he was worried she'd hear it from somewhere else. This was the type of news that Sasti Masti would run with and ask questions later. For a second, Jyoti considered the fact that if her parents' issues were brought to light, then they may be buried under the weight of this larger scandal. It was hard to know which tragedy was better gossip fodder.

"I'm sorry," Jyoti said finally, at a loss for words.

He managed a wry smile. "It's rather humiliating. But I guess you probably think I deserve that."

Seeing the pained look on his face made it hard to be cruel to him. Although there had been times when she'd wished ill upon him, even she hadn't contemplated something like this. She could see that the devastation on his face was genuine, and it reminded her of the looks he'd had during each of her miscarriages. He'd just lost another baby that he'd thought he'd get to hold in his arms and raise.

"No one deserves to feel the pain of losing a child, no matter what the circumstances are around it."

"I've been thinking a lot about our marriage," Ashok said, staring intently at her through the screen. "I'm sorry, Jyo. I realize I really let you down with the way I handled things."

She was shocked to hear this incredibly genuine apology leave his lips. For so long, she had dreamed of him acknowledging his part in the failure of their relationship. She had made peace with the fact that the apology would never come, rationalized that Ashok didn't have the capacity to understand that what he'd done was wrong so would never consider remorse. But now that it was here, her body felt a bit lighter, her feelings finally validated. It was one thing to make peace within yourself, but it was another to have the person who hurt you acknowledge their part in it.

"Thank you," she said softly. "It was hard."

"I can see that now. I was only thinking of myself and didn't give any weight to the life we'd built together. Things weren't going as we planned and my mom kept reminding me that time was running out. It felt like if I was going to have this part of my life work out and be a father, then I needed to do that quickly."

As much as Jyoti hated how he'd treated her, a part of her did understand his sentiment. If he knew he wanted children and she couldn't give them to him, then the suffering was always going to be there regardless of how and when they parted ways.

"It seems that kids aren't in the cards for me," he said. "But I kept thinking of what I wanted my life to look like without them, and I kept seeing you."

Jyoti jerked her head back and widened her eyes. This was the last thing she expected to hear from him.

He watched her carefully and continued. "I don't know where you are in your life. Maybe you've run off with some Italian man, but I miss our old life. I miss coming home to you. I hate to admit it but people were right. Radha was too young for me. I felt like an old man around her. She never understood my jokes or TV references or taste in music."

"I'm not sure age is the reason that she didn't understand your jokes," Jyoti said, finding herself falling back into their familiar banter.

Ashok laughed. "Maybe so. But she and I couldn't talk the way you and I did. I loved the way we used to work together at Taste of Ginger. We were a team. That's the dynamic I miss. Radha and I never had that. Think about it. What if you and I became partners again and revived the restaurant and that was our life from now on?"

She felt like the wind had been knocked out of her. "You want to get back together?"

He nodded.

"We got divorced and now you want to—what? Remarry?"

He shrugged. "We wouldn't be the first people to do it."

"We'd be the first people in *our* community to do it." She knew she was going to sound like her mother and all the aunties when she continued. She was going to sound like an earlier version of Ashok too, but she couldn't hold back the words. "What will people say?"

"Who cares?"

"Who are you? You cared about that so much when we were married. We both did."

"And maybe that was the problem."

She couldn't deny that. During her summer in Italy, she had learned to start trusting herself rather than always worrying about the opinions of others. Her situation with Tommaso and the failed first rehearsal dinner with the Fattorios had shown her that she needed to build her confidence from within so that it could not be shaken so easily by external forces.

She shook her head, trying to process what she was hearing.

"So, you want to get remarried, run the restaurant together again, and move back into our old lives in New York? You're now okay not having children and telling your mom that the line dies here and just living out the rest of your life child-free?"

"Well, there is one other thing," he said. "The cryobank hasn't destroyed the embryos yet, so if we wanted to try for kids, we still could. Or we could even look into a surrogate if you don't want to put your body through that."

"I'd thought you'd said surrogates were too expensive."

"They are, but I have my dad's life insurance money. I can't think of a better way to spend it than carrying on our family line and having the baby we wanted for so long."

Jyoti felt as if the room were spinning. In the aftermath of him leaving her, how often had she pleaded for exactly this offer that he was making to her now? She could go back to a life that was fully predictable. Fully accepted by their families and community. She and Ashok had been okay until they started having fertility problems, hadn't they? He was saying they could go back to that time. Back to those days of her recipe testing in the kitchen she loved, and him coming in and being her first taster. Back to having someone with her each night to cook dinner for so she wasn't microwaving frozen meals for one. The sentiment of turning death into life with the insurance money filled her with warmth. She'd longed for having a child without putting her body through more trauma, but had had to dismiss the thought because she could never have afforded that on her own. They hadn't been divorced for that long and their community could just sweep it under the rug if they got back together. No more ostracized middle-aged divorcée. No more being outside the fold along with Karishma. She'd never thought she'd be offered a do-over, but here it was, and she saw that Ashok's proposal was sincere.

"I don't know," she said slowly. "This is a lot to take in. I'm not sure what to say."

The hopeful expression on his face slid to disappointment but he quickly forced a smile. "I understand. Take your time and think about it. But just remember how happy we were before all the drama. Even though our parents introduced us, we chose each other, and we can do it again, only older and wiser this time around. And now we know that it would be forever because we've been through too much to get back to each other."

Jyoti nodded numbly and considered this. She'd thought that the last time, and she'd been willing to hold up her end of that bargain, but he had not. Could she ever trust him again? And even if she could, should she?

TWENTY-NINE

Karishma and Nalini came home about fifteen minutes after Jyoti ended her video call with Ashok, and she still hadn't moved from where she'd been seated at the dining table. Karishma was carrying two pizza boxes and the room filled with the smell of melted cheese and fragrant tomato sauce. Jyoti's stomach grumbled at the sight of the pizza like a Pavlovian response, even if she couldn't think about eating right now.

"What's up with you?" Karishma asked as she kicked off her shoes. "You look weird."

Nalini pushed forward to see Jyoti, and seemed to agree with Karishma's assessment and put the back of her hand against Jyoti's forehead.

"Are you sick?"

Jyoti brought herself to attention and shook her head. "No. I just got the strangest call from Ashok."

"Don't tell me he went ahead and sold the restaurant out from under you," Karishma said.

Jyoti shook her head slowly. "He wants to get back together and resume our married life."

Karishma nearly dropped the pizzas but recovered and quickly placed them on the dining table.

"Is he into polygamy now?"

Jyoti shook her head. "Their marriage is over."

Nalini's eyes widened and Jyoti suspected the shock on her mother's face mirrored her own. She'd always been a carbon copy of her mom. She filled them in on the conversation and they both stared at her blankly after she'd finished.

"This is a surprise," Nalini said, deadpan.

Karishma clasped her hands into prayer position. "You told him no, right?"

Nalini shot Karishma a look, and Karishma's shoulders sank. Jyoti's gaze moved from one to the other.

"I didn't tell him anything. I was too stunned to speak."

Nalini put a hand on her shoulder. "Beta, I know he hasn't always been the best in the past, but people change. Maybe you should consider this and give him a chance. It could make your road ahead easier."

Karishma's jaw tensed, but she remained silent. Jyoti had known what Karishma's reaction would be from the start. But Jyoti wasn't sure if she was as independent and brave as Karishma when it came to living life alone.

That evening, Chaya called Jyoti and she rushed to answer it, surprised to see her sister calling again so shortly after their last conversation. *What else could possibly be wrong?*

"Good, you're there," her sister said in a clipped tone. "I just saw Dad and he's a mess over this."

"Of course he is."

"I can't believe you let this happen. Those silly videos."

"It's not as if I planned for this." Jyoti's tone started to match her sister's. "No one could have predicted this, and you know it."

"Maybe not," Chaya said. "But Isaac and I have been doing some thinking and maybe we need someone with more family values to raise our kids if something happens to us. We wouldn't want our children to grow up learning that they should think about themselves without considering anyone else."

Jyoti felt the words cut through her like a knife. She knew her sister was mad, but this felt like a step too far. "Why am I being blamed for Mom's decision? I wasn't even there. I didn't even talk to her before she showed up here."

"She would never have done this without your influence, and you know it."

Having spent this past day talking to her mom for the first time in what felt like years, Jyoti didn't have a response. But she was certain that her off-the-cuff videos were not powerful enough to push someone in a direction unless they already wanted to be there in the first place.

"You're not being fair."

Chaya scoffed. "I'm not going to debate this with you. I only called to tell you that Isaac and I will leave Nitin and our future child with his brother's family if anything happens to us, so you are off the hook. You can flit about Italy or wherever, making whatever videos you want, and not be burdened with having to care for our children." She hung up.

Jyoti knew Chaya didn't like Isaac's brother's family so this news felt especially personal. Her sister would rather have people she didn't like raise her children than her sister who had helped raise her. Jyoti began to feel the hollowness that she had felt before, and that Chaya's news about her potentially being a guardian one day had helped fill. Part of what had made it easier for her to embrace a life without children was that she had begun to see that she still had children in her life. But now it felt like Chaya was taking that away. Jyoti couldn't help but think that going back to Ashok might solve this problem too.

★★★

That night, Jyoti lay in bed next to her mom, both women staring at the ceiling. Jyoti could feel the tension coming from the other half of the bed, knowing there were things her mom wanted to say but was holding back.

She pictured her mom chewing her lower lip, debating if she should speak aloud her thoughts. Unable to take the silence, Jyoti finally said, "Just say what you want to say."

Nalini sat up and turned toward Jyoti. Her face caught the moonlight, giving it an ominous glow. "You should consider what Ashok said."

"I can't stop thinking about it, but why do you think I should?"

"You are still young, and life can be so hard alone. I don't want you to suffer if you don't need to."

Jyoti sat up. "You just left Dad and want to live alone."

Nalini sighed. "This is different, beta. I am almost done with my life. You still have so much to go. I would not have wanted to be alone at your age, and I wasn't. I had Dharmesh. I had you girls. Don't you still want kids? You tried for so long. Ashok is offering a better way now."

"I don't know, Mom. Sometimes it feels like this is too old to start that. I'm going to be forty-three this year. Do I really want to be over sixty years old and attending a high school graduation?"

"More and more people your age are having kids like this. You had a lot of challenges and sometimes that can affect the mind, and now you are too scared to try again. But think of how much you have been through between then and now. Maybe this was Bhagwan's plan all along."

"I don't know, Mom."

Jyoti had stopped believing in Bhagwan's plan a while ago. Years of failed fertility attempts and her husband leaving her jobless had been enough to convince her that maybe not everything in life was for some higher purpose. But she also had the niggling feeling that there could be some divine intervention at play on some level. She'd already gone through the emotional upheaval of agreeing to destroy the embryos and thinking they—and her chance at any biological children—were gone. But now that she had learned they were still there in their frozen baby slurry, she wondered if this was the Universe's way of telling her that she'd previously made the wrong decision and she *was* supposed to become a mother. She felt lost in her thoughts and knew Karishma would tell her to meditate with some crystals and Jyoti was actually starting to think that maybe that would help her find clarity. Karishma had definitely rubbed off on her in these months.

"I just want you to be safe, beta. To know that someone is there to look after you when your dad and I are gone. I know you spend time with Karishma and think this life is a good one, but you two are not the same. I know my daughter, and you are not like her."

"What is that supposed to mean?" Jyoti felt her voice rising.

"She doesn't have the same sense of community and values as we do."

Jyoti didn't want to get into this tired conversation again. "You're wrong about her. She's as much family to me as you are."

Nalini flinched and her expression revealed that she wasn't pleased with occupying the same space as Karishma. "She can be alone all the time, but you need people. Even just to cook for so you can share your love with someone that way and not hole yourself up eating frozen pizza and drinking wine. Cooking is something we do for others even more than for ourselves."

Jyoti knew there was some truth to what her mother was saying. She hadn't done well when she'd been on her own for the first time after the divorce. She could understand why her mom didn't want to see that become the entirety of Jyoti's life.

She didn't want that either. Jyoti appreciated that despite everything, her mom still wanted to look out for her.

"I love that you care. But I don't know what the right decision is for me."

"Of course I care. I'm your mother." Nalini took a deep breath. "I've been wondering if this is all happening at this time because it means we are both meant to go back to our husbands."

Jyoti sat up straighter, rubbing her forehead. "You want to go back to Dad now?"

"I don't know. I thought I was making the right decision, but then seeing you go through this, I know that I think you are better off with a husband who can help you through the rest of life. Maybe I am seeing this through your eyes so I can make the right decision for myself too. I don't know how much life I have left, maybe it doesn't matter how I spend it and who I spend it with and I should just go back home."

Jyoti, too, would feel better if her mom were back with her dad and the two of them had each other to look after. To have someone at home to notice if the other fell and needed help, especially at their age. She understood her mother wanted that for her, too, so maybe the two women were more alike than they wanted to admit. It was scary to think of a life lived completely alone for however many decades she had left, but she also had mixed feelings about going back to the life she had known.

"Let's sleep on it," Nalini said. "But I'll make you a promise. If you go back to Ashok, then I will go home, too, and we'll do this next chapter together as we reconnect with our husbands."

Jyoti felt a lump form in her chest. No pressure.

THIRTY

The next day was the Fattorio dinner and despite the turmoil around her, Jyoti had to put it all aside and cook the best meal she could. Admittedly, the stakes seemed less high this time because if she went back to Ashok, she'd have the restaurant again anyway and no longer needed money for it. But even though the guilt of reuniting her family weighed heavy, she still hadn't decided what she was going to do.

She, her mom, and Karishma had loaded up Ben's car and crammed into it along with their produce and containers, trying not to jostle anything as they headed to the vineyard.

"This is beautiful," Nalini said upon arrival, scanning the rolling hills, charming stone villas, and endless rows of vines and olive trees. "I've never seen anything like this."

Jyoti thought about her mom's comment about wanting to travel. Seeing the wonder on her face as she took in the Italian countryside for the first time made Jyoti appreciate how much her mother had sacrificed. Jyoti had had the opportunity to visit Europe before this trip with Ashok and with friends, but her mother's trips outside of the country had all been to India. Immigrants who were lucky enough to be able to return home felt an overwhelming sense of responsibility to use their resources that way, especially knowing that so many others were forced to say goodbye to their home countries forever. Since her dad had retired and they could travel for longer, they'd often do a stopover depending on which airline they flew and spend a few days seeing Kuala Lumpur or Dubai. But she could see from the look on her mom's face that she craved more.

When they arrived, Mae was taking test shots. Ben had gotten her the photographer job for the evening and she snapped a few pictures of them coming up the walkway with their bags. She was introduced to Nalini, and then Jyoti, Karishma, and Nalini made their way to the kitchen to begin the prep. Jyoti was surprised that her mom had offered to help with what she'd always called servant work, but decided it was best to accept. She needed the extra hands, and who better than the woman who had cultivated her love of cooking?

It was Jyoti's third time in the Fattorios' kitchen and she was glad she had some familiarity with it. She began to set up stations for prepping each dish and then divvied out orders.

"Karishma, you add the herbs to the paneer and then stuff the squash blossoms. Mom, you make the samosa filling." Jyoti watched Karishma stare at the piping bag as if it were a foreign object, and then said, "Mom, maybe you help Karishma stuff the blossoms too. Let's just communicate when things come up and make the best dinner these guests have ever had."

Even though she was leading her mom and best friend, it felt good to be in a kitchen calling out orders again. The bustle of the kitchen was where she felt connected and calm. She began kneading the dough for the samosas, using her body weight to help bring the large quantity into a cohesively melded dough. Feeling flour and water transform from a sticky paste to a smooth ball grounded her. Bringing order from chaos.

She pinched off a tiny piece to taste for salt and jeeru and then began rolling out circles.

It was warm in the kitchen and she wiped away the beads of sweat dotting her forehead. When it was time for the first course, she carefully arranged her mandolin-sliced baby artichokes that had been dressed with a jeeru vinaigrette into a small pyramid. She then added a few vibrant parsley leaves and some toasted white sesame seeds to finish it. She wiped away any excess dressing from the sides of each plate with precision, while Nalini watched her. This was the type of fussiness that her mom did not understand—making a towel dirty just so the first bite would start off on a clean plate—but Jyoti was grateful there was no commentary today.

She walked to the outdoor table where the fourteen guests were seated. Greca, Fausto, and Ben were closest to her, which put her slightly at ease. Mae surreptitiously walked around, snapping photos of the diners and food.

Fausto clinked his wineglass with a knife to get people's attention. "I'd like to present our chef for the evening, who has imagined this very creative meal you are about to try. Please explain the menu, Jyoti."

She cleared her throat and looked at the eager faces around her. "I want to thank you for letting me be a part of this unique experience with you. The Fattorios have crafted some truly exceptional wines and it's an honor to be able to pair food that helps accentuate the notes in it. As you can see, I'm not Italian, and the menu tonight blends the flavors of my Indian heritage with some of the stunning local produce and ingredients here in Tuscany. Your first course is a shaved artichoke salad with a cumin and mustard seed vinaigrette that should set the tone for the rest of the meal. Please enjoy."

She heard clapping from behind her and turned to see Karishma and her mom peeking out to watch her give her presentation, both of them with wide smiles. The rest of the guests followed suit and shared in a round of applause before picking up their forks and diving in. Jyoti lingered a moment to watch them take their first bites. She watched the guests close their eyes as they savored the flavors before quickly returning for a second bite. In that moment, Jyoti knew she'd prepared something they loved. She went back to the kitchen for the next courses with a lighter step. This night would be a hit because she had allowed her soul to shine through in her food, and that was the recipe for success.

Back in the kitchen, the three resumed their work. Jyoti was careful to give Karishma tasks that involved more arranging than cooking. Her mom began frying the samosas, something she had done countless times and could do without a thought. Her mom and Karishma were polite to each other as they worked, but it was clear that Jyoti was the glue forcing them together and they'd otherwise have little desire to be in each other's company. But Jyoti couldn't focus on the kitchen dynamics right now.

By the end of the evening, after Jyoti had plated and presented a successful eight-course tasting menu, she took a moment to think about what she had accomplished. She could only imagine how the night could have been even better if she'd devoted less of her time to second-guessing herself, and more to trusting her creative instincts. But, based on the satisfaction on the diners' faces, she had a hunch that more opportunities were around the corner.

Jyoti and her mom were still in the Fattorios' kitchen, doing some cleanup, when Nalini glanced around and noticed it was just the two of them and shook her head.

"Some things never change."

Jyoti braced herself, anticipating some negative comment about this career path. But to her surprise, her mom said, "That girl always finds a way to disappear when it's time for the dishes."

Jyoti laughed. It was no secret that Karishma did not enjoy doing dishes. It was a large part of why she didn't cook at all. Mae had been coming in and photographing the plates as they were prepared but she, too, had ventured off somewhere.

"Mom, she's not that bad."

"I know she's your friend, but we will never agree on her values." Her mom turned from the sink to meet Jyoti's eyes. "I know you have a big decision to make, and I don't want you letting her influence you about this. You know she'll want you to join her on this alternate path she's taken even if it's not right for you."

"You're not being fair. She has been there for me when no one else has." Jyoti looked pointedly at her mom. "She probably knows me better than anyone at this point. And she has my best interests at heart."

"Jyoti, you are too gullible. You always have been. How can someone who got you drunk on the day of your sister's graduation have the same family values as you? She didn't even come to say sorry to Tanvi or Dharmesh and me after it happened. What kind of person doesn't even apologize?"

"Apologize for what?" Karishma asked, reentering the kitchen with a glass of red wine.

The color drained from Jyoti's face.

"You don't remember?" Nalini turned the faucet off and faced Karishma. "Of course not. It would be of such little importance to you."

Karishma looked like she knew she had walked into something serious, but she wasn't sure what. And Jyoti was certain she had no idea what was about to unfold.

"Remember what, Auntie?"

"Tanvi's graduation. You got Jyoti drunk and she missed it."

"Me?" Karishma looked at Jyoti. "What did I have to do with that?"

"See." Nalini turned to Jyoti. "Her values are not the same.

She doesn't even remember such a big event. And what else was so important? Wine? Day drinking, is that what you call it?"

"What is she talking about?"

If Jyoti could have sunk into the wooden floorboards and transported herself anywhere else in the world, she would have.

Karishma looked perplexed. "Didn't you miss Tanvi's graduation because of—"

"I'm sorry," Jyoti interjected.

"Because of what?" Nalini asked Karishma. "Because of you, right?"

Karishma's free hand flew to her chest in disbelief. "Me?"

"Mom, it wasn't her fault," Jyoti said.

"Still all these years later and you are defending her. Why? She is old enough to take responsibility for her actions."

"Mom, it wasn't her fault," Jyoti said, more forcefully this time. "I lied."

Both her mother and Karishma turned to her in confusion. Jyoti met Karishma's eyes, trying to convey an apology for what she was about to say. Then, turning to Nalini, she said, "I wasn't with Karishma that day. She's not the reason I got drunk and missed it. I was with Ashok and things had been getting serious and I knew an engagement was coming. I didn't want you to reject the match. So—" she dragged her eyes back to Karishma "—I said I was with Karishma since I already knew you didn't like her."

"You did what?" Karishma's face fell.

Nalini swayed uncomfortably. "All this time, you let me believe it was Karishma."

Karishma and Nalini exchanged a glance, realizing they were both on the same side of having been duped.

Suddenly, knowing settled across Karishma's face. "That's why Sasti Masti started ostracizing me and my family."

Now both Nalini and Jyoti looked guilty.

"I'm sorry," Nalini said to Karishma. "I didn't know. I

thought Jyoti wouldn't behave like that without some bad influence..."

"And you assumed it had to be me," Karishma said coldly.

"No," Jyoti said. "I told her it was you. I'm so sorry. I didn't realize how bad it would get for your family. And then you kept saying you didn't care what the aunties thought of you and I wanted to believe you, so I thought what was the harm in keeping it up? Ashok and I were getting engaged and I hoped it would all blow over."

Karishma crossed her arms, the wine sloshing up the sides of the glass as she moved. "I have always been there for you. Always. Why didn't you just tell me?"

"I know." Jyoti hung her head. "I should have. I meant to. I just never found the courage because the more time passed, the more I could see that it was having a bigger effect than I had anticipated, and then it felt too late..."

Jyoti knew her mom had run out and told the other Aunties the lies Jyoti had fed her and it was too easy for them to gobble them up given the biases they already had against Karishma.

"Hurting me is one thing," Karishma said. "But my mom—" her voice broke on the word. "She didn't deserve that." She met Nalini's eyes. "You were such good friends. And for you to let her be excluded from the group that way... You know how hard it was for all of you to find a community when you immigrated. Casting someone aside was so unfair."

Jyoti could see her mom filing back through the things she would have said and done at the time. "I thought I was protecting Jyoti." Nalini looked stricken. "I'm sorry, Karishma. You've been a good friend to my daughter, and I've treated you so poorly."

Karishma's jaw was still tense, and she looked directly at Jyoti. "And you've kept this from me for years. You threw me and my family under the bus and never had the guts to tell me.

And you never tried to fix it even when you saw what it did to my mother."

"You're right," Jyoti said. "It's why I've been so ashamed all these years. What can I do? I can send a group text to Sasti Masti right now letting them know the truth."

"You can't fix the last eighteen years with a text." Karishma turned and stormed out of the kitchen.

Jyoti and her mom were quiet as they cleaned and then loaded their cooking supplies into the bags they came with. The two glanced around to make sure the kitchen was exactly as they had found it before stepping outside into the cool night air. The stars shone above and an owl hooted in the distance. They saw the guests with their full bellies, eyes glistening from the wine, and knew they had served a good meal. But after what just happened, especially since none of this would have been possible without her best friend, Jyoti couldn't bask in the glow of her success. Ben met Jyoti and Nalini near the car and informed them that Enzo had come to pick up Karishma and Mae. His demeanor suggested he knew something was going on but was too polite to say anything more.

As they sat in the car, Jyoti looked solemnly out the window. "Thank you for your help today."

"There's no *thank you* with family," Nalini said, as she always did.

They drove the half hour into Florence in silence.

When they arrived, the door to Karishma's bedroom was closed and the lights were off. Jyoti pressed her ear against the door, but did not hear any sound. The two-bedroom apartment felt very small housing three people who were at odds with each other. Her mom settled into the bed, but Jyoti could not be in that close proximity after the events that had unfolded earlier. Disappointment radiated from Nalini, and she didn't want to be there to feel that energy. She took a blanket and curled up on the sofa, unable to sleep.

Moving quietly through the apartment, with only the moonlight coming through the living room windows and the light from her phone, Jyoti put on her shoes and went for a walk. It was well after midnight and the streets were not that crowded now that the bars were closed. The occasional group of young adults passed by speaking loudly, but for the most part she could enjoy her solitude. One of the things she loved about Florence was that it felt safe for her to walk alone at night. She'd never have done that in New York at this hour, and this was part of the charm of a city this size. There was no constant calling of sirens, whirring from exhaust fans, and rumbling from underground transport, so Jyoti could think without distraction.

The Ponte Vecchio was deserted as she began to cross it. The jewelry shops nestled against both sides of it were locked and boarded, and the river below glistened in the moonlight. During the day, the bridge was packed with tourists shopping for that signature piece of jewelry. She could hardly believe that she had the opportunity to be in this iconic place with no one else. She leaned against the middle of the bridge past the jewelers, in a spot that was normally clamoring with people taking selfies with the Arno River and classic Florentine architecture as a backdrop. She closed her eyes and thought about the history of this place and how many lifetimes this bridge had seen. Wars and peace. Plagues and famine. Countless commodities exchanged. Foot traffic from every nation on the globe. And now Jyoti had it all to herself to think about how her one small life had led her here, and where she should go next.

She'd never seen Karishma so hurt, and for the more than thirty-five years that they'd known each other, they'd never had a conflict of this magnitude. Jyoti chastised herself for throwing Karishma under the bus all those years ago, and even more so for staying silent when Karishma and her family were punished for her own actions. She had allowed herself to believe that her best friend was unfazed by the judgment, but Jyoti knew better. Karishma was resilient, but it didn't mean she was immune to wanting approval. And the worst of it was that their mothers had drifted apart during that time without Karishma's mom knowing what had happened to cause the distance. Karishma's family had found their own niche of other Gujarati immigrant families after the freeze, but they deserved to know the hand Jyoti had played in that fate, which would have felt monumental at the time.

Then there was Ashok and her own family. She thought about how easily she could step back into the old life that she had craved for so long. There would be some finagling of the gossip circles around it, but she knew in time that would subside because she'd be doing something that their community found familiar: living with her Indian husband and potentially raising a child with him while working in their small restaurant business. If she continued on the path she was on, one similar to Karishma's, then she would stay on the outside of their community circle. Jyoti wasn't sure that she wanted to be alone forever or never marry again. It was hard to fathom choosing a table for one for the rest of her life. But as she thought back on her marriage with Ashok, she knew it hadn't ended solely because of the lack of children.

Ashok had been raised with very traditional values and had certain beliefs about the role of women and men in society and within his home. The truth was that he had never matured and become independent enough to disobey the wishes of his mother, and she would be the one who ruled their lives—even if indirectly. Knowing that, Jyoti couldn't picture him ever agreeing to a life without children, and her priorities had now shifted. She'd had enough time to reflect and conclude that she'd only wanted children because it was what Ashok and their families had convinced her was expected of a good Indian girl.

Karishma, Ben, Enzo, and Mae had great child-free lives, and she found herself gravitating toward that for her future. If she didn't give herself permission to live that way without feeling like a failure, then no one else would either.

After a lifetime spent trying to please others, it was time for her to put her own desires first, and that started with learning what they were. She wanted to continue being a chef. She wanted to serve more meals like the one she had made tonight. She wanted to explore things that were yet unknown to her. She was excited for the possibility of what could come if the only person she had to answer to was herself. She could move halfway across the world, or stay put. She could continue with her career or change directions entirely. She had freedom and choice that she knew motherhood would not provide. And suddenly, she felt grateful. More grateful than she'd ever felt before that her attempts at fertility had failed. Having a child was for life and there were no do-overs. Her fingers grazed Karishma's labradorite prism necklace that still hung around her neck and wondered if her body had always known what she wanted even before her mind had.

On that bridge, with the calm silence of Florence around her and the moonlight glinting against the ripples in the Arno River, Jyoti finally gave herself permission to want a life that was different from the one that so many people whom she loved so deeply wanted for her. Their intentions were good, but she couldn't let good intentions force her into what she knew was wrong for her. She wanted to live in alignment with her soul. And that meant showing her true self to the people who mattered most.

THIRTY-ONE

When she got back to the apartment, she saw the light on in the guest room and gently pushed the door open.

"Why are you up?" Jyoti asked Nalini. "It's the middle of the night."

"I heard you leave. I wanted to make sure you came home okay."

Jyoti sat on the edge of the bed. There was a time not too long ago when she would have been annoyed that her mom was still treating her like a child and worrying if she got home okay. A time when she would have had an entire speech ready about how she was an adult and if something happened to her, what could her mom have done anyway? A time when she'd have been resentful that her mom thought she couldn't take care of herself or that Jyoti had the poor judgment to walk without considering whether it was safe. Tonight, though, realizing this was the only mother-daughter relationship she'd have during this lifetime, she appreciated the sentiment from which it came: unconditional maternal love.

"I needed some air and the city is so quiet at night. It's nice to walk when it feels like I'm the only one in it."

"I wish I'd known the truth about Karishma all those years ago," Nalini said.

Jyoti could hear her mother's guilt.

Nalini continued. "We were all so sure that Karishma was a bad influence and putting these thoughts into our children's heads about dating and drinking. So, we tried to protect you. We didn't want you to lose your ancestral bonds."

"I know, but her family wasn't treated fairly, and I was a big part of that. I'm not sure how I can make that up to her and her mom. I was a coward and I wish I'd been stronger." Jyoti traced her finger along the seams of the thin bedspread.

"I was also quick to believe you. I didn't question for even a moment that Karishma was the one at fault. We expected her to be drunk and careless. We all saw how independent she was. It was our biggest fear that our daughters would end up too *American* like her."

"Why was that so scary for you?"

Nalini pulled her knees to her chest and hugged her arms around them. "We gave up so much to come to America, and the values were so different once we arrived. Maintaining our culture was the only way we knew how to make sure you kids were on the right path. We had to make adjustments along the way from what we thought was right. Chaya marrying someone like Isaac wasn't in our plans. Tanvi not being married at all by this age wasn't either. Your divorce. Nothing worked out the way it was 'supposed' to. My fear was looking at you girls and not being able to recognize where you came from. For me, that would have been my biggest failure."

"But why is who we marry or end up with such a big part of our identity for you?"

Nalini shrugged. "It was what we knew. This love that you see in the movies in America wasn't part of our decision when marrying, and we have seen how fickle it can be. We understood marriage was to build wealth and family, so that the future generations could continue down the same path and our whole family line would grow and become more prosperous over time. It was our duty to the ancestors and none of us thought about doing anything else."

Jyoti stared out the window at the moonlight shining on the cobbles in the empty Piazza Santo Spirito, absorbing her mother's words. She knew this was one of the costs of immigration: that the next generation might not carry the same values as the one that had made so many sacrifices.

Turning back to her mom, she said, "Life doesn't always work out as we plan. I never expected to be divorced either. But I have spent most of my life living for you and for Ashok and his parents—I know you may not see it that way because things aren't exactly as you want them—but the reality is that I tried to give you everything. I just couldn't." Jyoti's voice caught and even she was surprised by the surge of emotion coursing through her. "I couldn't have a baby despite trying to force one out of my body every way possible."

Tears slid down her cheeks and her mom put her arms around her.

When Jyoti could speak again, she said, "I think the reason I couldn't have a baby is because I wasn't meant to. I think my body was saving me from a life that wasn't what I wanted. I let Ashok, and his parents, and even you convince me that my sole purpose in life was to have a child even though I knew I wanted to keep building my career at Taste of Ginger. And then when there were problems, everyone was so invested and I couldn't stand the disappointment all around me, so it became this failure that needed to be overcome. Whenever I mentioned to any of you that I didn't want to go forward with it, or that my body was done, everyone kept insisting that I had to keep trying. That the next time would be different."

"I'm so sorry, beta." Nalini's eyes were glistening. "I just wanted you to be happy and I thought a baby was what you wanted."

"I know. I'm finally realizing the difference between what I want and what everyone else wanted for me." Jyoti sniffled. "Mom, I was so alone when I was going through fertility problems. I felt like I had done something wrong and that was why this was happening to me."

"Oh, beta." Her mom pulled Jyoti to her. "You didn't do anything wrong. These things happen."

"I know, and now I'm glad it did. I don't want to have a young child right now. I don't want to be tied to Ashok for life. I don't want to be a stay-at-home mom. I want to build my chef career and introduce the world to our food. I know you thought a baby was the way to carry on our culture, but for me our culture has always been in our food. That is what reminds me of home, and I love being able to share that part of our heritage with other people. Legacies don't have to be children. There are other ways to leave a mark on the world for future generations."

"So, you won't go back to Ashok?"

Jyoti leaned back to face Nalini and shook her head. "He would want to go back to the way things were, and I don't want that. I don't think he'll ever be happy without carrying on the bloodline, and I don't want kids anymore. He will do exactly what he did during our entire marriage: he'll say he understands how I feel and then try to belittle me until he gets what he wants. It's who he is. It's the relationship he saw between his own parents so he doesn't know anything different. And he hasn't done the work he would need to in order to change that. I doubt he even wants to. In fact, I don't think he has the capacity to truly understand what was wrong with the way he treated me."

"I wish I had known you felt that way," Nalini said.

"Me too. I wish I'd been brave enough to say it before. Until I started sharing personal stories on social media, I didn't realize how many people felt the same way I did. I thought I was alone. And that there was something wrong with me that I'd even entertained the idea that I didn't want kids. What kind of woman feels that way? But then I met more people who have full, rich lives outside of marriage and kids and started feeling that was more aligned with the life I wanted. I started feeling happy again after having been depressed for the whole decade I spent trying to get pregnant."

Nalini's eyes brimmed with tears. "I should have seen how much you were hurting and stopped pushing."

"It's okay. Everything that I did or didn't do led me here. And I know it's hard for you to imagine my life without someone taking care of me, but people do it. Look at what Karishma has built here. She has friends who are like family and they help each other out. I think it's better to create a community of support rather than have one man who I'm fully dependent on for the rest of my life." She looked at her mom. "That's the one thing I always appreciated about you and Sasti Masti. When you immigrated, you found a community. I want to have that, too, even if mine doesn't look like yours."

Nalini nodded. "Beta, whatever you do is between you and Bhagwan. But I do understand some parts of how you are feeling."

She looked wistful, and Jyoti collected herself while her mom took the time to speak again.

"When I saw you cooking the dinner, I was so proud of you. I never knew you could cook like that. I see the difference between us now. You are a chef, but I was always just a cook."

"Don't say that, Mom. I learned everything from you. Without that, I would never have been able to do this."

Nalini nodded. "I loved teaching you. I loved teaching anyone." She now gazed off into the distance through the large window in the room.

Jyoti could see that her mom was having a moment and waited for her to feel ready to speak again.

"When I was in India, I had wanted to run a cooking school," Nalini said, turning back to face Jyoti. "But it wasn't sensible for women to have big careers back then, and certainly not ones that came before duties in the home. I had always loved cooking and I was good at it, but my parents thought it was servant work. So, I opened a small school in secret and started teaching classes, showing people how to make Gujarati classics like khandvi, handvo, khaman. I had some interesting takes on that food, interesting for that time anyway. Like green khaman with curry leaf paste or deep pink idli made with beetroot. Nothing as fancy as the things you made tonight. None of this fussy bussy with wiping the spots on the plates before people eat or adding chutney with a squeeze bottle."

Jyoti let out a chuckle through her tears. "I can't believe I never knew this."

"I'd been running the school out of the kitchen of my friend's family's restaurant. The restaurant was only open for dinner so she would sneak me and the guests in during the day while it was empty. Then she and I would race to put everything back the way it was so no one would know." Nalini laughed at the memory. "We knew so little about cleaning because we'd never had to do it before then, but we knew we could not involve the servants in the scheme. It had been fun being sneaky." Her face clouded. "But then, one day, we got caught. It was only a matter of time. Gossip travels like leaves rustling in the wind. Someone had noticed the kitchen lights on during the day and said something to my friend's father who came to investigate and found us in the middle of a class." She shook her head. "My parents were so ashamed when Uncle told them what we had been up to. I'd told them I was volunteering at an orphanage during the day, and they were mortified that I'd chosen servant work over humanitarian work."

Jyoti listened intently to her mother's story.

"My mother came to me that night and asked if I ever wanted

to be married and have a family. I told her of course I did. She explained the intricacies of the marriage market and said that if their circle learned what I'd been doing, then my marriageability would go down significantly. People were looking for well-behaved wives for their sons and my actions fell outside of that. She urged me to cook at home, as those skills were considered very desirable in a match. When faced with the choice of having a business or having a family, it was no choice for me. So, I stopped." She met Jyoti's eyes. "And I didn't regret it, because I had you three girls and I knew that was my purpose in life: to be a good mother. For so many years, I prayed to Bhagwan, expressing my gratitude for my parents leading me down the right path."

"And that's why you wanted that for me too," Jyoti said.

She nodded. "A parent's job is to make sure their kids don't make the same mistakes. When you first started trying for a baby, you were still working and those miscarriages felt like they were a response to you not prioritizing the right things. I'd thought that if you stopped, it would be better for you and your body. And I could see that Ashok was losing patience and I didn't want you to end up alone. That's why I was so against you continuing."

"He was losing patience. But that had more to do with him than me. Ashok was used to getting everything his way because that's how his parents pandered to him his whole life." She took her mom's hands in her own. "But I never realized you wanted to do anything outside of the home. Why couldn't you have started something after you moved to America? You were already married by then. Did you ever talk to Dad about that?"

"No, beta. Moving to America is not like moving from New Jersey to Manhattan. Things were hard and we had so many obstacles to overcome. We needed to survive from one day to the next and passions had no place in our lives. Assimilating into a new culture requires more focus, attention, and energy than anything else you do in this world. Raising children is difficult no matter where you come from, but raising them in a society that is completely foreign to the one I grew up in changed everything. We didn't have any family to lean on. Our Gujarati friends in America were going through the same struggle, so we couldn't burden them. Your father and I were alone to navigate how to give you girls a good life, so there was no room for anything else." She smiled wistfully at her daughter. "And I think we did okay in the end."

"You did better than okay. Look at us. We may not have the lives you thought we would, but we are smart, healthy, and relatively well-adjusted, all things considered." Jyoti managed a small laugh. "We are happy more often than we are not, and that's saying a lot."

Nalini's lips curled into a half smile. "No one can be happy all the time, I guess."

"I think they wouldn't be living if they were. It's inevitable that every risk we take in life won't pay off like we hope it will. I was devastated when my marriage ended. But after this time in Italy, I see clearly that I'm meant to be on a different path than the one I'd always expected for myself."

"Is there something I did to make you feel that way?"

"You were a great mom," Jyoti said. "I saw how much you gave up and sacrificed even before I knew you had dreams you had to leave behind. Maybe it's selfish, or just honest, but I'm not sure that at this stage of my life—when I'm finally figuring out who I am and what I want—that I'd want to put that all aside to be who someone else needs me to be. I've spent my entire life doing some version of that even *without* kids, and I want to live the way I want to for once."

Nalini nodded. "I can understand that. Children change everything and there's really no time for yourself. For me, that felt right. But I can see for you maybe it is different."

"But I want you to really think about the rest of your life

too. And if that means that you want to leave Dad and live on your own, then I'll support you in that. But I don't think our situations are the same. You and Dad fell into traditional roles because you *both* allowed that to happen. My marriage was different. I kept trying to convince Ashok to see me for who I was during the marriage. And whenever my views differed from his, he would gaslight me into thinking something was wrong with me. It took coming here to remind me of my confidence and begin to build it again. You and Dad aren't like that. I've seen you come together and work as a team, especially when it came to us kids. But I think that's the problem here. I think you've forgotten who you are without kids, and with Tanvi moving out, that must feel very lonely."

Nalini wiped away a tear. "I don't remember who that woman is who snuck into a restaurant to run a cooking school. The energy of the house has changed with Tanvi leaving. Even if I rarely saw her, I still needed to have meals cooked for her and do laundry and those things so they'd be ready when she needed them. Dharmesh and I spent over forty years making you girls our top priority. We lost ourselves in that process. And now—" her voice caught "—you don't need us anymore, so I really felt like I had to find something for myself."

"Oh, Mom. We still need you, but in different ways. Tanvi needs to learn to cook for herself and do her own laundry. She's going to be a disaster if she doesn't learn some basic skills. What we need are conversations like this. I needed to understand about your abandoned dreams. It's no wonder I love food and cooking so much…you passed that down to me. And now it's my turn to carry that dream forward for both of us."

Nalini sniffled. "What will Dharmesh and I do in that house alone? We hardly know each other. I thought that now that we've raised you girls, we did what we needed to do together in life and can go our separate ways for whatever years we have left."

Jyoti leaned over to grab a tissue from the box on the small desk near the window and handed it to her mother. "I think you need to learn who you are before you can expect Dad to know what you want. That's been a big part of my journey too. You should tell him how you are feeling and see what he says rather than assume he won't support you. If you still want to do something cooking related, you could still do that. We could even think about doing something together."

Nalini sat straighter at the suggestion, her eyes filled with hope. "Your father will likely be too angry to talk to me after this."

"You might be surprised," Jyoti said. "He's going to run out of that frozen food soon and nothing is more motivating than an empty stomach."

They both laughed.

"The world is different now," Jyoti said. "You don't have to choose between family and cooking like you did before. You just need to figure out what you want and communicate it. We all love you and want you to be happy. Let us help you after you spent your life helping us."

"It's so hard to take help from your children," she said. "It's supposed to be us helping you."

"There comes a point in every adult child's life when they need to start parenting the parents. You missed that period because you lived most of your life with your parents half a world away but trust me on this."

Her mom eyed her suspiciously, but the air around them was light. They'd never had such an honest and vulnerable conversation before and Jyoti realized how much they'd both needed it. She hoped this would be the start of many opportunities for them to release their past experiences and expectations and get to know each other as women, rather than parent and child. That was the next step in their evolution, and she would do everything she could to help them get there.

THIRTY-TWO

Jyoti waited at the dining table with a cup of chaa until Karishma emerged late the next morning. When she did, Jyoti leapt to pour her a mug as well. She reluctantly took it and sat stiffly across from Jyoti.

"I'm so sorry," Jyoti said. "I should have said something sooner. Actually, I should never have lied in the first place. I was young and still so scared of what my parents and Sasti Masti would think of me. I was being selfish trying to protect the reputation of the guy I wanted to marry without thinking about how my lies would affect you."

"Things make so much more sense now. I had always been the black sheep amongst that circle. I knew that, but then things were ratcheted up a notch and I never understood why. I know I said these things didn't bother me, and maybe I was okay, but I hated how it affected my mom. She's the one who didn't deserve it. That Sasti Masti group meant a lot to her and then one day she was on the outside of it."

Jyoti hung her head. "I know. I'll do whatever I can to help

Indira Auntie. I know my mom will too. Everything just spun out of control so quickly. I convinced myself that you didn't care."

"That's not really a great excuse," Karishma said. "Especially when you could see what was happening. I remember talking to you about how weird it all was and you just let me go on and on without saying you knew why."

Jyoti's eyes glistened. "I'm so sorry. You're right. I was a coward and don't deserve your friendship."

"I'd always thought we were each other's ride or die. It's humiliating to know that wasn't true." Karishma stood from the table. "I need to take some time. I'm going to Enzo's."

Jyoti watched Karishma walk out the door. In the last day, she'd reconnected with her mother only to lose her best friend in the process.

Jyoti immediately went to find her mom.

"You cannot blame her, beta," Nalini said. "And I know it's hard, but you cannot blame yourself either. You shouldn't have done that. There's no question that you should never lie like that. But I also shouldn't have taken it so badly. I should have trusted that you would make your own good decisions whether you were friends with her or not."

"I know. I just wanted you to like Ashok, and maybe you wouldn't have even cared about it if I'd told the truth."

Nalini shook her head. "You were right. We would have cared. Enough to stop the engagement—" she bobbed her head back and forth "—who knows about that? But family was everything and Tanvi had been disappointed not to see you there, so we were too."

"So was I. It was a bad mistake that I can't take back. But I will do everything I can to fix it now. It's never too late to hold myself accountable. I need to call Indira Auntie."

Her mom looked at her watch. "We both owe her an apology. And thankfully she is a morning person."

★★★

When Indira Auntie's beaming face filled the screen, Jyoti felt her hands go clammy.

"Hi, Auntie. I'm not sure if Karishma told you, but—"

"Is everything okay, beta? Karishma is fine?" Indira Auntie asked.

"Oh, yes, Auntie. I didn't mean to worry you. We are all fine."

It was clear Karishma hadn't said anything to her mom yet. Even in anger, Karishma was loyal, which only made Jyoti's heart sink lower.

"I'm calling because I need to tell you something I did a long time ago," Jyoti said, her tone serious.

Indira Auntie's expression grew more somber to match Jyoti's mood. She listened intently as Jyoti explained what had happened all those years ago, apologizing profusely along the way. After Jyoti had finished, she waited for Indira Auntie to speak.

There was a long silence. "It's good to have some answers."

"Do you think you can forgive me?" Jyoti asked. "I know a lot of years have been lost."

"Beta, I'm seventy-four. I have no time to hold on to hate. I'm glad to know now, and I wish I had known then, but the truth is that Bhagwan has a plan for us always. We had a difficult two years when we didn't know what was going on. Losing anyone is hard, but losing community when you are alone in a strange land is especially difficult. But then we found a new group outside of Sasti Masti. And, to be honest, I felt less pressure in that group. For me, for Karishma, and so maybe it was all for the best."

Jyoti marveled at the grace with which Auntie was responding to her. She wondered if it was the natural path of age that forgiveness came more easily. Jyoti saw her mom peek her head out of the bedroom and turned back to the screen.

"There is someone else here who would like to speak to you, if that's okay."

Indira Auntie nodded and Jyoti made space for her mom to join.

"Hi, Indira," Nalini said. "It's been a long time."

She nodded. "Yes, Nalini. It has been. But I hope you are well."

Nalini shrugged. "When Jyoti told me what she did, I had to look at my own actions too. I'm very sorry for how I behaved, Indira. It was wrong of me."

Indira Auntie nodded again, more slowly this time. "I know. But we were young then, and things change."

"Not that young, bhen. We were older than the girls are now, so it's hard to find excuses for my actions." Nalini tucked her hair behind her ear. "I'm happy you found a better community. I think you are right that Sasti Masti kept us in the same gossip circle for so many years of our lives. Maybe that's what happens when we aren't fulfilled as women. Je hoy te, I'm glad your family found a better group and you are happy."

"Oh yaar, as I said to Jyoti, don't be so hard on yourself. We all make mistakes, but we all find our path. It's all destiny, right? None of it is up to us."

"Hah, bhen. But we are never too old to make an apology even if it's eighteen years overdue. I've had the chance to see Karishma and Jyoti together here in Florence, and you raised a daughter that you should be very proud of. In fact—" she gave Jyoti a glance "—I think there is a lot my Jyoti could still learn from her. I'm very glad that my own daughter disregarded my wishes and they have been close friends for all these years. It is rare to have a friendship like the one they have."

Indira Auntie smiled. "They have been a great gift to each other and whatever has happened or will happen with us has nothing to do with it."

"When I return to New Jersey," Nalini said, "I'd like if we can meet. Just the two of us. A lot of time has passed, but I hope we can start something new."

Indira Auntie brought her hand to her heart. "Bhen, you have my number. I will await your call."

Jyoti turned to her mom after they got off the phone with Indira Auntie. "I've never heard you apologize like that."

"Maybe some of these American customs are soaking into me. I think it's better to say sorry when it's needed, and in this case, it most certainly was." She put her hand on Jyoti's shoulder. "And, beta, I'm sorry for everything you went through alone. I should have been there. I'm your mother and it was my job to make sure you were okay."

Jyoti shook her head. "Thank you for saying that, but it's *my* job to make sure I'm okay, and I'm finally starting to see that. That means listening to myself and honoring what my body, mind, and spirit want. I hope you'll always be there to listen and maybe offer some sage advice here and there, but one of the things I did wrong before was assume that someone else—like Ashok—was responsible for my happiness. I won't make that mistake again."

"I suppose that is a lesson we all need to learn in life," Nalini said. "I fear I did the same with you girls and Dharmesh, and maybe that is why I'm having such a hard time now."

Jyoti put her arm around her mother's shoulder. "This is something we can work on improving together. Not as mother and daughter, but as woman to woman."

Karishma came back to the apartment and as soon as Jyoti heard her key slip into the lock, she bounded out of the bedroom like a puppy who had been alone all day.

"You called my mom," Karishma said matter-of-factly as she tossed her keys into the bowl.

"It was the right thing to do even if it was many years too late."

Karishma sank into a chair at her dining table.

Jyoti sat down next to her. "You didn't tell her what I'd done."

"Of course not. What would it change now? And no point in her hating you."

"I don't deserve you."

"You really don't." Karishma folded her arms across her chest, but in a playful way. They would be okay.

Karishma's primary pain had been over someone hurting her mother. That was the way it always felt when parents were involved. Jyoti suspected Indira Auntie's forgiveness was what Karishma needed to give hers too.

"I'll do whatever I can to make this up to you and your entire family. Really. I can go to the next Sasti Masti event and explain it all, and—"

Karishma held up her hands. "Please don't."

Jyoti cast her gaze downward. "I know this doesn't make it okay, but you were always so polished and self-assured that I thought you didn't care and would bounce back in no time."

"I wanted everyone to think that." Karishma sighed. "I don't know. Maybe this was always how it was going to turn out. People were already talking about me before that, and I was always going to live the life I'm living right now, so I was going to be on the outside eventually. Maybe what you did just sped up the inevitable."

Jyoti understood her friend's sentiment and while she might be right, she hated that she'd had any role in the outcome. "I'm going to make sure everyone knows what really happened. Maybe it's too late to change anyone's mind, but at least we are better off living in truth." She looked at her best friend, her full heart on display. "I'm so sorry, Karishma. You've been nothing but loyal and supportive to me and I haven't always returned that. I was so caught up in what other people thought of me that I let them think the worst of you. I'll never let that happen again. They should be lucky if their kids grow up to have even half the integrity that you have. Any parent should be proud to have a daughter who carries herself with pride and is leaving such an important mark on the world by championing our culture's representation. You're preserving our heritage in a way that no marriage or kids would have."

Karishma smiled. "Thanks, Jyo. That means a lot. It's not easy fighting for future generations. I'm not even going to have kids that are part of them, but I can't stop this feeling of wanting the world to be a bit better when I leave it."

"It will be," Nalini said, emerging from the bedroom. "Even if you don't have kids, Chaya and so many others do, and when their parents take them to a library, they will see characters like them on the shelves. I never thought about the fact that you girls didn't have that. When we left India, we didn't think about what it would be like for our kids to not see themselves in books and media."

Karishma's eyes glistened as if she'd received praise from her own mother. "Thanks, Auntie."

"I'm sorry, too, beta," Nalini said, giving Karishma a hug. "I judged you harshly, and it wasn't fair. Then I took it out on your parents, who were such a big part of my life for so many years. I see how much you have been there for Jyoti through all her hard times and rather than commend you for it, I condemned you."

"It's okay, Auntie. What's done is done. Let's find a path forward."

Nalini broke their embrace and took Karishma's hand in hers. "Thank you for being family to my Jyoti when I wasn't."

Karishma smiled. "She's been there for me too—outside of this little lapse in judgment."

Nalini's free hand grabbed Jyoti's. "You two always stay by each other. No matter what happens or what any of the rest of us say or do, you are each other's family. And nothing should ever change that."

★★★

Karishma and Nalini went to pick up some pastries for Jyoti and Nalini's flight back to New Jersey. They needed an in-person family meeting, maybe the most important one of their lives. Ben and the Fattorios had been understanding of her need to return home early and she'd promised to send them some samosa spice mix and a recipe card. As her best friend and mom giggled about something as they walked out the door, she was overjoyed by their newfound closeness. She'd never seen them look forward to spending time together and she hoped this was the start of a new chapter for them as well.

Even though she was alone in the apartment, she closed the door to the bedroom to make her video call to Ashok. He smiled at her when he answered and she knew he expected her to acquiesce and agree to what he wanted. That had been the pattern of their entire relationship. He'd always gotten what he wanted by acting this way so he had no reason to change. She finally understood that she shared the blame in that.

"Did you think about what I said?" he asked, the grin on his face awaiting good news.

"I did. Quite a bit."

"And...?"

"I can't go back to the life we had," Jyoti said. "Or to you."

His forehead furrowed.

"I thought about how I'd said I wasn't ready for kids, and you insisted. And then how I said I wanted to keep working, and you said that was the reason the pregnancies weren't taking hold. And then how my body was depleted, bruised, and battered from all the attempts, and you wouldn't even consider adoption or surrogacy. And then after I finally found the courage to assert myself after a decade of giving in to you, you decided children were more important to you than I was."

He looked as if he'd been slapped. "But we both wanted kids. I was just doing what we needed to get us there."

"No, that's what I'm realizing. I didn't want kids when we started trying. You wanted them on your timeline and you manipulated me into doing everything the way you wanted. You and our parents and community and everyone else convinced me that I was a failure if I didn't have kids. All I wanted to do was go back to working at Taste of Ginger. That's when I felt alive, and you took that from me. You gaslit me, and you couldn't see how much damage it was doing. I felt so utterly alone during most of our marriage because I spent so much of it trying to please you. There was no energy left to think about myself."

Jyoti took satisfaction in the changing expressions on Ashok's face as he processed her speaking up for herself for the first time since they met.

"Don't make me out to be the bad guy. *We* decided to have kids. You were part of that decision. And then things got hard. No one is denying that. But it wasn't my fault it was that hard for you to conceive."

Jyoti managed a wry smile. "Not conceiving is the best thing that happened to me. It got me away from a life that would have been just like our parents'. We get to go our separate ways now, not tethered to each other at all. I'm so grateful that my body protected me until I was ready to see the life I was meant to have."

"And what kind of life is that?" Ashok asked. "One with no husband, no kids, and no job? How is that satisfying?"

"That proves my point. You think there's only one way to live. And that's fine. You can go live that way and have your parents find a third wife for you. It just won't be me."

"But we could do things differently. We don't have to try for a baby right away. If we are using a surrogate, then we have time."

"I don't want a baby. Not now, and probably not ever. I want to cook for others and find the people who make me feel like I'm home," Jyoti said.

"You'd be able to cook if you come back to Taste of Ginger and we restore it to what it was when we ran it together. Then once we're settled again, we can talk about kids."

Jyoti smiled to herself as she realized he would never understand. She surprised herself by saying, "I don't want Taste of Ginger back. It's your family's restaurant, no matter how much work I put into making it something else. You can do whatever you want with it. I'm going to start something that's my own. Or maybe even with my mom. But it has to be something that reflects who I am today."

She felt a spark inside her as she said the words, because she knew they were true. She was going to find her culinary place in this world, and she wanted to focus on building a new future rather than trying to resurrect the past. She didn't know if her mom would want to excavate her long-buried dream, but Jyoti was excited at the thought of them teaming up in the kitchen, like they had at the Fattorios' dinner.

"You're making a huge mistake," Ashok said, anger flashing across his face. "How could you possibly start over now, at this age?"

"That's another place where we disagree. How could I not? Haven't I wasted enough years living my life for other people?"

Ashok shook his head as though he could hardly recognize the person he was talking to, and that delighted Jyoti. She wanted to be this new version of herself and close the chapter on him completely.

"I hope you find what you're looking for, Ashok. I really do. I know I will. And if you do meet that third woman willing to marry you, then I hope you listen to her instead of just projecting your wants onto her. Every woman deserves that from her husband."

Her pulse was racing and her breathing was shallow when

she ended the call. She'd never stood up to Ashok before. When he told her he was leaving her, she'd been so depleted and numb that she absorbed the news in silent defeat. She didn't fight for him to stay or to notice what he had done and how unfair it had been. She simply let him go and moved back into her childhood home for her mom to take care of her for a month. But now, she was ready to fight for her life. Ready to take care of herself. And ready to call out anyone who stood in her way.

THIRTY-THREE

A Year Later

Jyoti felt the heat of the lights on her skin and the brightness made spots appear before her eyes when she looked directly at them. She could hardly believe this was happening and was so nervous. She wouldn't have been here if not for Karishma and Mae, so she had to deliver a stellar performance no matter what. They had believed in her before she'd learned to believe in herself. Ranting about her feelings on TikTok had been one thing while she was finding her way in Florence, but having her musings professionally filmed for others to see was something else entirely. She'd had people do her hair and makeup and select an outfit for her. That part had been a relief, because she was far from a fashionista. She'd given them a list of ingredients and equipment, and, as if by magic, it all rested on the counter before her now, including the herbs in pots that she'd insisted on rather than precut containers. Fresh herbs were something she'd promised to always have on hand after her time in Italy.

She lifted the handle on the sink to see if water would actually come out and was delighted to see that it did. She didn't know why that surprised her because water was essential to cooking. As soon as she closed it, an aide with a headset had swooped in with a towel and wiped away the droplets in the basin. She suspected they could tell that she was new to this and were giving her some leeway.

Out of the corner of her eye, she saw her mom smiling at her encouragingly. Her dad was on Nalini's left and Karishma was on her right. Her parents had just returned from their trip to Singapore and had raved about the food they'd eaten and the beautiful kaleidoscope of lights on the Supertrees at Gardens by the Bay, but both said there was nowhere in the world they would rather be than at the taping of her pilot. She could hardly believe that so much had changed in each and every one of their lives compared to where they'd been a year ago.

She'd been stunned when Karishma had stopped by to give her the news four months earlier. Since returning from Italy, she'd been doing some private cheffing but nothing consistent that felt like it could have been a career. She knew she had to start somewhere, so she didn't mind. Occasionally, her mom had helped her with a client or planning a menu. They'd really enjoyed their time in the kitchen together just as they had when Jyoti was a teenager learning to cook. Her mom even wanted to learn some of her "fancy bancy cooking," and conceded that chutneys dolloped onto the plates with squeeze bottles did make them look more appetizing. She had joined her on a TikTok Live while they taught the audience how to make khandvi, something Nalini had always been better at than Jyoti. They had received such a warm reception from her followers, that they did a second Live where they made samosas. That video had been her most popular and countless requests for the spice mixes had rolled in. Together, she and her mom packaged it up and began selling it through Jyoti's TikTok account. It had been fun to work together on that. She'd never thought about selling a product, but given the interest so far, it seemed like it could become a bigger business someday. Even if it didn't, she was starting to get offers for paid promotions on TikTok and had never dreamed that she could earn money doing what she had been doing for free in Florence. She loved that people were excited about and interested in the flavors that were her home.

Jyoti hadn't even known Karishma was in town until she had shown up at her apartment with a chilled bottle of champagne in hand that Ben had picked out. *The good stuff that is properly from Reims*, his note said.

"How much do you love me?" she asked Jyoti, spinning her around in a big hug.

Jyoti felt confused as she twirled. "A lot, but what are you doing here?"

"Promise me you'll remember me when you're famous," Karishma said, holding Jyoti at arm's length so they could see each other's faces.

"Care to tell me what is going on?"

"I might have done something over the summer while you were visiting..." Karishma looked mischievous.

"Out with it."

"I knew you were struggling a bit when you arrived and needed to get your cooking chops back. And the whole thing with Ashok and Taste of Ginger...it seemed like a lot could go wrong with that situation—"

"What did you do?" Jyoti asked.

"I reached out to some colleagues about pitching a cookbook that focused on how you weave Indian flavors into other cuisines, stuff like the Fattorio dinner you did, and I finally heard back."

Jyoti's eyes widened as she looked at her friend.

"There's a new imprint that is launching cookbooks and

pairing them with professionally produced cooking videos on their YouTube channel. I submitted a proposal for you."

"A proposal for what?" Jyoti asked.

"For the cookbook and YouTube series, silly. Keep up," Karishma said. "They loved it, and they want you to film a test pilot for it."

"What did you submit?"

"I had Mae take pictures of your food all summer, and then I took pictures of your recipes in your notebook so I could type them out later. Jyo, the world is finally ready to see your food and hear your stories."

Jyoti had never thought her TikTok videos and summer recipes could have led to a culinary path like the one she was on now. She'd assumed she'd go back to New York and find a small space and do the restaurant life again, but this was better. This gave her more freedom and more exposure to do what she most wanted: to share Indian flavors with a wide audience. To let them find the same comfort in them that she always had.

The publisher had been excited about her sharing stories about her culture, childhood, and life experiences, just as she had been doing on TikTok while she cooked. It was a dream come true and she could not believe that it was happening to her and this could be a real job. So much in her life had to go sideways from what she had expected and planned for her to get to this moment. Was it all part of some larger plan? Who was she to say? She only knew that she was finally happy with where life had brought her and she had needed every twist and turn in the road to reach this destination. She might not ultimately get her own cooking series, or her book might tank, but maybe she *would* get it and maybe the book *would* fly off the shelves. Since her time in Italy, she was more focused on possibility than probability.

She closed her eyes, allowing the moment to sink in. She

touched the Asha Patel Designs labradorite prism necklace that she, too, now wore every day. She let the protective energy flow through her and took a few box breaths. Her skin felt warm under the heat from the lights and she tuned out the din around her as the production crew moved about. She focused on the red blinking light on the camera directly across from her.

"Lights, camera, action!" the director called out. A clapboard snapped shut and a hush fell around them.

Jyoti began to share her story. "I learned everything I know about cooking from my mom, and last summer, I had the opportunity to learn who she is as a woman and not just a parent. We'd had some tough times leading up to this, but then she had the chance to see me cook a meal from my soul in the vineyards of Tuscany, and this first recipe I'm going to share with you is from that dinner. I hope more than anything that every child gets to learn who their parents are as people, and not just as parents. Learning my mom's story allowed me to appreciate the sacrifices she'd made and the roads she didn't travel because of my sisters and me. It is because of my parents' journeys that I am here today, pursuing my passion, which is bringing Gujarati flavors from my heart to your homes."

Jyoti smiled as she dropped curry leaves, dried red chili, cumin, and mustard seeds into the heated oil for the vaghar. They sizzled and popped as the camera zoomed in to catch the action.

★★★★★

ACKNOWLEDGMENTS

I will forever look back upon this book as my miracle book, because every word of this was written during the most personally traumatic year of my life. I wrote this novel while recovering from serious medical injuries that I incurred during the summer of 2022, and during the many months that I spent bedridden and in the worst pain of my life, Jyoti's story and her adventures in Italy allowed me a slight reprieve from my situation. For any readers who are going through hard times, I hope it provides you with that same escape. I wanted nothing more than to be gallivanting around Italy, creating new recipes, eating delicious meals, meeting new friends, and basking in the azure waters of the Amalfi Coast. Those moments when I could escape to Italy with Jyoti felt like salvation and helped me heal. So, given the condition I was in, when I look back on the year, I can hardly believe that I was able to write a book at all. Seeing this book on shelves will always remind me of what I've overcome.

First and foremost, this book is possible because of my parents. Unlike the families I write about, my relationship with my parents has always been very open, honest, and emotionally healthy. When I was injured halfway around the world in 2022 and got myself back to Los Angeles (through sheer adrenaline), my parents bought one-way tickets, without even knowing the extent of my injuries, to come and take care of me. None of us knew how long my recovery time would be, or that they would ultimately end up staying with me for four months before I could slowly manage to live on my own again. There is nothing more humbling than a self-sufficient adult becoming a child who needs her parents to take care of her again in her forties, but the grace, compassion, and empathy with which they embraced me will be what I carry with me for the rest of my life. Mom and Dad, I could not have written this book without you feeding me, driving me, applying medications, dealing with the annoying broken appliances, and making sure I always knew you were there. Thank you for always showing me the unconditional love that every child deserves.

I was also very fortunate to have a great medical team in place to help me recover, and I owe so much of my healing to Samantha Zarling. If all medical professionals were like you, the world would simply be a better place. I cannot thank you enough for your patience, intelligence, and kindness during such a difficult time in my life.

While my health was my top priority in 2022, my professional life was certainly second. I left my full-time entertainment lawyer career while I was recovering from my injuries to shift my focus to healing and writing. I am so grateful to my agent, Gordon Warnock of Fuse Literary, for believing in me and my work at a time when I really needed a win. Your editorial eye and business strategy are the stuff that authors dream of, and I know my career is in the right hands with you as my partner and advocate. You do not work alone, so I want to thank the entire team at Fuse who do so much behind the scenes, including making the best social media graphics.

This book would not be what it is today without the keen editorial eyes of Nicole Luongo of Park Row Books and Jennifer Lambert of HarperCollins Canada. Nothing has made this Canadian-born, American-raised author happier than seeing this novel launch in both of those territories. When I spoke with both of you about this book, your enthusiasm was infectious, and I could not think of a better duo to coax so much magic out of Jyoti's story. Thank you both for loving the setting, food, representation, and messaging that I hoped to convey. Behind these two outstanding women is a team of people who help turn words into an actual book that gets to readers, so I want to thank the entire Park Row and HarperCollins Canada teams for their dedication to making this book the best that it could be. I'm so grateful for the publicity efforts by Heather Connor, Sophie James, Kamille Carreras Pereira, Kali Luckhee, and Gareema Dhaliwal; marketing support from Randy Chan, Pamela Osti, Rachel Haller, Lindsey Reeder, Brianna Wodabek, Ciara Loader, Jaimie Nackan, and Neil Wahwha; and the eagle eyes of Tracy Wilson, Stephanie Van de Vooren, Bonnie Lo, Kimberley Conroy, Judy Brioux, and Natalie Meditsky. Designing covers is such an important job and I had such a great team designing both of mine. A huge thanks to Kathleen Oudit, Neethi, and Alan Jones for finding the right images to bring the essence of the story to life. I am a huge consumer of audiobooks and am honored to have Soneela Nankani give voice to my characters. Thank you for keeping up with the many accents I throw your way with my stories. I am honored to have such a stellar roster of people on my side.

My parents are not the only supportive family members in my life, and I am grateful to each of them for reading and championing this dream. My brother does anything he can to help promote my books, including spending a day making promo reels and trying to figure out how to stop books from flying off a spinning turntable. I also have to give a special shout-out to my cousin Kruti, who has become my official Gujarati-English transliteration expert. Thank you for patiently answering my questions about whether I should use "dal" or "daal."

Paulette Kennedy, we both had difficult years for different reasons, but I am grateful for the support and friendship you have provided through it all. It is happenstance that two girls from Missouri ended up in Los Angeles debuting books in the same year with the same publisher, but I'll always be grateful for the coincidences that brought us together and shared values that cemented our bond.

I had some challenges during the editing of this novel, and I'll be forever grateful to Mark Woods and Maggie Velasquez for meeting me in the Greek islands during the final push of my developmental edits and for getting my laptop charger back to me in true *Amazing Race* style. I literally would not have met my deadline without your help. I am also grateful to Maria Vandoulaki, the team at Parea on Paros, and the staff at Olea Bay Hotel on Milos for providing quiet, scenic places for me to write and be inspired, and for helping with the Laptop Charger Crisis.

The author community has been so supportive since I've embarked on this second career, and a special thanks goes to my fellow authors who are in the trenches and understand the journey: Namrata Patel, Lyn Liao Butler, Marjan Kamali, Jo Piazza, Sonali Dev, Saumya Dave, Jennifer Bardsley, Eden Appiah-Kubi, Elissa Grossell Dickey, Julie Buxbaum, Rochelle Weinstein, Kerry Lonsdale, Tif Marcelo, Phaedra Patrick, Jamie Varon, and Barbara O'Neal.

Tracy Russo, thank you for answering so many questions about Florence and Italian culture, letting me stay in your lovely guest room off Piazza Santo Spirito while I was researching this book, and always pointing me toward the best food in Florence. I'm glad our friendship can survive our differing views on truffle gnocchi. Thank you also for planning the most perfectly curated Praiano guide for me. I could never have imagined that trip would spark such a beautiful part of this book.

Research trips may be the best part of this job, and I must thank Gabi Lozano for traveling to Praiano and the Amalfi Coast with me. Writing those parts of the book made me feel like we were back in Hotel Tramonto d'Oro with that stunning view and spending our days with Frankie driving us around in his boat. I think we can both agree that there is something about the Tyrrhenian Sea that is deeply healing. To the amazing staff at Hotel Tramonto d'Oro, thank you for making me feel welcome and providing views that I did my best to capture in these pages.

Gennaro "Frankie" Capriglione (@frankieboattours) is indeed the best boat tour operator on the Amalfi Coast, and I was honored to spend as much time with him as I did. Thank you for showing me the best parts of the coast, introducing me to great restaurants, and always looking out for me. If anyone wants a tour of the Amalfi Coast, there's no one better than Frankie.

One of the best parts of writing is being able to highlight other amazing creatives, and Asha Patel (@ashapateldesigns) makes stunning jewelry that blends Eastern and Western aesthetics. Thank you for allowing me to feature your East-West prism necklace as Karishma's signature jewelry item. It is my favorite piece in your collection and I want it in every possible size and stone.

Writing is a solitary endeavor, so the friends who lift me up and support me are so important. Paula Sloyer and Kim Mills, you remain the best thing to come out of the innumerable WarnerMedia reorgs. I love you both for being early readers, wine companions, and travel buddies. Paula, I could not have gotten home after being injured in Bali without you, and I'll always be grateful. Jennifer Pastiloff, thank you for always believing in me, and for introducing me to my soul sister. Nicole Chambers, you are that soul sister, and I'm so grateful to have you in my life. Nicole and Jen, when life hit me hardest, you showed up. And I'll never forget that. To other friends near and far who have helped me on my journey, thank you, Jill Girling, Marion Karrer, Srivitta Kengskool, Elise Goldberg, Cynthia Wood, and Penelope Preston.

To my crew from Warner, Jeff Dossey, Kirby Chan, Nina de Guzman, and Candace Frazier, thank you for being the best studio team in the business and for supporting my transition out of Hollywood even though it meant more work for each of you. To Jackie Hayes, I wish I'd had more time with you as a boss. Thank you for your compassion as I made one of the most difficult decisions of my life, and for letting me go.

There are so many people involved in getting the word out about books, and I am grateful to the BookTok and Bookstagram communities for highlighting my work and helping me find new books that I want to read. It warms my heart to see the content you create, and I feel like I'm constantly learning from all of you. A special thanks to Saadia (@booksbookseverywhere) and Michelle (@nurse_bookie), both of whom have supported me from the start and whom I've had the pleasure of meeting in real life.

Thank you to Suzanne Leopold of Suzy Approved Book Tours, who jumped in and helped me when I really needed it. I hope we work on many more books together.

This novel is in many ways my desire to live out my culinary dreams without having to do the long, grueling, late-night hours of actually working in a restaurant. Cooking is my favorite thing to do when I'm not writing, and my love of cooking and food is captured in these pages. I must thank the fantastic chefs on social media from whom I took inspiration when creating Jyoti's character. Palak Patel (@chefpalak), Joanne Molinaro (@thekoreanvegan), Nik Sharma (@abrowntable), Priyanka Naik (@chefpriyanka), and Maunika Gowardhan (@cookinacurry), you have enriched the content in these pages and made my life more delicious.

I also want to acknowledge any readers who have had fertility struggles similar to Jyoti's or who have chosen of their own volition to be child-free. Regardless of the path that led you there, society doesn't make it easy. Like Jyoti does, I hope everyone finds the ending they deserve.

None of my words matter without readers, so my most heartfelt gratitude goes to each and every one of you who have read, recommended, reviewed, posted on social media, emailed me, taught my books in your classrooms (this one still makes me tear up), requested that your libraries carry my books, and talked about my work in any forum. The reception I have gotten from readers has been so thoughtful and supportive, and I could not ask for more. I get to have this second career that feeds my soul because you continue to show up for me, and I will never take that for granted.

THE WORLD'S EASIEST AND TASTIEST SAMOSAS

(Serves 6–8)

What's not to love about spiced potatoes and peas wrapped in a crunchy yet soft dough? The number of spices involved and keeping the flavors balanced are what make samosas intimidating, but with the pre-blended Magic Masalas crafted by my mom, all the guesswork is removed, and you can make foolproof samosas anytime the mood strikes. My mom developed these spice blends for my brother and me when we went to college so that we only needed simple grocery store ingredients to be able to taste the flavors of home no matter where we were. You can find the Magic Masala blends on my website, www.mansikshah.com, or on my Instagram, @mansishahwrites. You can also find video demos of all these recipes on my Instagram page. This recipe makes about 40 samosas, and they freeze really well for up to four months if you don't want to eat them all in one go. Although, no one would blame you if you did.

Ingredients for Filling

2 lbs russet potatoes
1 large onion, shredded
(I use yellow, but you can use whatever you have)
3 garlic cloves, chopped or grated
3 Tbsp neutral-flavored oil
1½ Tbsp Magic Masala #1
(use only 1 Tbsp if you want less spicy
and 2 Tbsp for more spicy)
1½ Tbsp Magic Masala #2
(use only 1 Tbsp if you want less spicy
and 2 Tbsp for more spicy)
1 tsp salt
Juice of 1 lemon (optional)
½ cup fresh or frozen peas (thawed)

Ingredients for Dough

2 cups all-purpose flour
⅓ cup coarse semolina flour (soji)
⅓ cup wheat flour (atta)
1½ tsp salt
1 tsp cumin seeds (jeeru)
(dry roasted will bring out more flavor,
but you can also skip this step)
5½ Tbsp neutral-flavored oil for dough
(I use grapeseed)
1 cup water
Neutral-flavored oil for frying

Directions

Bake or pressure-cook whole russet potatoes until fully cooked, peel, and then roughly mash to texture of chunky guacamole.

Note: The potatoes are ready when a paring knife easily slides into them.

Make Dough: Combine all-purpose flour, semolina flour, wheat flour, salt, and cumin seeds (lightly crush in your palm before adding to release some of the flavor). Add oil and enough water to make a pliable dough (approximately 1 cup). Knead for approximately 3–4 minutes to combine into a smooth ball (it should not be sticky or difficult to work with). Cover and set aside to rest for at least 20 minutes.

Make Filling: In a large saucepan over medium heat, add neutral-flavored oil. Once heated, add Magic Masala #1 and bloom spices in the oil for about 1 minute until fragrant. Add onions and cook for 3–4 minutes until onions are cooked through. Add garlic, mashed potatoes, Magic Masala #2, and salt, and stir to thoroughly combine. Then add juice of 1 lemon, if using. Taste for seasoning and add more salt if desired. To make it spicier/bolder, add more of Magic Masala #2 until you reach your desired flavor. Last, add peas and mix to combine.

Frying: Heat oil in vessel you are using to deep-fry the samosas. Oil should be around 400°F. You can test it by placing a small piece of flattened dough into the oil, and if it sizzles and floats to the top quickly, then it is ready.

Separate the dough into about 20 equal-sized balls and roll each into a 7-inch circle, about ⅛-inch thick. Using a knife, slice the circle in half. Take one half and bring the corners of the straight edge together to shape into a cone, pinching the dough together at the center point and then pressing the seam to create a tight seal. Take about 2 Tbsp of filling and press into the cone, leaving about ½ inch of dough to seal it closed. Pinch the excess dough together to create a flat seal, being sure to seal all the way to the filling so there is no air left inside. If the dough feels dry, dip your finger in water and spread a light layer of water on one side to act as a glue to bring the two sides together.

Assembled samosas should be covered with a damp cloth and set aside so the dough doesn't dry out while you make the others.

Drop them into the hot oil in small batches (being careful not to crowd them) and bring down the temperature of the oil. Fry for 1–2 minutes on each side until golden brown.

If you intend to freeze some of them, then I'd recommend flash frying them for about 15–20 seconds on each side (they will still be pale colored), letting them cool completely, and then freezing them in a single layer that you can then transfer to a freezer-safe sealable bag. To finish cooking them, place them directly from the freezer onto a wire rack and place them in the oven at 325°F for about 35–45 minutes until golden brown.

Enjoy while warm and serve with green chutney (recipe below).

Note: This recipe is naturally vegan.

Variations

Given how easy the filling is to make with Magic Masalas, the more time-consuming part of this recipe is making the dough and assembling the individual samosas. If you want some shortcuts that will still give you great flavor, here are a few options.

Make the filling, spoon it into store-bought puff pastry sheets, make turnover-style triangles, and then pop them in the oven according to the package directions.

Make the filling and then shape the potato mixture into patties and coat with breadcrumbs. Then place the patties into a skillet on medium heat with a little bit of oil to crisp up the breadcrumbs. Place the finished patties between 2 slices of toasted and buttered bread and enjoy an Indian-style sandwich. My personal preference is using brioche buns and spreading a layer of green chutney on them before eating.

Make the filling and put into a tortilla or flatbread and wrap like a burrito for a take on an Indian Frankie.

SAAG PANEER RAVIOLI

(Serves 4)

While there are several components to this dish, they are easy to tackle step-by-step, and the finished product is truly as good as Jyoti describes in the book. Many of the components can be made in advance and refrigerated or frozen so you can always have the ravioli and chutney on hand when a craving strikes. The Indian spices are easily available at local Indian markets or online.

PANEER

Paneer can be purchased at Indian markets, and I've seen it at certain mainstream stores like Whole Foods, but there is no substitute for homemade, and given how easy it is to make, I'd suggest giving it a try. Paneer can be made in advance and refrigerated for up to 3 days or frozen for up to 3 months.

Ingredients

½ gallon whole milk
¼ cup lemon juice or white vinegar

Directions

Pour the whole milk into a thick-bottomed pot and heat it on medium heat, stirring often to keep the milk solids on the bottom of the pot from burning.

When it starts to form bubbles on the surface and has heated to just below boiling, add the lemon juice or white vinegar to separate the curds and whey. Stir vigorously and you'll see the curds begin to form and a greenish liquid (the whey) separate from it.

Once the curds and whey are separated, pour the mixture into a colander lined with cheesecloth over a large bowl.

Save the bowl with the whey for another purpose. I use it in soups in place of water or broth, or to cook pasta to give it some extra tang and flavor.

Rinse the paneer curds with cool water to stop them from cooking, ensuring they remain soft.

Squeeze out as much of the whey from the curds as possible by making a tight ball with the cheesecloth.

Once it cools, it is ready to be used for the ravioli. If, however, you want paneer cubes for a different purpose, then at this stage, add 1 tsp of salt and form the cheesecloth into the shape you want for the paneer, using pressure to squeeze it together. If you have a tofu press, you can place it in there to condense it for a few hours or until it has your desired density for slicing.

SAAG PANEER FILLING

This filling is wonderful in the ravioli but also delicious with rotli, paratha, naan, or rice if you want a simple meal. It also freezes quite well for up to 4 months, so you might want to make a double batch. It starts off as saag paneer, and you can eat it that way if you want a more traditional Indian dish. The addition of a couple extra ingredients gives it the creaminess and softness that makes for a satisfying bite of ravioli. I prefer to use weight measurements over volume but have included both as this is not a recipe that requires fastidious precision to be delicious.

Ingredients for Saag Paneer

1½ Tbsp ghee (17 g)
1 medium white onion (200 g), diced
4 large garlic cloves, roughly chopped
1 serrano pepper, seeded if you want to reduce the heat, and roughly chopped
1-inch knob of ginger (8 g), grated
3 tsp dhana jeeru (cumin and coriander seed powder)
¼ tsp turmeric
⅛ tsp cloves powder
⅛ tsp cinnamon powder
¼ tsp ground cardamom
1 tsp tomato paste
16 oz fresh or frozen greens, thawed and liquid drained (I like 8 oz spinach, 4 oz Tuscan kale, and 4 oz mustard greens, but feel free to use all spinach—which would make it palak paneer—or other greens to your liking)
1 tsp salt
½ cup water or broth or whey leftover from making paneer
Zest of 1 lemon
240 g paneer

Ingredients for Ravioli Filling

240 g whole milk ricotta (strained)
2 Tbsp heavy cream (optional)

Directions

Place a large saucepan on medium heat and then add the ghee.

When the ghee becomes hot, add the onions, garlic, serrano pepper, ginger, and a sprinkling of salt, and cook until it is softened and brown (about 15 minutes). If the mixture starts getting too dry and begins to scorch, then add 1 Tbsp of water as needed and leave the saucepan covered.

After the onion mixture has cooked through, add the dhana jeeru, turmeric, cloves powder, cinnamon powder, and cardamom.

Let the spices cook through and add a touch of water if it feels too dry and seems as if it might burn.

Once the spices are fragrant, add the tomato paste, the greens, approximately 1 tsp of salt (to taste), and water (or broth or whey, depending on what you are using).

Let it all cook down until the liquid is fully absorbed. You don't want excess liquid in the mixture because it will lead to soggy ravioli. If it seems too wet after everything is cooked, put the mixture in a cheesecloth and strain out the excess moisture.

Add lemon zest.

Place the mixture in a food processor and pulse a few times to chop up the greens.

Add the paneer, whole milk ricotta, and heavy cream, if using, and pulse until you have a homogenous mixture. If you want it creamier, add more ricotta.

Taste and season with salt if needed.

To make this vegan: Substitute crumbled tofu for the paneer, use vegan ricotta, use oil instead of ghee, and omit the heavy cream or use a vegan option.

VEGAN CILANTRO-LAMINATED PASTA

For pasta or any type of dough, I like to use weight measurements to ensure accuracy. If you don't want to go through the step of laminating with cilantro, it will still taste great, as the lamination is more for aesthetics than flavor. And you can always make this dish with your favorite fresh pasta recipe or store-bought fresh pasta sheets.

Ingredients

300 g 00, all-purpose, or fine semolina flour
(approximately 2⅓ cups)
180 g vegan eggs (¾ cup)
(recipe below)
1 Tbsp olive oil
1 Tbsp water
1 tsp salt
Washed and dried cilantro leaves
(optional, for lamination)

Directions

Pulse all ingredients, except the cilantro leaves, in a food processor for 90 seconds. Because different flours absorb liquid differently, you might need to add more water 1 Tbsp at a time until you have a texture like wet sand that will stick together when pressed between your fingers.

Remove the dough from the food processor and knead it for a few minutes to bring it together and make a homogenous ball.

Cover with plastic wrap and leave to rest for at least 30 minutes (up to 6 hours).

Cut into 4 portions and roll each through your pasta roller, starting on the thickest setting and getting to the desired thickness for ravioli. If laminating and using a KitchenAid pasta roller attachment, I roll it until a thickness of 7.

To laminate, place cilantro leaves on half of a sheet of pasta and fold the other half over it (lengthwise, so the width of the pasta remains unchanged). Then use a rolling pin to ensure the two sides stick to each other.

Lastly, roll it through the pasta roller until you reach your desired thickness. After laminating, I roll it at a 5 on the KitchenAid pasta roller attachment and continue until a thickness of 7 or 8.

Place pasta sheets under a damp cloth to avoid them drying out until you are ready to make the ravioli.

To assemble the ravioli, take 1 Tbsp of the saag paneer filling and spoon it onto the bottom half of your pasta sheet, leaving about 1 inch of space in between each of your dollops. Then fold the top half of your pasta sheet over the filling and press around the filling to create a tight seal, being careful to avoid trapping any air inside the pasta. Then using a knife or pasta cutter, cut the ravioli into squares.

VEGAN EGGS

I have become such a fan of this recipe that I use it as a healthier alternative to eggs anywhere I can. I use it for pasta dough, brownies, cookies, omelets, and the list keeps growing given how easy it is to make. Simply place all the ingredients below into a high-speed blender and blend until smooth. These ingredients are easily found at any Indian market or online.

Ingredients

½ cup moong dal, soaked for at least 6 hours
½ cup coconut milk
¼ tsp black salt
(this gives it the eggy flavor, so you can add more or less based on your preference)
¼ tsp salt
1 Tbsp avocado oil
½ tsp turmeric
¼ tsp onion powder

1½ tsp nutritional yeast
2 Tbsp rice flour
¾ tsp baking powder

Directions

Blend all ingredients together in a high-speed blender until you have a smooth, creamy consistency.

Store in fridge for up to 1 week or in the freezer for up to 3 months.

GREEN CHUTNEY

This is a bright, bold, spicy chutney that is good on everything, and forms the base of the sauce for the saag paneer ravioli. This is also the perfect accompaniment for the squash blossoms.

Ingredients

1 bunch cilantro (okay to use stems)
1 jalapeño or serrano pepper
(remove seeds if you want less heat)
½-inch piece of ginger (about 1 tsp)
1 Tbsp lemon juice
1 Tbsp shredded coconut
(fresh is best, if you can find it,
but unsweetened dried will also work)
½ cup cashews,
soaked at least 15 minutes in hot water
½ tsp cumin (jeera)

½ tsp salt
20–25 mint leaves
½ tsp sugar (optional)

Directions

Blend all ingredients together in a high-speed blender until you have a smooth, creamy consistency that is perfect for dipping snacks into.

Taste and season with any additional salt or heat as needed.

This can be stored in the fridge for 2 days, and also freezes beautifully for up to 4 months if you want to make a double batch so you have some ready for samosas and the squash blossoms.

SPICY TOMATO SAUCE

There are many uses for this sauce as a general alternative to ketchup or other tomato-based condiments. This is great with the ravioli but also delicious with homemade mozzarella sticks, slathered on sandwiches, as pasta sauce, and so much more.

Ingredients

1 tsp ghee (can substitute neutral oil or butter)
8 oz tomato sauce
½ tsp Calabrian chili paste
(can use more or less based on your spice preference)
½ tsp salt
¼ tsp dhana jeeru (cumin and coriander seed powder)
1–2 Tbsp coconut milk (optional)

Directions

Warm the ghee in a small saucepot, and then add the remaining ingredients and stir until combined.

Blend the mixture until it is smooth and has the consistency of ketchup. If it's too thick, you can add more coconut milk or water. If it's too thin, continue to cook it down until you get the desired consistency.

For dressing the ravioli, I recommend a squeeze bottle, but you can also use a fork to drizzle or a spoon to dollop.

LEMON YOGURT SAUCE

This is about as easy as it gets and is a refreshing sauce for the ravioli, but you'll be able to find other uses too. Add it anywhere you want to add a cooling brightness to your dish.

Ingredients

1 cup yogurt
1 tsp lemon juice
(can add more depending on how tart you want it)

Directions

Mix the yogurt and lemon juice together until combined.

For dressing the ravioli, I recommend a squeeze bottle, but you can also use a fork to drizzle or a spoon to dollop.

To make this vegan: Use a vegan yogurt.

SAAG PANEER RAVIOLI

Now that all the components are ready, the assembly of this delicious dish is quick and easy.

Ingredients

24 saag paneer ravioli (6 per serving)
2 Tbsp ghee (can substitute neutral oil)
¼ cup green chutney (recipe above)
Salt to taste
Lemon yogurt sauce for dressing (recipe above)
Spicy tomato sauce for dressing (recipe above)
Cilantro leaves (optional, for garnish)

Directions

Bring a pot of salted water to a boil, then add the ravioli. They will only need a few minutes to cook. After they rise to the surface, boil them for another 20–30 seconds, and then they are done.

In a medium saucepan, melt the ghee. When warm, add the green chutney. Also add a ladle of pasta water from the ravioli to bring it all together and emulsify until you have a smooth green sauce.

Taste and season with additional salt if needed.

To plate, ladle a spoonful of the green chutney sauce on the bottom of the dish. Then arrange 6 ravioli onto the dish. Finish by dressing with the lemon yogurt sauce and spicy tomato sauce. As a final touch, add some cilantro leaves for freshness. Note: If you aren't using laminated pasta for the ravioli, then you can transfer the cooked ravioli directly into the pan with the green chutney sauce and coat the ravioli with sauce before arranging them onto the plate.

CREAMY, CRISPY SQUASH BLOSSOMS

(Serves 3–4)

My first time frying squash blossoms at home was in preparation for this book and the results far exceeded my expectations. This is now my absolute favorite way to eat squash blossoms, so definitely give this recipe a try when you see those beautiful orange blooms at your local market or in your garden.

Ingredients for Filling

10–12 squash blossoms
¼ cup crumbled paneer (50 g)
⅓ cup ricotta (strained) (75 g)
Zest of 1 lemon
¼ tsp cumin seeds (jeeru),
roasted in a dry pan and then lightly crushed
½ tsp crushed green chilies
(can add more to increase the spice)
½ tsp salt
(may need more as you taste)

Ingredients for Batter

Neutral-flavored oil for frying
¾ cup club soda or sparkling water
(helps keep the batter light, but you can use
regular water if that's all you have)
½ cup all-purpose flour
2 Tbsp cornstarch
Salt and pepper to taste

Directions

Wash and thoroughly dry squash blossoms, as you don't want any moisture left on them.

In a small bowl, mix together the paneer, ricotta, lemon zest, cumin seeds, and green chilies, and add salt to taste.

Fill a piping bag with the mixture (I find this to be the easiest way to fill the blossoms, but you can also spoon the mixture into them).

Fill each blossom with the mixture, making sure there are no air pockets and to leave a bit of room at the top to twist them closed.

Heat neutral-flavored oil to about 350°F in vessel you are using to deep-fry the squash blossoms.

Prepare your batter only when the oil is at temperature because the batter will become thicker the longer it sits.

In a shallow dish large enough to dip the blossoms, mix the club soda or sparkling water, flour, and cornstarch, and season with salt and pepper to taste.

Carefully dredge each blossom in the batter and then slowly drop them into the frying oil, in small batches, being careful not to crowd them, and bring down the temperature of the oil. Fry until golden brown, which should take about 2 minutes.

Place the blossoms on a paper towel to catch any excess oil and sprinkle with salt.

These are delicious on their own, but dipping them in green chutney (recipe above) takes them to a new level.

To make this vegan: Use 125 g of vegan ricotta and omit the paneer.

GUJARATI SHAAK-INSPIRED RISOTTO

(Serves 3–4)

Every culture has a creamy rice-based dish that serves as the ultimate comfort food. In Gujarat, that's kitchari, a savory long-grain rice and lentil stew packed with vegetables. In Italy, it's a heaping bowl of risotto made with starchy short-grain rice. Fusing risotto with Gujarati flavors created a tantalizing dish that takes the best of both worlds and brings them together into one delectable bite. This dish is savory, creamy, loaded with vegetables, and has just the right amount of spice from the green chilies and bite from the mustard seeds to cut through the richness.

Ingredients

2 cups mix of cauliflower and romanesco,
cut into bite-sized pieces
(can use only one type if that's what you have)
Salt to taste

Pepper to taste
(I prefer white pepper for this dish, but black will work fine)
3 cups vegetable stock
2 Tbsp olive oil
1 garlic clove, minced
1 large shallot, diced
1 cup arborio or carnaroli rice
1 cup dry white wine
(can use more vegetable stock if you prefer to omit)
¼ tsp turmeric
¾ tsp crushed green chilies
½ cup grated Parmesan cheese

Ingredients for Vaghar

2 Tbsp ghee
¾ tsp black mustard seeds (rai)
Leaves from 2 sprigs of curry leaf plant

Directions

In a pan on medium-low heat, sauté the cauliflower and romanesco with a sprinkling of salt and pepper. When cooked to al dente, transfer to another bowl for use later in the recipe.

In a saucepot, warm the vegetable stock and leave it simmering.

In the same pan in which the vegetables were cooked, heat olive oil over medium-low heat.

Add garlic and shallot, with a sprinkling of salt and pepper, and cook over low heat for 3–4 minutes until translucent, but don't brown them.

Add rice and increase heat to medium. Toast the rice for 3 minutes until white center is visible.

Add wine and cook until most of the wine is absorbed.

Add 1 cup of the warmed vegetable stock, turmeric, and green chilies, stirring constantly and adding more stock 1 cup at a time once absorbed. This could take 20–30 minutes.

When the rice is nearly al dente and only needs 1 more cup of stock, add the vegetables to the rice along with the final cup of stock, so that the vegetables can warm through.

In a small pot over medium heat, make the vaghar with the ghee, black mustard seeds, and curry leaves. The black mustard seeds and curry leaves should sizzle and pop in the ghee, and then you can remove them from the heat.

When the rice is al dente, turn off the heat, and then add the Parmesan cheese and vaghar mixture, and mix until the rice is glistening and the consistency is creamy and a little runny. Taste and add any additional salt or pepper.

Serve immediately. Risotto needs to be eaten right from the stove.

To make this vegan: Use vegan butter in place of ghee, and vegan Parmesan cheese. You can also omit the cheese entirely and make sure there is a little extra stock or vegan butter to keep it creamy.

PAV BHAJI

(Serves 2–3)

Pav refers to an Indian dinner roll and *bhaji* refers to a mix of vegetables. This dish is the ultimate comfort food with the flavorful mix of vegetables cooked in luscious butter and slathered onto buttered and toasted bread. It's perfect to warm you up on a cold night, or to help mend a broken heart, like it did for Jyoti. In this dish, more butter definitely means more better, and it's no surprise that this is the dish that went viral.

Ingredients for Bhaji

½ lb cubed potatoes (225 g)
⅓ lb mixed fresh or frozen chopped vegetables (160 g) (this can be any vegetable you like, but I prefer a mix of carrots, peas, green beans, and cauliflower)
3 Tbsp butter (but it's always okay to add more)
1 small onion (110 g), finely chopped
3 garlic cloves, chopped

1 small tomato (100 g), finely chopped
½ tsp grated ginger
1 Tbsp pav bhaji masala
(available at Indian grocers and online)
1 tsp salt
Juice of half a lemon

Ingredients for Pav

Any soft bread you like
(dinner rolls, soft French bread, or even sandwich bread)
(My favorite is dinner rolls)
Butter

Ingredients for Garnish

¼ medium onion (30 g), diced
2 Tbsp chopped cilantro
Lemon juice to taste
Salt to taste

Directions

Cook the cubed potatoes and chopped vegetables in a pressure cooker, Instant Pot, or in boiling water on the stove.

Drain the excess water from the vegetables after they are cooked and then roughly mash the vegetables so that it resembles a chunky guacamole.

In a saucepot over medium heat, add the butter. When the butter has melted and is warm, add the onion and garlic. Let it cook for 3 minutes until the onions are translucent.

Add the tomato and ginger and allow them to cook through.

Once cooked, use a masher to mash the garlic, onion, tomato, and ginger mixture in the saucepot.

Add the remaining mashed vegetables and add the pav bhaji masala and salt, mixing thoroughly and letting the spices cook through for a couple minutes.

Add the juice of half a lemon and now taste for any additional salt. If you want it spicier or more flavorful at this point, then add more pav bhaji masala ½ tsp at a time until you reach your desired flavor level. The bhaji is now done.

In a warm skillet, toast your buttered bread until you see crisp brown spots on the buttered side.

In a small bowl, mix together the garnish ingredients of onion, cilantro, some lemon juice to taste, and some salt to taste.

To assemble, heap some bhaji onto your toasted bread and then top with the fresh garnish and dive in.

To make this vegan: Use vegan butter.